**He had come back into her life—
with a vengeance**

Darcy tried to twist out of Heath Chapman's strong arms—arms even stronger than she remembered from when they last had held her years before—but she was helpless.

"Heath," she said desperately, "when I left you I vowed never to feel emotion for a man again. I'm dead to the kind of love you want."

His lips were against her ear and she felt a shock run through her and she exhaled sharply. "See," he whispered, "you felt that, didn't you?"

"Yes . . ."

His lips burned their way across her cheek to her mouth. "You'll feel this, too," he murmured just before their lips joined. "And this . . . and this . . ."

Tears welled up in Darcy's eyes . . . tears of passion . . . tears of pain . . . as she entered once again the heaven she longed for and the hell she feared. . . .

DEFY THE
SAVAGE WINDS

Big Bestsellers from SIGNET

DEFY THE SAVAGE WINDS

JUNE LUND SHIPLETT

A Sequel to
THE WILD STORMS
OF HEAVEN

A SIGNET BOOK
NEW AMERICAN LIBRARY
TIMES MIRROR

*This book is dedicated to all of my
wonderful friends at the Mentor Public Library,
in Mentor, Ohio, for their thoughtfulness
and help in researching all of the novels I've
written, and for being such grand people.
Thanks!*

PUBLISHER'S NOTE

This novel is a work of fiction. Names, characters, places,
and incidents are either the product of the author's
imagination or are used fictitiously, and any resemblance
to actual persons, living or dead, events, or locales is
entirely coincidental.

NAL BOOKS ARE AVAILABLE AT QUANTITY DISCOUNTS
WHEN USED TO PROMOTE PRODUCTS OR SERVICES. FOR
INFORMATION PLEASE WRITE TO PREMIUM MARKETING DIVISION,
THE NEW AMERICAN LIBRARY, INC., 1633 BROADWAY,
NEW YORK, NEW YORK 10019.

SIGNET, SIGNET CLASSICS, MENTOR, PLUME, MERIDIAN AND
NAL BOOKS are published by The New American Library, Inc.,
1633 Broadway, New York, New York 10019

First Printing, July, 1980

1 2 3 4 5 6 7 8 9

PRINTED IN THE UNITED STATES OF AMERICA

❦ 1 ❦

Port Royal, South Carolina—November 1796

It was close to midnight as Heath galloped along the dusty road. Sweat turned the mass of dark hair beneath his top hat to ringlets, and dampened the shirt beneath his frock coat. He knew he was pushing his horse too hard, but off in the distance the sky above the Broad River was bright orange, with wisps of black smoke drifting through it like storm clouds on the horizon.

Rounding a slight bend in the road, he reined up abruptly, the silhouettes of six horsemen coming toward him. His horse snorted, pawing the ground as he waited impatiently for the men to approach. They were soldiers, and rode hurriedly, alert for anything out of the ordinary.

"Halt!" the sergeant in charge yelled.

Heath glared as they surrounded him. "Do I look like I'm going anywhere?" he asked breathlessly.

The soldiers stared as the sergeant went on.

"We're checking all the roads," he said forcefully. "There's been an uprising."

"Where?"

"River Oaks."

"My God!" cried Heath. "My sister's at River Oaks."

"Your sister?"

"I'm Heath Chapman. My sister's the Duchess of Bourland. Her husband's aunt owns River Oaks, and she's been staying there."

"Well, there's nothing left now but the house, sir," said the sergeant, studying Heath curiously. "And I'm

1

afraid your sister's husband's been murdered. At first they couldn't figure out how it happened, since nobody saw any of the slaves get into the house, but then someone said they remembered seeing the upstairs maid wandering around during the ruckus with a butcher knife in her hands. Most of the slaves have escaped downriver on a ship that was docked at the wharf."

"That would have been the *Eagle Hunter*," offered Heath hurriedly.

"Right, sir. But some of them didn't make the ship and we've got orders to run 'em down."

"My sister?" asked Heath quickly.

The sergeant glanced at his men, then back to Heath. "She's missing," he answered. "So are the boy and his nurse."

Heath frowned. "You're sure she's not at the plantation?"

"No, sir. The captain had soldiers all over every foot of ground. They're afraid maybe some of the slaves may have kidnapped her to use as a hostage."

Heath's horse stirred restlessly as he took a handkerchief from his pocket and wiped the sweat from his forehead, removing his hat momentarily. He thought of his half-sister, Rebel. For years she'd been in love with Beau Dante, the son of a Tuscarora Indian chief. In fact, her son, Cole, who was now almost two years old, was really Beau's son, born nine months after Rebel's marriage to Brandon Avery, the Duke of Bourland. Brandon had made life miserable for her because of the boy, and when Beau, a privateer, had been commissioned by the French to capture her because she was the wife of the governor of British-held Grenada, in the Caribbean, Rebel and Beau had been reunited. But Beau hadn't turned her over to the French. Instead, he and Heath, who had been first mate on their ship, the *Golden Eagle*, at the time, discovering that the French had planned to imprison Rebel and her son, had rescued them and brought them here to Port

Royal—to her and Heath's mother, Loedicia, and her stepfather, Roth Chapman, Heath's father. During the crossing from France, Rebel and Beau had resumed their former relationship, and by the time Rebel's husband had discovered where she was and come after her, she was already expecting another child by Beau. When she refused to return to Brandon, he'd kidnapped her and taken her to River Oaks.

Beau had been ready to storm the place to get her back, and it had taken all they could do to argue him out of it and warn him to wait until they could find another way. The fact that Rebel had mysteriously lost her expected baby didn't help matters. There were rumors that her miscarriage was the result of a beating from her husband. Heath's father's foreman, Silas Morgan, had warned them that something strange was in the wind at River Oaks. Had Beau taken advantage of the unrest?

Heath put his hat back on as he watched smoke still filtering through the crimson sky. Then he turned to the sergeant. "Am I free to go, Sergeant?" he asked anxiously. "Maybe I can be of some help."

The sergeant stared at him hard for a minute, making note of the fancy gold velvet frock coat, beaver hat, buff breeches, highly polished boots, and the shiny gold earring that graced his right ear. A memento from his days as a privateer, so some said. He'd heard of Heath Chapman, all right. He was twenty years old and his father owned the Château, a large plantation next to the River Oaks, and he'd caught glimpses of him a few times in Beaufort, where the troops were stationed.

"Go ahead," he finally said, maneuvering his men back into a military line behind him. "But be careful. Some of the escaped slaves are armed."

Heath assured him he'd be extra cautious, then watched as the small squad of soldiers moved off once more toward Beaufort. As soon as they melted into the darkness, he whirled his horse about and once again plunged forward down the dark road. But when he reached the crossroads, he pulled up rein, and instead of turning left toward River Oaks, dug his horse in the ribs and headed upriver.

Sometime later, he reined up in front of the small house he had helped Beau build, on the land Beau had bought. He and Beau had been living there since shortly after their arrival in Port Royal, and he had a suspicion that inside he just might find his sister.

As he dropped from the saddle and turned, the door opened, letting out a crack of light, and he realized they had pulled the curtains across the windows.

"Aaron?" he challenged, as a large figure slipped through the doorway, and the big man frowned, his voice unsteady.

"Mistah Heath?"

"What's going on, Aaron? Is Rebel here?" he asked, but Aaron cautioned him.

"Shhh! Don't say nothin' till you gets inside, Mistah Heath," he said, and pulled him as Heath stumbled through the door; then Aaron slipped back out, shutting it behind him.

Heath straightened, pulling his hat from his head, while Aaron hurried to stable his horse. He stared across the room at the other two slaves, Job and Liza, who were standing in front of the fireplace, watching him nervously.

"Is Rebel here?" he asked, and saw the conviction in their eyes.

"It was awful, Mistah Heath," said Job. "She come lookin' for Mistah Beau. The slaves were runnin' all over the place shootin' and cuttin', and she couldn't find the boy. She was frantic. Me and Mistah Beau and Aaron, we went back to River Oaks while Liza took care of her and we found that boy. That is, Mistah Beau found him. That man of hers locked him and his nurse, Hizzie, in a dirt cell in the wine cellar. He was gonna kill the boy, but Mistah Beau killed him instead."

Heath gasped. "Beau murdered Brandon?"

Job shook his head, but didn't get a chance to answer.

"No, sir," said Hizzie from the shadows at the other side of the room where she'd been sitting on the sofa holding Cole. Hizzie was Cole's nurse. She was a black girl Rebel had brought with her from Grenada. Heath could barely make out her rounded figure and frizzy head of hair. "It wasn't that way at all, sir," she said. "Mistah Brandon tried to kill Mistah Beau, and they fought. It was self-defense. I seen it all."

Heath moved over slowly, and touched Cole's face, running his hands through the boy's hair, gazing into his deep green eyes.

"Is he all right?" he asked Hizzie.

"Yes, sir," she said proudly. "I took real good care of him." She smiled, the teeth in her dark face shining unusually white. "I always takes care of him as if he were my own," she said. "There isn't nothin' gonna happen to this child long as I can help it!"

"Where's Rebel?"

Hizzie nodded toward the bedroom, embarrassed. "She's in there with Mistah Beau. He said he wanted to tell her what happened himself."

Heath straightened, heading for the bedroom door.

In the bedroom, Rebel lay beneath Beau, luxuriating in the aftermath of his lovemaking, and his lips were warm on her mouth.

"This is one hell of a time to be making love," Beau whispered softly against her mouth now that the strain and tension was gone from his body. He was still inside her, and she never wanted the moment to end.

"I heard some commotion out there before," she said; then her violet eyes widened. "Oh, Beau . . ." she stared up at him. "I didn't think . . . they won't arrest you for killing Brandon, will they?" Her fingers dug into his back as he buried his face in her neck, his lips close to her ear.

"The only one who saw me do it was Hizzie," he told her. "And the only ones who know I was even there are Job, Aaron, Liza, Hizzie, and you. Besides, it was self-defense."

Suddenly there was a soft knock on the door. "It's Heath!"

Beau raised himself and looked down at her. "He might as well come in," she whispered. "I think he knows we haven't been talking in here all this while."

He slipped from her and lay at her side, pulling the covers up. "Come in."

Heath opened the door, then stopped for a minute before stepping in. "You crazy fools," he said softly as he shut the door behind him and looked at his sister and Beau together in bed. "Don't you know the whole countryside's looking for Rebel and the boy?"

Beau sat up, black hair rumpled, green eyes alert. "Oh, God, I hadn't thought of that. All I thought of was keeping her safe."

Heath shook his head. "I met some soldiers on my way back from Beaufort. They've got an alarm out for them. The soldiers told me about the uprising and about Brandon being killed. They think the slaves have kidnapped Rebel and the boy, and it seems nobody can figure how one of them managed to get into the wine cellar and put a knife in Brandon, since nobody knew any of them were in the house." He glanced quickly at Beau. "But don't worry, you're clear. Somebody said they saw the upstairs maid running around with a butcher knife during the fighting, so I guess they aren't going to press the issue too far. I was going to ride over to take a look around before coming home, but thought better of it." He looked at his sister. "If they find you here, though, they just might start asking some nasty, embarrassing questions."

Beau glanced down at Rebel. He had to get her out of here. "Where are the patrols?" he asked Heath, and Heath gestured with his hand.

"Everywhere. Most of the slaves made it to Brandon's ship, but some are still running around loose. I bypassed the rest of the patrols."

Beau bit his lip. "Heath, can you ride to your mother's and get Casey to bring the *Interlude?*" he asked, and right away Heath knew what he had in mind. Casey was captain of Heath's father's private ship. "And for heaven's sake, bring some clothes for Rebel," he said. "She showed up here in her nightgown." Heath disappeared out the door, and Beau slipped from the bed. "In the meantime, we'll have to find someplace for you to hide, just in case they come around," but she shook her head of flaxen hair vigorously.

"Beau, I'm safer right here than anyplace else," she said. "They'll search the grounds, figuring the slaves might be hiding, but it'd be an insult to search your bedroom."

He wasn't sure she was right, but she proved it a short while later when a contingent of soldiers rode up and searched the place, even the barn, then moved on while she, Hizzie, and Cole huddled in Beau's bedroom.

It was almost four in the morning when Heath arrived with Casey and the *Interlude.* "Every time we saw a boat, I used the excuse that I was helping in the search," explained Casey as he waited while Rebel put on some clothes. "I'll tell you," the helmsman went on, "that Mrs. Grantham and her manager, Mr. Minyard, should have gotten worse than what they got for the way they treated those slaves. And we can be thankful the runaways decided to leave in the ship instead of taking it out on the rest of Port Royal."

Beau agreed. He'd seen the results of slave uprisings. They weren't very pleasant.

They learned from Casey that Roth and Loedicia had gone to Beaufort and were due back the next morning, and Rebel was apprehensive as they made their way to the ship tied to the pier. She wasn't quite sure how Roth and her mother were going to take all this. Heath wanted to go with her, but Casey insisted that it was better he stay. He knew what to do, and so did Silas, and they'd handle the whole thing fine.

Beau kissed Rebel good-bye, promising to come over first thing in the morning, then kissed Cole's cheek while he lay with his head on Hizzie's shoulder fast asleep; then Beau and Heath watched silently as they boarded the ship and it slipped from its moorings.

"Well, it looks like your life's settled," said Heath as he glanced at Beau. "Once this all quiets down, you and Rebel can get married, and everything'll be fine."

"You sound cynical," said Beau as they watched the ship move into midstream.

"You think I was with Cora tonight, don't you, Beau?" he said, and Beau looked at him surprised. Cora was the wife of Senator Victor McLaren. She was twenty years younger than her husband, with hair the color of thick honey and brown eyes that glinted like smoky topaz when she was aroused. Heath and Beau had rescued her five years before from Indians, then lost track of her when they'd been shanghaied aboard a ship in Philadelphia. Now she was here, and so was Heath, and they had picked up where they'd left off.

"You weren't with her?" asked Beau.

Heath hung his head. "I was with someone else." There was anger in his voice; then he swore as they turned and headed for the house. "Dammit, Beau, what makes a woman do things like that to a man? I thought Cora . . . I guess it was because she was the first, I don't know. Then I met her and it was as if all the rest of the women didn't even exist."

"Not even Cora?"

"That's the trouble," complained Heath. "I can't get rid of Cora, and if she finds out Darcy and I know each other . . ."

"Darcy?"

"Senator McLaren's daughter," he explained helplessly, and now Beau understood. He'd heard about the senator's daughter. She was all of seventeen, and spoiled rotten. A tempestuous redheaded vixen, he'd heard someone describe her. It was rumored she'd turned down half a dozen proposals the first year she came out.

"You spent the evening with her?" Beau was surprised.

"Well, in a way," Heath said. "We spent it fighting."

"Fighting?"

"Why does she have to be so stubborn, Beau?" he said as they went into the house. "What's wrong with a man asserting himself?"

Beau smiled. "I take it the lady has a mind of her own."

"Just like my damn sister," Heath said as he tossed his coat on a chair. "But what I want to know is, how do I tell Cora?"

"That," said Beau, "is a problem." He shrugged. "But then, what can Cora do? Threaten to expose you? She can't do that without exposing herself. Think about it, Heath."

Heath walked into his room and flung himself on the bed. He closed his eyes and tried to tell himself Cora didn't matter, but he knew she did. He didn't love Cora. They shared a bond. Like growing up together. Darcy! He remembered the way her cat-green eyes had flashed when he'd told her he didn't want her father to know yet that he was seeing her.

He remembered the first time he'd met her. The senator had been out of town and he'd slipped into Beaufort to be with Cora. It was exciting and adventurous at first; now it was irritating. Cora had slipped away from the house through the back garden, and he'd escorted her back, kissing her good night beneath the rose arbor. He watched her move into the house, then turned to leave when he heard voices. He pulled back into the shadows as a man and woman came through the back gate and started up the walk.

"I told you before, just one kiss, Harold," the woman was saying as they stopped near the rose arbor, but the man wasn't satisfied.

"One kiss? You call that a kiss?" he complained. "You barely let me touch your lips."

The girl laughed. Heath could tell now that it was a young girl rather than an older woman, and the young man with her sounded put-out.

"I don't think you're being fair at all, Darcy McLaren," he said. "You've kissed other men. More than once, too, so I've heard."

"Well, you heard wrong," she insisted. "In the first place, Harold, the evening was a horrible bore, and I'm sorry I even took the risk of sneaking out with you, and in the second place, all those men who brag that they've kissed Darcy McLaren are nothing but liars. Not that they didn't want to, naturally. However, I don't go around bestowing passionate kisses on just anybody. Only a few of my close men friends have the privilege of kissing me like that, and you, Harold, are not one. Now, if you don't mind, I'm tired. Good night, Harold."

The young man shoved his hat on his head angrily. "Good night, Miss McLaren," he said irritably and stalked off.

She stood watching after him for a long time, then picked one of the roses and turned so the moon was full on her face. God, she was beautiful. Her hair was the color of burnished copper and her pale green eyes were masked with thick dark lashes, and from what he could see in the moonlight, her mouth was full and provocative. Heath had heard of Darcy McLaren. She'd arrived from Columbia, South Carolina, a few days earlier, but he'd never laid eyes on her until now. He watched the moonlight play on her face; then she walked toward the gate to fasten it, moving into the shadows of the wall.

He stepped from where he was hiding and glanced quickly at the house to make sure Cora wasn't watching, then moved into the shadows directly behind her.

"If you lock the gate, how will I get back out?" he

asked softly, and Darcy gasped as she whirled around, her hand over her mouth.

"Who . . . who are you?" she asked, trembling, and Heath smiled that long, luxurious smile of his that could charm the devil himself, and his dark eyes snapped as he looked at her.

"You mean you don't know?" he asked, and he sensed her embarrassment.

"Am I supposed to?"

"Not really."

Her tone changed, became more spirited. "Then what are you doing here?"

Heath's voice dropped to barely a whisper. "I needed a place to hide."

"A place to hide?"

. He nodded. "From some men who were chasing me."

She eyed him skeptically. "You're spoofing."

"I wish I were," he said seriously. "But you see, there are these three men. I killed their brother in a duel, and they don't think it was a fair fight. It wasn't my fault, he was a poor shot."

Her eyes narrowed as she looked at him. "You expect me to believe that?"

"Well, how about this, then?" he said casually. "I owe them money and they think I ought to pay it back."

He saw a smile begin to play at the corner of her mouth. "Just what are you really doing here?" she asked curiously, and he straightened as he stepped closer and looked down into her pale green eyes with their long thick lashes that were shadowed in the darkness.

"How about this?" he whispered intimately. "I was waiting for you. I wanted to find out just what your lips were really like," and he pulled her into his arms, his mouth covering hers. For a moment she'd struggled; then, as he held her close, he could feel her lips move beneath his, warm and alive, and he knew no one had ever kissed her like that before, in spite of the gossip. That passionate kiss had started the whole affair.

He had told her who he was, but made her promise secrecy because his father, Roth, and her father were on opposite sides of the political fence.

They'd been meeting the past few weeks whenever he could get away from Cora, and Heath knew this was different. Darcy was somebody special. But then, what of Cora? What did he owe her? He put his hands behind his head, and that's the way he was still lying when he woke up a few hours later.

Roth and Loedicia arrived back from Beaufort early that morning, having heard the news of the uprising and rumors that Rebel and her son were missing. Rebel explained everything to them as soon as they arrived at the Château, and by the time the authorities were notified that Rebel was safe and sound, their story was unshakable.

They told the authorities that Rebel had been frightened when the commotion started, and worrying for her safety and that of her son, had slipped unnoticed from the house and made her way, with her nurse, Hizzie, and the boy, to the Château, where she'd gone directly to her old room, not bothering to wake the servants, since she still had her own key to the house and her parents weren't home. Rachel Grantham fumed, but there was no way she could deny it without admitting that her nephew, Brandon, had been keeping the boy in the wine cellar and his wife a prisoner.

The tale was believed, although many thought it strange that Brandon's beautiful blond widow attended his funeral two days later with dry eyes. Rebel couldn't cry for Brandon. Once she had felt sorry for him because she'd been unable to return his love, but eventually even her pity for him had turned to hatred. She stood at his funeral dry-eyed, realizing her son was the new Duke of Bourland, since Brandon had left no will, and her heart was empty of any feelings toward Brandon except bitterness. Since Rebel was an extremely attractive woman, it was no surprise when a few days after the funeral, Beau Dante began making frequent calls at the Château, and before long rumors began circulating that he and the young widow, who were often seen about together, would someday wed.

Heath smiled some weeks later as he left the house, leaving Beau and Rebel on the sofa in each other's arms. It was funny to think of the stern, stony-faced Captain Thunder, as Beau had been known in his days as a privateer, reduced to playing on the floor with a toddler, and staying at home nights to sit by a fire. Not for him. There was so much to do out there in the world.

He thanked Aaron for saddling his horse, and mounted, heading down the drive. Tonight he was meeting Cora. Victor had gone to Charleston, and she'd sent word that she had to see him, so he headed for the usual place. Cora always drove the buggy herself; that way she didn't have to worry about servants talking. The room Heath had rented was at the top of the stairs at the inn, but Cora always went in the back way, making sure her face was covered.

He tied his horse to the hitching post, then sauntered to the side of the building and peeked around to see if she was here yet. Her horse and buggy were out back, so instead of going to the taproom first, he went directly upstairs. The inn was a small one close to the outskirts of Beaufort, where few people stopped. He nodded to the innkeeper on his way.

"I thought you'd never get here," said Cora nervously as he walked in, and she moved to him languidly, her arms moving up about his neck. He kissed her long and hard.

"What is it? You're trembling," he said, and she half-smiled.

"I guess I'm a bit nervous, that's all."

"Did someone see you?"

"Oh, no, Heath." She studied him for a minute. He

was nothing like the shy young man she'd taught how to make love five years ago. Heath was strong and virile, like Beau had been then, and he was so handsome it made her warm all over to look at him. What a man he'd become. His lovemaking was enough to set any woman on fire. She sighed. If he was like this at twenty, what would he be like at twenty-five or thirty, when a man was considered a man. She hadn't wanted to fall in love with him. It was supposed to be a game like she'd played before her marriage dozens of times. But this time it was different. And now, what if she lost him? What if he didn't want her anymore?

"You said you had to see me," he said as he watched her wringing her hands. "What is it?"

"I don't know how to tell you," she said painfully, "but . . ."

"The best way is just to say it."

She looked up into his dark eyes. "I'm pregnant, Heath," she said softly, and he stood for a minute, not saying anything.

"So?" he finally said.

"You don't understand. It's your baby."

"Mine? How do you know it's mine? You do have a husband, Cora."

She shook her head. "That's just the trouble," she replied. "Victor will know it's not his."

"How?"

"Because I'm two months. Victor was gone for over a month before elections, remember? This is the end of November. How could I have conceived if he wasn't here?"

Heath closed his eyes and moved to the window. What a damn fool he'd been. Before, it was always slight flirtations, a night of romance, never any lasting affair, just a woman to fill his needs. He should have listened to Beau.

"You're sure you're pregnant?"

"Positive. I've missed twice already, Heath." Her eyes caught his. "I'm going to have to tell him soon."

"Can't you pretend it's his?"

"I'm scared, Heath," she said softly. "Victor has a violent temper. What if he gets suspicious?"

Heath reached out and took her hand; it was cold, like ice.

"Oh, I wish we could get married," she said anxiously. "I wish I could tell him the truth and he'd set me free and you and I could get married."

Heath turned from her and stared out the window. He didn't want to get married. He didn't want to settle down and have children, especially not with Cora. She was all right for a diversion, but to spend the rest of his life with her? He was only twenty. His stomach tugged at his insides, churning it until he felt sick.

"Cora . . ." He turned to look at her, his face pale. "I didn't dream anything like this would happen."

"You think women don't get pregnant?"

"I didn't say that. I just thought you knew when it was safe and when it wasn't."

"No woman knows that, Heath," she said, and her eyes faltered as she looked at him. "You don't want the baby, do you?" she asked.

He looked at her curiously. "Well, do you?"

Her lips trembled. "I want you, Heath," she said. "Baby or no baby. I want you. I made a mistake when I married Victor, I know that now. I need the kind of love you can give me, not the clumsy attempts he makes."

She put her arms around his waist and pressed her head to his chest. "I love you, Heath," she said softly, and he cringed.

He wanted to run, to disappear, but he couldn't; instead, he put his arms around her and held her close for a few minutes. "Look," he finally said, "Victor's in Charleston right now. You said he'd be gone a week. When he comes back, hint around to him about babies and see what his reaction is. Then, if he seems receptive, tell him about the baby and he'll probably be happy about it."

"But you don't understand," she said stubbornly. "I don't want to stay with him and have the baby. I want to be with you."

His face hardened. "You can't, Cora, don't you understand?" he said firmly. "You're his wife. He won't give you up. Besides, it takes forever to get a divorce decree, and anyway, I have no money to support a wife."

Cora stared at him, her eyes blinded by tears.

"If you didn't already have a husband, I'd marry you, you know that, but you do, and it's the only solution. Pretend it's his, Cora. We can still see each other if you want, but there's no way in hell he can prove that baby's not his. You'll see. When he comes back from Charleston, you'll see."

Heath felt like a cad as Cora reached up and pulled his head down until their lips met. She was asking him to take her again, and he knew it, but he didn't really want to. Not anymore. Somehow all the joy had gone out of it for him, but he let her arouse him anyway. What did it matter? After all, the damage was already done.

The next day was Sunday. Heath rode into Beaufort again. This time he rented a carriage, then picked up Darcy at their usual meeting place and headed out of town. He drove for a long time in silence.

She laughed. "Are you still angry with me for the other night?"

He smiled cynically. "I should be."

"But you're not?"

"No."

"Then what's the matter?"

He straightened as he flicked the reins, hurrying the horses. "Nothing's the matter."

"But you look so serious."

Darcy had packed a picnic lunch, and Heath pulled off the main road, moving through narrow buggy tracks that led to a small, secluded picnic spot. He tied the horse so it could graze, then helped her down, and they walked across the field to a small stream beneath a stand of trees. It was quiet and peaceful here. They had been here once before, and Darcy loved it. She spread the tablecloth out, emptying the picnic basket, then sat down beside him, her lemon-yellow dress spread out, covering her feet.

"I'm sorry I made you angry the other night," she said as she finished eating, and he smiled.

"You're not really sorry," he said, and she smiled back.

"In a way I am."

He leaned over, his eyes devouring her. "Why?"

She flushed. "Don't look at me that way, Heath, it makes me nervous."

"What way?"

"Like you wanted to eat me."

"Maybe I do." He reached up and touched her face, and she felt a shock run through her. "I know I want to kiss you," he said softly, and leaned closer.

She didn't move; she couldn't. Since the first night he'd held her close and kissed her, Darcy'd known what it was to thrill to a man's touch. No one before had ever kissed her like that, as if she was the last woman on earth . . . as if he was a part of her.

"Darcy?" whispered Heath, and she leaned toward him.

His kiss was gentle at first, like sweet honey; then, as her lips moved beneath his, Heath felt his blood begin to grow hot, and he pulled his mouth from hers breathlessly. He'd better watch himself. It was one thing to lie with Cora, but Darcy was something else, and her kisses were something else too. He always felt them clear to his toes, and his head was still reeling from the onslaught of her last kiss.

He leaned back on his knees, then sat up straight, trying to keep his mind off the low décolleté of the dress she was wearing, and he turned to the stream, picking up a twig, throwing it in the water.

"There you go again," Darcy said stubbornly as she

moved over and sat beside him. "Why do you kiss me like that, then act like I'm not around? Don't you like my kisses, Heath? If not, then why do you kiss me at all? Why do you even bother with me?"

He closed his eyes and lay back in the grass, then opened them again as he felt her hand on his chest, her fingers unbuttoning his shirt. "For God's sake, Darcy, what are you doing?" he asked anxiously, and her eyes shone like pale green peridots.

"I've never felt a man's chest, Heath," she answered softly, and her hand moved beneath his shirt. "I've always wanted to. I've seen men bare to the waist chopping wood, and watched the muscles as they worked." Her hand moved across his chest, where only a scattering of hairs was curled, but the gesture made him go weak inside. Her fingers pressed into his flesh, burning their way across his chest; then suddenly she leaned over, her lips touching the base of his throat, and he felt himself hardening.

"Darcy!" he gasped, and she drew her head back, looking at him, her eyes warm and limpid.

"I never wanted to do that before," she said breathlessly. "Not until now. . . . Heath, I feel strange . . ." She moaned as she stretched out, her head on his shoulder, her hand still warm on his chest, and her body tingled all over with sensations she'd never felt before. "Oh, Heath! What's wrong with me?" she gasped. "I feel so strange, as if . . . as if . . ."

He gazed down into her eyes, feeling her body pressed against his. "As if what?" he asked huskily, and she let out another moan, her body beginning to move sensuously against him.

He tried to fight off the desires that were overwhelming him. He was on fire, every nerve in his body pulsating vibrantly, and he moved up, rolling her onto her back in the soft grass. It was no use, he couldn't fight it. Not something as strong as this.

His mouth came down on hers, and he kissed her longingly, his tongue opening her lips, searching the exciting warmth of her mouth as his hands fumbled with the buttons on the front of her bodice. Her breasts burst forth full and ripe, and his lips left her mouth to cover them, teasing the nipples until they rose in hardened peaks and there was no going back. He had to have her, but he knew it was her first time.

His hands moved gently, caressing, teasing as he lifted her skirts. Her voice was soft, begging, whimpering, groaning with ecstasy as he pulled off her bloomers and felt the soft skin of her thighs beneath his hand. Then his hand moved across her stomach and down to the hair that curled, and his fingers dipped into the hair, touching, probing sensuously.

"I love you, Darcy," he whispered softly, and meant it for the first time in his life as he looked into her eyes staring up at him glazed and warm, her face flushed.

"Oh, Heath, I love you too," she sighed, and he reached down, unfastening his pants, letting his swollen manhood free to find its solace.

He spread her legs anxiously, yet held back. His tongue, his hands, his lips pleasured her, thrilling her body until she could hardly stand it; then, when he was sure she was ready, he moved into her. She cried out at his first thrust, and tears welled up in her eyes.

"Heath!"

His mouth covered hers again, and he thrust harder this time, feeling her groan beneath him as her maidenhead gave; then he stopped inside her, waiting for the first pain to ease. His lips moved against hers again, his tongue flicking in and out, parting her lips, and slowly he began to move inside her.

The pain was suddenly gone, and Darcy felt warm and weak, thrills pulsating through her like she'd never felt before, setting her loins on fire. She wanted more. Arching her body up to meet him, she clung to him, fighting for something that seemed to drive her. Then, as Heath plunged deep inside her, she let out a startled cry and felt a thousand explosions shake her insides, leaving her trembling in a rapture she never knew existed.

Heath felt it too, she knew, because he shook violently, then lay against her quietly, his lips sipping at hers slowly, as if he barely had the strength to move.

"Heath," she whispered against his mouth. "I had no idea it was anything like this."

He drew his mouth from hers and buried his face in her warm neck, smelling the intoxicating fragrance that seeped up from her gorgeous coppery hair. "Are you surprised?"

"Very."

He was still inside her, and he started to move away. "No," she pleaded softly. "Push it in again. I want to feel it inside again, Heath."

"I can't keep it up much longer," he said against her ear. "Once it's over, it takes a while to make it hard again."

"Why?"

"You ask the strangest questions." He thrust forward and discovered he was still hard enough to make her sigh; then he felt it softening and pulled out. He pulled down her skirts and straightened them, then gathered her into his arms, holding her close. "Now, see what you started," he teased against her hair. "I should spank you for that."

"I've never done anything like that before, Heath. I never wanted to," she said. "But when I'm with you . . ."

He kissed her, and they lay in the grass for a long time talking, and when it was time to leave, neither of them wanted to go, and for the first time in his life Heath knew no other woman would ever satisfy him the way Darcy had. They made arrangements to meet next Sunday afternoon as he drove her back to the town, but the meeting never came.

On Wednesday afternoon Victor McLaren returned from Charleston. Cora was as nervous as a cat all through supper, although she hid it well, thanks to Darcy's continuous chatter.

That evening at bedtime, she put on her favorite nightgown. It was soft and clung to her figure, emphasizing her full breasts, the tiny pink rosebuds that cascaded down the front contrasting with the sheer, filmy panels of white that covered the pink satin beneath. She let her hair down long and flowing, brushing it to make it shine.

"I'm certainly glad I came home early," Victor said as he undressed on the other side of the room, with one eye on his pretty young wife. "It's nice to have a wife to come home to who enjoys going to bed."

Cora sighed. "Why shouldn't I?" she said sensuously. "After all, look who I'm going to bed with." If she buttered him up, it wouldn't hurt. Then she made her fatal mistake. "Victor," she asked cautiously, hoping not to sound too eager, "what would you say if I told you I was pregnant?"

She heard a gasp from behind her, and whirled around. Victor was standing on the other side of the bed staring at her, his heavily jowled face white, eyes round like saucers, his hairy chest, above his protruding stomach, heaving dangerously.

"What did you say?" he asked slowly, hesitantly, and she looked at him, her lips trembling.

"I . . . I . . . What's the matter, Victor?" she asked softly. "What have I done?"

"Did you say you were pregnant?" he shouted, and she shook her head.

"No . . ." she cried hurriedly. "I said, what would you do if I said I was. I'm not . . . I'm not pregnant."

But he didn't believe her. He stalked out from behind the bed, still in his underwear, his face contorted with rage. "You lie!" he yelled viciously, and grabbed her arm, pulling her from the vanity bench so she almost fell to the floor. "I want to know, Cora! Tell me the truth. Are you pregnant?"

His eyes were boring into hers like hot coals searing

her soul. "Yes," she gasped trembling as his fingers bit into her wrist. "Yes!"

His nostrils flared as his face reddened. "Who's the father?" he asked, and she winced.

"You are!"

"No!"

"Yes!"

"Never!" he shouted, and his free hand struck the side of her face with such force she felt her jaw crunch. "I asked you, who's the father?"

Her lip was beginning to swell. "I told you!" she cried hysterically. "You are!"

Suddenly there was a knock on the door. "Father, are you all right?" It was Darcy.

"Go to bed, Darcy, this is between Cora and me!" he yelled, but Cora's voice drowned out his words.

"Help me, Darcy! Please!" she screamed. "Help me!" and Darcy stood in the hall, uncertain, as the housekeeper came running up the stairs.

"My word, what's going on?" she asked, and Darcy shook her head as Cora screamed again for help.

Darcy couldn't listen anymore. She knew her father had a violent temper, and she reached down, turning the doorknob, throwing the door open wide, but her father had no idea she and the housekeeper had entered the room.

"I'll tell you why I can't be the father of your baby," Victor was shouting hysterically. "Because when Darcy was little and had mumps, I had them too, and the doctor said I'd never father any more children. I can't father any more children, Cora. So I'm asking you again, who's the father of your baby?"

Cora choked in a sob, her world shattering into pieces. "I can't tell you!" she cried helplessly, but he raised his hand to hit her again. "I . . . Heath!" she gasped, sobbing as she stared at his raised hand. "Heath Chapman! It was Heath Chapman, Roth's son." Neither of them saw the stricken look on Darcy's face at Cora's confession.

"Roth's son?" asked the senator through clenched teeth, and Cora confirmed it.

"Yes . . . Heath!" she sobbed.

"When?" asked Victor, his voice rumbling with rage, and tears streamed from Cora's eyes.

"We've been lovers for months. I knew Heath before, a long time ago . . . Please, Victor, you're hurting me," she begged as she tried to twist her wrist from his hand, but he was like a madman.

"That's the truth?" he asked, and she nodded, licking the tears as they ran into her swollen mouth, wiping her face with the back of her hand.

He let go her hand and walked to the dresser. Cora sighed. "Please, Victor, forgive me, I didn't mean to hurt you," she said, and the housekeeper moved close to Darcy, whispering softly.

"We'd better leave, Miss Darcy," she said, but Darcy didn't answer; she stood transfixed, staring at Cora, listening to the words stumbling from her mouth. Then suddenly the housekeeper glanced toward the senator, and her face went white. "Oh, my God, no!" she screamed, but it was too late.

The explosion was deafening, and Cora stared in disbelief as she felt the searing pain in her breast; then slowly a warm feeling began to flood over her, and the room began to spin around. She saw Victor with the pistol in his hand, and the housekeeper, and Darcy . . . Darcy looked so funny . . . and then she saw Heath stretching his arms to meet her, but he was moving away. . . .

"Heath! Heath!" Cora mumbled, then slumped to the floor in a pool of blood.

The next morning the whole of Beaufort was shocked by the news that Senator McLaren had been arrested for the murder of his wife, naming Heath Chapman, son of Congressman Roth Chapman and his wife, Loedicia, as Cora's lover and the father of the child she'd been carrying. There was no way they could keep the details quiet, because the housekeeper was determined to talk, and all of Beaufort listened, then talked with her, and the word spread.

Loedicia paced the floor of the parlor at the Château, then stopped and stared again at her son. "Why?" she asked, shaking her head of dark curly hair, her beautiful violet eyes weary. "Were you in love with her?"

Heath reddened. "I thought so once."

"But another man's wife. Heath, even Roth and I can't help you now."

Loedicia looked at her husband, hoping for an answer. She had married Roth the first time some twenty years ago, back in 1775 when she thought her first husband, Quinn Locke, had been killed by Indians. Then, a little over two months after the ceremony, Quinn had come back—he hadn't been dead—and she'd returned with him to the wilderness on the shores of Lake Erie. Heath had been born nine months later, and as the boy grew, they both knew he was not Quinn's son, but Roth's. It had almost destroyed their marriage. In the spring of 1794, while returning from a trip to England, where Quinn had reclaimed his title of Earl of Locksley, he was accidentally killed when Beau and Heath's privateer captured the ship they were sailing on. After Quinn's burial at sea, Heath had brought her to his father. She had always loved Roth. He was a tall man, impressive and good-looking, and had just recently been elected congressman for his district. Life with him had been wonderful. Now this. Her heart was heavy.

Roth felt her eyes on him and stood up, studying his son, his dark eyes scowling. "The only thing you can do now, son, is go away somewhere and hope maybe they'll forget in time," he said.

"And if I stay? After all, I didn't kill her."

"If you stay," said Loedicia, "they'll treat you like an outcast. No mother will let you so much as look at her daughter, and no respectable man will admit you're his friend."

Heath looked at Roth guiltily. "I guess I let you down, didn't I?" he said. "I wanted you to be proud of me. I was going to ask you if I could come live here and learn all about the place, but I guess I'm too late. This won't hurt your political career, will it?" he asked Roth.

Roth shook his head. "I don't know. Rachel's having a field day with your mother's reputation, but I think we can weather it."

Heath saw the hurt in his mother's eyes.

"Where will you go, Heath?" she asked. "You don't know anyone to go to." She began to cry. "There's nowhere I can send you. Fort Locke isn't even there anymore," and she burst into tears.

He reached out and pulled her into his arms, holding her tightly. "Don't worry, Mother, please," he said softly. "I know people all over the world, and I've been restless lately anyway. I'll keep in touch and I'll be fine." She couldn't see the tears in his eyes, but she could hear them in his voice. "Beau's ship, the *Duchess*, is sailing out tomorrow, and I'll be on it." He pushed her back so he could look at her, and fought the tears that tried to cloud his vision. "Now, don't worry. It's my fault. I've been stupid and dumb, and now I'll pay for it, but there's something I have to do, Mother, before I go, someone I have to see. I'll go to Beau's to tell Liza to pack my things, and I'll say good-bye now." He kissed her and hugged her, then released her as he turned to Roth. They embraced; then, without another word, he left, walking out into the warm afternoon sunshine.

He didn't want to go. He'd begun to like it here. And Darcy—all he could think of was Darcy. Beautiful, wonderful Darcy, and what she was thinking. He had to try to explain before he left.

He rode upriver to Beau's place first, where Rebel spent practically all of her time. He'd expected a tongue-lashing from her, but surprisingly, none was forthcoming. Instead she tried to act like nothing was wrong and promised to help Liza pack his things, if he'd really made up his mind to go.

That evening, when he finally headed toward Beaufort, he was in a bit better spirits than he'd been for the past few days. It was Sunday. He and Darcy were to have met again today for their ride in the country, and as he remembered last Sunday, his heart grew heavy. It seemed like he was always having to leave places for one reason or another.

It was pitch dark when he reached Beaufort and rode toward the senator's house, dismounting outside the garden where he'd first met her. He opened the gate slowly and slipped inside, closing it quietly behind him. Darcy had told him she usually came out in the garden every evening just before going to bed because it was so quiet and peaceful, but would she still keep to the same ritual?

He moved into the deeper shadows and waited what seemed like an eternity. Then, when he was about ready to give up and just go barging in, the back door opened and someone stepped outside. He held his breath, watching as a shadow fell across the walk in front of him, made by the light coming from inside the house; then he sighed as Darcy stepped into view. She stood for a long time staring off into space, then moved toward the gate and started to lock it.

"If you lock it, how will I get back out?" Heath asked softly, parroting the words he'd said to her the first night they'd met, and she whirled around, her hand covering her mouth, her eyes wild. "Please, Darcy," he begged as she stared at him, "just give me a minute."

She lowered her hand to her breast, and he saw that her heart was pounding. "What do you want?"

"To explain."

"You think you can explain away Cora? You think anything you say will make a difference?"

"No, I don't suppose it will," he said. "But I have to try." His eyes looked directly into hers. "I don't know why Cora happened, Darcy. I guess because women meant nothing to me. Not really. They meant a warm bed, a bit of pleasure, and I took it whenever I could. Then I met you. I fell in love with you, Darcy, but it was too late. Cora was already there and the wheels of fate were already turning against me. I can't go back and undo any of it, but I wanted you to know. I'm leaving in the morning, and I don't know if I'll ever be back, but before I go, I wanted you to know that I never meant to hurt anyone, least of all you, and that I'll always love you."

He reached out and grabbed her, pulling her to him as his mouth covered hers in a long passionate kiss. Darcy tried to fight him, but it was no use. She felt her body responding to him as her lips kissed him back. Then, as suddenly, he released her and looked down into her face.

"I hate you, Heath Chapman," she whispered savagely, tears glistening in her eyes. "I hate you," but he only smiled that charming smile of his that at the moment was covering the sadness in his heart.

"I know," he whispered softly. "Good-bye, Darcy." He walked out of the gate, leaving her standing alone in the garden with her heart torn to pieces, and the next morning he sailed from Port Royal and out of her life.

On December 20, 1796, five days before Christmas, on a cool, misty morning, Senator Victor McLaren, despondent over having killed his unfaithful wife, and unable to face the trial he knew was ahead of him, committed suicide, hanging himself in his prison cell.

ᘛ 2 ᘚ

Mud splashed against the wheels of the carriage, bogging it down at times as it made its way farther and farther away from Beaufort. Inside Darcy clung to the cloak about her, trying to ward off the chill that had come with the rain. It had been a perfect day to leave, because it was a day that required no looking back. And that's what she wanted, no looking back.

She had stood in the doorway last evening, looking out into the garden, and vowed she never wanted to see the place again. There were so many memories. Memories she wished had never been.

She leaned her head back against the cushioned seat and closed her eyes, listening to the rain beat its tattoo on the roof of the closed carriage. Her heart was torn inside. Why was life so cruel? All she'd wanted was love. Was that so wrong? To be loved? Tears glistened at the corners of her eyes. She'd loved him so much. Never again, she told herself. She'd never let another man do to her what Heath had done. She'd forget him. Put him out of her life and her thoughts.

She shivered, her mind suddenly recalling the feel of his hands caressing her, his mouth sipping at hers, his body covering hers. How could she ever forget? She straightened in her seat guiltily, opening her eyes abruptly as her aunt spoke.

"Are you all right, Darcy?" she asked.

Darcy sighed. "Yes, Aunt Nell." But Aunt Nell frowned.

"I know it's been hard on you, what with everything

28

that's happened, and then the funeral," she said, leaning forward, reaching across the seat to touch her niece's hand and squeeze it affectionately. "But I warned your father about that woman, and he wouldn't listen."

Nellida McLaren leaned back again, and sat erect against the seat, her stern face unsympathetic. She was still single at the age of forty. Whether by choice or not, Darcy never knew, because no one ever discussed Aunt Nell much. She was just there. She had always lived with them and had taken over the running of her brother's household when his first wife became ill and died, filling the job of hostess until his marriage to Cora, and supervising much of Darcy's time afterward, when Cora seemed uninterested in her young stepdaughter. She'd warned Victor heatedly that his ridiculous love for a woman young enough to be his daughter would lead him to ruin. Now it had. It had led to his death and disgrace. But nobody ever listened to her. After all, what did she know of love and marriage? She was a spinster. Who was she to give advice?

Darcy glanced at her now, seeing the gray streaks in her dark auburn hair, her brown eyes curiously animated.

"Your father was a fool," she went on angrily. "A stubborn, childish old fool to even think that woman would be true to him." She bit her lip irritably, straightening the skirt of her black wool traveling suit. "In a way, my dear, I'm glad I didn't arrive before that young man left town." She had arrived in Beaufort the day after her brother's suicide, in time to make the funeral arrangements and help Darcy settle his affairs. "Because if I had," she went on, "I probably would have gone to see him and told him exactly what I thought of him."

Darcy flinched. "It wouldn't have done any good, Aunt Nell," she said softly.

Her aunt spluttered. "Probably not," she said. "But to think he had the nerve to expect Victor to accept the child as his own. To fool with a man's wife like that . . . It's no wonder Victor went out of his mind. That vicious woman. She was no good for my brother. Poor Victor!"

Darcy's jaw tightened. "Please, Aunt Nell, do we have to talk about it? It's a long way to Columbia, and I'd rather forget."

"Poor child," she cooed softly. "You're going to have so much to live down now. I'm just glad I was able to shelter you through most of this. Can you imagine? That young man's father is a congressman. Why, you might even have met him if you'd been down in Beaufort sooner, and things could have been worse. From what I've heard, he's quite a ladies' man. Used to be a pirate or some such . . . wears a golden earring in one ear, can you imagine?"

"Aunt Nell, please," Darcy cried, trying to hold back the tears. "It's over and done. I just want to go home and forget the whole thing." She stared at the handle on the door to the carriage, having nothing better to look at while Aunt Nell studied her face intently.

There'd been something about Darcy. Ever since her arrival, Nell had been uneasy. Naturally, her father's death had been a blow, but Darcy and her father hadn't been too close over the years. In fact, Darcy had been indifferent and cool toward her father for some time, and Nell was certain the girl had discovered her father's infidelities against her mother during her early teens. Darcy's mother had been extremely ill long before she'd taken her final breath, and even though Nell had cautioned Victor, he'd been a virile man and she knew her warnings would do little good. It was natural that Darcy resented him for it, so it seemed unusual that she'd be drained so emotionally by her father's actions. She was, though. She was lifeless. As if she too had died, and it didn't seem right.

"Darcy, are you sure you're all right?" she asked again.

Darcy nodded, her face pale, then settled back again

against the seat. But she wasn't all right. Not really, and she never would be. Nothing would ever be the same again. She'd go back to Columbia, to the house she'd been born in, her father had left her well provided for, but nothing would ever be the same again. They had spent Christmas alone, just she and Aunt Nell, without a tree or presents or friends. It didn't even seem like Christmas, and the next day they'd clothed the furniture with dust covers, shut the house, and left for Columbia, and she closed her eyes again, glad she was going home.

They had been in Columbia for three weeks already. New Year's Eve had gone by, as had Christmas, lonely and unhappy. Now there was the long wait for spring.

Darcy stood in front of the fireplace, staring at the logs, the embers, glowing deep red, taking the chill from the room. It looked like they were in for a cold snap. She wished the weather would stay warm. The cold seemed to go right through her, and she hated it. She held her hands out toward the heat, wondering what time Aunt Nell would return from visiting her friend, yet dreading the moment, but she had to tell her, there was no other way, and the quicker, the better. Poor Aunt Nell. As if she hadn't been through enough.

Darcy rubbed her eyes, then pinched her cheeks, hoping to put some color into them as she heard the front door open. She waited, motionless.

"Oh, here you are," exclaimed Nell a few minutes later as she entered the parlor, rubbing her hands together. "I must say it's certainly gotten cold outside. I wouldn't be surprised to see ice on the puddles in the morning." She stepped up beside Darcy and followed her suit, holding her hands out toward the flames. "My goodness, it hasn't gotten this cold for years." She rubbed her hands together briskly.

Darcy tried to make light conversation, but it was no use, her voice failed her.

"You look pale, dear," said Nell as she glanced over at Darcy, and Darcy swallowed hard.

"I haven't been feeling well lately," she replied.

"It's this weather. Cold like this gets to everybody. Remember when you were a little girl, the way you used to end up in bed whenever there was a cold snap?"

"Aunt Nell, that's not it," said Darcy. "It's not the cold."

"Oh?"

"No . . . it's . . ." How could she say it? How could she tell her?

"It's what?" asked Nell, frowning, and Darcy took a deep breath.

"It's . . . it's that I'm pregnant," she murmured breathlessly, and the words seemed to echo in the room.

Nell stared at her niece, her eyes never leaving her face, her hands going numb; then slowly she groped for the nearest chair and lowered herself, her eyes stricken.

"Pregnant?" she gasped helplessly, and Darcy shook her head.

"I didn't want to tell you. But I knew I had to."

"But how . . . how could something like this . . . ? Who?" she asked, and Darcy cringed, swallowing hard.

"Remember on the way home when you said you were glad I hadn't been in Beaufort long enough to meet Heath?"

Nell's face went white. "Oh, God, no!"

Darcy bit her lip. "Please, Aunt Nell," she said. "It wasn't what you're thinking."

"You let Cora's lover touch you?"

She tried to hold back the tears. "You make it sound so dirty," she cried. "And it wasn't."

Nell stiffened, trying to keep herself composed. "What do you call it, Darcy?" she said. "He was your stepmother's lover."

"I know . . . I know . . ."

"Then how can you say it wasn't cheap and degrading.

Darcy fell to her knees at Nell's feet, her hands clasping Nell's desperately. "I loved him, Aunt Nell, don't you understand?" she sobbed, her heart breaking. "I loved him and . . . and I still do. I hate him, yet I can't forget him. I wish I could die!" She buried her face in her aunt's lap, and Nell stared at the back of her head, tracing the outline of the soft flowing ringlets of deep coppery red. Darcy's body was heaving with each sob, her young heart tearing into pieces.

Slowly, as Nell stared at her, tears filtered into the older woman's eyes. She wiped them away before reaching down to stroke the girl's head.

"What have you decided to do?" she asked, sniffing back to keep from crying.

"I don't know," said Darcy, having momentarily halted her flow of tears. "I heard about a girl last year who went to a lady who did something to make her lose it."

Nell's hand curved on the back of Darcy's head, and she held the girl's head tightly in her lap. "No!" she said angrily. "You'll do no such thing." Darcy looked up abruptly. "You'll not go to one of those butchers," Nell went on, and stared off beyond Darcy's head toward the fireplace. "I have a better idea," she said slowly; and looked down into Darcy's pale green eyes, the lashes thick with tears. "I was planning on going to Boston this summer to visit a close friend," she said. "Instead, we'll go now. The two of us, You can have the baby there."

"How will that help?"

Nell stroked her cheek and wiped away a tear. "We'll find someone to take the baby," she said. "Maybe my friend can keep it for you. She loves children and has a big house." ·

Darcy stared up at her, her eyes misty. "You mean, give the baby away?" she asked, and Nell nodded.

"It's the only way, dear," she said. "You're not even

eighteen yet, and without a husband . . . Your father was a wealthy man. He left you well provided for, but you'd never be able to hold your head up in society. Yes, that's what we'll do. We'll find someone to take the baby."

Darcy stared at Aunt Nell. To give away something so sweet. A part of Heath. How could she do it?

"You have to, dear," said Nell, seeing the indecision in her eyes.

"There's no other way?"

"Can you think of one?"

She hung her head, sniffing back tears. "No."

"Then it's settled." Nell gave her a handkerchief, making her dry her eyes, then insisted she have one of the servants bring her some hot tea, and they sat in the parlor until quite late while Darcy told her the whole story and they made their plans.

Darcy had thought they'd go overland to Boston, but Aunt Nell made other arrangements. She was afraid the long ride would be too much for Darcy in the winter because of the snow in the North, so they traveled to Wilmington, a port town in North Carolina, and had only a short time to wait for a ship, then sailed, arriving in Boston the second week in March.

"Isn't the coastline beautiful?" exclaimed Nell as they stood at the rail watching the ship approach Boston Harbor.

Darcy nodded unenthusiastically. She'd been sick for most of the voyage, and today was no different. "Do all women feel like this?" she asked her aunt.

Nell's eyes clouded momentarily. "No, dear, not from what I've heard." She couldn't tell her niece that she'd been sick too. That she'd gone to one of those butchers and almost died. That the young man she'd loved, the father of the baby she'd gotten rid of, had been lost at sea, and the man her parents had arranged for her to marry had disappeared when he'd learned of her indiscretion, and that because of it she could never have children. No. She'd never tell Darcy about young Nell McLaren, but she could understand, and she could make sure the same thing didn't happen to Darcy.

She put her arm about Darcy, helping her back to the cabin to lie down, and by the time they left the ship, she was feeling somewhat better.

Emily and Will Exeter lived in a comfortable home on the outskirts of Boston, not far from the Charles River. It was surrounded by plush meadows and rolling hills, the trees on them bare now to the late-winter sun.

Darcy had been cold for days, and the sweep of brisk winds off the river drove the chill even deeper in her bones as the carriage made its way along the river, snow covering its banks and the hills beyond. What if the Exeters weren't as pleased as Aunt Nell was sure they'd be? After all, they had expected Aunt Nell to arrive alone, and in June, not with her in March. Aunt Nell had sent a letter on ahead, but they hadn't waited for a reply, and now, as the carriage pulled into the long drive, Darcy, staring ahead at the white boxlike structure, with its upstairs dormers and bleak appearance, was uneasy.

Even standing at the doorstep waiting for the door to open unnerved her.

"Yes, ma'am?" asked a thin, unattractive woman, her New England accent heavy as she opened the door, staring at them, and Nell smiled.

"I'd like to see Mrs. Exeter," she said, surprised to see a new housekeeper. The last time she'd been here, which was three years before, the housekeeper had been a plump woman in her late fifties, not quite as young as this one, who looked to be closer to thirty-five, and Nell hadn't remembered Emily having written that she'd dismissed her old servant.

"The Exeters are out at the moment, ma'am," she explained, her stern countenance unfriendly. "If you'd care to leave your name, I'll tell Mrs. Exeter you called."

Nell frowned. "That's impossible," she said abruptly. "We just arrived in Boston and all our luggage is outside in the carriage. We can't possibly ride back to town."

The woman stared at them, her pale eyes irritated. "Was Mrs. Exeter expecting you?"

"I did send a letter."

"She didn't say," she said curtly, then opened the door wide, motioning inside. "But I guess you'd best come in until the matter's settled."

"Our trunks?"

"Have the driver put them in here." She gestured about the foyer as Darcy stepped inside.

Darcy was glad to get in out of the bitter wind while Aunt Nell returned to the carriage to give the driver instructions. A few minutes later, she and Aunt Nell stood in the parlor, in front of the fire, listening to the wind howl past the corner of the house, and Darcy felt the warmth begin to penetrate beneath her dark gray velvet with its long sleeves, high waist, and pearl buttons down the back. Soft ribbons of pink satin edged the bodice of her dress, and the matching gray bonnet she handed to the housekeeper, along with her gray pelisse and hooded cape, had rosettes of pink satin ribbon on each side. Even her pelisse and cape together hadn't been enough to keep the New England weather at bay on the ride out, and she was chilled to the bone.

Nell straightened the skirt on her green wool, rubbing the warmth back into her hands. "And I thought it was cold back home," she said breathlessly. "Gracious, I never dreamed winters in the North were like this. I've only been here during the summer months."

"I thought you said spring began in March."

"I'm sure it does," she said. "But I presume the weather in Boston can be just as unpredictable as the weather in South Carolina."

Darcy glanced toward the window as huge snowflakes began to fall, and she shivered. Would she never get warm?

It was after dark when the Exeters arrived home,

shortly before the evening meal. Darcy was curled up in a chair in front of the fire, her red curls gleaming orange-gold in the firelight as they rested on her shoulders, the dark lashes on her sleeping eyes caressing her cheeks that were reddened from the heat. For the first time in days she was finally warm. So warm that she resented having to move. Yet, as she became aware of voices around her, she reluctantly stirred, then stared at Aunt Nell, who stood across the room talking to someone.

"I'm glad you're awake, dear," Nell said, glancing over toward Darcy, and Darcy straightened, her feet once more touching the floor as the two women walked toward her.

Emily Exeter was a contrast to Aunt Nell. Her hair was dark like a black cloud piled atop her head, wisps of it falling loosely to form soft, thin ringlets near the hairline, and her blue eyes were not the blue of the sky, but the deep blue of a stormy ocean with the sun glistening on it, causing gold flecks to dance in their depths. Her brows were heavy, yet well arched above a small pert nose and full pouting mouth. Her face was slightly rounded, as was her figure that was gently bulging beneath a striped wool dress in varied shades of mauve.

On the trip to Boston, Aunt Nell explained that Emily and she had been best friends since schooldays, and it was only her marriage to a sea captain that had separated them.

"He's given up the sea now, though," she'd said as they'd both stood at the rail of the ship watching the pounding waves. "Now he has a chandler's shop as well as owning ships of his own."

Darcy stared at Emily Exeter, noting the warm smile and affectionate way she looked at Nell.

Aunt Nell's thin mouth tightened severely, her amber eyes discoloring to match the red still streaking her hair in the firelight. She stared down her classically tapered nose at her niece, and Darcy realized she must have been an attractive woman when she was young. She could almost imagine seeing the women together as young girls. They must have been a lovely pair. But the years had deepened the lines in Nell's face, hardening it severely, and it was rare for her emotions to ever give way to tears. Strong and independent, she watched now as Darcy swallowed apprehensively.

"I've told Emily everything, Darcy," said Nell as she saw the girl's questioning look.

"And I'll do all I can," responded Emily. "Only, I won't be able to keep the baby here, dear," she went on. "Will and I are getting rather old to be raising a child. But I'm sure we can find a suitable couple somewhere who'd be willing to take on the task."

Darcy flinched. All the way to Boston she had been mulling over the prospect of giving her child away. How could she do it? How could she separate herself from a part of Heath that had meant so much to her? She'd never forgive him for what he'd done, but couldn't deny the fact that she still loved him. She had consented to come to Boston because Aunt Nell had been so insistent, and she knew it was impossible to stay in Columbia. But to give the child away? The reality of it was still far from settled in her mind or her heart. Her flame-flushed cheeks turned a deeper crimson, knowing that Mrs. Exeter knew of her predicament already, and she felt the woman's deep blue eyes studying her intently.

"There's no hurry," Darcy murmured self-consciously.

Emily saw the distress in Darcy's eyes. "Of course there isn't, dear," she replied. "Nell said you're not due until sometime in September, so we have months yet to decide what's to be done."

Darcy was grateful not to be pressed, and glanced at Aunt Nell, relieved, as Will Exeter cleared his throat to warn them, then stepped into the room.

Although of average height, Captain Exeter, as he was still respectfully called, was a man of commanding presence. His stomach had expanded some over the years, and pressed uncomfortably against a striped silk vest, but the black velvet frock coat with turned-down collar and double pocket flaps of black satin fit generously across his broad shoulders. Unlike a number of men whose legs became spindly with age, his breeches, silver buckles at the knee, covered fleshy, muscular thighs, with striped silver-and-white hose above black patent shoes. He wore a clipped beard, enhanced by the pale apricot stock about his neck, tied over a ruffled shirt, and his gray hair curled about his ears. His face was warm, yet firm, the mouth broad, eyes large, wide-set, and deep gray. They caressed his wife lovingly, then settled on the young girl in the chair, her red hair disheveled, pale green eyes shining in the firelight.

In that one long, searching look Darcy knew that he too had been told, and she wondered what he must think of her.

"So this is the young lady," he said as his eyes appraised her. "Thought perhaps she'd be a homely little goose, since the lad won't make things right with her." He cleared his throat again, and it was obvious he didn't know the whole truth. "The young man must be crazy to let a pretty little thing like her slip through his hands."

Emily touched his arm when she saw Darcy redden. "I think she'd rather not talk about it right now, Will," she cautioned, and Darcy saw her give Aunt Nell a knowing glance. So they were both keeping the full truth from the captain. Well, that was their affair.

Aunt Nell introduced her properly, and although the captain seemed to have reservations, his wife had none, and welcomed her warmly.

The next few days seemed to fly by as they settled into the routine of life with the Exeters. A life far different from that to which she was accustomed. There weren't as many servants, only the housekeeper, who also served as cook, and a cleaning girl who lived in an attic room above the dormers. Darcy had to do almost everything for herself, and there were no parties, teas, or social affairs.

Every afternoon she'd stroll across the meadow to the river and watch the changing landscape as the snow melted and gave way to spring flowers, and it was here, one warm day in April, that she met John McGill.

Carriages were frequent on the road that carried people up the Charles River, and often, as she watched from a distance, they'd slow down to admire the scenery. On this particular afternoon, however, one of the carriages stopped, and she watched apprehensively as a man stepped down, straightening his brown frock coat, adjusting the pale blue cravat that graced his plain white shirt.

She could see that his hair was completely gray as he removed his beaver hat and strolled toward her, but his face, in spite of the sallow complexion and age lines, held a pair of dark eyes that sparkled yet with the warmth of youth, reminding her of Heath's dark, almost black eyes. His chin was strong and firm, the cheeks thin, forehead broad. He would have been handsome as a young man.

"Hello," he said, greeting her from a distance, and she stared, frowning. "Don't be upset," he offered. "I believe you must be Will's house guest, Miss McLaren. Am I right?"

She didn't answer, so he continued trying to put her at ease.

"I should wait until we're properly introduced, I know," he said, smiling at her warmly, "but you see, you've taken my favorite spot. The dead log you're sitting on is where I usually spend all my time when I come to visit, and you've rather taken it over."

"Who are you?" she finally asked, surprised that instead of frightening her as most older men did when they approached her in such an offhand manner, he didn't. Instead, she felt drawn to the warmth that shone in his face.

"I'm John McGill," he answered, sighing. "An old friend of Will's."

There was something about his face. "Are you all right, Mr. McGill?" she asked as she saw him catch his breath as if in pain.

His eyes steadied on her, taking in her windblown curls trying to escape the straw bonnet. He liked the way the spring breeze caught at her white muslin dress with its daintily embroidered yellow flowers, plastering it against her shapely legs, exposing her kid shoes.

"I'm fine at the moment," he replied; then his smile broadened again. "You remind me of someone," he said, his eyes once more sparkling. "I hope you don't mind."

She smiled back. "Who?"

His eyes suddenly clouded as he looked off toward the river. "The girl I married twenty-five years ago."

"She's dead?" she asked hesitantly. She didn't know how she'd known; it was something in the look on his face.

He nodded. "We had ten beautiful years together."

She felt sorry for him. It was obvious that he still grieved for her. She watched as he bent down and picked a few spring beauties, savoring the fragrance as he held them to his nose. If it weren't for the hollows at his cheeks and shadows beneath his eyes, John McGill would still be a very handsome man. His clothes, too, though, hung on him as if he'd recently begun to lose weight, and she began to wonder.

"For you," he said, addressing her once more as he handed her the flowers, and she flushed, reaching out to take them. "I suppose I should go on to the house," he said, straightening, then looked back toward the river. "But it's so lovely here. Especially in the early spring, when everything's coming to life." He tugged at his coat sleeves. Perhaps you'd let me walk you across the meadow to the house," he said, and she stood up,

catching her hand on the bonnet to keep the wind from
whipping it off.

"I think I'd like that," she said, and he smiled,
pleased as he raised his hand and motioned for the carriage that had brought him to go on ahead.

They strolled across the field slowly, breathing in the
warm spring air, the scent of earth, grass, and sky clear
on the wind. She liked John McGill. He talked of the
most interesting things. He'd been around the world
dozens of times, to strange exotic places few white men
had ever been, and his stories fascinated her.

The more she talked to him, the less she cared that
he was three times her age. He was like the father she
could never relate to and had lost, yet with the keen
wit and sensuous heart of a young man. His eyes held
a depth of longing that eased from inside him, and
Darcy, alone, needing someone to care, caught hold
and wouldn't let go.

By the time they reached the house, they were
laughing like old friends, and neither saw the frown
that creased Aunt Nell's brow as she was introduced to
him, nor the wariness that crept into Emily's eyes, nor
the anger that flooded the captain's face when he came
home.

John McGill had moved into his father's import-ex-
port company as a young man and traveled the world
as an agent, selling and buying. He'd met his redheaded young wife in Ireland, married her hurriedly so
she wouldn't get away, and taken her with him around
the world, where he'd run into Will Exeter. It was
Will's ships that carried much of his trade, even now.
After the death of his wife from a disease caught somewhere in the tropics, he spent more and more time in
Boston, finally establishing a home of his own and in-
heriting the business when his father passed away. He
was an extremely wealthy man and had never remar-
ried.

But as Darcy watched him at dinner that evening,
the meager food he consumed, the frown that occasion-

ally creased his forehead for no apparent reason, she sensed that something was wrong. He was trying too hard to hang on, and it was after his carriage had driven away that she had the courage to ask the Exeters about him.

"Mrs. Exeter, what's wrong with Mr. McGill?" she asked as they sat in the parlor after the gentleman had left.

Captain Exeter glanced at her, frowning. "What makes you ask?" he said before Emily could answer.

She shook her head. "I don't know. I just feel . . . he's ill, isn't he?"

Will glanced quickly at Emily. They had seen the look in John's eyes whenever he'd talked to the girl, and both of them had also come to the same conclusion months ago that Darcy had, yet John had told them nothing.

"If he is, he's been closemouthed about it," Emily replied as she knotted the thread on her embroidery. "I think maybe it's just that he's been away from the sea for a few years, and a man like that needs the sea to live."

Darcy didn't agree. It was something else, and in the days to come, when John arrived at the Exeters' more and more often, spending a good deal of his time with her, she knew she was right.

Then one day John came over earlier than usual. It had only been a few weeks since their first meeting, but already she felt at ease with him. Never once had he been out of place. He'd never held her hand or said anything to make her feel uncomfortable, and she knew that soon she'd have to tell him the truth about herself. The truth Aunt Nell had stated was none of his business.

Will had been in a panic ever since John's first appearance at the house, and just last evening cursed to himself for letting the man spend so much time with Darcy.

"Why not, he's happy for a change," Emily argued, but Will was insistent.

"My dear, he's an old man. What can possibly come of it?"

"Who cares?" she'd answered. "Have you watched them together? She and John get along so well. Perhaps it's good for them both. The girl misses her father."

Will still didn't like it.

Darcy had accidentally overheard the conversation, and she had seen the displeasure on the captain's face whenever John came to visit. She wasn't sure just how she felt about the situation herself. She had to admit that she missed John when he wasn't around and had begun to depend on his company. It wasn't fair for the captain to act so displeased just because she was happy for a change and seemed to be making John happy.

It was early afternoon and Darcy was strolling across the meadow toward the river when John arrived. She saw the carriage come up the road, and stopped, waving as John climbed down and strolled toward her. He usually came later toward evening unless it was a weekend, and she was surprised to see him.

"What a beautiful day you've picked for a visit," she said as he approached, and she watched the sun dancing in his gray hair as the breeze ruffled it softly, his dark eyes devouring her.

"I was hoping you'd be outside," he said, and held out his arm. "May I escort you the rest of the way to the river?"

She took his arm. "Thank you, sir."

They both laughed; then John grew serious.

"Darcy, there's something . . . I've been wanting to talk to you, and time's running so short."

She looked at him, puzzled, her pale green eyes reflecting the gold of the afternoon sun as they walked.

"Sit down," he said, and ushered her to the old log on the riverbank where she'd been sitting the first day they'd met.

She studied him. He'd become even thinner in the past few weeks, the hollows in his cheeks more prominent. She frowned. "What is it?"

He half-laughed. "I don't really know how to say it," he said self-consciously, his long tapered fingers fidgeting with his beaver hat. Then he sank to the log beside her, fumbling awkwardly for the right words, "Darcy, I know I'm almost old enough to be your grandfather," he began, "but . . . How can I say it?" He cleared his throat. "I want you to have my name, Darcy," he said hesitantly. "I want you to marry me. I want you for my wife."

She stared at him dumbfounded, her heart pounding. She'd never dreamed. It had been so nice to have someone to share things with. Someone who didn't expect favors in return. Someone her heart didn't have to worry about censuring, and now.

She tensed, her body rigid, the warmth driven from her like a stormy tidal wave. Marry him? God no! Tears welled up in her eyes, and one slid down her cheek.

"I didn't want—" she began, but he stopped her.

"Hear me out first, Darcy, please," he begged, and she stopped, swallowing hard, knowing she was losing another friend as he went on. "I know why you came to Boston," he said anxiously, and saw her face flush. "Will told me last night. He thought I was playing the fool and wanted to warn me, but you see, it only makes more sense now," he said. His face sobered seriously. "Darcy, I'm a sick man. The doctor says I'll be lucky to see the Fourth of July, and here it is May already. I'm lonely. My house is large and empty except for the servants. Meg and I had no children. Please, let me take you there. You need me, Darcy. Let your child bear my name. Let what I have be yours, everything. The house, the company, everything I own, in exchange for making my last days on earth happy ones."

He saw her frightened eyes, trembling lips. "Darcy,

all I ask is that you let me hold you sometimes and
touch you." His face paled, then reddened. "I'm sorry,
Darcy, I can't do more than that, my dear." His voice
broke. "Physically I can no longer share a bed with
anyone, let alone a young thing like you." Her eyes
met his. "But just to have you near . . . I'd be content.
Please, Darcy, make an old man happy. Say you'll be
my wife."

Darcy was speechless. He knew! He knew all about
the baby, and yet he'd asked her. She watched the dark
eyes shining as they looked at her from a face that was
becoming paler with each day. Not see the Fourth of
July? Tears overflowed her eyes, and suddenly her
heart went out to him. He wasn't that old. Perhaps in
years, yes, but in his heart he was still young. She'd felt
it when they'd talked and laughed together. He should
be robust yet, like the captain. Virile and strong, able
to take a wife who could still give him children. But he
wasn't.

"Oh, John!" she sighed. "I don't know what to say.
I vowed I'd never let a man into my life again."

He took her hand, his fingers unusually cold. They
tightened on hers. "Darcy, this young man, the father
of your baby. You loved him?"

She nodded, unable to speak, the answer choked in
her throat.

"Will said he'd heard you and your aunt discussing
giving the baby away. Is that what you want?"

"No."

"Then let me give it my name." His voice deepened.
"I can't give you the kind of love he gave you, Darcy,"
he said softly. "But I need someone now more than
ever, and I want that someone to be you."

She stared at him, her heart in a turmoil. Here was
the answer to her prayers. But could she do it? He said
all he wanted was to hold her and touch her.

"But what would people say? I'm not yet of age."

"I don't care what others say. I don't feel like an old
man, Darcy, not inside. When I'm with you, I'm young

again. Would you deny me a few months of happiness?"

He watched the indecision in her eyes. He was crazy for wanting her, he knew, but she'd become so dear to him the past few weeks. It was like having Meg with him again, warm and vital.

"Darcy, you have your whole life ahead of you, and you have the child to think of. He or she could have a home and all the luxuries of life," he went on. "You're young yet, and as the Widow McGill no one will think anything of the fact that you have a child."

She shuddered, her eyes misty. "Don't even talk like that, John," she said, and reached up, touching the side of his face, running her fingers across his sunken cheek. Dying! He was dying. This man who she knew had once been so vibrantly full of life was dying, and she'd become so fond of him.

"Would it be fair to you, John?" she asked. "I don't love you, at least not as a husband, only as a friend."

"I know." He sighed. "I'm not asking you to love me like that, only that you're kind to me in the days I have left. I think it'd be worth your while."

"Don't put it like that, please."

"But that's the way it'll be. I'll give you respectability, Darcy. All I ask is to have you near."

She saw the eagerness in his dark eyes. They were like Heath's, so dark it was hard to tell exactly what color they were. Could she make him happy? It would be a marriage in name only. He said he could no longer make love to a woman. Oh, how that must hurt. She remembered Heath's strong young body, then glanced at the shoulders of the man before her. He was becoming more frail with each day.

She choked back tears and swallowed hard. She could gain the world and keep her baby, but what a cruel way to do it.

"Darcy?"

She licked her lips, watching him hesitantly. Not for myself, she thought, not all for myself, and she knew that what she was about to do was going to cause an uproar in the Exeters' austere New England household, yet . . .

"Yes, John," she finally whispered, her heart in her throat. "If you're sure it'll make you happy. Yes, I'll be your wife."

Relief shone in his eyes as he lifted her hands to his lips and kissed them, and she could have sworn she saw them glistening momentarily with tears.

It was not as easy to convince Aunt Nell, however, nor the Exeters. The captain called John an old fool, and denounced Darcy for using him abominably for her own wicked, selfish ends, and even Emily wasn't sure the whole thing was right.

But in spite of the furor it caused, and in spite of the condemnation from others who were close to John, Darcy McLaren and John McGill were married on the tenth of May 1797, in a quiet ceremony, and she and Aunt Nell moved into John's home on the other side of town, overlooking the harbor. It was a beautiful home, elegantly decorated and furnished with a staff of servants to care for their every need, and for the first time in months, Darcy quit feeling sorry for herself.

John demanded little from her as her husband, and was content to merely gaze fondly at the wonder of her beautiful young body, and caress her affectionately at times, running his hands gently over her breasts, using his hands and mouth to try to bring her some pleasure, his heart filled with rapture, eyes filled with love. These were the hardest times for Darcy, however, because every caress and sensuous gesture brought back memories of Heath, and sometimes she wished John were able to do more. Perhaps it would still the longing inside her that his hands and mouth aroused.

By the middle of June, even these attempts at love-making had come to an end and John was completely bedridden. Now he merely held her hand and smiled weakly as she read to him and straightened his bedding, trying to make his life more bearable. What little bit of life he had left.

On August 2, John died in Darcy's arms, and Darcy wept. She'd grown to love this warm, gentle man. Not the way she'd loved Heath, but as a dear, close friend, and even the stares she evoked at his funeral, when she stood beside the coffin, her swollen stomach proclaiming to the world her advanced pregnancy, didn't diminish the sense of loss she felt inside.

One month later, on September 3, Heather McGill came into the world and life in the McGill household took on an air of urgency, centered around the new arrival. Life had become worthwhile again.

But Darcy didn't stay in Boston. Three years later, with her tiny red-haired daughter, and Aunt Nell by her side, Darcy, unable to face another bleak New England winter, and no longer a naive young girl, sold John's big house, turned the running of the company over to an agent, and returned to Columbia, South Carolina. Not to the big house she was born in, with its servants and memories, but to a small house on the other side of town, as the Widow McGill.

ॐ 3 ॐ

Port Royal, South Carolina—May 1800

Soft breezes stirred the curtains in the huge elegant
parlor of the big plantation house, as Loedicia stared
out the open window, down the front drive, to the road
that led to town. How terribly long it had been since
Heath had headed down that road, leaving family and
friends behind. Yet, the scandal had never been left to
die. Someone was always keeping it alive one way or
another.

January had brought with it a new century, and she
hoped to God it would be better than the last, at least
for Heath.

She turned, violet eyes alert at a noise behind her,
then relaxed as her adopted daughter, Ann, entered
the room.

Ann was tall for her age. She had just turned eleven
last month and already was past Loedicia's shoulders.
But then, Loedicia was a small woman, only an inch or
two over five feet, and she was as petite as Ann was
statuesque. The girl was half English, half Delaware
Indian. Loedicia and Roth had found her in a Delaware village when she was barely five and had
promptly fallen in love with her. Since she was an or-
phan, the tribe had no reservations about letting them
take her, and she'd been legally adopted into the
family.

Her eyes were like ebony, long and sloe, her skin a
tawny hue, but the rest of her was a contrast. The sun
glinted golden on her amber braids as she approached,

white ruffled lace pantalets and blue dimity dress covered with dirt.

"Gracious! What happened to you?" asked Loedicia as she saw the angry tears in her daughter's eyes.

Ann's bottom lip pushed out as she sniffed, trying to wipe away some of the dirt. "If Martin Engler ever asks to ride with me in my cart again, tell him he's not allowed, Mother," she said, acting older than her years. "He said he wanted to drive, then ran the cart off the lane into the ditch." She brushed at her dress vigorously. "For someone who's supposed to be thirteen already, he's stupid," she added, and Loedicia held back a smile.

Martin Engler lived a few miles away on another plantation downriver, and often rode to the Château on his horse. Loedicia was sure he was smitten with Ann; however, Ann always treated him abominably, and seemed unaware of his youthful admiration. It amused Loedicia, although she wondered if she'd be as amused if the situation persisted into the future. Martin was rather disappointing and could have had more in his favor. He had sandy hair, freckles, and what Roth called a big mouth. Not physically, but verbally. Always butting in when he had no business, and acting as if he knew all there was to know. Maybe that's why Ann treated him with such indifference most of the time.

Ann gave up trying to rescue her dress from the dirt, and sighed. "I'd rather have ten Wilton Chalmerses around than just one Martin Engler," she exclaimed as she stared at her mother disgustedly, and this time Loedicia couldn't hold back the smile.

Wilton Chalmers was another neighbor to the south, also thirteen years old, and completely the opposite of Martin. No backbone, no confidence, and afraid of his own shadow. Whenever he came over, they hardly knew he was around.

Ann frowned. "What's so funny, Mother?" she

asked pertly, and Loedicia's smile broadened even further.

"You, dear," she said softly. "I wonder if you'll be so demonstrative about Martin and Wilton a few years from now."

Ann straightened proudly as she walked over beside her mother and gazed out the same window.

"A few years from now I shouldn't care a thing about either one of them," she said with confidence, then turned to face her mother. "Do you think if I wrote another letter to Heath that he might possibly get it?" she asked suddenly.

Loedicia felt a tug at her heart. They had written so many letters to him the past four years, and received only one. He'd been in India somewhere at the time, trying to find where Loedicia had been born and raised. Her father's old regiment was still there, he'd written, and he'd met some people who had known her, but she had lived there so long ago. There'd been no indication that he'd received any of their letters, and no hint of where he might be headed next.

"You could try," she told Ann. Whenever she thought of Heath she felt so lost. He was such a strong part of her. He was Roth's son. Hers and Roth's, and although she had fought against it over the years, and tried not to show it, there'd always been something special in her feelings for Heath.

"I thought I'd write to him about the trip to England we're going to take later this summer," Ann said, ignoring the forlorn look on Loedicia's face. "Who knows, he might even be able to meet us there." Her eyes shone as she glanced at her mother. "Wouldn't that be something, Mother?" she said. "I'd not only get to meet Teak for the first time, but get to see Heath again too." She smiled wistfully. "It seems strange to think that I have two brothers, and one I've never even met."

Strange? Loedicia frowned. Yes, it was strange. Heath and Teak, her sons. Teak was in England, had been for six years now. She and her first husband, Quinn, had left him there, at his own request, so that he could go to Oxford. When Quinn was killed during their crossing home, Teak became the new Earl of Locksley, refusing to come back to America where he'd been born. He'd been fifteen at the time, and she'd heard little from him over the years. An occasional letter came from Mr. Briggs, the agent they'd left in charge of him and the estate, with a small note from Teak enclosed, but that was all. He was twenty-one now, and Loedicia felt it was time she paid him a visit, since it was obvious he wasn't about to come see her.

Roth had to go to Portsmouth, England, on business later in the summer, to inspect the businesses left to him there by his father years before. He'd had agents running them for him, but always liked to check things out for himself. Loedicia was taking advantage of the trip, and she and Ann were to accompany him. While there, they'd all go to London to see Teak.

Ann had never met her stepbrother, and the thought of having a big brother who was an earl fascinated her. She just knew she'd love him as much as she did Heath. Well, maybe not quite as much. After all, she was planning to marry Heath when she was old enough. Martin always told her she was crazy, that you couldn't marry your brother, but she knew he was just a dumb boy and didn't know any better. After all, she and Heath weren't really brother and sister. So what did it matter.

Stupid, dumb, Martin, she thought to herself as she stared out the window thinking of Heath. Then suddenly her eyes narrowed and she squinted.

"What is it?" asked Loedicia as she saw the startled expression on Ann's face, but Ann was speechless.

Then, "Heath!" she cried, and Loedicia's eyes followed her daughter's gaze down the long drive to where a rider was slowly cantering toward them.

My God, she thought, a hand flying to her breast to

still the heart that was pounding beneath the soft folds of her pale lavender gown. The squared shoulders, the easy way the rider had of sitting in the saddle, and, as he turned his head, looking first this way, then that, the sun glistening off the golden earring in his right ear, and she knew for sure.

She grabbed Ann's hand, and they raced from the room, through the plant-filled foyer, to the front door, and burst through it together, standing on the veranda to wait, watching him slowly approach.

He wore a coat of crimson with buff breeches and well-worn riding boots, his beaver hat dusty, as if he'd traveled a long way, and a bulky bundle was perched up behind his saddle.

They waited breathlessly, hardly believing their eyes until he rode up to the hitching post, slid from the saddle, and stood motionless, staring at them, the close-cropped beard he now wore making him look older than his twenty-four years.

Loedicia couldn't believe her eyes. "Heath!" she burst out, and her knees trembled as she lunged forward. "Oh, Heath!" and in seconds his arms engulfed her and he was holding her so tightly she thought for a minute she'd be crushed.

Although he tried to conceal it, she felt the tears on her neck as he held her to him, and her own tears fell freely.

"My goodness," she sniffed, when he finally let go. "Why didn't you let us know you were coming?"

He smiled wearily, the dust and tears making crow's feet at the corners of his eyes. "I didn't know myself until I started riding," he said. "Then there just didn't seem to be anyplace else to go."

Loedicia wiped her tears and her nose ineffectively with the back of her hand, and he reached in his pocket, handing her his handkerchief; then his eyes rested on the young girl standing anxiously behind his mother, her face all smiles, eyes shining.

When he'd left four years before, she'd been a toothless seven-year-old with scrawny legs and bony elbows; now she was a young lady with a full set of beautifully white teeth. Her scrawny legs were longer than before, like a young colt's, but beginning to fill out, although Heath had no knowledge of this, since they were concealed beneath her pantalets; all he could see was that she had grown taller and begun to fill out in the right places. The change was highly noticeable.

He held out his arms, and she sprang into them, hugging him for all she was worth. "I thought you'd never come home again," she said happily. "I was going to write you another letter today."

He held her from him, his eyes intent on her young face. "What do you mean, another letter? I haven't gotten the first one yet."

She stared, bewildered. "That can't be. I wrote all the time."

"And sent them where?"

She blushed, looking up at him sheepishly. "Well, you see, I'd write all the time and save them, then, when we'd hear you were someplace, I'd send the letters on, all at once, hoping you'd get them. You didn't?"

"Not a one. I probably left again before they arrived. I've been moving around quite a bit the past few years."

"It must have been terribly lonely for you," said Loedicia, and he looked over Ann's head at his mother.

"Let's forget it, shall we?" he said, then looked back at Ann. "You can bring me up-to-date on everything, how's that?" and Ann beamed, swinging her long thick braids back over her shoulders.

Heath was home! Home at last.

By the time they went into the house, with Ann noisily leading the way, Mattie was waiting for them in the foyer, and Jacob, a big black who had worked about his father's place for years, greeted him from the back door.

"Your father's up at Tonnerre with Rebel and Beau," explained Loedicia as she led him to the parlor and made him sit down while she told Mattie to fix them something to eat. Mattie had been with them since before Loedicia's marriage to Roth, and she was as glad to see Heath as his mother was.

"We'll take a ride up after lunch. Wait till you see the place, Heath," Loedicia went on when Mattie was through her fussing and left for the kitchen. "Beau's done wonders with it. The house isn't finished yet, but they've added an upstairs, cleared off about twenty more acres of bottomland on the north side, and put in more cotton."

"And they have a new baby, too," added Ann. "She'll be a year old in July. Her name's Lizette."

Heath glanced at his mother. Lizette had been the name of Loedicia's best friend. A Frenchwoman who had lived with them in the wilderness at Fort Locke for twenty years, traveled to England with them, and stuck by her after Quinn's death. She had died at the hands of two Seneca Indians when Loedicia too had almost lost her life. It was an honor for Rebel and Beau to name their daughter after her.

"And Cole must be about five by now, right?" he said.

"He was five in February," Loedicia confirmed. "And, oh, Heath, he looks so much like his grandfather."

"Like Telak?"

Telakonquinaga, or Telak as most people called him, was chief of the Tuscarora Indians who lived along the shores of Lake Erie near their old home at Fort Locke. Beau was the son of Telak and his fourth wife, who was half Indian, half French. It was this Indian heritage that had made Beau forsake his love for Rebel for so many years. Now he'd learned to cope with it, and it no longer bothered him.

"He's going to be better-looking than Telak," she said, nodding. "But the resemblance is going to be so striking, except he has green eyes. So does little Lizette, and both of them have hair as dark as ebony. They're such beautiful children."

"And you're a doting grandmother?"

Loedicia sighed. "I guess I am, at that." She smiled, and he smiled back.

She may be a grandmother, he thought, but she looked little like one. At least not the typical grandmother most people were used to. But then, she had never looked much like a mother either, nor acted like one, and his smile deepened as he remembered the many times over the years she'd embarrassed him with her unconventional, unmotherly behavior. But then, she wasn't just anybody. She was his mother, the former Lady Loedicia Aldrich, then Loedicia Locke, the Countess of Locksley, now Loedicia Chapman, wife of Congressman Roth Chapman. A very unusual lady.

At the age of forty-five, her hair was still black and curly as it had been when she was young, with barely a trace of gray near the temples, and her face was unlined, figure firm, lithe and petite. Yet her deep violet eyes held a maturity that contradicted their vibrantly youthful liveliness. She loved life and lived for love, and it shone in her face.

"Your father's going to be so glad to see you. So will Rebel and Beau," she said as he watched her face warming softly with her love for him.

"And the rest of Port Royal?" he asked, knowing the question couldn't be avoided.

Her eyes dropped from his as she glanced quickly at Ann. Ann had been too young to understand all the scandal that had accompanied Heath's sudden departure four years before, and Loedicia felt she was still rather young to learn the facts now. She had no way of knowing that Ann knew some of the rumors. Distorted ones, but with enough truth in them to make Heath even more glamorous in her eyes.

"The rest of Port Royal we'll discuss later," she said,

and Heath too glanced at his young sister, and understood.

They ate a light lunch, then had Jacob hitch the buggy while Ann changed her soiled dress, and she and Loedicia got their bonnets. Heath freshened up; then the three of them headed down the drive and upriver toward Tonnerre, with Heath driving.

It was so good to be home again, he thought as they rode along. Strange he should call Port Royal home, but it had started to become home to him. The first home he'd had since leaving Fort Locke when he was fifteen. Now he savored the sweet smell of the magnolias, the damp smell of the Broad River, and the earthy smell of the newly hoed young cotton plants being tended in the fields. But it brought back memories, too. Memories hard to erase that became even more vivid as they neared Tonnerre.

The place was shaping up beautifully. Another few years and it'd be as grand as the Château. Neither plantation had slaves as such. Both Beau and Roth bought slaves, gave them a working wage, and let them work off their initial cost, then set them free, hiring them back to work for them and helping them every way they could. It was a practice done by few Southerners and one looked down on and resented by the other planters, and it sometimes caused trouble for both plantations. In spite of the fact that the other planters said it wasn't practical, both plantations were prospering.

When they arrived, they were told that Rebel was at the back of the house watching some of the slaves putting in a flagstone terrace that would overlook the river while she tried to help Hizzie entertain Cole. Liza, the housekeeper, who remembered Heath with a motherly hug, told them to come in, she'd bring her to the parlor, but Heath wanted to surprise her. A few minutes later as they walked down the side lawn, Rebel stopped what she was doing, frowning, surprised to see her mother and sister coming to visit at this unusual hour of the day. She hesitated momentarily, then suddenly yelled in disbelief as she spotted her brother turning the corner of the house.

"Heath!" she squealed, and stumbled as she forgot about her son and rushed forward, tripping over the skirt of her pale green muslin, her blond hair, curled and piled atop her head, losing a couple of hairpins in the process. "My God! How did you get here?" she cried, hugging him as he whirled her around and around; then he set her back on her feet again.

"He just rode up to the front door as if he'd never been away," said Loedicia as Rebel looked him over carefully, to make sure she was really seeing right.

"You're going to stay?" she asked.

He looked beyond her to the young boy tugging on Hizzie's hand, then back to his mother and Ann, then again to Rebel. "I don't know," he finally said. "There are some things I have to do first before I'll know."

She stared at her brother intently, her violet eyes, so much like her mother's, noting the sadness in his face. "Like what?"

"I have to find out how good the memories of the people of Port Royal are for one thing," he said. "Then there's someone I have to find."

"Senator McLaren's daughter?"

He frowned. "How . . . ?"

"Beau told me," she said, and he glanced at his mother.

"You know too?"

She nodded. "Yes."

He straightened, sighing. "Is she still around?"

"Victor McLaren committed suicide in his cell a few days before Christmas. She left the day after Christmas with her aunt. No one's seen her since. Rumor is she went back to the capital. I know she hasn't been to Beaufort."

"She sold the house?"

Loedicia shook her head. "I don't think so. At least from what I hear. They say some of her distant relatives are living in it, but no one seems to know where she is."

He looked out across the back lawn, toward the river, the image of Darcy's pale green eyes before him, unaware of the strange, hauntingly hurt look on Ann's face as she watched him.

Ann had heard Senator McLaren's name being linked to Heath's over the years, but only members of her family had ever mentioned anything about the senator's daughter. It had always been hush-hush. She didn't even know her first name, only that she was his daughter and something horrible had happened to the senator. Something Heath had been blamed for. She didn't really know what it was all about. But she did know by what was said, and the way it was said, that Heath's feelings for this girl, this senator's daughter, whoever she was, were far deeper than she liked them to be. She didn't know the whole story of what had happened back in those days, but she did know that whatever happened had been scandalous. It was so bad no one would even talk about it in front of her.

She had heard bits and pieces about the senator over the years. Partly from eavesdropping on grown-ups' conversations and partly by what Martin had heard people say and repeated to her. Whatever it was, people thought it wasn't nice, but she knew in her heart that Heath couldn't do anything wrong. Not her Heath. And now to think that just mentioning the senator's daughter had any effect on him, and could bring that look to his eyes, hurt.

Oh, Heath, don't you worry, she said to herself, someday when I grow up, I'll make you forget her. I'll make you forget everyone else but me, and she took a deep breath as Heath turned back to Rebel, changing the subject.

"Where are Beau and Father?" he asked.

Rebel glanced quickly at her mother, then back to Heath. "They rode upriver," she said. "Beau wanted Roth to look over some land he's been thinking of buying. There's a good stand of timber on it, but the access may be a problem. He wanted his opinion."

By the time Beau and Roth returned from their ride, which was shortly before dinner, Heath had become acquainted with his new little niece, given Cole numerous piggyback rides, and he and Ann were still entertaining the children in the yard while Loedicia accompanied Rebel inside to change for dinner.

Ann was in her glory. She had Heath all to herself. Well, almost all to herself, anyway. Cole and little Lizette didn't really count, but she frowned, gazing across the lawn, watching now as Beau and Roth strolled up from the stables. Heath hadn't seen them as yet. He was without his frock coat, shirt sleeves rolled up, giving Cole a toss into the air and letting him fall almost to the ground so he'd squeal, when Cole too saw the two men coming.

"Papa!" yelled Cole as he wriggled away from Heath before he had a chance to throw him again, and Heath watched as his nephew raced across the lawn and flung himself at Beau, who caught him, hefting him into his arms; then Heath glanced at his father.

The lines in Roth's face seemed to suddenly vanish as their eyes met and he held out his hand. Their hands met, and Roth pulled Heath into his arms, slapping him on the back affectionately before releasing him.

"Why the devil didn't you let us know?" he asked, astounded as Heath greeted them both. He saw the intense look in Beau's eyes as the two old friends met.

Heath shrugged. "I didn't really know myself," he said. "I just started riding one day, and here I am."

Roth sighed, shaking his head in wonder. "My God, it's good to see you."

"You're staying for dinner," said Beau.

Heath smiled. "Rebel already made sure of that."

Beau's swarthy good looks were a contrast to Rebel's fairness. Although his coloring was dark, he looked little like his Indian father. Instead, he resembled his grandfather, who had been a French-man. It seemed strange to Heath to see him in this new role as father and husband, because for years they had recklessly traveled the globe together and become as close as brothers, some of their adventures quite start-ling. He was pleased knowing that Beau turned to Roth for help, because Beau was the type who asked few men for help.

Roth Chapman was a strong man, but now the sight of his son tore at his heart. It seemed that he always found him, only to lose him again. For years he hadn't even known that Heath existed, and then suddenly, when he discovered his presence in the world, a new life had opened up for him. He'd been so proud. How-ever, Heath's scandalous behavior with Cora McLaren had almost ruined Roth both politically and emotion-ally. He'd survived, though, and now he welcomed his son home with open arms, hoping this time he wouldn't lose him again so soon.

Beau plopped Cole back on his feet as he studied Heath. "Well, you don't look much the worse for wear, I'll say that," he said.

Heath rubbed his clipped beard with the back of his hand. "I've seen a few things . . . been a few places."

"What are your plans now?" asked Roth.

Heath began rolling his sleeves down, fastened the cuffs, and slipped back into his frock coat, then put an arm about Ann, who was glaring at her father and Beau, disappointed because they'd interrupted them.

"I guess I'll stay around long enough to find out which way the wind blows," he said.

Ann leaned against him, her young body molding to the curve of his hip, but he didn't seem to notice. Nei-ther did the other two men. She savored every moment of his nearness, her dark eyes looking up at him ador-ingly, and it startled her when little Lizette crawled over, grabbing her pantalets. She tried to pull herself up, but couldn't, and Ann was forced to leave the solid warmth of Heath's body to pick up the baby.

She frowned as the men went on talking as if she wasn't even around. Men were so selfish. She hefted Lizette up angrily, irritated because the baby was drooling on her clean pale yellow organdy she'd put on just to impress Heath. How would Heath ever think she was growing up? First she'd been covered with dirt, now baby drool. Oh, how she hated being eleven years old. People hardly paid you any attention except to order you about and tell you not to get dirty, and exclaim about how you'd grown, then ignore you. Nobody thought she ever had feelings.

Heath put his arm around her again, unaware of her disturbed expression, and he chucked the baby under the chin as the three men kept on talking. Then he took the baby from her and instructed her to grab Cole's hand and they all headed toward the house.

"Come on, you little nuisance," exclaimed Ann under her breath as she grabbed Cole by the arm, pulling him away from a worm he'd been trying to pick up, and she followed the men into the house, dragging Cole with her.

For the next few days Heath divided his time between the Château and Tonnerre. Ann was by his side as often as possible, and he seemed to enjoy her company, but there were times he went off by himself while she sat at home in agony, wondering who he was with and what he was doing.

By the end of the first week it was obvious he was more restless than usual. Even Loedicia noticed as she, Heath, and Ann sat on the terrace at the back of the house in the early twilight, overlooking the river dappled with the golden hue of the sun that had just set a short time before, while Roth was in the library working on a speech.

"What is it? What's the matter, Heath?" Loedicia asked, watching him pace uneasily. He frowned.

"They don't forget, do they?" he said.

Her eyes clouded. "No, not so soon, anyway."

She knew what he meant. One of the neighbors was

planning a ball on the coming weekend, and although
most of Port Royal was invited, it had been specifically
noted that Heath Chapman was not asked to attend,
and the suggestion that he might call on any young
ladies in the neighborhood had also met with cold dis-
approval.

"Do they think a person never pays for his sins?" he
asked angrily, and Loedicia put a finger to her lips.

"Not in front of Ann, please Heath," she said.

Heath glanced quickly at Ann, who was toying with
a stuffed doll, pulling at its yarn hair absentmindedly,
pretending she wasn't listening.

"Afraid my little sister might hear something terrible
about her big, bad brother?" he asked, looking at his
mother again.

"Heath, don't. You're only hurting yourself," she
admonished.

"It's better than hurting others, isn't it?" He paced
back and forth on the flagstones, then stood at the end
of the terrace, watching the darkening sky. "It seems
like I'm always hurting others, doesn't it?" he said bitterly. "From the day I was born, someone's gotten
hurt, haven't they?"

"Will you stop that!" she cried, and Ann flinched,
watching out of the corner of her eye as her mother's
violet eyes flashed angrily. "You know better than
that!"

He turned and knelt at his mother's feet, clasping
her hands in his, holding them tight. "Mother, I can't
stay here," he said softly. "I've tried. I thought I could,
but I can't." He hesitated, then found his voice again.
"I'm going to Columbia," he said softly. "I'm going to
see if I can find her."

"And if you do?"

"I'm going to ask her forgiveness again and hope
that this time . . ."

"Heath, let me go with you?" she asked.

He stared at her hard. "Why?"

"You've been home such a short time. It would

mean I'd be with you longer." She glanced over at her daughter. "Ann could come too. She's been so happy since you've been home, and she was hoping you'd stay awhile."

He took a deep breath, turning to Ann, who left her pretense at listless daydreaming. "Well, what do you think, Annie," he asked, a carefree manner masking what he really felt inside. "Would you like to take a trip north? Only as far as the capital of this fair state, but we could have some fun on the way. Maybe we could talk Father into going too."

Ann was delighted, and forgot about the doll, shoving it aside as she once more became a part of the conversation. There were so many things she wanted to find the answers to, and for now going to Columbia with Heath would be a start. Maybe she'd find out at last.

But she didn't. All she found out was that their trip uncovered nothing. The young woman they were looking for was nowhere to be found. The house Senator McLaren had once owned had been sold three years before when the daughter had decided to stay in Boston where she'd married, and Heath returned to Port Royal with a heavy heart.

For the next few days, even the constant attention of his young sister couldn't seem to cheer him up, not completely. Finally, after much misgivings, he pulled up stakes once more and left Port Royal. But this time he joined the United States Navy, where he hoped his life would find some sort of meaning, while his father, mother, and little sister packed for their coming trip to England.

The next few years went by slowly with Heath gone. It was late spring, 1806, and the midmorning heat was promising a sultry afternoon at the Château as a hard, resounding slap echoed through the stuffy stables. Ann's eyes steadied on Martin's, her face flushed. At seventeen, her birthday having been in April, she was lithe and graceful, almost as tall as he. Her long amber hair, in one large braid wound and coiled at the nape of her neck, contrasted with the burgundy riding dress she wore, making her hair look even more golden. Her small firm breasts beneath the frogging on the bodice rose and fell quickly with every breath.

"You'll take that back!" she cried breathlessly, but Martin Engler sneered, blowing a lock of sandy hair back from his narrow forehead, the imprint of her hand showing across his freckled cheek.

He wore a brown riding coat that did nothing for his sallow complexion, visible beneath the freckles, and his mouth formed the words precisely, above his deep-clefted chin. "I'll not take them back because they're true," he said arrogantly.

She glared at him, her sloe eyes snapping viciously. "You have no right to say that about Heath!"

"Then if it isn't true, why doesn't he stay in Port Royal?" he said. "Why is it you never hear from him? Because he's a blackguard, that's why."

"He's not! He's not!" she screamed. "You take that back, Martin Engler, or I'll . . ."

"You'll what?"

Ann clenched her teeth furiously, her eyes misty. It wasn't true. Not Heath.

Something had happened, yes. But it wasn't what Martin said. He'd said Heath and another man's wife . . . But it couldn't be. Not Heath. Not her Heath. Oh, if he'd only come home. It had been so long, and she hadn't heard from him for over three years. She'd been eleven when he was home last, and at first, when he'd left, the letters had come often. But the past few years, nothing.

"I'll . . . I'll never speak to you again," she said defiantly.

He laughed. "I don't know why you're always defending him, Ann," he said, watching her closely. "He doesn't even know you exist."

"Oh, doesn't he, now?" she said, tilting her chin up.

"I'll have you know he's just waiting for me to grow up. He even said so the last time he was home."

"He's been saying that for years."

"He meant it!"

"Don't be silly. It's just something grown-up men say to little girls, that's all. It makes them feel important."

Tears welled up in her eyes. "That's not true," she insisted. "You don't know Heath. You'll see. And he didn't do all these things you said he did. I don't ever want to see you again, Martin, do you understand?" she went on. "Don't ever come over again. You're no friend of mine."

Martin sobered, his eyes hard on hers. "You'll be sorry, Ann," he said boldly. "You can ride by yourself, for all I care. I'll go riding with someone else. After all, I'm nineteen, it's time I started looking for a wife. Father's been after me to start getting serious about someone for a long time now, you know." He pulled at the sleeves of his riding coat affectedly. "For a while I think he thought I was getting serious about you, and did I get a lecture."

Her dark eyes narrowed. "Tell him he needn't worry," she retorted. "I wouldn't marry you if you were the last man on earth."

"Who said anything about marriage?"

"But you said . . . ?"

"I said he thought I was falling in love with you. It could complicate my life if I did, you know. After all, marriage would be out of the question, you being Indian and all."

"Yes, marriage would, wouldn't it?" she said curtly. "For a minute I forgot who I was. And we wouldn't want to taint the Engler bloodline, now, would we?"

He flinched. "Oh, come on, Ann. I can't help being an Engler, no more than you can help being what you are."

"That's just the trouble," she said. "What am I?"

His eyes stared into hers, and he suddenly felt

strange inside. My God, she always made him forget
everything his father told him. Maybe his father was
right. Maybe he should spend less time with her. More
and more each day he was conscious of the way her
breasts pushed against the material of her clothes, and
the sensuous lines of her slim ankles when they waded
in the river. And that day they got caught in the rain
and her dress had clung to her. He'd seen every line
and curve, and he'd had a wet dream that night. He'd
never thought about love before, not the kind of love
he'd heard men speak of, not with Ann. Hell, he'd
known her since she was just a toothless little girl. But
maybe . . . it was possible. Maybe his father was right.

"What are you looking at me like that for?" she
asked abruptly, seeing the strange glint in his eyes. One
she'd caught glimpses of occasionally, but never seen
with the intensity that seemed to radiate from him now.

"I was just thinking," he said softly, and she
frowned cautiously as he went on. "Maybe my father
was right after all and I am in love with you," he said.
"It does make sense, you know. I've been coming to
see you for years, and I couldn't really tell you why."

"Don't be silly." She half-laughed, but he went on
seriously.

"You know, you're not a little girl anymore, Ann."
His brown eyes sifted over her and made her uneasy.
"You're almost all grown-up, and I just realized why I
keep coming back here all the time taking your abuse,
letting you yell at me and boss me around the way you
do."

"This is ridiculous!" She started to walk away, but
he grabbed her arm, pulling her back, drawing her
hard against him, and he held her tightly.

"Is it?" he asked huskily, and she stared into his
face, noting the flush beneath his freckles and the
glazed look that veiled his eyes. His breathing had
quickened, and his heart was pounding heavily beneath
his riding coat. She tried to pull away, but he wouldn't
let her. "My father was right," he said slowly. "I

should have looked at other girls, Ann, but I didn't."
His voice was dreamy, wistfully passionate. "All I
cared about was you. Riding with you, talking to you,
looking at you!"

"Martin, stop it!" she said angrily. "Let go of me!"

"I can't," he whispered. "Oh, God, Ann, I can't let
you go! I want you, Ann!"

She pushed against his chest, her eyes blazing, realizing the predicament she was in. They were alone in
the stables, all hands out in the fields, and for the first
time in her life she was suddenly afraid of Martin.
Mother had warned her that he was in love with her,
but she'd never given it a serious thought. She knew
Wilton Chalmers was. He followed her around like a
sick puppy, but he was harmless, she could handle
him. Martin was a different matter.

"Martin, don't be foolish," she said, hoping to sound
convincing. "Nothing can come of it. I'm part Indian,
remember?"

"It doesn't matter," he whispered. "We don't have
to get married, Ann. But we can be together. Father
doesn't have to know. I'll take good care of you, darling. And when you're ready, I'll get a house in
town . . ."

"A house in town?" Suddenly she was no longer
afraid, but mad. Just plain mad. A house in town? His
mouth started to descend toward hers, and she lifted
her foot, bringing it down as hard as she could so the
heel of her riding boot caught across the arch of his
foot, and she felt him gasp, his face turning pale.

Taken by surprise, he loosened his arms, and she
took advantage, twisting from him, at the same time
kneeing him in the groin. He doubled over, grimacing
as he looked over at her, holding his hands in front of
him to protect his aching privates.

"A house in town!" she exclaimed through clenched
teeth. "You'd get me a house in town? And you say
you want me? Well, neither you nor any other man will
ever have me under those terms, do you understand,

Martin Engler?" she cried. "The man who will have
me is the man who will love me and make me his wife,
knowing that I'm half Indian and not caring!" She
stopped for a moment to catch her breath and stared at
him, then continued. "I have feelings just like anyone
else," she said. "I can love and hate, and right now I
hate you. A house in town! I won't be your whore or
anyone else's. Ever! Besides—she lifted her head, dis-
missing him as she headed for the door—"there's only
one man I'll ever give myself to, and that's Heath!"

Martin's pained laughter stopped her as she reached
for the latch. "You're a fool, Ann," he gasped. "You'll
end up a spinster before that ever happens."

She whirled to face him, her sloe eyes closed for a
moment as if she were trying to control her temper;
then she opened them again, addressing him slowly.
"Then I guess I'll be a spinster," she said, looking
squarely at him. "At least that's better than being your
mistress." She started to leave again, then turned back
once more. "And don't bother to come over anymore,
Martin," she said, "Because I won't be home to you.
Go find yourself a wife who'll pass society's inspection.
I don't ever want to see you again," and she left the
stables, heading for the house, feeling as if she'd suddenly grown up.

That evening at dinner, Loedicia was surprised Martin wasn't around. Usually when he came over to visit
he stayed until evening, having dinner with them and
playing games with Ann in the parlor. Roth still
thought he was an arrogant know-it-all, and Loedicia
felt he could have more charm and finesse, but Ann
usually enjoyed his company and didn't seem very serious about him, so they never complained.

Roth glanced over at Loedicia, then looked at Ann.
"Didn't I see Martin over this morning?" he asked.

She frowned. "You won't anymore," she said, and
both parents looked at each other in surprise; then
Roth looked across the dining-room table at Ann.

"What do you mean?" he asked.

Ann set down her fork and straightened the napkin in the lap of her crisp white muslin. She was wearing long dresses now, as of last year, and they too made her feel more grown-up. She blushed.

"I told Martin not to come over anymore," she said hastily. "He was starting to act too serious."

Loedicia frowned. "I was afraid of that," she said. "And from what I hear, his father wants him to start courting the Van Sweringens' daughter, Priscilla. I guess he's been over there a few times with his parents, and the two seemed to get along well." She gazed at Ann thoughtfully. "You aren't unhappy about Martin not coming over anymore, are you, Ann?" she asked. "After all, you have been friends for a long time. I never thought you might care for him."

"I don't," she said abruptly. "But even if I did, it wouldn't matter because Martin couldn't marry me if he wanted. You see, Mother, I'm part Indian. Most young men have an aversion to marrying an Indian."

"But you're not full-blooded."

"That doesn't really matter."

"Beau's Indian, and they accept him."

"They don't know."

Roth studied his daughter's face as she talked with Loedicia. "She's right, Dicia," he said, interrupting them. "Unless someone knew Beau's background intimately, they'd never dream he was an Indian. At least not until they got a good look at Cole. Then maybe they'd wonder. But Annie's eyes . . ." He looked into her sloe eyes, so beautiful, yet such a dead giveaway. "One look is all it takes." He straightened. "But all people aren't like the Englers, Annie," he said, his own dark eyes warm with the love he had for her. "There are always people who care little for bloodline and heritage and more for character. Someday you'll find a young man. You've got a few years to wait." He smiled, the smile lighting up his handsome face, and once more Ann was reminded of Heath as she always was when she looked at her adopted father.

Heath had always been a youthful copy of Roth, and even though Heath had been gone six years now, he had been kept alive for her because of Roth. Always Roth was there to remind her that someday her big brother was sure to come home.

"Oh, I'm not worried," she finally said softly, continuing to pick once more at her dessert. "It'll be a long time before I'm ready to settle down to marriage, and when I do, I have my own ideas of what I want."

"That's my girl," said Roth, and he smiled at Loedicia. "Good Lord," he went on, "I hope Martin doesn't change his mind and start hanging around again. It was bad enough before having his big mouth to listen to, if he started mooning around here acting lovesick like Wilton Chalmers, I don't think I could stand it," and Loedicia and Ann both laughed, agreeing with him.

Ann hadn't dared tell her father everything about her argument with Martin. Especially about what he tried to do, or what he'd accused Heath of. She wouldn't dare. There were just some things one didn't tell one's parents. So after dinner, when they retired to the parlor, she slipped off to her room at the top of the stairs and took the small carved wooden chest from her drawer and once more read over the letters from Heath, even though she knew them all by heart.

The last one was dated in the spring of 1803 and he'd said he was being reassigned to a different ship that was heading somewhere out into the Mediterranean, and he'd write again as soon as he could to let her know where to send his letters. They hadn't heard from him since. That had been three years ago. Where was he? What was happening to him? So many times she felt she'd die from not knowing whether he was alive or dead, and when she finally went to bed that evening, she prayed harder than she'd prayed in months that he'd hurry and come home, because she was almost grown up now. Not quite, but almost.

Two months later, late in the afternoon, as the Fourth of July neared and Port Royal readied itself for what had become its annual celebration, Ann headed for the stables to find a groom and have her horse saddled. Martin's engagement to Priscilla Van Sweringen had been announced at church last Sunday, and she'd been relieved. After all, she had never been in love with him. He had merely been someone to bide her time with and do things with because Heath wasn't around. Maybe now he'd quit pestering her as he always did when they accidentally met in town or at one of the neighbors' get-togethers.

It was a beautiful day, with a soft breeze blowing across the river, carrying with it the muddy, earthy smell of the water. And the birds cavorting around the walk to the stables acted more like it was spring rather than the end of June. Ann was wearing a new riding suit of deep blue silk. The matching hat had plumes that cascaded down onto her shoulders. Her long hair was caught up and held with a large blue ribbon so that she could ride with ease.

She'd been humming a tune, and now she stopped abruptly, staring toward the road off in the distance as a large coach that had been ambling down it stopped in front of the drive. She stared curiously, watching as the driver bent down and talked to someone who had alighted. Now as she continued to stare, the driver straightened in his seat, flicked the reins, and the coach moved on, leaving someone standing in the middle of the road.

That's strange, she thought, and she squinted, one hand above her eyes, trying to see more clearly in the sunlight. The drive was long and tree-lined, and as the lone figure moved into the shadows, she wasn't sure, but the walk looked so terribly familiar. Her hands tightened on her riding crop as she stared; then suddenly her mouth went dry and her knees weakened.

He was home. It was Heath! It had to be! The walk, the rhythmic way his shoulders swayed back and forth with each step. He was tall, broad-shouldered, slim-hipped. It had to be Heath. It couldn't be anyone else.

She let out a cry and began to run, very unladylike, her riding boots kicking up the dust as she left the walk and headed down the drive.

He was halfway to the house when he spotted her, and suddenly the bundle he had on his back slipped off, hitting the dust of the drive, and he lunged forward, shortening the distance between them. They met in the middle of the drive and she leaped into his arms. He whirled her around and around, then set her back down again.

"My God, Annie!" he said as he held her back away from him and looked at her. "I made it home!" Then he hugged her again before releasing her.

Annie looked up at him, her heart in her eyes, but he didn't see the young woman who stood there. All he saw was the little sister who had begun to grow up while he was away, and she was like a breath of spring to him.

He kissed her hand, then dragged her back to where his bundle lay in the road, picked it up, slinging it once more onto his shoulders as he held her hand, and they headed for the house.

"Where are Mother and Father?" he asked as his eyes sifted eagerly over the landscape, taking in the beauty of the large white columns that graced the veranda and the well-cared-for grounds that surrounded it.

"Mother's in the library answering invitations to some of the soirees being held over the holiday week," she answered anxiously. "And Father's back by the wharf somewhere checking on a cargo they're loading on one of the ships."

He sighed, releasing her hand, pulling her tightly against him, putting his arm about her shoulder affectionately, feeling her arm encircling his waist.

"But where have you been?" she asked, the feel of his sturdy body against hers making her tingle inside.

He glanced down at her, smiling that rare smile of his that could charm Medusa. "That, my dear little sister, is a long story," he said, and she heard it that evening at the dinner table after he'd received a warm welcome from his parents and been given a chance to clean up.

"I was transferred to a ship called the *Philadelphia*," he said as they sat around the dining-room table feasting on a number of delicacies he hadn't seen in years.

He had changed his clothes and was wearing clean black breeches and a white silk shirt open low at the throat. He had on the same old boots that someone had tried to polish in spite of the worn creases, but they looked fine, and he was quite oblivious of the effect his obvious virility was having on his young stepsister. He continued his narration while consuming the food lustily.

"We were dispatched to the Mediterranean along with the *Constitution* and some other ships, to blockade the harbor in Tripoli and try to put an end to the pirates who've been victimizing shipping there. But the *Philadelphia* ran aground, thanks to our overzealous captain. We hardly had a chance to defend ourselves."

"We heard about the *Philadelphia*," exclaimed Loedicia. "I guess everyone has, but we had no idea you were on board."

"I know," he said reluctantly. "Unfortunately, I neglected to tell my commanding officers that I had any next of kin." He glanced at his mother sheepishly. "I was rather upset when I left, remember? I was hoping to forget who I was."

"Then you were a prisoner?" asked Roth.

"I spent two years, up until June of last year, in one of the pasha's dungeons," he said bitterly. "I was never so glad to get out of a place in all my life. It cost the government sixty thousand dollars ransom to get them to turn us loose, and it wasn't any too soon. I think another year in that hellhole and I'd have gone mad."

Loedicia sat quietly with her fork resting in her food, her violet eyes misty, trying to brush away the thoughts of what he must have gone through. "Last

June?" she said, her voice subdued. "You took so long coming home."

He toyed with his food. "We went to Europe first. There've been a lot of things to forget." Then he looked up at her and smiled. "But that's all in the past. I'm home now. So how has everyone been in Port Royal?" he asked.

His parents exchanged glances. "I'm afraid the people in Port Royal don't forget too easily, Heath," Loedicia said, and he hesitated for a minute. He'd been afraid of that.

He glanced over at Ann, looking into her dark eyes as she stared at him from across the table. For a moment they reminded him of the Indian maidens when he was a young man at Fort Locke. And her golden, tawny skin . . . But then his eyes caressed her hair. It was the color of lightly scorched honey, with gold flecks running through it, and instead of wearing it in tight curls atop her head and tucked against her ears as was the latest fashion, it was long and straight, held in place with a curved comb on each side, and the combs were covered with small artificial blue flowers that matched the delicate embroidered flowers on her white muslin gown. And that too had changed. Her dresses were now down to the floor, hiding the long slim legs that had once been encased in pantalets.

"You're going to be a lovely woman when you grow up, Annie," he said suddenly, changing the subject, and she blushed.

"I *am* grown up, Heath," she said, "I'm seventeen already."

He chuckled. "Ah, seventeen." He gazed at her affectionately. "I remember when I was seventeen." He reached over and chucked her under the chin, tilting her head so the light from the candles in the chandelier sparkled in her dark sloe eyes. "Someday, my sweet young thing, you'll really be grown up," he said, "and when you are, I just might come back and marry you. That is, if some handsome knight on a white charger hasn't already come along and stolen your heart by then."

She inhaled, trying unsuccessfully to keep her heart from pounding, the touch of his hand and warmth in his eyes turning her insides to jelly.

"And if I go to the balls and soirees during holiday week, and no one else dances with me, you'll dance with me, won't you, little sister?" he asked, and she nodded, her voice unsteady.

"I'd love to dance with you at the parties, Heath," she said happily, and he tried to stifle a frown.

"See, Mother," he said as he turned toward Loedicia. "Maybe I'm good for something after all." Then he asked in a more casual tone, "By the way, how was your trip to England? Your letters were so evasive. How is my brother Teak, and how goes the Locksley estate?"

He was surprised by the sudden tension his question evoked.

"I'm afraid your brother has little use for his family anymore," Loedicia said softly, and Heath hesitated.

"The title's gone to his head?"

"Not the title, my dear," Loedicia's face reddened. "Heath, Teak resents my marriage to Roth and everything that's happened over the years," she explained, a tear reaching the corner of her eye. "He's truly his father's son, Heath. There's more of Quinn in Teak than I ever dreamed there would be, yet he seems to lack his father's compassion and understanding."

"It's the English influence," said Heath. "That was the worst thing you could have done, leaving him in England."

"Well, we did," she said, sighing. "It's not the only mistake I've made over the years, but I admit it's certainly the hardest to accept."

Roth reached over and took her hand, caressing the fingers affectionately, his eyes alight with his love for her. "Don't worry, darling," he assured her. "Someday you'll have all your children together again, and everything will be all right, you'll see."

She gripped his hand tightly, her heart turning over inside her because of the intense look he gave her. To love a man so much . . . he had been her strength ever since her first husband's death. He was her life now. Oh, God, whatever else happens, don't ever let me lose him, she prayed, then turned to Heath again, questioning him once more on his adventures over the past few years.

By the time the Fourth of July rolled around, Heath had been able to gauge the temperament of the people of Port Royal, and he wasn't pleased. At thirty, he was no longer the young irresponsible man that had brought scandal and shame to his parents, but people couldn't seem to accept it. To them, he was still only a handsome, devil-may-care wanderer who would steal the hearts of all the young ladies, and everyone just knew he was up to no good. He had attended two parties with his family, and been treated coolly at both. Not so much by the young ladies—they were all atwitter over his return—but by everyone else, including the young men, who resented Heath's good looks and charm.

It was the evening of the Fourth of July, and after a day of horse racing, cock fighting, and general merriment, Heath had accompanied Loedicia, Roth, and Ann to a ball at River Oaks. It was the first time he'd been on the plantation since the dreadful fire and slave uprising back in 1796, when Rebel's husband, Brandon Avery, the Duke of Bourland, had been killed. He had hoped Rachel Grantham, Brandon's aunt by marriage, who was the Dowager Duchess of Bourland and owner of River Oaks, would have sold the place and moved away by now. After all, titles in America meant nothing. But as his mother explained on the way in the carriage, Rachel never gave up, and she was determined one way or another to try to make life miserable for her.

"She hasn't succeeded," said Roth as he put his arm about his lovely dark-haired wife. "And she never will, if I can help it. But Rachel's stubborn and petty," and now as they entered the ballroom at River Oaks, Heath understood what he meant.

Rachel, dressed in a frothy ball gown of daintily embroidered pink organza, swept everyone else aside as she greeted them, paying rapt attention to her greeting of Roth. If it hadn't been for the fact that Roth was still in Congress, and Rachel was acquainted with a number of politicians and members of the political factions in South Carolina, Roth and Loedicia wouldn't even have attended her ball. But it was expected by his constituents, so they had no other recourse.

Heath watched her now. The way her hazel eyes coveted Roth while she tilted her head full of tightly wound chestnut curls provocatively. Her overseer had been killed during the uprising back in 1796, but other than that the River Oaks had changed little. She still had the same manager, although tall, thin Alan Minyard had aged considerably. His once dark hair was completely gray, and his face had taken on a more sullen, haggard look. They had bought more slaves and treated them no differently than the last unhappy ones. Even Rebel, who had been socially forced to accompany her husband to the ball this evening, had remarked about the tomblike atmosphere that still permeated the main house.

But tonight, in the ballroom, everything was gay and carefree. Even the slaves who waited on the guests seemed in a good mood.

"It's so good to have you back again, Heath," Rachel gushed as she greeted him, turning her attention reluctantly from his father.

Heath thanked her for inviting him, then glanced about the room, aware that he was being stared at by more than one uneasy pair of eyes, and for the rest of the evening, no matter whom he asked to dance with him, except for Annie or his sister, Rebel, their hostess, or his mother, he was met with an icy reproach. Often he stood in the corner seething, the color of his face almost matching the crimson of his frock coat as he downed another glass of punch.

"I certainly can't understand what's the matter with all the females in South Carolina," exclaimed Ann as she stood next to Martin Engler, who had searched her out while Priscilla dutifully danced with her father. "Heath is just the handsomest man here tonight, except for my father perhaps, and they're treating him like he's some kind of an ugly toad." She motioned with her head toward Heath, who was being rejected by still another pretty young maid whose mother was bearing down on her forcefully from across the ballroom floor. "Don't you agree he's handsome?" she asked, and Martin took his eyes from Priscilla, moving them across the room to glance at Ann's brother.

Handsome? Well, there was something about him. What was it Priscilla had said? Devastatingly gorgeous? He wouldn't go quite that far, but those had been her exact words and he had to admit the man was attractive in a flamboyant way. He still wore the short clipped beard he'd worn six years ago, with that gaudy earring in his right ear. His pants were buff, and clung tightly to his muscular thighs and calves, leaving little to the imagination, and the way his red velvet frock coat broadened his shoulders and enhanced his physique was irritating. His silk shirt and ruffled cravat only added to the charm. He had a way with women, that's for sure, and the men in the room envied him, as did Martin, although he wouldn't admit it, even to himself.

"Oh, I expect he's handsome enough," he said curtly. "But then, I believe everyone in the room knows what kind of a man your brother is, Annie. You can't very well blame them if they don't want their daughters associating with him."

Ann clenched her teeth angrily, her golden skin turning pink next to the whiteness of her ball gown. It was yards of delicate lace with diamanté sprinkled about the skirt, with white velvet ribbons decorating the bodice and low décolleté. She had twisted her long hair into a chignon, and now a short stray strand fell onto her neck. She tucked it back up angrily as she turned toward Martin.

"You make me furious!" she cried, her dark eyes snapping. "Heath has been gone for six years. He was fighting those Barbary pirates, and in prison two of those years, and this is all the thanks he gets for trying to help his country."

"So that excuses what he did?"

"What did he do? Just what did he do?" she said viciously. "Nobody will even say." She threw up her hands in disgust. "Oh, they hint around, and drop innuendos here and there, but nobody, I mean nobody, has the guts to tell me what he did that was so wrong."

Martin turned to her abruptly, his face set, then sighed. "You want to know what he did?" he asked.

"Yes."

"What he really did?"

She looked at him skeptically.

"Don't worry, I know," he said, glancing quickly about the room to see if anyone was close enough to overhear their conversation. "Everybody's been talking about him since he came back, so I asked my father. Come on," he said, and grabbed her arm, ushering her toward the French doors at the side of the ballroom that opened onto the side lawn.

She hesitated in the doorway, staring at him. He'd been trying to get her off to himself all evening, and she didn't know whether to trust him or not. Being engaged hadn't seemed to change him all that much.

"Well, I don't intend to tell you in here," he said disgustedly, and she frowned, then took a deep breath and let him lead her outside into the warm moonlit night.

"Well," she finally said as they stopped near where all the carriages were parked. "Just what did he do?"

Martin cleared his throat, watching the moonlight nestling on Ann's figure, bringing it to life. God, she was a beauty. Too bad she was part Indian. If only she weren't so stubborn. "You know this Senator McLaren you've heard mentioned?" he began, trying to keep his mind off her low neckline.

"Yes."

He looked away from her so as not to get too distracted. "To put it in plain language, it seems your brother Heath had an affair with the senator's wife and she got pregnant with Heath's baby. When the senator found out, he shot her. Then after he was arrested for her murder, he hung himself in his cell. Your brother got off scot-free."

Annie stared at Martin silently, her face unreadable. Then suddenly, after several seconds, she found her voice. "You're lying," she said softly.

"I am not."

"How . . . how did they know it was Heath's baby?"

"Mrs. McLaren said it was. The housekeeper was there when it happened. She said the senator told his wife he couldn't have any children. Something about having had mumps or something when he was younger." His eyes sifted over Ann hungrily. "Oh, it was quite a sordid affair," he said, trying to mask his longing for this long-legged girl he'd grown up with. "Do you wonder now why your precious Heath can't be trusted around women?"

She turned from Martin and stared off into the darkness, at the moonlight resting on the carriages, and she wasn't sure . . .

"What about the senator's daughter?" she asked suddenly, and Martin shrugged, the cleft in his chin deepening.

"He had a daughter, I guess, but the scandal didn't have anything to do directly with her."

"What was her name?"

"I have no idea."

She was puzzled, and glanced at him furtively, not quite sure she should believe what he told her. "If you've lied to me, Martin Engler. . . ."

"Now, why would I lie?"

"Who knows." She shook her head. "You've always hated to hear me talk about him, and made fun when I said I was going to marry him someday. "I just can't imagine . . ."

"Why not?" he said, and reached out, running his finger up her arm.

She slapped his hand away, then faced him. "I didn't come out here to let you paw me, Martin," she said. "I came out here to hear your version of Heath's fall from grace." She scowled, tilting her head up defiantly. "I'm not sure I believe it either."

"Suit yourself."

"You'd better go in now," she said, glancing toward the French doors as she heard the music stop. "Before Priscilla thinks something's going on."

He laughed, his broad mouth turning up at the corners in a sinister smile. "Don't worry, Annie love, Priscilla's so naive. That offer still goes, you know," he said, lowering his voice. "I could set you up in a beautiful town house with servants . . ."

"Martin, you disgust me," she exclaimed, and it was she who went inside, leaving him standing by the carriages, a smirk on his face.

Someday she'd be glad to take him up on his offer, he thought carelessly. Either that or end up a spinster. After all, what eligible young man in South Carolina would have the audacity to marry a girl who was so obviously his social inferior? Yes, he'd marry Priscilla, but someday, when Annie grew up and realized her true place in society, and the only place for girls like her, she'd come crawling to him. He straightened arrogantly and followed her inside.

The music was starting up again by the time Ann reached the refreshment table where she had planned to quench her thirst, and she stopped suddenly, staring

across the room. Heath was dancing, and it wasn't with
Rebel, or Rachel Grantham, or even his mother. He
was dancing with an attractive young woman Ann had
seen him staring at earlier in the evening, and she had
watched Heath's eyes as he'd appraised her. She was
the wife of one of Roth's political friends whom Ann
had met previously at another party, but she didn't
remember Heath having been introduced to her.

Heath's eyes were on the woman's eyes, and he
seemed to be enjoying himself for the first time this
evening.

I wonder where her husband is, thought Ann as she
glanced about, but he was nowhere in sight. Ann accepted a glass of punch from a gentleman beside her as
her eyes once more rested on Heath and his lovely
partner. The woman had deep auburn hair, large
brown eyes, and Ann hated her. She was so engrossed
watching, that she was paying little attention as to who
had given her the punch, and just kept nodding and
answering vaguely. Shy, unassuming Wilton Chalmers
didn't seem to mind, though. His pale blue eyes never
left her face, and he seemed content just to be near.

The dance ended, and Ann gasped as she saw Heath
talk to the woman for a few minutes; then the two
headed for the same French doors Ann and Martin
had entered only minutes before. Ann gulped her drink
quickly, then for the first time turned to Wilton, realizing whom she'd been talking to, and when the music
started up again, he was surprised to suddenly find
himself out on the floor dancing with her. Only he
wondered why she kept dancing so close to the French
doors, stretching her neck, trying to peer out.

Outside, Heath started to stroll toward where the
carriages were, then changed his mind, remembering
another ball at this same house when he and Cora had
met again after so many years. They had met alone
here, near the carriages. He glanced at the woman by
his side. She reminded him a little of Darcy. The same
small features and red hair. She hadn't the saucy

pertness that Darcy had possessed, but she was lovely and had accepted his invitation to dance. The only woman besides his sister, his mother, and the hostess who'd had the nerve. This in itself made him wonder.

"Beautiful evening, isn't it?" he said, trying to make small talk. It was hard to know what to say to her. After all, he didn't even know her name. Her eyes had caught his from across the room, and for the first time tonight they hadn't avoided his, but had boldly looked back at him. He hadn't hesitated, but walked over and asked her to dance.

She smiled up at him as they walked, then glanced toward the moon. "I love the climate here in Port Royal," she said softly. "It's so marvelously balmy, even at night."

"You're not from Port Royal?"

"We live in Charleston. It's so terribly hot there this time of year." She looked back at Heath, her eyes soft and sultry. "Do you ever get to Charleston?" she asked, and he warmed to the invitation in her voice.

"It's been a long time," he said, watching her closely, noticing the distinct change in the rhythm of her breathing as he stopped in the middle of the path. "But then, I didn't know Charleston had such enchanting attractions to offer."

Her smile deepened provocatively. "And now that you do?"

She was wearing a low-cut emerald-green gown, and he reached out, his hand resting on her bare shoulder, turning her toward him. "Now, why would you say a thing like that?" he asked suddenly, and her face flushed self-consciously.

"You mean you wouldn't like to come to Charleston?"

"It all depends," he said. "Why did you accept my invitation to dance when everyone else has been refusing me all evening?"

"Because I wanted to."

"That's no answer."

She glanced down at her hands, then back to Heath. "Because I wanted to find out how much truth there is in all the stories I've heard about you."

His face hardened. "You know who I am, then?"

"Yes."

"And?"

"I haven't really had enough time to find out, now, have I?" she said.

His eyes bored into hers, and for a minute he wanted to hit her; then suddenly it all seemed so ridiculous. She was a beautiful woman, they were standing in the moonlight, and from the look on her face he knew she was asking him to kiss her, and he'd been a long time without a woman. Then why didn't he? Maybe because it was too easy. He hadn't noticed earlier. Now he reached down, taking her hand, and he brought it up as if to kiss the fingertips, but instead, he stared at the rings gracing her third finger. He was too late, however, and he realized it unhappily as a voice behind him cut through the balmy night air.

"Elizabeth!"

Elizabeth's eyes widened as she stared beyond Heath's shoulder to the man standing behind him, partially obscured in the shadows made by the trees on the lawn. She swallowed hard, trying halfheartedly to laugh, but there was nothing to laugh about, and Heath felt a deadly sensation in the pit of his stomach as she spoke.

"Homer?" Her voice was too high, too loud. "Oh, Homer, darling," she said, brushing Heath aside quickly, rushing toward the man as Heath turned to face him.

The man stepped out of the shadows, and Heath could see him clearly now. He cringed. His hair was gray and he was thick through the middle, with heavy jowls. It was Victor McLaren all over again, and Heath's first instinct was to run, but he didn't. Instead, he straightened to his full height and took a deep breath, prepared to explain.

"If you'll forgive me, sir," he said, apologizing to the man, who was glaring at him with hatred in his eyes, "but your wife," and he said it regretfully, "neglected to tell me she was married."

Elizabeth glanced quickly at Heath, her eyes no longer soft, but cold and calculating. "That's a lie, Homer," she said softly. "I told him I was married, but he didn't seem to care."

Heath's fists clenched at his sides, and he wanted to throttle the woman. "If that's what you want to believe, sir, believe it then," he said angrily. "I don't much care anymore. I came tonight to dance and enjoy the evening. I saw your wife, whom I did not know was your wife, standing by herself, and asked her to dance. She accepted. Then I asked her to step out for a breath of fresh air. She accepted. Nothing happened. I assure you."

The man named Homer grabbed his wife's arm, pulling her partway behind him, his face livid. "My wife doesn't lie, sir," he exclaimed. "She's an honorable woman, and you, sir, have debased that honor."

Heath sighed. If he didn't watch it, he'd end up fighting a stupid unnecessary duel. My God! How could he get himself in so much trouble without even trying? He inhaled, his jaw tightening, but before he had a chance to contradict the gentleman, Ann interrupted them.

"Oh, there you are. I've been looking all over for you, Heath," she called anxiously as she headed down the path toward them, knowing that things weren't going well for him. She had made quick excuses to Wilton when she saw the woman's husband heading for the French doors, and had left the young man standing alone in the middle of the dance floor. "Father wants to talk to you," she lied, trying to think of something to break the tension. "I told him I'd find you for him." She turned then to look at the couple who were both staring at Heath. "Oh, Mr. and Mrs. Argyle, hello," she said politely, pretending nothing was wrong. "I didn't know you were out here with Heath. But I must take him away. Father wants to see him about something very important."

Heath frowned as he grabbed Ann's arm. "I'm afraid it'll have to wait, Annie," he said, but she shook her head.

"It can't wait," she said stubbornly. "Please, Heath." She clenched her teeth, her jaw set firmly. "If you don't come, Heath," she said through her teeth, trying to fake a smile, "Father's going to be terribly upset." She addressed the Argyles. "Forgive me, please, for dragging him away, but my father is an important man," she rambled on, letting them know that they'd better have a good reason before trying to cause trouble. "If he says go bring Heath, I go bring Heath. You do understand, Mr. Argyle?"

Homer Argyle stared at the girl, fire in his eyes; yet what could he prove? That his wife preferred a younger man? He should defend her honor, but against a man like this? A man who was known to be a fantastic swordsman and an accurate marksman? A man who had once been a pirate?

Heath never flinched, but stared at Homer Argyle, waiting for the challenge he was sure was coming, but instead the man straightened, pulling his shirt sleeves affectedly.

"I dislike scenes, Mr. Chapman," he said, his voice brittle, unsteady. "So I'll accept your apology this time, but believe me, I intend to let everyone know just what kind of a man you are." He turned and grasped his wife's arm. Heath saw her flinch. "Come along, Elizabeth," he said, "we'd better join the others," and they headed back toward the French doors while Ann breathed a sigh of relief.

She looked up at Heath. "Good heavens," she admonished as he watched the couple disappearing into the ballroom, "don't you know any better than to step outside with a married woman?"

"I had no idea she was married," he said, his voice low, barely audible.

"You could have looked at her hand."

He frowned, suddenly realizing how close he'd come to fighting a duel and perhaps killing a man he didn't want to kill. "Will it always be like this for me in Port Royal?" he said absentmindedly, as if talking to himself, and he was surprised when she answered.

"It will be unless you find yourself a wife."

"A wife? They won't even let me near their precious women. How can I find myself a wife?"

She straightened, trying to look as grown-up as she could. "Maybe you just haven't looked close enough or tried hard enough," she said, but he only laughed.

"Oh, I've looked, all right," he said bitterly. "I've looked and I've liked, but not well enough to put up with the reception I've received around here for the rest of my days." He smiled bitterly, then glanced down at his young stepsister, not realizing she was offering herself, and treating her offer casually. "I guess I'll just have to wait for you to grow up after all, Annie," he said. "Nobody else will have me." He looked back toward the French doors, listening intently for a moment to the music drifting toward him across the lawn. "In the meantime, I think I've overstayed my welcome."

Her heart sank. "You're going away again?"

"I have to."

"But why?"

He put his arm around her shoulder affectionately, and held her close as he had when she was a small child. "Because all I ever cause is trouble," he said.

"I don't care!"

"You would if you knew."

She hesitated; then, "I do know," she said softly, and felt his muscles tense.

"What do you know?"

She looked up at him, her eyes misty. "I know all about why you left Port Royal back then, Heath," she whispered. "It was because you got another man's wife pregnant and he shot her, wasn't it?"

He winced. "Yes."

"Well, I don't care, that was a long time ago. You're . . ." She couldn't tell him how she really felt, not yet. "You're my brother, Heath, and I love you and I know you had a reason for what you did, and that you're sorry and have paid enough for it."

He squeezed her shoulder, and she felt the anger inside him. "I'll never stop paying for what I did, Annie," he said, and she wanted to cry out for him to stop, but couldn't. "I'll keep on paying and paying and paying for as long as I live!"

The next morning, regardless of Roth's protests, Loedicia's pleadings, and Ann's tears as she passionately kissed him good-bye, Heath once more left Port Royal with only the clothes on his back, a meager bedroll on his saddle, and a horse beneath him.

ꙮ 4 ꙮ

Locksley Hall, England—January 1, 1812

The smell of plum pudding, roast duck, and ever-green bows filled the halls at Locksley, and the fire in the hearth warmed the library, adding a glow to the silver bells that hung above the mantel, casting shadows across the face of the man who sat at the large ornate desk. Teak Locksley, the Earl of Locksley, spread the three letters out in front of him and stared at them again for a long time, then rose from his chair tall and erect and walked to the window, watching the snow fall.

His hair, the color of faded dandelions basking in the summer sun, looked more deep golden than usual in the firelight, but his gentian-blue eyes were still as bright as the sky on a clear day. An inch or two over six feet, he was ruggedly handsome, his tanned face and muscular frame attesting to his athletic prowess, and the clothes he wore fit him like a glove, the soft green velvet of his coat stretching comfortably across broad shoulders.

His hands moved behind him, where they locked together as he stood thinking. He knew all three letters by heart. The first was from his mother. It had been written eighteen years ago, and in it she had informed him of the death of his father, Quinn Locksley, the former Earl of Locksley. How many times he'd read that letter over to himself. He'd been fifteen then and had stayed in England so he could go to Oxford and his parents had sailed for America. That was so long ago. He was thirty-two now, would be thirty-three in a few weeks, and he'd only seen his mother once since. She'd come to England to visit, and he had to admit he hadn't treated her as warmly as he should. She still wrote occasionally, but he'd never answered. He should have, because he'd loved her very much, but how could he? He'd loved his father too, and she'd betrayed him. Heath was proof of that. And if it hadn't been for Heath, his father would still be alive. After all, he'd been killed saving Heath's life. Half-brother! Bastard was more like it, and then she'd had the nerve to marry Heath's father. She hadn't even waited the customary year.

He felt an ache in his chest when he thought of the hurt that letter had brought to him, but it had taught him a lesson too, and he'd never truly trusted a woman since. Not until he met Darcy.

A smile twitched at the corner of his mouth as he thought of the letter from Darcy. She'd written it shortly after her arrival back in the States. Beautiful, vivacious, Darcy. The woman so many men wanted and only he'd attained.

He'd met Darcy first some years ago in Europe. He'd taken a trip to Italy for Mr. Canning at the Foreign Office, let's see, that was seven or eight years ago. Italy in the summer, with its olive groves, pimentos, blue skies, and the intoxicating smell of a hundred blooming flowers in the air. Its ancient ruins and passionate music were so conducive to romantic evenings, and he'd spent a great number of those evenings with Darcy McGill.

She was a widow visiting with friends, having left her small daughter in America with an aunt. His first impression of her had been dislike, for she held her coppery head high and proud, pale green eyes distant and cool, and before the first few days of her visit were over the men were referring to her as the lady of ice. Not even Lord Trumble's charming way with the ladies had melted her reserve enough to allow a man to so much as hold her hand or sneak a flirtatious kiss, and she was exceptionally quiet, listening, but saying little, giving her admirers no encouragement whatsoever. Still, they tried.

Maybe that's why he'd stayed clear of her at first. It wasn't until that day he'd met her near St. Peter's Square that he began to change his opinion of her.

He'd spent the morning at the embassy arguing over what he considered minor infractions by two of his men, but what his superiors felt held more importance, and he was in a rather foul mood. Often when he was troubled or irritated he'd walk off his anger, giving no thought really to where he was going.

He'd walked through the square and was starting down a side street when he heard a woman's voice protesting vigorously. This in itself would have been nothing, but the woman was decidedly American and she was violently disturbed. Making his way to where a crowd had formed, he shoved his way into it, elbowing through, and stood face to face with Darcy McGill, her eyes flashing dangerously as she stood looking at the mess all over the front of her dress and all over the floor and seat of the carriage she had been riding in. From what he could make out by all the shouting, a horse hauling a cart with a load of ripe farm produce had been frightened by something and bolted, careening down the street without a driver. The carriage Darcy had been in had pulled into the intersection at an unfortunate time, and unable to get out of the way, the carriage had collided with the cart. One of the carriage wheels was broken, and ripe vegetables and fruit had flown from the cart, smashing into the lone occupant of the carriage. There was even a smashed strawberry sticking to the side of Darcy's cheek, and for a moment as he stared at her, Teak wanted to laugh.

Her eyes relaxed slightly as she recognized his familiar face. "Lord Locksley, thank heaven," she cried in tears. "Will you please do something? My dress is ruined, my carriage broken, and these horrible people don't understand a word I'm saying!"

He reached up into the carriage and lifted her out, standing her up on the pavement, brushing the assortment of fruits and vegetables off her beautiful white silk dress, then pulled her aside while the carriage driver and the farmer who owned the vegetable cart tried to explain the incident to the police.

"You're not hurt?" asked Teak solicitously, and her face reddened to match her hair.

"I'm mortified," she answered, and he couldn't help laughing.

"You look delicious."

"I feel like yesterday's garbage."

He glanced over to where the carriage driver was still arguing with the farmer and the police. "Well, one thing is for certain. You can't return to your lodgings in the carriage. Not with a broken wheel."

Her eyes caught his in consternation. "Oh, heavens, I can't return there anyway. Not today. Lady Brithelwaite is staying at her cousin's for a few days and has closed down the villa while she has some redecorating done. I was on my way to the hotel where I'd intended to stay in the first place when I'd first booked passage. All of my luggage is there already, but I can't appear like this. What'll they think?" She looked down at the streaked and splattered dress.

He studied her thoughtfully. She was quite beautiful, and up close her long dark lashes seemed almost unreal. "Mrs. McGill, may I make a suggestion?" he finally said. "Now, you don't have to abide by it, but I think, under the circumstances, it'd be the best thing for you to do, since it seems you don't speak Italian. Am I right?"

She nodded. "What is it?"

"I have friends here in Italy. I usually stay with them when I visit, and although they aren't in residence at the moment, I have permission to use their villa whenever I wish, and I've been staying there since I arrived. The servants are very discreet, and if you like, I can take you there. The maids would be glad to repair your dress, and"—he looked at the sky—"since it's close to the noon hour, we could have something to eat while we're waiting. Then I could deposit you clean and presentable again at the hotel."

She stared at him for a long time, her eyes suddenly cold again.

"Believe me, madam, if you'd rather appear at the hotel as you are, I have no objections."

Her eyes fell beneath his gaze as she looked at her dress. Lord Locksley? He was the tall, quiet fellow who always brought a hush over the ladies when he walked into the room. She had heard all the remarks. One of the most eligible bachelors in England, but elusive. More than one mother had shoved her daughter his way without results. In fact, he was extremely select about the ladies he chose to escort about, and shied away from any commitments. Some said he must have been disillusioned as a youth because he regarded most women critically, often referring to them as the deceitful sex and although she'd been properly introduced to him, he was the only gentleman at the soirees who didn't fall all over himself to claim a spot at her side. She looked up again and met his blue eyes. "Thank you, Lord Locksley," she acknowledged with a smile. "Your offer is quite generous and gladly accepted."

She waited while he went down the street and commandeered a carriage for them, offering the driver enough lire to make it worth his while, then seated her in the carriage, climbing in beside her.

"Whatever possessed you to come to Italy when you can't speak Italian?" he asked as the carriage began to move.

"I'm fairly good at Spanish, and some stupid fool made the mistake of telling me that Spanish and Italian are almost identical."

He laughed. "Shoot him the next time you see him."

She scowled. "It was a she, not a he, and I'll strangle her instead."

"You said you hadn't planned to stay at the Brithel-waites'. . . ?"

She smoothed her hands over the soiled skirt. "I met Lady Brithelwaite on board ship, and since she's a dear friend of my aunt's, I couldn't very well refuse her invitation, although I must say I haven't seen much of Italy in the week I've been here. I think I've seen the inside of every ballroom, cabaret, and opera house, but have yet to see the sights. That's why I was near the basilica. I thought at least I'd get a glimpse of that before I have to leave. Tonight there's a ball at the American embassy that I've promised to attend, and tomorrow afternoon Lady Brithelwaite's cousin has insisted I join them for a lawn party." She frowned. "And I suppose by then she or someone else will have the next day all planned for me." Suddenly she looked at him, and her face flushed. "Oh, I am sorry," she apologized. "You aren't at all interested in my dull, boring life." She turned and looked ahead again, her head held high in that lofty manner. "It's just that sometimes I find people rather exhausting."

He studied her profile. It was classic, her cheekbones high, with faint hollows shaping the side of her face, and her nose was exquisite. "I thought all women liked parties and balls and meeting important people," he said with an air of cynicism, and she looked at him, frowning.

"I enjoy balls sometimes," she said, "but not as a regular diet. It may sound ridiculous, Lord Locksley, but I'd love to see the ruins of the Colosseum, the Roman Forum, and the Palatine, and to be able to admire the wonderful statues and paintings of the great artists, then walk through a few of the museums and perhaps eat at one of those small inns I've heard about where they serve the meal from huge bowls and you have to break the bread with your hands. And I'd like to see how wine's made and what an olive grove looks like. It matters not to me whether I shake hands with ambassadors or kings. I came to see Italy, not just the people who live here." She smiled sheepishly. "There I go rattling off again. I am sorry."

"Don't be," he answered, quite amazed, for if rumor was right and from what he himself had observed, Mrs. McGill had talked more freely in the past few minutes than she had during the whole week of her visit so far. "I'm relieved at your honesty." He smiled. "And all the time I thought you were enjoying your stay."

Her eyes flashed momentarily, then narrowed suspiciously. "Did I look like I was enjoying myself, Lord Locksley?" she asked.

"Now, that's hard to say, because I have nothing to compare. Now, if, when you're pleased, you act cold and aloof and frigid, then yes, I'd say you were enjoying yourself. But then, on the other hand, if, when you're pleased, you become warm, natural, relaxed, and human, I'd say no, you were not enjoying yourself. Not half as much as you are right now."

She flushed as she turned and looked at him out of the corner of her eye. He was right. She was enjoying herself. The carriage was taking them through some of the prettiest parts of the city, parts of Rome she hadn't seen as yet, and the sights were fascinating. There were fountains in the middle some of the streets, where women were washing clothes as they talked, and marketplaces crowded with peasants. She'd almost forgotten completely about the mess on her dress, and it was only when one lady gave her a strange look that she remembered it.

"Where do these friends of yours live?" she asked, ignoring his question.

He nodded. "A short distance ahead." Some ten minutes later the carriage stopped in front of a beautiful house with dozens of balconies, flowers cascading from window boxes, and fountains gracing the lawns. The house was not overly big, but the decor was delightfully elegant, with marble floors, hand-carved woodwork, and plush furnishings.

When Teak ushered her inside, the small dark-haired woman who answered the door was aghast at the sight of Darcy's dress, but assured him they'd try their best. They ate pasta with creamed mushroom sauce, Italian sausage, and fresh vegetables washed down with a sweet red wine, but when they finished, the dress was still not ready.

Darcy had slipped on Teak's red silk robe that clashed abominably with her coppery hair, but accentuated her well-developed curves, and Teak was very aware of them as he ushered her into one of the sitting rooms.

"Where are you from in America?" he asked, and she hesitated a moment before answering.

"Columbia, South Carolina," she answered slowly, and saw a flicker of annoyance in his eyes. "Do you know someone from there?" she asked, tensing unexpectedly.

"No," he lied, "no one," and she turned away relieved.

"Oh, I thought perhaps . . . you have been to America, though, haven't you?"

His eyes held a strange, almost haunted look. "I was raised there," he answered slowly, then wondered why on earth he'd told her that. He wasn't accustomed to talking about his past with anyone.

"I rather guessed it might be something like that," she confessed. "You don't have the typical British accent that usually accompanies a name like Lord Locksley. You sound more like an American."

"And you, ma'am, do not have a typical American accent."

She smiled. "It's typical if one lives in the South, sir. All Southerners talk like this."

His eyes flickered over her. "How charming."

Her face reddened. "You're poking fun at me, sir."

"Not at all. I never poke fun at a lady." He walked to a mahogany cabinet and opened it, reaching inside. "Would you care for a game of piquet? It'll make the time go faster," and she was amused. Men had offered to do a lot of things with her and to show her a thousand dubious games and parlor tricks to while away the time, but never would she have dreamed that a man would offer to while away the hours with her playing piquet. What a strange man Lord Locksley was.

"I'd be delighted," she accepted. "I'm not too good at it, however, and you'll have to be patient with me," but he didn't seem to mind.

The rest of the afternoon was spent playing cards, and Teak had to admit it was the quickest three hours he'd ever spent. Darcy was quick-thinking, a natural-born wit and mimic, and when she was relaxed with no thought to proper conduct and not having to worry about persistent suitors, her conversation was both colorful and revealing. They laughed and relaxed over their bottle of wine and the piquet game and it wasn't until late afternoon when the little housemaid finally presented herself with the sad news that the signorina's dress was beyond repair.

"The stains are too deep," he translated to Darcy. "If the dress hadn't dried on the carriage ride here . . . They've tried everything to soak them out."

Her eyes faltered. "What'll I do?"

"We could send a note to the hotel asking that one of your dresses be sent over."

Her hand flew to her breast. "Do you realize what that would imply?" she asked, but he only laughed.

"You're certainly worried about propriety."

"Perhaps your hostess has something I could borrow, just for tonight," she suggested, but he frowned.

"The lady of the house is about two inches shorter than you, my dear, and about double your width. I'm afraid there's nothing."

Darcy was scowling, her cheeks pale, and she walked to the balcony looking out. What was she to do? She couldn't appear at the hotel in that horribly stained dress and she certainly couldn't wear Lord Locksley's robe.

"I have another suggestion," said Teak as he walked

up behind her. "The maid can take your measurements, and since the shops are closed tonight, first thing in the morning I'll send her in to fetch a gown for you. We'll send a note to the hotel that you're delayed one more day and will arrive tomorrow, and you can spend the night here. There are plenty of rooms."

She turned slowly, the scowl still on her face as she looked up into his handsome face. "You didn't happen to arrange this whole thing on a dare or a bet, did you, sir?" she asked suspiciously, and he laughed. "Don't laugh!" she snapped angrily. "It's been tried before, and I never thought it amusing."

He sobered as he stared at her. "You mean men have actually tried to trick you into situations like this?"

"Tried and failed, yes," she admitted. "You must feel proud at succeeding."

"I have succeeded at nothing but making you angry, madam," he said stiffly. "I apologize. But I assure you the whole thing was completely unplanned."

Her eyes studied him warily. "I don't know whether to believe you or not."

"Madam, I have no need to use tricks or subterfuge to get a lady into my boudoir. There are many who would be only too eager to come if I wished it."

She turned crimson. "That's not what I meant," she said defiantly. "It's just that . . . well . . . I'm well aware that men refer to me as an iceberg behind my back, sir, and make remarks about my lack of warmth where they're concerned, and because of it many think it a joke to make bets on my"—she cleared her throat—"my 'conquest' would be the best way to put it, I guess. They've bet everything from money to horses on their ability to . . . to compromise me."

"I had no idea," he said. "Believe me, madam, I've no intentions of compromising you. I was only trying to help a lady in distress."

She sighed. "I want to trust you . . ."

"If you'd like, I'll go to a hotel," he suggested, but she shook her head.

"Oh, I couldn't put you out . . . please . . . I . . . give me a few minutes to think," and she turned again toward the balcony.

He watched her from the back, the well-rounded hips, small waist, and she was full-breasted. Why did a woman with attributes like that not use them? She'd been married once. Didn't she miss the pleasure a man's body could bring her? But perhaps she'd never found pleasure in the joining. Some men had no idea how a woman liked to be treated; all they knew was how to use a woman, not enjoy her or give her anything in return.

Darcy turned, catching his eyes looking at her longingly, and almost changed her mind. She hesitated; then, "If you promise that no one will find out I've been here and think we . . . well, if you promise, I'll stay," she said, and suddenly she laughed almost recklessly. "Besides, you owe me two games of piquet," she said, "and if we have to stay up all night playing, I intend to win them."

Halfway through the evening she remembered the embassy ball. They'd been playing cribbage this time, and he was beating her royally when she thought of it.

"I forgot to send a note that I wasn't coming," she exclaimed.

"I wouldn't worry if I were you," he said, "but if you want, we'll send a message now. Late's better than never," and she agreed.

They ended the evening with a glass of wine and a walk through the garden in the moonlight, and although Teak had the deuce of a time controlling himself, he kept his distance, so it surprised him very much when he deposited her at the door to the room Maria said she could use and she reached up and touched his face.

The wine had warmed Darcy more than what she was used to, and she felt strange inside, almost giddy.

Lord Locksley had been the perfect gentleman—she couldn't deny it. Maybe that was the trouble, he'd been too perfect, and she frowned.

"What's the matter?" he asked as her hand touched his cheek and she studied the way his hair fell into place and the long curve of his jawline, then looked deep into his eyes.

"I was wondering why."

"Why what?"

"Is there something wrong with me, or is it you?"

"You mean because I haven't tried anything with you?"

"Mmmhmmm. You're strange. I'm sure you want to."

"But do you want me to?"

Something stirred inside her. A remembrance, a long-dead desire that began to creep slowly into her body, making her warm inside. "I . . ." His blue eyes held her mesmerized; then slowly she stood on tiptoe, and her arm moved behind his neck, pulling his head down. Her lips met his and a shock ran through her to her toes and suddenly his arms were about her and he was holding her close, his mouth returning her kiss urgently; then, as abruptly as it started, the kiss ended.

"Good night, Mrs. McGill," he said softly, and she stared at him, her face warm and flushed.

"Good night, Lord Locksley," and she watched him walk down the hall to his bedroom; then she turned and went into her own room, stretching across the bed wondering. Now, why in heavens name did she do that? It was the first time she'd kissed a man for . . . how many years? She closed her eyes, remembering painfully, then lazily fell asleep.

That night was the start of it. The next day, after her dress arrived, Teak took her to see the Colosseum and they ignored Lady Brithelwaite's cousin's lawn party and that evening they visited the ruins of the Palatine by moonlight and he kissed her good night properly. By the end of the week everyone was talking about them, and although Teak would have given almost anything to make proper love to Darcy, he kept his distance; but the shock to everyone, however, when Darcy's visit was over, and instead of begging her to stay, Teak kissed her goodbye, waving to her from the pier with the rose she'd given him, was unnerving. They had been so sure that the perennial bachelor had finally been caught and the ice lady had melted.

He hadn't seen Darcy again for almost two years. She'd come to London to visit a friend and he'd bumped into her at a dinner given in honor of one of the men from the American Foreign Office, and the friendship that had started in Italy continued. This time when she returned to America they corresponded, and then four years later when they were both in Italy again, Teak realized he wasn't getting any younger. If he was to marry and have an heir, it would have to be soon. Of all the women in his life, Darcy came closest to what he wanted in a wife, and he was sure what he felt for her must be love. She was beautiful, intelligent, sensible, and although she was the only woman in his life he'd never been able to bed, he'd asked her to marry him, and much to his surprise, she'd consented. But the marriage would be delayed for a while. Her daughter was fourteen now and she wanted to tell her first before the wedding, so they made their plans. She'd leave Italy and return home, explain everything to her daughter, then they'd catch a ship to London. She returned to America on the next boat out of Italy, but when she arrived home, there was trouble with her daughter and her aunt. The wedding would have to be postponed until she could persuade them to her way of thinking. She wouldn't marry anyone without her daughter's full approval, and it would take a little time.

Teak glanced toward the desk, at the other letter that stared back at him. It was from his superiors. He'd worked in the Foreign Office since giving up his commission in the army some years before, but now they wanted him to take on a special mission. When the letter first arrived, he'd dropped everything he was doing and headed for the London office to find out what it was all about, because as the rumors of possible war began to float around the Foreign Office, it had been like a three-ring circus and the message had been marked urgent.

It had been late afternoon when he'd arrived in London, and he'd gone straight to headquarters. "So what's it all about?" he asked Viscount Robert Castlereagh as he hung up his greatcoat and rubbed his cheeks that were red from cold.

"Sit down, Teak," the viscount said, motioning toward the chair in front of his desk, and Teak sprawled into it, his long legs looking for room. "We have a strange mission for you."

"It must be unusual, with you giving the orders."

Viscount Castlereagh, the foreign secretary, cleared his throat. "It's one I hope you won't refuse."

"Refuse?"

"It's delicate." Teak eyed him curiously. "That's why I wanted to talk with you about it myself instead of leaving it to someone else."

Teak straightened as best he could in the chair. "Just what is this mission?"

"First of all, I have to make sure my facts are right. Your father, the former earl, was an American, right?"

Teak frowned. "He was born in England and went to America when he was fifteen."

"And you were born in America."

"That's right."

The viscount stood up and walked around his desk, clearing his throat again, then sat on the edge of it as he looked at Teak. "Do you remember any of your childhood there? I mean, you were almost fifteen, I believe, when you came to this country. Your father, from what I've heard, was a backwoodsman, and I imagine, as such, he taught you the rudiments of living in the wild."

Teak's eyes narrowed as he stared at the viscount. "Go on."

"We need a man on the American frontier, Teak. Someone who can mix in and pass for an American. Someone who knows the wild, who can get along with the Indians, yet someone we can trust."

"In other words, you want me to become a spy."

"If you wish to call it that, yes, I guess that's it. Lake Erie's a strategic area. If war comes, it's going to be one of the decisive areas, and you're familiar with it."

"That was a long time ago."

"A man of your stature doesn't easily forget, Teak."

Teak pulled himself from the chair and stared at Castlereagh for a long minute, then turned and walked to the window, staring out at the cold November afternoon, where the smell of a first snow hung in the air. Twenty years ago, and they were sure he'd remember. How could he ever really forget. He'd hated his life then. The lonely days on the trail, learning to track and hunt and survive. That's one thing his father insisted on. Even his sister, Rebel, knew how to survive if caught alone in the wilderness, and it was a lesson not easily forgotten. He remembered the buckskins, the one good suit of clothes, and the simple fare at the table, and most of all he remembered the Indians. The sloe-eyed savages with their strange customs and equally strange emotions. He'd hated it all, and now they were asking him to go back to it. He turned to face the viscount.

"Do you know what you're asking, Robert?" he asked belligerently, and the viscount scowled.

"I'm asking you to serve your country, Teak. You do consider England your country now, don't you?"

"Of course I do. It's just . . . I hated that life, Robert, that's why I'm here. I didn't enjoy roaming the woods and living like a savage. I like what I have here. Having servants to take care of my needs and money to spend when I want it and everything that goes with having a title. You're asking me to go back to a life I detested."

"It won't be forever. Just until this damn thing is over one way or another. If war comes, we need you out there."

"And what happens if I get caught?"

"We know nothing about you, naturally."

"Then I'm completely on my own?"

"We'll make arrangements for financing. Naturally there'll be times when you'll need money and materials. You'll account to no one but me. You'll have a password to use, and all the military will know it and be instructed to honor it, but I want your true identity kept a secret, so you'll be referred to as Warbonnet, even by our troops."

"In other words, I'm to be a nonentity."

"That's about it."

Teak hadn't wanted the assignment, but what could he do? England had been good to him. He'd lived in luxury the past almost-twenty years; he couldn't turn his back on them.

"Only one problem," said Castlereagh.

"What's that?"

"Your family and your fiancée. They're Amercans."

"As far as my family's concerned," answered Teak, "I haven't seen my mother for some years. We aren't on very good terms, and Darcy . . . The marriage has been postponed for a while, so I guess they're really not obstacles."

"Then you'll do it?"

He shrugged. "Have I any choice?"

The foreign secretary shook his hand, and the bargain was sealed, and now Teak stood in the library at Locksley Hall, watching the snow fall, probably the last snow he'd see in England for a long time. Today was New Year's. It had been a lonely Christmas and a lonely New Year's Eve, but tomorrow would be even

lonelier, because tomorrow he'd leave all this behind
him for an uncertain future.

He turned and walked to the desk and gazed down
again at the three letters, then gathered them up and
put them in one of the drawers and locked it for safe-
keeping before he left the room.

The next morning early he was up and dressed,
smothered in his greatcoat as he stood at the door. He
hadn't even been able to tell Mr. Briggs where he was
going, but the old man seemed to understand. After all,
Lord Locksley was an honorable man, and working for
the Foreign Office the way he did, there were times his
trips were of the utmost secrecy.

Mr. Briggs had been with him since the day his
parents had sailed for America and left him in England, and it was to Mr. Briggs that Teak had turned
for comfort at the death of his father. He was Quinn
Locksley's agent, a firm, well-disciplined man, and the
two had become very close, but now Mr. Briggs was
old, his hair white, and although Teak wasn't his son,
he felt as if he were as they shook hands and parted.

Teak rode into London where he boarded one of His
Majesty's ships of the line, which by the next afternoon
was clearing the channel and heading out to sea.

The second week in March 1812, with a spring thaw
in his wake, he was making his way down the St.
Lawrence River in a canoe, his greatcoat and fancy
clothes exchanged for buckskins, fur robe, and a rifle.
The weather was still cold, and snow lay thick along
the riverbank. It was strange to be alone in the wilderness again, especially a wilderness into which he'd
never traveled. He'd been north as far as Black Rock
with his father the summer before going to England,
but had never been on the St. Lawrence. The river was
fascinating. He slept along its banks wherever he found
shelter, and fished its waters for his food.

By the end of March, as buds began to come to life
again on trees and bushes and the birds began to wend
their way back to their summer haunts, where spring

flowers were beginning to carpet the forest floors, he pulled into the Canadian side of the river at a place called Kingston, on Lake Ontario.

Activity was heavy in Kingston. The French had once built a fort here, but the British had burned it down and were now building ships and sailing them. In fact, just last year the first steam-powered ship on the lake had sailed from Kingston.

It was after dark and quite late when he arrived. Teak pulled his canoe onto the beach and secured it in the bushes some distance from the center of the settlement, hefted the rifle onto his back, and headed for the cluster of buildings set back a short distance from the water's edge. One building in particular was his destination, and lights burned inside.

"Sorry, sir," said a redcoated regular as Teak stepped up to the door of the building, "but you can't go in there," and Teak stopped, his steady gaze sifting over the young man.

"Is this where I'll find Sir James Yeo?" he asked, and the man nodded.

"Yes, sir, but no one enters without permission, sir."

"Then I suggest you get me permission," stated Teak. "Will you please inform Sir James I'd like to see him."

"Who shall I say requests permission to enter, sir?" he asked, and Teak's mouth tightened.

"Tell Sir James one word. Warbonnet," he said, and the man stared at him.

"Just Warbonnet?"

"That's all that's needed."

"Yes. sir."

The young soldier turned and knocked on the door, and it was opened from inside. He passed the word to the man who answered, and the door shut again. Not five minutes later the door was opened and Teak was ushered in. He was taken directly to the office of the fleet commander. Sir James Yeo studied him curiously as they shook hands.

"What do I call you?" he asked solemnly, and Teak gazed about the room.

"Warbonnet will do."

"My orders are to cooperate with you in anything you request, so how may we help?"

"I have to reach the American side of Lake Ontario by the shortest route," said Teak, "so I assume one of your ships would suffice."

"Where's your destination?"

"For the moment it's Niagara."

Sir James frowned. "We'll set you down after dark."

"Good, but one thing I must ask. I also board ship after dark and stay in the cabin unseen during the voyage. Not even your captain is to know what I look like. Is that understood?"

"Don't you think the precaution a little unnecessary, sir?" he said. "After all, you've been seen here in Kingston."

"By the men outside your door and you, sir," he said quietly. "The fewer people who know what I look like, the more successful I'll be." He looked closer at the sparsely furnished room. "I was told you could show me a fairly recent map of the area. It's been a number of years since I've been here, and the place has undoubtedly changed."

Sir James walked to the far wall and pulled a rolled-up map from a shelf, then returned to his desk and unrolled it, setting paperweights on the corners to hold it flat, and Teak studied it thoroughly. The lines were the same, but settlements had been added that hadn't been there before, and forts had sprung up. New trails were marked and old trails abandoned. His mind took it all in, even gun placements and naval forces. When he was satisfied, Sir James put the map back.

"How soon can you have a ship ready?" Teak asked as Sir James slipped the map into place on the shelf, and he turned abruptly.

"I can get you out tonight yet if you want it," and Teak nodded.

"Good."

"Give me three hours," he suggested, "and in the meantime you can catch a nap in my private room."

This Teak didn't mind at all. He was tired of sleeping on the hard, cold ground. Sir James led him to another door which opened onto a small private sleeping room where Sir James spent most of his nights, and it felt good to stretch out on a bed again even if the mattress was lumpy. Oh, how he missed the comforts of home, and he dreamed of Locksley Hall.

He slept better than he had in weeks, but his sleep was short-lived. At three in the morning Sir James nudged him awake, and with one of the commander's cloaks covering him sufficiently, hiding his buckskins and rifle, he slipped aboard one of the ships in the harbor and they set sail for Niagara.

On April 1 in the dark hours before morning, his feet touched shore only a few miles from Fort Niagara. His only words to the men in the longboat who brought him ashore were "thank you"; then like a phantom he melted into the night, leaving Sir James's cloak behind.

⟫ 5 ⟪

The warming weather was making everyone feel better, and Heath stretched out under the oak tree, his long legs uncomfortably bent to make room for one of the men. He lay back with his hands behind his head and stared up at the night sky, wondering just what the hell he was doing here anyway. He'd come a long way since Tripoli. Not economically—he was still as broke as he'd been that morning he'd left Port Royal back in 1796.

How long ago that was. Sixteen years! Sixteen years of bouncing around the world, trying to find a place to roost. He'd gone to Boston first, curiosity mostly, then shipped out for Asia with a merchantman, and left the ship in India, where he looked over the land where his mother said she'd been born and raised, but a few years later as the old century ended, he found himself once more aboard ship heading for the States, and in the summer of 1800, his feet took him up the road that led to Port Royal.

But it wasn't the same. Roth was absorbed with politics and the plantation; his mother was busy as the wife of a congressman, mistress of the Château, and in her new role as grandmother; and Beau and Rebel, solidly married with a new baby sister for Cole to play with, had little time for him. Besides, the people of Port Royal were slow to forget. Annie had been upset when he left, but it had to be.

Heath had sat in the living room at the Dante plantation, aptly named Tonnerre, and stared at Beau. He looked no different from the handsome Captain Thunder, who'd set the British Navy on their heels except for the look of contentment that filled his eyes when he looked at his wife. From adventurer to hearth, with love. For Beau it had been enough, as it was for many men, but Heath had lost the one woman who'd begun to mean anything to him.

He'd tried to find Darcy that summer, but she was gone. She'd disappeared from sight shortly after her father's suicide, and he couldn't blame her. But he'd told her the truth that night in the garden, and when he finally left Port Royal again, his heart was heavy. Even little Annie's passionate promise to wait for him to come back someday to marry her couldn't soothe his aching heart.

The next five years found him in the United States Navy. That is, until October 31, 1803, when the ship he was on at the time, the *Philadelphia*, during the blockade of Tripoli in the Mediterranean, ran aground and was captured, and he along with Captain William Bainbridge and the rest of the crew were held prisoner for two years, until the United States and the pasha decided to come to terms.

By the time of his release, he had seen all he wanted of Tripoli and foreign shores. When he reached the States in the summer of 1806, and after a brief unsuccessful attempt at making a life for himself in Port Royal, he decided to see how much the country had changed. For the past few years he'd been roaming the Ohio Valley trapping and scouting. His knowledge of the frontier, taught to him by his stepfather, Quinn Locke, was proving invaluable to men such as Governor Jonathan Meigs of Ohio, for whom he'd been not only confidant and scout, but personal friend. So here he was, duly elected a special ranger for the Ohio Militia, and still without a home to call his own.

"You know, you'd think at my age a man would have learned something," he said to the beefy sandy-haired man who fell down beside him, and the man grinned.

"You tryin' to tell me something, Heath?" Eli asked.

Heath sighed. "You'd think at thirty-six I'd be farther along in this world than a rifle and the clothes on my back," he complained, and the beefy man smiled. He'd been with Heath for three years now. Ran into each other that first year on the Scioto River, and after wintering together, they'd become fast friends.

Eli Crawford was a wanderer, same as Heath. "Lost a wife and two young 'uns to the Shawnee ten years ago, and can't seem to light in one place no more," he'd explained one evening before the fire in the cabin they'd resurrected from an early grave, and from that day on the two men had been together.

Eli was hard, relentless, his body as solid as a rock. He could hold his liquor and take his women anyway they came—black, red, or white, made no difference as long as they knew what a bed was for, but he never took one without her permission, and he always prided himself that when he hit a settlement he spent few lonely nights. "And for a man with a face like mine, that's quite a feat," he'd often remind Heath.

Heath glanced at him now, his sandy whiskers bobbing on his square chin as he talked, his gray eyes twinkling. "I think you oughta find yourself a woman, Heath," he was saying, his eyes intent on his friend. "You always get restless 'bout this time of the month." He shook his head. "You know, I swear some men get horny just like the ladies do at times. Know what I mean? There's times I don't care one way or another whether I have a piece of ass or not, and there's other times they drive me crazy. I think maybe this is one of those times for you, lad. Why don't you wander into town and see what you can find?"

"Won't do any good, Eli, and you know it," he said. "When I get like this, there isn't anything can please me, so why try?"

"You oughta head east then and see if you can find

that gal again," he said. "Get it over with once and for all," but Heath shook his head, the dark mass of curls touching the tips of his buckskin collar.

"Sixteen years is too long, friend. Thanks for the thought, but she's married now and probably has half a dozen children anyway. As my dear mother would say, yesterday is the beginning of tomorrow, and if tomorrow isn't everything it should be, we have only ourselves to blame, but remember, there's always another tomorrow."

"So what does that mean?"

"It means it's my own damn fault for what I'm doing, so I should shut up, make the most of it, and quit bellyaching."

Eli shuffled his feet as two of the men got up and wandered off toward the other side of the meadow they were camped in. They'd been waiting for what seemed like ages for General William Hull's arrival. General Hull had been given command of the Northwestern Division of the army and as governor of the Michigan Territory, he was to lead the men to Detroit.

Out of the thirty thousand Ohio militiamen called out by Ohio Governor Meigs to join Hull, close to fifteen hundred of the best had been chosen along with special scouts Heath Chapman and Eli Crawford to show the way, and now the waiting was getting on everyone's nerves.

"He'd better get here soon," said Eli. "You're not the only one getting restless. The men are achin' for a good fight."

"Eli," reminded Heath, "war hasn't been declared yet."

"It will be." He straightened, picking a twig from his bushy head of hair. "Why else is Madison sendin' men out there?" He gazed over at his friend. "Don't I remember you sayin' you got a brother in England?" he asked, and Heath frowned.

"My half-brother. Haven't seen him for over twenty

years. He's an English lord. Money, horses, the easy life."

"Seems funny, you havin' an English Lord for a brother."

"Nothing funny about it," answered Heath. "Teak and I never did get along. He was only twelve the last time I saw him, but even then he was obnoxious and spoiled. My sister said he took to a pampered life in England like he was born to it."

"Then I guess there's no chance of you ever seein' him again, is there?"

"I doubt it. England holds no attraction for me. In fact, it's strange. When I was young I used to stand and look out over the lake and wish I could sail off into the horizon and just keep going. I guess I always have been a wanderer, and even though I balked at life in the backwoods, I almost feel more at home here now than I ever did."

"It gets in your blood."

"I guess so." He frowned. "Only, sometimes it can get mighty lonesome."

"It don't have to."

Heath gazed up at his friend, at the intent look in his eyes. "All right," he exclaimed as he stretched and stood up shrugging, "come on, Eli, let's go into town and see what they have to offer. You won't let me rest until I do," and the two men started off across the field that was scattered liberally with militiamen, but this time their minds were on women instead of fighting.

On May 25 General Hull and his entourage finally arrived with wagonloads of much-needed supplies. He was welcomed warmly, although there were some disgruntled remarks from some of the men because the fifty-nine-year-old general had also brought with him his son, who served as one of his aides, his daughter-in-law, and two grandchildren, and allowed various of his other officers to bring their wives.

The day they arrived, Heath and Eli stood to one

side watching the line of wagons unloading and the men and women pitching tents, trying to set up camp.

"Damn foolish thing to do, bringing women," said Heath as they watched the flurry of confusion. "They're only going to get in the way."

"That one over there can get in my way anytime she wants," exclaimed Eli as he motioned with his head toward one of the wagons where a woman was struggling vainly to untie a tent from its side.

Heath glanced quickly, then steadied his eyes on the woman. She was perhaps in her late twenties, extremely well built, her curves emphasized by the severe cut of her dark green traveling suit. As his eyes sifted over her figure, stopping at the chignon of coppery hair resting at the nape of her neck, a sweet ache went through him and he was reminded of Darcy.

The woman turned, and his eyes softened as he agreed with Eli. She was beautiful, extremely so. She stood with arms akimbo staring toward the general's wagon, her face set stubbornly; then, evidently not seeing her husband among the men around the general, she went back to her struggle with the ropes that were holding the tent.

"I think the lady could use some help," said Eli as he watched her struggle, and Heath smiled.

"Maybe she does at that," he answered, and straightened. "Shall we oblige?"

Eli grinned back. "After you, my friend," he said, gesturing in a low bow, and the two scouts wandered toward the wagon.

"Excuse me, ma'am," interrupted Heath as the woman angrily made one last violent effort to free the tent, and as she whirled around abruptly to look at him, pulling hard on the rope, it finally gave way and with a small cry she fell, landing on her rear in the dirt at the side of the wagon, her blue eyes staring up at him in surprise.

"What . . . !" she exclaimed as the tent poles fell

into the dirt in front of her, followed by the rest of the tent and ropes, and Heath tried to keep a straight face.

"I was going to offer to help," he said as Eli began gathering up the ropes and poles. "I didn't mean to frighten you." He leaned over and held out his hand. "Here, let me help you up."

She stared at him, speechless, her face turning deep crimson.

"I'm sorry," he apologized, his hand still held out. "Please let me help."

She eyed him curiously, her face still tinged pink; then gingerly she held up her hand, letting the tall handsome stranger pull her to her feet. She dusted her skirt off, glancing surreptitiously at him as she did, taking in his worn buckskins, black hair that curled in masses above his fringed collar, matching the dark penetrating eyes that stared at her; then her eyes stopped on the gold earring decorating his right ear, and she looked puzzled.

He smiled sheepishly as his hand moved to the earring and he fingered it. "A memento of my misguided youth," he explained, and again she turned the color of her hair.

"I didn't mean . . . it's really none of my business, sir," she said as she straightened her waistcoat, then turned to Eli. "Here, sir"—she held out her arms—"I can take it now," but Eli protested.

"Not at all, ma'am. Show me where you intend to put it up, and I'll carry it there for you."

"There's no need, really," she flustered. "I'm quite capable," but both Heath and Eli insisted, so she led them to a spot some fifty feet away.

"My husband said to put it up over here," she said as she pointed out the spot. "I wanted him to help me, but it seems the general's tent comes first." She glanced toward the general's wagon, where the soldiers and militia were as thick as flies. "It seems the general's comfort always comes first," she complained disgustedly, "but then, I guess I should be used to it by now. My name's Janet Putnam. My husband's Captain Mark Putnam, the general's chief aide."

"Heath Chapman and Eli Crawford, at your service, ma'am," introduced Heath as Eli set down the scrambled parts of the tent. "Would you like a hand at putting it up?"

She took a look at the sorry mess on the ground at her feet, then shrugged. "You might as well help me. I doubt if I can even tell which end is which in that mess," she accepted, and they dug into the poles and ropes, sorting and twisting, with Mrs. Putnam shaking her head as she watched, and within a short time the tent was erected in one piece.

"I never would have believed it," she said as she gazed at the finished product.

"It's a matter of knowing how," said Heath.

"Oh, I understand that. It's just that I never knew how. This is the first time I've ever come with Mark, and it's not at all like I thought it would be."

"What did you expect?"

She blushed again, delicately this time. "You know how women are . . . it sounded romantic."

"The glorious West? Something like that?"

"Something like that." She looked downcast. "All I've had so far is hard work and trouble." She looked at him quickly. "Oh, I don't mind the hard work, really," she said by way of redeeming herself. "It's just that . . ." She looked off toward the general's wagons again.

"I presume the general keeps your husband fairly busy."

"Busy?" Her laughter was tinged with bitterness. "Oh, yes, Mr. Chapman, that's one thing he does do, keep Mark busy," and he saw the snap to her eyes as she said it.

The tone of her voice should have warned him then, as well as her eyes. In fact the color of her hair should have warned him, but with the mood he'd been in lately, he probably would have paid little attention to the warning anyway, and she smiled at him openly as she talked.

"Tell me, are you and Mr. Crawford part of the militia, Mr. Chapman?" she asked.

Heath shook his head. "No, ma'am. Eli and I aren't soldiers. We'll be doing the scouting for the general."

She was impressed. "Scouts. No wonder you knew what you were doing," she said as she glanced quickly at the tent.

Heath smiled, "All in a day's work, ma'am." His eyes held hers, and he liked what he saw. "If you need further assistance—"

He was interrupted by a harsh voice from behind him. "What's going on here, Janet?" her husband asked as he eyed the two men, disliking their casual appearance.

Heath turned to meet the man's eyes, and his impression was one of surprise. Captain Mark Putnam was short compared to Heath's tall, well-built frame. About five-foot-eight or -nine, he was well-built, his army uniform emphasizing broad shoulders and slim hips. However, though he was only in his late thirties, his hairline had already receded far back, leaving his scalp shiny and smooth, yet the dark hair at his temples was still without frost and moved on down across his chin and above his mouth in a clipped beard and mustache. He was still an attractive man, but his work with the general had added premature lines to his forehead and an arrogant tilt to his head.

"May I ask who you are and what you're doing here?" he asked irritably, and Heath acquiesced.

"Your wife was in need of help, and unfortunately you weren't anywhere around, Captain," he explained. "I'm Heath Chapman, and this is Eli Crawford. I hope you won't mind, we helped her with the tent."

Captain Putnam looked at the tent, then to his wife. "I thought you wanted to learn to do things yourself," he said sternly. "That was your argument for coming along, or don't you remember, Janet?"

Her lips tightened angrily. "I remember perfectly well," she retorted. "But you were supposed to show me what was to be done, not let me try to learn without any help. You didn't say I had to stumble along blindly, without any instructions. We've slept in the wagon all the way out here, and now you expect me to know how to pitch a tent without being shown first. And it was the same with the cooking. You were so busy helping your precious general that you didn't have time to show me how to make a fire or hang pots or anything. I said I wanted to learn, Mark, but in order to learn, a person has to be taught."

Mark's eyes hardened. "I knew the trip would be too much for you, Janet, I warned you," he said; then he turned to Heath. "My wife has the notion that traveling through the wilderness is no different from a trip to her Aunt Mary's, gentlemen," he went on, his eyes denoting his reservation at using the word "gentlemen." "I explained to her before granting permission to let her come that it was hard work and there was nothing exciting about tramping through this godforsaken land." He straightened, his hazel eyes steady on his wife's flushed face. "I thank you for your help, sirs, but in the future I must ask you to forgo any assistance you might be tempted to offer. She made the decision to come, so let her do the work herself. Is that clear, Janet?" he asked, and she bit her lip, her hands clenching angrily. He was treating her like a spoiled child, not like a wife.

"It's perfectly clear," she answered furiously. "Now, if you'll excuse me, gentleman . . ." She addressed Heath and Eli. "I want to thank you for your help," she said softly. "Thank you," and she walked away without so much as looking at her husband.

Mark Putnam watched her stalk off. "Women!" he exclaimed as she walked briskly to the wagon and began climbing into the back. "I'm sorry, sirs, I don't like to sound like a blackguard, but we've been married thirteen years and I've never brought her along before. I shouldn't have now."

"Then why did you?" asked Heath curiously.

"Pressure, sir, pressure," he admitted. "My wife is a good friend of the general's daughter-in-law, and since she was allowed to come . . ."

"At least the nights won't be lonely for you this time," offered Eli, and Mark Putnam frowned.

"On the contrary, sir," he remarked as he watched Janet struggling to get some boxes out of the back of the wagon. "Janet can be a stubborn bitch when she wants to be, and a man with a wife along doesn't dare find someone else to share his bed. No, Mr. Crawford, I must say I've had lonelier nights this trip so far than I ever had before," but he never caught the look the two woodsmen gave each other.

They talked for a few minutes longer and Heath halfheartedly promised they wouldn't run to Janet's aid again, then walked away slowly as the captain headed back toward the general's wagon and Janet began her struggle with the boxes.

"I don't think it's at all right," said Eli as they watched from a distance while Janet carried the boxes from the wagon to the tent, and Heath agreed, but there was nothing they could do. She was the captain's wife, and what he did with his wife was supposed to be his own business.

A couple of times Janet stopped momentarily and smiled at Heath, and he felt a little reassured. At least she wasn't angry at them. She even managed to build a fire and start some food cooking, and Heath had to admit she was trying, regardless of what the captain thought.

For the rest of the afternoon and all the next day he watched her from a distance, and she knew he was watching. Their eyes would meet and she'd smile and he'd smile back; then sometimes if he saw she was doing something wrong, he'd walk by nonchalantly, dropping hints without being obvious, and she'd pretend he

hadn't said more than a quick good day, yet silently
she thanked him for his help.

It was the afternoon after the general's eloquently
stirring speech to the men that Heath bumped into
Janet away from camp. He'd taken a stroll and was
walking back toward the clearing when he spotted her
standing a short distance away looking first one way,
then the other, as if she didn't know where she was.

She whirled, startled by his approach.

"Are you lost?" he asked curiously, and she sighed,
hefting a big bundle of clothes higher on her arm.

"Probably," she answered. "I was looking for the
creek so I could wash these clothes. I've got four days'
wash here, and Mark said it was in this direction."

"Your husband was wrong," stated Heath. "Come
on, I'll show you."

She hesitated. "Won't that be against my husband's
orders?"

"What he doesn't know won't hurt him. Come on."

He led her farther into the woods, then half-circled
the camp until he came onto a wide stream where the
grass at the edge had been trampled by people kneeling
to wash their clothes in the clear water.

She glanced back from where they'd come. "Now,
why would Mark tell me the creek was back there?"
she asked, frowning, and Heath didn't comment, but
sat down on an old log at the edge of the water to
watch.

"I'll walk you back again so you don't get lost," he
offered as she dropped her bundle of clothes and began
unfastening them, and she was thankful for his company. The woods were quiet and spooky so far from
camp, especially since the sun had already started to
sink low on the horizon.

"Why have you waited so late in the day to wash?"
he asked as she dipped one of Mark's white shirts in
the water, then began rubbing the lye soap on it.

"In the first place, I hate washing clothes, and sec-
ondly, Mark had to wear this shirt in the ceremony this

afternoon; then he insists he needs it again tomorrow afternoon." She shrugged. "Besides, with everything else there is to do all day, I really didn't have time to do it until now. I'm not as efficient as the other women, I guess."

"What on earth ever made you decide to come with him?" Heath asked out of curiosity. "He said it's the first time you've come with him in the thirteen years you've been married."

Her face reddened, but she didn't answer.

"I suppose it's none of my business."

Leaning back, she stared at the wet shirt in her hands as if contemplating. "I guess I just got tired of waiting all the time," she finally answered softly, then began rubbing the collar of the shirt again. "I was seventeen when we married. At first Mark was stationed near New York and we were together all the time. We had a small house near headquarters, and he was allowed to come home regularly; then a year later he was transferred to Fort Pitt. That wasn't too bad either, because I was still allowed to be with him. But after two years at Fort Pitt, he was made adjutant to General Hull and he said it was impossible for me to go along. Most of his time the past ten years he's spent in the Michigan Territory, and home was a place he dropped into two or three times a year to visit." She twisted the shirt viciously in her hands and the flush grew deeper over her face. "I'm young yet, Mr. Chapman," she confessed shortly. "I need a husband more than two or three times a year." She turned her head, embarrassed at her frankness and also ashamed of the tears that welled up in her eyes.

"Was it worth it, Janet?" he asked, and she couldn't look at him, her fingers toying with the shirt in her hands.

She began to scrub the collar again slowly, absent-mindedly, letting his question sink in. How many times she'd asked herself the same question the past few months. Mark hadn't wanted her to come, she was sure of it. He claimed he loved her, yet he was perfectly

happy with the arrangement as it had been, and his
reaction to her insistence about coming annoyed her. It
didn't seem to bother him that he could only make love
to her two or three times a year. At least it didn't seem
to bother him the way it bothered her. How many
nights she'd lain awake aching to feel his body against
hers, wanting to feel the warmth of a kiss, the love she
knew was being denied her. Even though his lovemaking had never been the ideal she'd expected it to be, it
was better than none at all. Didn't he feel the same?
Didn't he want her near him?

The question had plagued her a hundred times since
they'd left home, and now Heath Chapman's question
was added to her turmoil.

"Well, was it worth it?" he asked again, and she
threw the shirt to the ground and sat back on her
heels, disgusted.

"I don't know" she answered dejectedly. "I just
don't know." She looked up at the trees overhead, not
really seeing them. "I thought it would be. I thought
once we got out here, Mark would forget his stupid
aversion to taking his wife along, but he's worse. Sometimes I wish I hadn't come. Nothing's working out the
way it should . . . he doesn't want me . . . not here.
He only wants me as a change of variety two or three
times a year."

He studied her wet hands that were spread firmly on
her thighs, dampening the dark brown skirt she wore;
then his eyes moved to her breasts heaving angrily
beneath her white cotton shirtwaist, and he knew she
suspected what Mark had confessed to them only the
other day.

"Are you sure?" he asked, and she swallowed hard,
rubbing her hands harder on her skirt.

"No, I'm not sure," she answered. "I'm not really
sure of anything, but it's the only logical reason I can
think of why he doesn't want me here. Why he's been
content to leave me behind all these years." She looked
at Heath, anger clouding her eyes. "Why are men like

that?" she asked suddenly. "Why do they think it's all right for them, but not for us? I'm expected to be a dutiful wife and stay put until he decides he wants to play husband. Well, I'm tired of staying put. I'll bet his nights haven't all been spent in empty beds like mine have. But if I were to do something like that, he'd kill me and everyone would say he was justified. The unfaithful wife! Why?" She leaned over and attacked the shirt again savagely. "I'll tell you why," she ranted furiously, "because it's a man's world, that's why. I can't accuse him of adultery. People would only laugh. Mark himself told me men aren't expected to live celibate lives." She rinsed the shirt in the clear water of the stream and began wringing the water from it. "Well, neither am I," she retorted viciously, then her face flushed again as she shook the shirt out and looked for a place to put it, having forgotten to bring a basket.

Heath reached out and took the shirt from her, and her eyes faltered as he looked at her.

"I'm sorry," she said apologetically. "I shouldn't be telling you all this," and she reached for her husband's underwear and began dowsing it in the cool stream.

"Why not?"

"Because it isn't proper."

"And Janet Putnam always tries to do what's proper, right?"

She began soaping the underwear and glanced at him sheepishly. "Janet Putnam is a fool," she said softly. "She should have stayed home and thanked God for the roof over her head and a comfortable bed, even if it was empty."

"Then you do regret coming?"

"Only because it hasn't worked." She stopped rubbing the underwear together for a minute as she stared at him. "I wouldn't mind the work so much. In a way, it's fun trying to adjust, but Mark treats me like an intruder." She looked away again and rinsed the underwear, then wrung it out, and he took it from her. "If your wife wanted to come along with you, would you think she was intruding?" she asked, and Heath smiled.

"I don't have a wife."

"But if you did?"

His eyes sifted over her thoroughly, and she blushed under his scrutiny. "If she looked like you, I'd never consider her an intruder, no matter where she wanted to follow me," he replied.

"You're a flatterer, Mr. Chapman."

"The name's Heath."

"All right . . . Heath." She went on with her washing. "What am I going to do, Heath?" she asked as she scrubbed one of her blouses.

"You're asking me?"

"You seem to know everything else about survival in the wilderness. Can't you suggest a way for a poor neglected wife to survive?"

He didn't answer, and she looked up to catch his eyes watching her, desire openly revealed on his face.

"I'm afraid any suggestions I might have would be quite improper," he whispered softly. "You're a lovely woman, Janet."

In spite of the cold creek water, she felt a hot flush run through her. "You're not supposed to say things like that to an old married woman like me," she told him self-consciously.

"But it's true. You are lovely."

"You'll be turning my head with such nonsense."

He held her wet clothes in one hand and reached out with the other, catching her chin in his fingers so she was forced to look directly into his eyes. "Your husband's the fool, Janet," he murmured softly, "a damn fool. If I had a wife like you, I'd never let her out of my sight."

Her heart was pounding in her ears so loud it was suffocating, and her lips trembled. She'd realized when she'd first laid eyes on Heath that he was far more attractive than any man had a right to be, and now, as she looked into his eyes, she wanted to melt to the ground. His eyes were so dark they looked black, the pupils blending into one intense, penetrating orb that held her spellbound, and his mouth was sensuously inviting.

"I'd better finish the wash," she whispered breathlessly, her lips trembling, and his fingers caressed her chin affectionately as he stared at her.

"Maybe you'd better," he finally said wisely, and his hand dropped from her chin.

She turned from him and swallowed hard, her hands shaking as she picked up her husband's pants, plunging them into the cold water, trying to still the beating of her heart as she scrubbed them and began rinsing off the soap. "I'm sorry, Heath," she said nervously, her voice unsteady as she dunked the pants up and down in the water. "I don't want you to think I was trying to throw myself at you."

"Did I accuse you?"

"No."

"Then forget it." He rested the wet clothes he'd been holding across his buckskinned knee and reached out, taking the heavy pants from her, his big, sinewy fingers twisting the water from them easier than her small hands ever could have done. "Now, why don't you let me help you with the rest of this wash so you'll get finished before dark?" he insisted, and she leaned back, relieved, as the tension broke between them and they relaxed back into an easy relationship.

Heath enjoyed Janet's company. She was witty, unpretentious, quick to catch on to things, and eager to learn, and in spite of her husband's refusal to let anyone help her, as the days went by she managed to glean enough from her brief encounters with Heath to survive.

On June 1 General Hull, with his son, daughter-in-law, and grandchildren in tow, followed by the rest of his men and their wives, with the Ohio Militia bringing up the rear, headed up the road toward Urbana, where they'd meet with the Fourth Cavalry and from there they'd start their next 170-mile trek to Detroit.

The road to Urbana was hot and tiring, and although Heath and Eli traveled far ahead of the main column, Heath's thoughts often wandered back to Janet struggling along thanklessly somewhere behind them, trying to please a man who was becoming ever more impossible to please as the days went on.

When they reached Urbana, Heath, as head scout, accompanied colonels Duncan McArthur, John Findlay, and Lewis Cass of the Ohio Militia to General Hull's tent for special orders.

"It seems the colonels are to go meet the Fourth Cavalry coming up from Vincennes and escort them into town when they arrive, and the general wants me to go along," he told Eli later when he returned from the general's tent, and his friend nodded.

"So that's why the old man's got the men decoratin' the town with them evergreen boughs," he said disgustedly. "Got an eagle right in the middle of that archway across the main road, and one of the men's makin' a sign to hang up over it."

"Well, we do have to make the Fourth feel welcome, Eli," Heath explained sarcastically. "After all, they're veterans, heroes."

"So we gotta kiss their asses, I suppose."

"General's orders friend," said Heath, and he straightened his buckskins, trying to smooth the curls from his hair before going to see if Janet had made out all right, but the curls refused to lie flat, and he shrugged, walking away.

The next afternoon as Heath stood to one side watching the three colonels of the Ohio Militia meet with the Fourth Cavalry a mile out of town and escort them in, he knew the men of the Fourth weren't exactly thrilled. They disliked the thought of fighting with men whose commanding officers wore makeshift uniforms and whose men had none of the hard discipline of the regular army, and one man, Colonel James Miller of the Fourth, protested loudest of all.

Ohio law demanded that the three Ohio colonels take their rank with them into federal service, but by doing so they relegated Colonel Miller, who was actually a lieutenant colonel, to fourth in command behind General Hull, and he didn't like it. He felt he should be second in command, and General Hull was at a loss. He had no idea how to settle the dispute and his only alternative was to send to Washington for a solution. Naturally the answer would take months in coming, and in the meantime their march to Detroit had to go on in spite of the tension that existed between the regulars and the militia, but it wouldn't go on until still another matter was settled.

Some of the militia started complaining about not getting the pay they were promised. They were yelling and threatening to turn back, refusing to march, and Colonel Miller, his back up, irritated already by what he considered the ragtail appearance of the militia, arrested three of the worst troublemakers and had them brought to a court-martial, condemning them to be dishonorably discharged. It was only by the intervention of General Hull, who pardoned the men, that the affair was smoothed over.

Heath and Eli, who weren't part of the regulars or the militia, watched from the sidelines, shaking their heads. Men were stubborn even when they couldn't afford to be, and they wondered just how the march would make out, with discord already building in its ranks. As scouts, both men were scheduled to leave two days before Colonel McArthur and his men were to start, and the night before, Heath moved about restlessly, his mind miles away from the job he had to do.

Heath and Eli always camped away from the others, and he left the fire where Eli sat whittling and wandered across the field to where the soldiers' tents were pitched in a neat row, sauntering slowly between them. He picked his way, at random, so it seemed, but there

was one tent that caught his eye, drawing him unconsciously.

He stood in the shadows and stared at Janet, the
firelight falling on her copper hair, turning it to fiery
red-gold as she stood at the entrance to the tent, her
dressing gown pulled about her, staring toward General Hull's tent, where Mark was disappearing inside. It
was late, close to eleven, and he wondered if they'd
had another quarrel. He knew they'd been arguing regularly ever since the march began.

She turned his way as she heard the footsteps approach, then relaxed when she recognized his tall
frame.

"Duty or disagreement?" he asked as he motioned
toward the general's tent, and Janet knew what he
meant.

"Some of both, I guess," she answered, and wrapped
her arm about the pole that centered at the tent flap.
"What does it matter anyway . . . the results are the
same."

"Janet!" She looked at him sharply. Their eyes met
and held for long moments, and neither of them said a
word; then, "Would you like to go for a walk?" he
asked, more subdued, and she continued to stare at
him, her eyes softening dangerously.

"Why not?" she replied, straightening solidly, then
brushed a stray hair from her face. "Yes, why not?"
and she stepped away from the front of the tent, looking off in both directions. "Which way?"

"This way," he said, and took her arm, ushering her
to the back of the tent, to the next row, and beyond it
to the edge of the field, where the trees began to
thicken and the air smelled like fresh earth and grass instead of cookfires and crude sanitation.

"Mark said you're leaving tomorrow morning," she
said by way of making conversation, yet she was very
aware of him.

"Eli and I have to blaze the trail and mark the
route."

"Isn't that dangerous?"

He shrugged. "Sometimes. The Indians have been pretty friendly this spring, though, and the general's waiting to see their reaction when they see so many troops on the move." They moved farther into the cover of the trees and on to the edge of a small meadow where it was quiet and secluded. "Besides," he went on, "I'm used to trouble. It seems to follow me like the plague."

She stopped in the shadows of a huge oak and turned to look at him. "Why are we doing this, Heath?" she asked suddenly, her face strained and drawn, and he frowned as his eyes met hers, and a warm glow went through him. Her voice broke. "We're always making small talk and acting like nothing's happened . . ." Her eyes flashed passionately as her voice lowered. "I'm afraid Janet Putnam is about to say something shameful, Heath. You'd better stop her," she begged anxiously, but instead he stepped closer and pulled her against him.

"No. I won't stop her," he whispered, "never. I want you to say it, Janet." His voice vibrated fervently. "Say whatever shameful thing comes into your beautiful head, because I've been thinking it myself for days now."

His hand moved into her flaming hair. It was loose tonight, falling about her face in a halo of silken wonder, making her look like an innocent girl, but the eyes that stared up at him were far from innocent. They were the eyes of a woman struggling with her desires and losing the battle, their blue depths enslaving him.

"Say you'll miss me when I'm gone, Janet," he pleaded softly. "Say you care what happens to me . . . say you want me to touch you, kiss you . . ." His voice broke. "Let me make love to you before I leave, Janet, please!"

"Heath!" Her eyes were wide, her lips parted as she held her breath, the world around her reeling. Since the afternoon she'd looked up from where she fell in the dirt beside the wagon, into his wildly handsome face, she'd known her feelings for Heath Chapman were not the feelings a married woman should have for another man. She'd tried to tell herself it was because he was concerned for her and because Mark was being such a stinker, but it wasn't, and she knew it now. She'd known it earlier tonight when Mark left for the general's tent and she hadn't cared, but to let him make love to her? No man had ever touched her except Mark. "Oh, Heath!" she murmured. "I . . . I don't know," and he pulled her closer in his arms.

"You know what's been happening between us, don't you?" he asked, his lips brushing her cheek. "You know I can't keep my mind off you. You almost said it yourself."

"I know . . . I know." Her body was on fire, vibrant sensations pulsating through her, and her hips moved involuntarily against him, searching for release to the yearning that filled her loins. "But to let you . . . this wasn't supposed to happen, Heath, not this," she gasped breathlessly, her hand caressing his neck, sending chills down his spine as he kissed her temple lightly, then let his lips slip to below her ear. "We don't have any right," she went on, holding her breath as he kissed her neck and face again and again, weakening her defenses. "We were supposed to just be friends . . . I shouldn't be here . . ."

"But you are." His lips were against her ear, and warm sensations exploded inside her. "I'm falling in love with you, Janet," he whispered softly. "I didn't want to, but it's no use pretending anymore. I need you."

His mouth covered hers, and she couldn't help herself as she melted against him, kissing him back. She needed him too. She needed the love she was sure he could give her. The love she'd tried to find in Mark's arms and couldn't.

Heath drew his lips from hers and pulled her into

the soft grass so she was on her back and he was look-ing into her face.

"What if someone sees us?" she asked nervously, and he smiled as he untied the sash on her dressing gown and pulled up her nightgown, his hands stroking her hips, then moving to her breasts.

"No one will, love, I promise. We're a long way from camp." He bent down and kissed her as his hand reached her breast, the fingers teasing her nipples, ex-citing her even more.

Only the night sounds about them penetrated the darkness as Heath made love to her, bringing her to life, making her ache for him; and he slipped from his buckskins and she felt his strong thighs against her as he moved on top of her.

"Heath!" she whispered from beneath him, and he hesitated as she held her breath. "I've never known an-other man, Heath," she gasped, frightened, and sud-denly she felt his manhood touch her, hot and moist, and a moan of ecstasy escaped her as he slowly began to penetrate, little by little at first; then he plunged deep, driving forward.

She clung to him, desperately afraid of the wonder-ful feelings that began flooding her.

"Relax, love," he coaxed against her mouth, "let me give you pleasure . . . relax . . . hush!" and slowly, for the first time in her life, as he kissed her and thrust into her, she forgot she was supposed to please him, and instead she lost herself in the rapture he was giving her, and when she finally came, it was like a violent force erupting inside her over and over again until she could hardly breathe and her body was writhing in ec-stasy. Her hands clenched against the back of his buck-skin shirt, and she trembled against him.

"What have you done to me?" she asked breath-lessly, and he bent down, kissing her lips softly, run-ning his tongue delicately along the line that separated them.

"Has Mark never made love to you like this, Janet?" he asked, and there were tears in her eyes.

"No . . . he . . . he never made me feel like this." Her eyes were glazed, as if she were drunk.

"Would you like to feel it again?"

"Again?"

He began to move inside her, slowly at first, then thrusting in and out in a rhythm that flooded her with wonder, and she wanted to cry out for joy at what he was doing, her body yielding to his in sweet surrender, and again she felt the same peak of pleasure that had thrilled her only moments before. She quivered, lifting her hips, arching herself to meet him, and he knew what she wanted.

"Now, Heath, now!" she cried, and he gasped as he thrust forward hard, exploding inside her, his body shaking spasmodically; then he relaxed on top of her, his face buried in her neck, his breathing heavily labored.

She sighed, her body content, and reached up, stroking his dark curly head as he lay above her, keeping her snug and warm. What could she say? How did you tell a man he'd made you feel like a real woman for the first time in your life and she wondered if she'd pleased him as much. "Heath?"

"Mmmhmmm?"

"Did I please you?"

He buried his lips in her neck, smelling the warm sweet smell of her. "Mmmhmmm!"

"May I ask you something?"

"Mmmhmmm."

"You won't get mad?"

"No."

"You're sure."

He kissed her neck again and caressed her shoulder with one hand. "I'm sure."

She hesitated, then inhaled sharply.

"Well?" he asked, and lifted his head, looking into

her face, trying to see it in the darkness beneath the oak tree.

"Were you ever married?" she asked quietly, and saw him frown.

"No."

"Were you ever in love?"

His hand moved to her face, and he caressed her cheek. She reminded him so much of Darcy, yet that was so many years ago. "Yes," he finally said softly. "A long time ago there was someone."

"Why didn't you marry her?"

He kissed her gently. "It's a long story," he answered, "and not a very nice one. You don't really want to know."

"I'm sorry."

"It was my own fault." He kissed her again. "I'll be truthful with you, Janet. The first time I saw you, I was reminded of her. Your hair and your smile are the same, but that's not why I fell in love with you . . . I would have loved you even if I had never known her. That was sixteen years ago." He slipped from her and stretched out beside her, pulling her into his arms. "I wish I didn't have to leave in the morning."

She snuggled closer against him. "So do I."

"I won't see you again until we reach Detroit."

"I'll die inside."

"You have Mark."

He felt her stiffen in his arms. "Oh, God, Heath, how can I go back to him?"

"We haven't any choice." His arms released her, and he stood up, picking up his buckskins, pulling them on; then he helped her to her feet, and she straightened her nightgown and pulled the dressing gown around her, tying the sash.

"Why couldn't we have met years ago?" she said, and he knew she was on the verge of tears.

"Because life is cruel." He thought back to Cora and Darcy and everything that had happened in his life; then suddenly he reached out and slowly pulled her into his arms. "Janet, I'm sorry," he said softly. "I shouldn't have lost my head. I should never have made love to you."

She put her hand to his mouth. "Don't say that. Don't ever say that. I'm not some silly young girl who expects you to fight Mark for me and carry me away with you. I knew what I was doing, and I wanted it as much as you did. I seduced you, Heath, whether you realize it or not, and I'm not sorry. You're everything I thought you'd be. Everything I've ever wanted or dreamed of, so there's nothing to be sorry about. I'll go back to Mark because I know I have to, but that doesn't mean I'm going to like it."

He took her fingers from his lips and bent down, kissing her deeply, sensuously, telling her how much he loved her; then they started back to camp.

❧ 6 ❧

The next morning, June 9, shortly before dawn, Heath and Eli slipped from General Hull's tent and headed out of Urbana, moving north toward Kenton, some forty miles away, the next step in the chain. A road was to be built through the wilderness, started by Colonel McArthur's Ohio regiment, and Heath and Eli were to blaze the trail for them, marking trees for clearing and leaving markers where the road would be laid. The going was rough, the weather far from ideal. One day was too hot, the next too wet, but the two men moved on diligently through Indian territory, moving closer every day toward what was called the Black Swamp.

They kept two to three days ahead of the colonel and his men, then from Kenton on, Colonel Findlay and the Ohio Second took over from McArthur's men and Heath and Eli still moved ahead. This section of the road led through Wyandot country. It was the watershed between the Ohio River and the Great Lakes Basin, and Heath and Eli headed into the swamps, mosquitoes plaguing them, ankle-deep in mud, with heavy rains soaking them. The men behind them were going to have one hell of a time putting a road through this, they knew, yet behind them, Findlay and his men pushed on in spite of the quagmire they were working in.

When the Second Regiment finally reached one of the forks of the Maumee, they built a fort, which was immediately named Fort Findlay, and in short order they were joined by Colonel Lewis Cass and his Third Regiment, preceded by the Fourth Army Regulars along with General Hull's troops. After dragging their wagons through mudholes axle-deep where carts turned over and the horses and oxen faltered under the loads, and weary beyond endurance, the general promptly decided they needed a rest and they settled in for a while at the fort.

Heath and Eli were still up ahead blazing the trail, and Colonel Cass and his men were still behind them. Weather and swamps had slowed them, but in spite of everything they were still moving and the road was still being laid, but with less enthusiasm.

Then on June 26, word reached General Hull from Washington that they were to hasten with all speed to Detroit.

"Is that all the message says?" he asked Captain Putnam as he sat in his tent by the Sweetwater, and Mark nodded.

"That's all, sir."

"Nothing about war?"

"Nothing, sir. See for yourself," and he handed him the paper.

The old man shook his head uneasily, but the order was clear. They were to get to Detroit as quickly as possible, but still no sign of war. "All right, tell the men to push on," he said, and the trek once more began.

Meanwhile, up ahead a few days past the old battle-grounds of Fallen Timbers, deep in Indian country, Heath and Eli, who were being extremely cautious, rounded a bend in the trail, then dropped flat to the ground, crawling into the underbrush as a band of unfriendly Wyandots emerged ahead on the trail.

Both men lay in the bushes quietly, hardly daring to breathe as the Indians moved to within ten feet of them, talking all the while, and they strained their ears, translating the Indians' dialect as they spoke.

"I say we should attack them now," said the Indian in the lead, but the one directly behind him disagreed.

"I say we wait and join Tecumseh first. We are not strong enough without Tecumseh."

"Bah! You are an old woman, Bright Feather," said the first warrior again, and the rest of the braves grunted agreement.

They stopped on the trail, continuing to argue. "You call me an old woman, then call Warbonnet an old woman. When the words of Warbonnet told the British soldiers war had begun, they also said we were to gather the rest of our braves and return to Fort Malden and join with Tecumseh when he arrived. You would disobey the words of Warbonnet's message?"

The other Indians stared at him, then began nodding.

"He is right," said one of the others.

"Warbonnet's words are wise," said another.

The first Indian stood motionless, staring at his comrade. "You are well to remind me, Bright Feather," he said. "But I still say our warriors could do better to attack General Hull's army before it reaches Detroit. After all, Warbonnet's words also said General Hull does not know yet that the war has started."

"And if they outnumber us and we lose? Warbonnet's messengers have said the army moving this way outnumbers the braves from our camp, and Warbonnet's words have always been true."

The others nodded. "With Tecumseh and the other tribes, we will be invincible," one of them said.

"Then you think we should return to Tecumseh?"

The braves all nodded in unison.

"Then I will not interfere," the first warrior said. "My father will hear the words of Warbonnet only. We will return to fight with Tecumseh," and with that they laughed, calling on the great spirit to guide their feet and bring them victory against their enemies, and they disappeared down the trail, leaving a pregnant silence in their wake.

Heath moved slowly from beneath the bushes and crawled onto the trail, meeting Eli halfway, and both men stared down the trail where the Indians had disappeared only moments before.

"What do you make of it?" asked Eli, and Heath's eyes darkened.

"I think the general's walking into a trap."

"Surely he knows already."

"You heard the Indians. And he won't know if they've waylaid his courier. Those Indian braves could get back long before the general reaches Detroit, and he could have an unpleasant welcoming party when he arrives." Heath stood up, and Eli stood up beside him.

"Maybe we'd better backtrack," he suggested, and Heath agreed. After all, they weren't building the road anymore, only marking the right trail for the general to follow. The roads this far north had already been built.

"I'd rather take the time to go back than end up bringing them into an ambush someplace."

"Then let's go," Eli agreed, straightening his buckskins; then he rubbed the sandy hairs on his chin. "But first, have you any notion yet who this Warbonnet is?"

Heath frowned. "Not yet, my friend," he said. "At least, nothing I can put into fact, but I've been keeping my eyes and ears open. That's what they sent me here for, and that's what I intend to find out. Come on," and they moved back down the trail the way the Indians had disappeared, but this time they were even more cautious, every nerve on edge, and two days later they joined Colonel Cass and his men, whose only word from the general had been to keep moving forward.

Heath and Eli also kept moving, but in the opposite direction, back toward the general, and they ran into his camp on June 30 at the banks of the Maumee across from Fallen Timbers, where he had stopped long enough to visit with his niece and nephew who lived in a settlement close by in Frenchtown.

Captain Putnam was in the general's tent when they

arrived after dark the evening of the thirtieth while the general, his son and daughter-in-law, and grandchildren were being entertained away from camp by their relatives.

"What are you doing here?" Mark asked as they walked into the tent, and Heath stared at him sternly, then glanced about the otherwise empty tent.

"Where's General Hull?"

"He's busy this evening."

"Busy?"

"That's right, and he isn't to be disturbed. It's the first chance he's had to relax since he left Washington."

"We have to see him right away," said Heath. "It's important."

"Important? Come, now, Heath, as the general's adjutant, you know I can handle the matter, there's no need to see him. I'll see he gets any message you want to leave."

Heath looked at Eli, then back to Mark. "Have you heard of the war?" he asked hesitantly, and Mark's eyes narrowed.

"I know it hasn't been declared yet."

"But it has," stated Heath. "That's what we came to tell the general. We ran into a band of Indians on their way out from Fort Malden."

"Indians?"

"They were talking about the war, had no idea we were even around."

Mark stared at them thoughtfully. "And that's your source of information? Some savages strolling through the woods?"

"They said war had been declared," replied Heath, "and I believe them."

Mark glanced at Eli. "And you agree with Heath?"

"Yes, sir."

"And when was this war declared?"

Heath looked disgusted. "They didn't give a date, Captain. A date wasn't necessary."

"Heath, a date is necessary. What am I to tell the general? War's been declared, but I don't know when?"

Heath exhaled. "I don't care what words you use, Mark," he exclaimed angrily, "but I suggest you tell him."

Captain Mark Putnam straightened. He didn't like Heath. The man was nothing but a roustabout, a backwoodsman, yet he walked about like a man of breeding, as if he was somebody. Who was he, anyway? The man didn't even have a home to call his own, from what he'd heard, and rumor was that he had once been a pirate—Mark's eyes centered on the small gold earring in Heath's ear—but yet the general treated him like some kind of god just because he knew the Indians and the country. Besides, he didn't like the way he always had his eyes on Janet, talking to her whenever he was around camp, and he had seen some of the looks that passed between them. No, he didn't like Heath Chapman, and he wasn't sure he believed him. Indians indeed! He was probably panicking over nothing. Well, he'd humor him and get rid of him.

"All right, Heath," he said. "If you'll write your message, use your own words, I'll see the general gets it," and he motioned toward the general's desk, where quill and ink were handy.

Heath hesitated, not sure whether to trust him, then shrugged and walked to the desk, picking up the quill, dipping it in the ink, and he began to write. When he was finished, he sanded the paper, blew on it to make sure it was dry, then held it up to the candlelight on the general's desk and read it over. Satisfied, he handed it to Mark.

Mark turned it toward the light, glanced over it, then nodded to Heath. "I'll give it to the general as soon as he gets back," he said, his chin thrusting out arrogantly. "Now, I suggest you return to your assignment, gentlemen," he said, stroking his dark clipped beard. "We still need our road marked."

Heath exhaled. "You expect us to start back now?"

"I expect you to rest no longer than is necessary, since your services are doubly needed, gentlemen," he advised. "And I'm sure the general will agree."

Heath glanced quickly at Eli, then back to Mark. "As long as the general gets the message, I guess that's all we've come for, thank you, Captain," he said, then turned, touching Eli's arm, and they left the tent.

Mark stared after them, then read the message again and sneered. Ridiculous! Indians! The man was crazy. He walked to the table, holding the message over the candle, watching flames begin to eat at it. If war's declared, there'll be a message from Washington. He wasn't about to let the general be the first to fire shots in a war that hadn't been declared yet on some backwoodsman's say-so, and he watched the message burn until there was nothing left but ashes.

Heath stopped a few yards from the tent and stared off toward the rest of the tents on the banks of the river. He didn't exactly trust Mark, but it was obvious he'd had no other choice. Oh, well, it was in his hands now, and Heath's eyes moved to a tent that was familiar.

"Eli," he said, his voice hushed, "you don't want to start out this early, do you?" and Eli glanced at him surreptitiously.

"You got somethin' else in mind?"

"Why don't you sit over there by the captain's tent for me, in the shadows, real quiet like, where nobody'll see you, and whistle something if you see him coming."

Eli cocked his head and looked at his friend. "She ain't worth gettin' killed for, Heath," he said, but Heath didn't agree.

"She's worth more than you'll ever know," he answered, then smiled at his friend. "Besides, you're not supposed to know a thing about it."

Eli's gray eyes sharpened dangerously. "You be careful, friend," he cautioned, and Heath put his hand on Eli's shoulder.

"I won't be long, Eli," he promised, "but I have to

see her," and the two men walked cautiously toward the rows of tents; then suddenly Eli dropped to the ground, into the shadows at a good vantage point close to the captain's tent where he could watch the general's tent.

Heath made his way toward the tent he knew had to be where Janet was. Strange how he recognized it by the careless way she always put it up and by the way she set the fire before it with the kettle hanging lopsided.

It was hot tonight, exceptionally hot as he stepped up to the dark opening of the tent and softly called inside. "Janet?" There was silence. "Janet?"

Then he heard someone stir, and a slight noise. The tent was dark inside, and suddenly the sweet scent of her floated out to him and her voice whispered close behind it. "Heath?"

He ducked inside, and she was already there against him. His arms went about her, holding her close, and his mouth found hers in the darkness. He kissed her long and deep, his hands moving up her thinly clad body to frame her face; then his lips left hers and he tried to see her face, but there was no light.

"Oh God, I've missed you," he groaned softly, and she sighed.

"I've missed you, too."

"How long will Mark be in the general's tent?"

"Until the general returns, about midnight. He already told me he's not to leave for anything, in case something important comes in. General's orders." She put her hand on his chest, feeling the strength beneath his buckskins. "But what are you doing here?"

He put his arm about her shoulders, and they walked to her bedroll and sat down while he told her about the Indians.

"Then there's war for sure. I was hoping they'd settle things without a fight."

"Mark has the message to give to the general, but I'm not sure he believed us."

"Have you told anyone else?"

"No. I wrote out a statement. It's up to your husband now." He leaned close and kissed her bare throat, his hand covering her breast over the sheer lawn of her flimsy nightgown. "He ordered us back right away, but I couldn't go without seeing you."

Her hands caressed his face as she drew his head up and gave him her lips to kiss, her body yielding to the plea of his hands as she lay back on her bedroll.

"What if Mark comes?" she asked breathlessly, and he assured her Eli would let him know.

"You told Eli about us?"

"Eli and I understand each other," he explained softly, his lips against her hair. "Don't worry, darling, I'd trust him with my life."

"Oh, Heath!"

"Just love me, Janet, please," he begged. "I had to see you, and it was the only way. Don't scold me like a bad little boy."

She ran her hand up inside his shirt, feeling the warmth of his skin beneath her fingers, and her heart turned over inside her.

"I could never scold you, Heath," she whispered, her lips caressing his ear. "I'm only afraid for you. If Mark should find out . . ."

"He won't. Now, forget about Mark and Eli and everyone except us," he said. "I only have a few hours. I expect to be far away from here by dawn," and his mouth found hers again in the darkness, and the world around them was forgotten as he made love to her.

When he finally slipped away, he left Janet happy and contented, and half an hour later Mark found her sleeping peacefully, Heath long gone, and not a sign that he'd been there.

The next morning Janet stirred in the bedroll and opened her eyes, looking up into Mark's flushed face.

"Janet, wake up," he demanded, shaking her nervously, and she stretched lazily.

"What's the matter?"

"Do you have to sleep so late?" he asked. "My God, I never saw a woman who could sleep so sound."

She pushed his hands away as she began to sit up. "All right! All right!" she exclaimed as she rubbed her eyes with her fingers, then looked at him. "What is it?"

"You'll have to get your things together right away. The general's sending all the ladies and the baggage on upriver so he won't have to worry about dragging all of you the rest of the way over the rough roads."

"Upriver?"

"There's a boat on the Maumee, came in this morning. A merchantman named the *Cayauga*, out of Buffalo. She sailed into the river last night, and the general gave her captain sixty dollars to make a run to Detroit. They're loading everything on already. You'll have just enough time to get dressed and pack your things. I'll meet you later in Detroit."

"But you said there were British forts on the Detroit River." She pushed the hair back from her face, puzzled. "What about the war?"

He stood up. "It hasn't been declared yet. There's plenty of time. You can all reach there safely without all the bother. Now, come on, get ready."

She was about to protest when she remembered that she wasn't supposed to know about Heath's visit last night and the message he'd brought. But what could she do? If Heath was right and war had started, by traveling upriver by boat they'd be heading right into British hands.

"Will you quit daydreaming?" Mark cried, flustered. "You don't have that much time," and Janet pulled herself reluctantly from the bedroll.

What was she to do? She began dressing, trying to think of something. Evidently Mark hadn't believed Heath and had kept the message from the general, and if she told the general . . . Oh, God! What a mess to be in. If she told the general about Heath's visit, he'd confront Mark, and Mark would want to know how he found out, and Mark would know she'd been with

Heath . . . and Mark would get in trouble with the general for not giving him the message.

She was in a daze as she hurriedly finished dressing, slipping into her deep green traveling suit, and packed what clothes needed packing, then pulled her hair into a chignon at the nape of her neck and put on her green velvet hat, leaving the ungainly tent to find someone to carry her trunks, since Mark had left to see if the general needed him.

The *Cayauga* sat at anchor while it was loaded with the heaviest baggage of the army, a few men who were sick, the bandsmen and all their instruments and General Hull's personal belongings, including his field desk stuffed with all his private papers, parade states, sick reports, inventories on stores, and his orders from Washington, and last on board were some thirty or so soldiers to guard the army's property, his daughter-in-law and grandchildren, along with the army wives who'd accompanied their husbands, which included Janet Putnam.

Mark had kissed Janet good-bye without batting an eye. As if he'd never received the news from Heath last night, and she wanted to scream at him, asking him why, but she didn't dare. It was all she could do to stand at the rail of the ship and wave reluctantly, knowing they were sailing directly into the enemy's hands. She thought of telling the captain of the *Cayauga* after they'd sailed, but it would do no good. Why would he believe her? After all, her husband didn't seem concerned, and she watched with an ache in her heart as the boat moved into midstream along with another, smaller boat that had been hired with it, and she wondered if she'd ever see Heath again.

Without the excess baggage and women now, the army packed up and moved out. There were regular roads ready to follow this time; they only had to keep to the trails Heath and Eli had marked so they wouldn't end up on the wrong route, and the Fourth Army Regulars decided to lead the way.

The general had received a report from the east that
Tecumseh was headed west with some fifteen hundred
braves, on his way toward a rendezvous with the
Wyandots, and he frowned, wondering why he hadn't
had a report from his two scouts since the night they'd
warned him that about two hundred Sioux had been
spotted near Brownstone. One of Cass's men had
brought the message in for them shortly before they
reached the Maumee, but Heath and Eli had sent nothing to him for the past few days.

That day, after watching the *Cayauga* depart with its
cargo, with the army forging ahead satisfactorily, General Hull had Captain Putnam put the men to erecting
his tent for the night, secure in the knowledge that all
was going well.

It was shortly after midnight, however, when he was
shaken awake and handed a dispatch that had just
been brought in. He stretched and yawned as Mark
turned the watch lantern brighter for him to see by;
then the general read the letter, his face turning white.
The short message said war had been declared, and it
had been dated the same day as the message he'd received on the twenty-sixth telling him to proceed to
Detroit with all haste. He stared at it, unbelieving.
Somehow the letter had been held up in post, and
now . . .

He turned and looked at Mark, his tired eyes bewildered. "The *Cayauga*, Mark," he blurted anxiously,
and he thrust the message in Mark's hands, watching
him read it. "We've got to stop the *Cayauga*," but it
was too late.

Horsemen were sent out, but the ship had already
cleared the Maumee and was well on its way across the
lake.

On July 2 Janet stood at the rail of the *Cayauga* and
watched, holding her breath as the ship began to move
up the Detroit River past the British-held fort at
Amherstburg; then she sighed in dismay, knowing
Heath had been right, when a longboat, covered by the

guns from the British ship *General Hunter*, pulled away from shore and drew up alongside and Lieutenant Charles Rolette of the Provincial Marines boarded and informed them they were all prisoners.

She watched, her heart in her throat as everyone was ordered ashore, but she held her head high, refusing to cry as the other women were doing. Instead, she marched off, not angry with the British, but angry with her husband for refusing to believe Heath's message and with herself for being a coward and not telling the general herself.

A few days later the general caught up to Heath outside the town of Detroit. Heath and Eli watched, frowning, as the army moved forward.

"Where are all the wagons and baggage?" questioned Heath as he stood halfway down the slope watching them march down the road toward town, and Eli shook his head.

"You don't suppose he left them back at Maumee, do you?"

Heath started down the hill. "Let's find out!" He moved along the line hurriedly until he spotted the general on his horse, then made his way into the column of men, ignoring the angry look on Mark's face as he sat his horse beside the general.

"General Hull, sir, may I have a word with you?" Heath asked anxiously as he trotted along beside him, and the general frowned wearily as he pulled his horse to the side of the column of marching men and reined to a halt.

"You have the information we need about Fort Malden?" he asked Heath, and Heath nodded.

"Yes, sir, but tell me, where are the rest of the men and the wagons and the women?"

General Hull gazed off toward the river. "That, my boy, is a question I think perhaps you'll have to find the answer to. They left the Maumee the morning of the first on the ship *Cayauga* sailing for Detroit."

"On the first?"

"I didn't receive the message from Washington until midnight about the declaration of war. By that time they were already gone."

"On the first?" he questioned again in disbelief, and the general was irritated.

"That's what I said, Heath, the first."

"But I left the message—" Heath glanced behind the general to where Mark had reined in his horse, and Mark interrupted him.

"You did what, Heath?" Mark asked haughtily, and Heath stopped, staring at him, frowning; then he turned to the general.

"I left a message with Captain Putnam here on the evening of June 30, sir," he said formally, his face hard as granite, "and in that message I informed you that the British already had confirmation that the war had been declared."

"You what?"

"I gave the message to Captain Putnam at your camp on the banks of the Maumee," he stated angrily. "You were visiting relatives."

The general turned to face his aide, but Mark's face showed only arrogance.

"The man's lying, sir," he replied calmly. "I was in your tent all evening, and I received no message from him."

"Why, you liar!"

"Come, gentlemen, please." The general turned to look at Heath. "We'll settle this when I officially reach Detroit," he said wearily. "Right now I'm tired and discouraged, and all I want is some rest." His eyes softened. "Meanwhile, Heath, can you see what you can find out about the *Cayauga*? My daughter-in-law and grandchildren were on her too."

Heath inhaled as he stared at Mark Putnam. "I'll be back," was all he said, then turned and walked away.

"The man's out to discredit me," offered Mark as Heath walked away with Eli at his heels, and the general wanted to know why. "Because he's a ladies' man, sir," explained Mark as he watched Heath stride up the hill, the summer sun turning his hair iridescent like the feathers on a raven as it curled about his head. "I've seen him making eyes at Janet. He'd like nothing better than to get me out of the way."

"Oh, come, now, Mark," admonished the general, "the man's been all around the world and had his pick of women. What makes you think he's after your wife?"

Mark's eyes narrowed as he continued to watch Heath until he disappeared. "A man just knows, that's all."

"Did he give you a message, Mark?" General Hull asked, and Mark shook his head. He didn't dare let him know the truth or how badly he'd bungled things.

"No, sir. He didn't," he lied. "Ask anyone if he was in camp that night. No one's seen him since we left Urbana, and he's always sent couriers back with messages. Why would he come himself?"

General Hull was bewildered. Governor Meigs gave Heath Chapman the highest recommendation, and he'd gotten to like the man. He seemed honest and willing, regardless of danger to himself. Yet, he'd known Mark for some ten years now. He'd been a personal aide and he'd never known the man to lie or make an enemy for himself. But then, he'd never brought his wife along with him before, either, and as much as he tried to shrug it off, the general had to admit she wasn't an average-looking female. He snorted as he pulled his horse about and Mark followed. Damn women anyway, he thought to himself. What men won't do because of them. Well, he'd settle the matter later. The damage was already done, and he rode off, following his men into the town of Detroit that numbered somewhere around eight hundred people in and outside the fort.

Late the next afternoon Heath showed up at the general's headquarters with the news that the *Cayauga* was indeed in British hands. "The prisoners have been removed from Amherstburg to Fort Malden," he said.

"Can you negotiate a release, Heath?" asked the general, and Heath studied him solidly.

"I can try, but it won't be easy. They'll probably want concessions."

"No concessions."

"Then what am I supposed to negotiate with?"

"Self-respect, sympathy . . . can't you persuade them?"

"General Hull, they're soldiers."

"That's right, and I'm counting on that fact. Women and children shouldn't be plunder of war."

Heath glanced quickly at Mark, who was standing behind the general, and he almost brought up the episode of the message again, then changed his mind. What use would it be anyway? The general probably took Mark's word on the matter; after all, he'd known him longer.

"Give me three days, four at the most, and I'll see what I can do," he said, and the general nodded.

"You'll need an escort," suggested Mark, and he looked at the general. "May I go along, sir?"

The general opened his mouth to answer, but it was Heath who spoke up first. "Eli and I go alone or I don't go at all," he said stubbornly. "I'll not have some hysterical husband on my hands if things don't go right."

"You mean you don't want a husband on your hands period," countered the captain. "I've seen the looks you give my wife. I know why you're so eager to go alone."

The general reached back and put his hand on Mark's sleeve. "Let it be, Mark," he cautioned, at the same time noticing the flush on Heath's face. "Perhaps Mark's suspicions are right, I have no way of knowing, Heath," he said angrily. "But I'll not have the two of you jeopardizing this command with your personal quarrels." He stared at Mark. "You can settle the matter with Janet when and if she returns." He turned to Heath. "I'll give you four days at the most. Today's the sixth, I'll expect to see you no later than the tenth either way. Is that clear?"

Heath saluted casually. "Yes, sir," he said, then turned and walked away, leaving the two men standing alone in the general's office.

Janet was restless. It had been days since their capture. She had no idea where the men had been taken or where the rest of the women were, because they were still keeping her in a room by herself. Fortunately her trunks had been brought to the room, even though they had been ransacked first, but at least she had clothes to wear.

She walked to the window, smoothing the skirt of her pale green silk, and looked below, out over the parade ground of the fort. Why were they keeping her here away from everyone else? The other day some men had come in and asked her all sorts of questions about Mark and the general. Some she could answer, some she couldn't. Her mind was in a turmoil. If she'd only told the general about Heath's message regardless of the consequences.

She heard the doorknob rattle, and seconds later the door opened and a tall blond man entered. A man she'd never seen before. He was wearing buckskins similar to those Heath wore, but the fringe was heavier and there was beading across the yoke that covered his broad chest. He was taller than Heath by an inch or two, meaning he was over six feet, and his intense blue eyes studied her appreciatively as he closed the door behind him.

"Good afternoon," he addressed her, his manner gentlemanly, his voice deep and resonant.

"Who are you?" she asked, but he only smiled.

"The name isn't important." He strolled over and stood gazing out the window to see what she'd been looking at. "But if you have to address me, you may call me 'sir.'"

She studied him. He must be in his thirties, and quite handsome. Undoubtedly a backwoodsman by the clothes and tanned face, but for some reason he didn't ring true. Eli and Heath were both casual and relaxed. This man was tense, alert. To Janet he seemed ill-at-ease.

"May I ask why you're here, sir?" she asked, and he straightened, looking directly at her, his eyes on her hair, and she flushed.

"Your hair's beautiful," he mused, as if to himself, then thrust the thought aside. "Our reports tell us you're the wife of Captain Mark Putnam, is that right?"

"They've already been through that, yes."

"And discovered nothing."

"Because I know nothing. My husband was not a man to confide in his wife, sir, and even if he had, I doubt I'd tell you. Besides," she added, "from what the men who talked to me before have already said, I understand they learned everything they needed to know from the papers they found in the general's private desk."

"Not everything, I'm afraid."

"Oh? What didn't they learn?"

"There's a scout working for the general. He came here with the Ohio Militia. You know Heath Chapman?"

Her face suddenly turned rigid. "I know him, yes."

"He's not an ordinary scout, Mrs. Putnam."

Her forehead wrinkled as she stared at him. "What do you mean, not an ordinary scout?"

"He was sent here not just by Governor Meigs, but by special interests in Washington." His eyes flickered dangerously. "Have you ever heard of Warbonnet, madam?"

"Warbonnet?" She half-laughed. "I've heard of Tecumseh and Little Turtle, and a dozen others."

"Warbonnet is not an Indian chief, madam," he said. "Warbonnet is a white man on the side of the British, and your scout Heath Chapman, from what we've been told, was sent to track him down."

Janet cocked her head and took a good look at the man in front of her. "Warbonnet? A spy? So why are you telling me this?"

He smiled cynically, his eyes amused. "We also have it from good sources that you and Mr. Chapman are"—he cleared his throat—"shall we say, lovers, madam? Am I right?"

Janet's mouth fell and her voice wavered. "What are you talking about?"

"I'm talking about your affair with General Hull's scout."

"How dare you!" Her hands clenched nervously as she gasped out the words, her face pale.

"I can tell by the look on your face that it's true, madam," he said nastily. "So there's no use denying it. Besides, unfortunately for you, your exploits with the gentleman have been observed."

"You're lying!"

"Am I? Then shall I be explicit? In Urbana you and Heath Chapman took a long walk into the woods and found the grass in the meadow was an ideal spot for making love." She turned crimson, her eyes flashing. "And back at Maumee, he visited your tent for three hours during your husband's absence," he went on. "Is that sufficient proof, madam?"

Janet's lips quivered. "You had no right! What I do with my life is my business!"

He laughed. "Exactly, madam, but we made it our business."

Her voice lowered. "What do you want?"

"We want you to continue to have your affair with Heath Chapman, but we want you to try to find out how much he's learned of Warbonnet's activities."

"You want me to spy on him?"

He shrugged, then touched her chin, tilting her head upward. "Must you be so crude, madam? We merely ask your cooperation in a delicate matter."

"And if I refuse?"

His fingers tightened on her chin as he stared at her.

Her hair was like Darcy's, but her eyes were blue instead of pale green, and just looking at her like this aroused him. She was sensuous and alarmingly attractive. No wonder Heath was smitten. He always did have an eye for the ladies; only, now he evidently wasn't as shy as he had been at fifteen when Teak had last seen him.

"If you refuse, madam, you'll remain a guest of the British Army and will be shipped out on the next boat back to Niagara, and from there you will depart for England, where you will spend the rest of your days languishing in a cell in Newgate Prison."

She stared at him dumbfounded. She had heard of the horrors of England's Newgate Prison. "You can't mean that."

"Oh, but I do."

"No!"

Teak released her chin, his hand covering her cheek, his fingers toying with her earlobe. "It'd be a shame to shut someone so lovely up where no one can appreciate her," he said softly. "I imagine you're used to having men singing your praises."

"Don't ask me to do this, please," she begged, but his eyes hardened.

"Perhaps I can persuade you," he whispered, and leaned toward her, but she wrenched, turning away from him.

"Keep your hands off me!"

Startled, he frowned angrily; then he reached out and grabbed her shoulders, spinning her around. "Don't ever turn away from me!" he yelled arrogantly.

She grabbed his hands to pull them from her shoulders, but his fingers dug in and he pulled her against him, his arms engulfing her, pinning her arms to her sides, his mouth only inches from hers.

"You'd let Heath touch you, but I'm not good enough, is that it?" he asked furiously, and her eyes blazed at him.

"Who are you?" she cried, and his smile broadened.

"You're Warbonnet, aren't you?" she gasped, trembling in his arms, and his smile faded.

"I'm a man, madam," he cried passionately; then his voice lowered seductively: "a man who hasn't enjoyed the pleasures of a decent woman for a long time and who's been wanting you from the moment he stepped into this room," and his mouth came down on hers violently.

He kissed her hard at first; then his lips softened as he slowly felt her mouth begin to move beneath his. She tried to fight him, but it was no use as his mouth brought a stirring deep within her. She didn't want the response he was forcing from her, but her body betrayed her as sweet sensations flowed through her and his hands began to caress her fervently.

He'd been hard and demanding at first, almost frightening, but now he was maddeningly gentle, loving, his lips sipping at hers hungrily, his hands stroking her. Why did she feel like this? She didn't even know the man who was giving her body so much pleasure.

She tensed, trying to keep the warm flood of desire from totally filling her as he took his lips from hers, brushing them softly across her cheek, kissing her closed eyelids, then dropping to the throbbing pulse in her neck as his fingers unfastened the front of her dress, his hand moving beneath her chemise.

His hands were gentle, his lips passionate, his words tender as he took his hand from her breast and picked her up in his arms. "You're beautiful, lovely," he whispered, his lips against her ear, "intoxicating," and he carried her to the other side of the room, laying her gently on the bed; then his mouth covered her nipple, sending a throbbing shock through her that exploded vibrantly between her legs.

This couldn't be happening. He had no right! She wouldn't let him. She couldn't, no matter how much her body craved it. Not this stranger. How could he do this to her? How could he make her feel this way? If she kept her eyes closed, she could almost imagine it was Heath making love to her. Heath!

"Oh, please," she begged breathlessly. "Don't do this to me. I don't want any part of you. Please . . ."

He raised his head from her breast and looked down into her face. Her eyes were open now and her heart was pounding so hard he could see the rise and fall of her breasts, and her eyes were full of tears as he stared at her. He smiled cynically, his face flushed with desire.

"It'll be easy, you'll see, better than with Heath," he whispered passionately. "Don't be afraid, Janet, you're a woman. Your body is made for this, for what a man can give you."

"No!" she cried helplessly. "I don't want you! I want Heath, not you. I want him to do this with me, not you. With you I'd hate it!"

He bent down. "No . . . you won't." His lips were warm on her neck as he pulled up her dress and began stroking her legs, his hand moving to the warm spot between her thighs, and she knew she was lost just as she was when Mark touched her. She didn't love this man any more than she loved Mark, but her body couldn't separate the loved from the unloved. Her body could only feel and respond as nature had intended it. With the right coaxing, it could betray her so easily. Only her heart and mind could sort out the difference. Her body responded by instinct as his hands caressed her and the tears at the corners of her eyes ran down her cheeks, falling onto his lips as he kissed her neck while he unfastened his pants and moved over her.

He hadn't lied. He was gentle, and she responded to his lovemaking involuntarily. She would rather he'd raped her violently than what he was doing to her now, and when she could fight it no longer and finally gave in to him and came, it was no different than it always was with Mark, a shallow taste of what Heath could give her, because it was without love, and she trembled. Not from happiness, but from misery.

When he was through, his own pleasure gratified, he

lay above her and looked down into her face, remembering the passionate way she'd responded to him, and his voice was hushed when he spoke. "Now, tell me truthfully, Mrs. Putnam," he asked softly, "did you really hate it so much?"

She closed her eyes and her jaw tightened angrily as sadness gripped her heart. "Yes," she whispered, and her tears flowed freely, "I hated every moment and I wish I were dead!"

Teak stared into her face, watching the tears fall on the pillow beneath her head, and his jaws clenched viciously. She really meant it. This was no act. Her tears were in earnest, and he cursed to himself. Any other woman would have reveled in his lovemaking. They always did, but this . . . this . . . she'd reminded him of Darcy.

His eyes narrowed. "You lie!"

"Do I?" she sobbed, her voice breaking. "Do you think you can ever compare to Heath? No one can give me what he's given me. I love him!"

"Love! What do you know of love?" He was still inside her, and he rammed in harder, watching her flinch. "Heath Chapman's a bastard, do you hear? And you'll leave this fort and do what you're told, do you understand?"

She closed her eyes. "May I get up now?" she asked weakly, and he wanted to throttle her. She looked so much like Darcy. Darcy, who'd never let him touch her, but who'd be his wife when this stupid war was over. He could enjoy this woman if she'd only let him. Why did Heath have to spoil everything for him?

He lifted himself from her and stood up, fastening his pants. She pulled her skirt down halfheartedly and turned to the wall, not even bothering to replace the bloomers he'd pulled from her, and she could feel the moist warmth between her legs. Curling up, she buried herself against the wall, and Teak suddenly felt ashamed.

He'd never taken a woman like this before. Always

they'd been willing, and she would have been willing too, she would have enjoyed it if it hadn't been for Heath, but he shouldn't have taken it out on her. Janet was a lovely woman and he regretted what he was doing to her, the role they were going to force her to play. He knelt down by the bed and reached out, touching her hair, stroking it gently as he would that of a hurt child.

"I'm sorry, Janet," he whispered softly, "but sometimes a man can't help what he does."

She hugged the wall, trying to hold back the tears, her heart heavy. "And neither can a woman," she answered, sniffing in, and he laid his hand on her shoulder.

"You're still going to have to do what we ask," he said, and she shook her head.

"I can't . . . I love him so much."

He stood up and stared down at her. "I think you will. I think you love life enough."

She moved, turning toward him, and sat up, fastening the front of her dress, her eyes misty. "Why do I have to do this? Why can't you just capture him and ask him yourself?"

"Heath's closemouthed, he'd never tell us a thing." He hesitated, then went on. "As soon as you consent to our wishes, you'll go free."

She looked up at him, studying him intently. He was an impressive man, actually attractive in many ways, but there was a cynical bitterness that dominated his actions, and he was unable to suppress it enough so no one would notice, and she wondered who he really was. She tucked her hands in her lap and lowered her gaze from his. "I'm sorry, sir," she said finally. "It's something I'll have to think over."

"You don't have time to think it over, Janet," he said firmly. "I have to have the answer now. You see, your lover arrived the other day to negotiate for your freedom and that of the other prisoners. The men we've refused to release, the other women are already back in Detroit by now, they've held you here at my request until I arrived. I told them I had to talk to you first. Heath is due back later today to find out if we're going to release you, and I have to have your answer by then."

Her face paled. "I can't betray Heath." She bit her lip. "Oh, God!" Her eyes closed and she held her breath, trying to think.

"If you refuse, you'll never see him again. He'll be told you're dead. I'm sorry. That's the way it has to be."

She swallowed hard. She had to see Heath, be with him at least one more time, and she made her decision. "What do I have to do?"

The corners of his mouth tilted sardonically. "You'll try to pry from him any information he might have concerning Warbonnet. No matter how insignificant it may seem."

"And what do I do with it?"

"You'll have a contact who will identify himself with one of these," and he gave her a small piece of leather with a feathered warbonnet beaded on it. "You'll keep this for your own identification and turn over any information to the bearer of one of these. It may not be the same person every time, for safety's sake."

"What happens if I back out after I'm released?"

His eyes narrowed. "There are still ships that sail to England regularly, my dear, but first I think your husband would be pleased to discover your infidelity; perhaps then he wouldn't miss you so terribly much when you mysteriously disappeared."

"You have it all figured out, don't you?" she said, and stood up, walking past him to the window, where the sun hung hot in the July sky. "Even if I wanted to say no, I couldn't."

He walked up behind her, his hands on her shoulders, his lips against her hair. "In another time and another place, Janet, if we'd been introduced properly ... I meant it when I said you were a lovely woman."

"It doesn't matter," she said sadly. "Nothing matters anymore."

He turned her to face him. "I'm not really cruel," he said, and she looked up into his blue eyes.

"Aren't you?"

He released her shoulders and turned, walking to the door. "I'll come for you when it's time," he said, then left.

She stared at the door that closed behind him, then down to her hands, to the beaded piece of leather she was holding, and huge tears began to well up in her eyes and make their way down her pale cheeks. This was it. There was no turning back. She'd see Heath again for just a little while; then there'd be no more love or happiness for her ever again. She'd made her decision, the only one she could make, and she knew that when she too went out that door, out to meet the man she loved, she wouldn't be walking to her freedom, but to her doom.

❦ 7 ❧

Heath didn't like it one bit. All during the journey back with the other women, he'd racked his brain trying to figure out why they hadn't released Janet. There was no logical reason for them to keep her. He'd deposited the other women at Detroit and retraced his steps cautiously back to Fort Malden, and now he was even more puzzled. This time he'd been prepared with even more arguments to convince them to release her, but to his surprise, when he arrived they'd informed him that they'd made a mistake and she was to be released promptly.

He waited now outside the main building with Eli, saddle horses, and two pack mules that were to carry her trunks. "What do you think's going on, Heath?" asked Eli as they shuffled from one foot to the other under the eyes of the redcoated soldiers who were milling about, and Heath shook his head.

"We'll have to see if Janet can tell us anything," he answered, and he glanced up quickly as a door opened and some men brought out her baggage and helped tie it on the horses; then they left, and Heath and Eli waited some more.

On the second floor of the building, Teak glanced furtively out the window and gazed down at his half-brother standing in front of the building. Yes, he'd have recognized him anywhere. They were both older, but he was still so much like Roth. Bitter memories clung to his thoughts for a few brief moments; then he turned to Janet.

"It's time," he said softly, and she nodded.

"I'm ready."

He walked to the door, opening it, and she stepped out into the hall, where two soldiers flanked her; then she glanced back, frowning as she looked at him.

"You're not coming out with me?" she asked tonelessly, and he shook his head.

"No, Janet, I'm not coming out," and she turned her head, tilted her chin high, forcing back the tears, and he watched as she walked down the hall; then he closed the door and walked back to the window, concealing himself behind the sheer curtain again.

A few minutes later he watched her leave the front of the building and join Heath. Their meeting was awkward, he could tell, with everyone watching, but they conversed for a few minutes, Heath helped her onto the horse he'd brought for her, and Teak smiled to himself, satisfied, as they headed out of Fort Malden.

Heath kept glancing at her curiously as they left the fort, wondering what had happened. Janet's eyes were no longer warm and caressing. They held a vacant stare that haunted him as they rode, and more than once he could see she was close to tears, but it wasn't until nightfall that he questioned her. They'd ridden along all late afternoon, and she'd barely conversed with him.

Eli had built a fire, and she sat in front of it now, her feet drawn up, arms clutching about her knees, and Heath dropped down beside her while Eli went for more firewood.

"Janet? What's the matter? What have they done to you?" he asked, and was startled as she let out a sob, turning to him, her face pale.

"Oh, Heath, I love you!" she cried, and tears flooded down her face unchecked as she threw herself into his arms and he held her close.

"Janet, darling, please. What is it?"

"Just hold me," she sobbed against his chest, and he

was still holding her, letting her cry, when Eli returned and Heath motioned for him to get lost again.

He held her close, stroking her hair, talking to her, soothing her, and little by little, after a while, the crying subsided and she sniffed in, cuddling even closer in his arms.

"Heath?" she finally said, her voice trembling, and he bent down, kissing her forehead.

"Yes?"

"I have to tell you . . ."

"Go ahead."

She moved in his arms and looked up at him, her blue eyes wide and frightened. "I don't know how," she said softly.

"Begin at the beginning."

She nodded, sniffing in. "At first we were all put in the same room together. I mean the women. Then they came in and asked our names and wanted to know why we were on the ship. We told them, and we stayed there all night, sleeping on the floor. The next day they came and brought us to Fort Malden, and this time they took me to a room all by myself, where some men came and asked me all sorts of questions that I couldn't answer; then they left again." She hesitated, then knew she had to tell it all, but she couldn't look at him, and laid her head against his chest. "Then earlier today a man came into the room, one I'd never seen before."

He could feel her heart beating frantically against him, and his arms tightened about her. "Go on."

Her hands clenched his buckskins, the knuckles white. "He told me that you weren't just a scout, that you were a spy sent to find out about a man named Warbonnet." She felt his muscles tense, yet went on, "He said he knew you and I were lovers and if I didn't cooperate with him and try to get you to tell me all you'd discovered so far about this man they called Warbonnet, that he'd have me sent to England, where they'd put me in a place called Newgate Prison."

Heath listened to her, his breath quickening as she went on.

"I told him I couldn't, that I was in love with you, but he wouldn't listen. He talked about you almost as if he knew you."

"Did he say who he was?"

"No, he wouldn't give me his name. Told me to call him 'sir,' but I think he was really Warbonnet."

Heath eased his arms from around her and held her so he could see her face again. "Are you sure?"

Her eyes fell before his gaze. "No, but he was wearing buckskins and he didn't look right in them, not the way you and Eli do."

"What did he look like?"

She fingered the fringe on his shirt, unable to look into his eyes. "He was taller than you, well-built, hair very blond, and his eyes were the brightest blue I think I've ever seen. He talked more like an English nobleman than a frontiersman, yet there was something almost American about him."

Heath's heart began descending to his stomach as Janet spoke, and the bits and pieces began to fit together, and he felt sick. "I wonder . . ." he mused softly.

She scowled, looking directly at him this time. "What did you say?"

"Janet, what else did the man say or do?" and once more her eyes grew withdrawn, afraid, and she swallowed hard. "Please, Janet, I have to know."

Her lips quivered. "He made love to me," she confessed softly.

"He raped you?"

"No!" She shook her head, tears glistening on her lashes. "He didn't have to rape me, not like that. He . . . oh, Heath, I didn't want to respond to him, but he wasn't violent, he did what you do, caressing and teasing and . . . all the time he kept telling me I'd enjoy him better than I did you, that if I could give myself to you willingly I could give myself to him. When he mentioned your name, it was as if he was talking about someone familiar. I kept begging him to stop, and then suddenly my body didn't seem to care anymore, but when it was over and I told him I still wanted you, that what he did to me was loathsome, he became so angry." She closed her eyes so she wouldn't have to look at him. "I'm so ashamed, Heath," she murmured. "But I know something now I wasn't completely positive about before," and she opened her eyes again, but kept them lowered.

"What's that?"

"What I feel for you isn't just the lust of a frustrated, lonely, unsatisfied wife. Before you, the only man I'd ever known was Mark, and I thought perhaps what you did to me could be done by anyone, because I was ripe and vulnerable for it, but even though this other man made love to me as you would, it left me as empty inside as Mark's lovemaking." She raised her eyes and looked at him, the firelight dancing in his dark eyes, and her own eyes softened. "I know I truly love you, Heath, and no man will ever fulfill me the way you do."

He stared at her and for a moment her words echoed a memory inside him. A memory of a young man of twenty trying to tell the girl he loved why he'd made love to another. The body was a strange, fickle member, so unlike the heart.

His hand moved up to her face, and he touched her cheek, then buried it in her coppery hair, pulling her mouth up to meet his. The kiss was long, and it spoke more than words; then he held her close and thought over everything she'd told him, and slowly a feeling of dread began to seep into him and he shuddered.

"What's wrong?" she asked as she felt him tremble.

His voice was husky. "Janet, you pretended to go along with him and spy on me, didn't you?" he asked, and she nodded, unable to speak because of the lump in her throat. "Oh, my God," he blurted anxiously, "but you never planned to go through with it, did you?"

"No," she said. "I could never betray you, Heath."

"And when they find out?"

He felt her gulp back the tears. "That's the chance I'll have to take. I had to see you . . . to be with you at least once more."

He held her closer. Suddenly he was afraid. Not for himself, but for her. Warbonnet was ruthless, he knew, and more than one man had lost his life because of him. Would they hesitate at killing a woman? If Teak was really Warbonnet, as he suspected, surely he'd think twice before hurting Janet. Or would he? Could he have changed that much? And how could he be around to watch over her?—he was gone from Detroit most of the time doing the general's bidding.

He hugged her against him, his heart pounding. "Oh, Janet, you little fool," he whispered softly. "I love you so," and she knew no matter what happened from here on, one moment with Heath was worth whatever lay ahead.

They arrived back in Detroit the next afternoon, and Janet was dutifully turned over to her suspicious husband, a fate she dreaded. Nothing more was said of the message that hadn't been delivered, and Heath felt it best just to forget it. As long as the women were all back safe and sound, why make a fuss? The general would have enough explaining to do to Washington as it was when they discovered he'd let the enemy confiscate his desk and all his papers.

Meanwhile the general made plans to invade Canada, and on July 12 the offensive was begun. Their first objective was the settlement across the river at Sandwich, and from there they would have marched on Fort Malden except for the Indians. Tecumseh and his warriors were everywhere.

For the next month the battles seesawed back and forth. The Ohio colonels established themselves extraordinarily well. McArthur at Lake St. Claire, Cass at Tarontee River, but although all three urged General Hull to press the attack and take Fort Malden, he was hesitant. The much-needed supplies hadn't come through yet, and without them he felt a siege on the British should be held off.

People began to disparage his leadership, and rumors ran rampant. During that time Janet was approached three times by men carrying the beaded pieces of leather. It was at the market and on her way to the shops, and each time her answer was the same. She'd learned nothing.

She and Heath had decided that maybe by not seeing each other there would be nothing to report. They knew his men were watching them, and this way they could foil this man who was called Warbonnet. Not seeing Heath nearly killed Janet. And Mark! Mark was even more abusive than before. He became upset over the derogatory remarks bandied about by the men in regards to the general, and he was more than suspicious of her ride back to Detroit with Heath, and he'd been listening to gossip from his men and their wives regarding her behavior. If he had known she and Heath had already been in each other's arms, he'd have killed her. As it was, he sniped at her, questioning why she'd been held, demanding an explanation she was unable to give, then trying to prove to her that his lovemaking was far superior to anything she could expect from any other man, unaware that she already knew otherwise.

Often Janet stood in the window of the rooms she and Mark shared and stared out at the settlement, wondering where life was taking her. Wondering whether she would ever be with Heath again and wondering why she'd ever left her soft lonely bed back home, then regretting the thought as she remembered Heath's arms. One night in his arms was worth risking even her life for, and she craved him like a drowning man craves air and was dying inside without him.

It was on just such a day that she stood at the window staring out, when a knock came to the door. Frowning, she moved to the door and opened it, expecting to see one of the other officers' wives or someone from the fort, and her heart flew into her mouth as a pair of intense blue eyes stared at her from a well-tanned face.

He was dressed like an American soldier, his blond hair covered by an army hat, but the smile was the same, cold and cynical. "Good day, madam, I would speak with you," he said formally, and gave her no chance to reply as he stepped into the small sitting room and removed his hat.

She shut the door quickly behind him and turned, her hands shaking nervously. "What are you doing here?" she asked hesitantly, and he straightened arrogantly, towering over her.

"I've come to find out if you've forgotten about our bargain, madam," he said harshly, and she tried to remain calm.

"How could I forget it?"

"Yet my men say you have told them nothing."

"There's nothing to tell."

"Why?"

She walked back to the window and glanced out, then faced him again. "I haven't see him since my return, and you know it," she said. "For one thing, my husband is overly suspicious, and for another, the general keeps him busy."

"A poor excuse." His eyes narrowed, then sifted over her, remembering the last time they'd been together. "When a man wants a woman, my dear, nothing can keep him from her. I suggest you let him know you're here for the taking."

She bit her lip. "I can't do that. What if Mark finds out?"

"That's your problem. And remember, Janet, I don't take kindly to being double-crossed. Warbonnet's activities are necessary to the British. He dares not be stopped by Heath Chapman or anyone else, so I suggest you play the role I've allotted you, whether you like it or not. Understood?"

She nodded, her heart heavy. "Yes," she said slowly.

"The next time, I'll come for the message myself, and there'd better be one, or by God I'll see you never see your lover again."

"And you said you weren't cruel."

He put his finger beneath her chin and tilted her head up, looking into her eyes. "It all depends, my dear," he said softly. "Perhaps if you were to forget your husband and your lover and do everything I ask, forgetting any other loyalties except to me, when we take over Detroit I could show you that I'm not really cruel." His fingers caressed her cheek. "Did I hurt you when I made love to you, Janet?" he asked, and she swallowed hard.

"Not physically, no."

"That's right. What I do, I do for survival only. The same as anyone else. remember that." His hand dropped, and he walked toward the door, then turned back. "I'll give you a week, Janet, that's all," he said, then left.

She stood for a long time staring after him, then walked into her bedroom and flung herself on the bed, trying to figure a way out.

When Mark arrived home, he was in a temper and didn't notice that she was upset. They'd received word that the mail caravan on its way back east had been attacked by Tecumseh and his Indians, and now the supply route from the Maumee was completely cut off.

"Things are going bad all along the coast," he complained to her as they sat down to supper. It wasn't bad enough Lieutenant Hanks had lost Mackinac Island to the British and Mark had sat in the general's office listening to the number of tribes massed against them, but today he had to listen to the report of the defeat of Major Thomas Van Horn and the mail train. "It isn't fair," he complained to her. "They're blaming the general for everything, when it should be that scout who is blamed."

She looked at him sharply. "What do you mean?"

"He's supposed to know the Indians and help get them back on our side. A lot of good he's done. The few Indians on our side are a drop in the bucket. That thieving Warbonnet's got them all worked up against us, and Chapman isn't doing a thing about it."

She sat across from him silently, listening to his tirade.

"That's it," he said bitterly. "Don't say anything against your precious hero." He clenched his spoon until the knuckles on his hand turned white. "Have you been talking to him again?"

She flushed angrily. "Don't be ridiculous. How could I see a man who spends all of his time in the woods?"

"Well, he's back now," he stated angrily. "He has been for two days, but if you so much as speak to him I'll kill you, do you understand?"

She nodded, sighing. Warbonnet didn't give her many choices, did he? And she was sure the tall blond giant was Warbonnet, even though he'd never admitted it.

The next afternoon Heath stood in the doorway of his quarters and stared at the note given to him by the young boy; then he frowned and excused himself from the men with whom he was talking and headed away from the fort toward town, first making sure that Mark was busy in the general's office and would be for a few more hours. His knock on the door of Captain Putnam's rooms was answered promptly, and as he held Janet in his arms, the past few weeks seemed like a bad nightmare.

"I've missed you!" he whispered softly, his lips on hers, and she wanted to die inside. Every moment with him could be her last, and she knew it and never wanted their time together to come to an end. She told him nothing of Warbonnet's visit until their lovemaking was over and their need for each other satisfied.

"He was here," she said as she lay in his arms afterward, and she felt his muscles become rigid.

"Here in Detroit?"

"He was dressed in an American uniform."

"What did he want?"

"If I don't have any information the next time he
comes, he'll carry through his threat."

"The next time he comes?"

She moved in his arms and looked down into his
face. "He said he's coming again the next time himself," she said, "and I have a plan."

He looked at her warily. "What?"

"You want Warbonnet, and I'm sure he's Warbonnet,
although he's never really said so. When he comes to
get the message, you and some men can be waiting for
him." She saw the fear in his eyes. "Heath, it's the only
way. With him in your hands, I won't have to worry."
She got up and began to dress, and he followed her
lead, pulling on his buckskins.

"Do you realize what happens if we fail?" he asked.

She let him fasten the back of her dress, then
turned, gazing into his dark eyes as he stared back.
"And do you realize what will happen when I have no
information for him?"

"I could give you some. I could tell you enough not
to make it obvious that it was on purpose. He'd be satisfied."

"And then he'd be back for more."

"So let him, Janet." He held her by the shoulders as
he looked at her. "I can't let you try to lead him into a
trap. I can't let you take that chance, and I won't.
Besides, even if we caught him, I'd have to turn him
over to General Hull, and he'd make sure Mark
learned everything. I can't do that to you. We'll stall
him off as long as we can, and maybe with time I can
catch up to him where I want to, on my terms." He
pulled her into his arms. "Oh, what a fool I've been to
let you fall in love with me. If anything happens to you

. . ." He kissed her again deeply, his heart aching for her.

It had been a week since Teak's last visit to Janet, and he frowned as he stirred from his hiding place. Close to midnight on August 13, when the *Queen Charlotte* had dropped anchor, setting General Isaac Brock ashore to join the forces at Fort Malden, his first act was to send Teak for Tecumseh. The meeting was over now, the plan was being put into action, and Fort Malden was preparing for its attack on Detroit, but first Teak had a visit to make.

He'd slipped along the riverbank last night, hiding his canoe in the bushes, then waited until this afternoon, and now he was on his way toward town. Heath was getting closer, he was sure. Just three days before, Heath had almost caught him near Sandwich when he was on a scouting mission with some of Tecumseh's men. There were spies at Fort Malden; he knew that too, and there were spies among Tecumseh's men, Indians who were loyal to Heath. He had to know who they were before the definite hour for the attack was made. His men could watch Heath, but that's all. It took someone close to him to find out who his contacts were and how much he knew.

The sun was high in the sky as Teak made his way into town, the buckskins he wore blending in as if he belonged, and a fur hat hiding his crop of light hair. His men had said she'd been with Heath twice since his last visit; then she should have something. Names of men who could hamper their plans, or a clue that would show him how close Heath was to discovering who he really was.

His eyes were alert as he made his way toward the marketplace where he knew she always shopped, and he waited for a long time, then sighed as he saw her at the other end of the street. Her pale yellow dress, contrasting with the red of her hair, was easy to spot, and she looked ethereal as the sunlight fell on her, playing in her hair and about her face. She didn't see him at first; then, when her eyes did meet his, there was something in hers that puzzled him. He shrugged it off and approached, his face studying hers intently.

"May I help carry your things, madam?" he suggested calmly as he took the basket from her arm, and she hesitated nervously, then relinquished it. "What's the matter?" he asked, and she shook her head.

"Nothing. You just startled me."

He glanced about them, then ushered her along, helping her select the vegetables she was to buy as if it was a natural thing to do, and when her basket was full they set off toward her house.

"Now, what news do you have for me?" he asked, and she sighed.

"You're so sure of yourself, aren't you?"

"I'm waiting."

She started to open her mouth to give him the information Heath had purposely given her, when there was a sudden scuffling behind them and they turned to see a detachment of soldiers converging on them, shouting for both of them to stop.

Teak glanced quickly at Janet, his eyes blazing. A trap! She'd laid a trap for him—that's why the strange look in her eyes. He dropped the basket and grabbed her wrist as he bolted, pulling her stumbling after him and started running down the street.

She tried to break loose, but it was no use, his hand was like iron about her wrist. They moved down alleys, running for dear life, and Teak tried to head for the canoe, but it was impossible. Instead, they ended up at the north end of town, plunging into the underbrush, with the soldiers still in pursuit, going farther and farther away from the river as they ran, and deeper and deeper into the Michigan woods.

Sergeant Beirne, at the head of his men, stopped to reconnoiter as the couple moved off among the trees. They were new to these woods, and the buckskin-clad figure with the captain's wife in tow was moving as if he knew his way. In minutes they were out of sight, and, frustrated, the sergeant stood now looking around, trying to figure which way they might have gone. He knew nothing of reading trails, nor did any of his men, so he turned them around and marched them back to Detroit to report to the captain.

Heath was in General Hull's headquarters reporting to him, standing out of view of the door, when Mark Putnam burst in without knocking, his face livid with rage.

"What's the meaning of this?" shouted the general as he stared at Mark and Mark saluted hastily as he spoke.

"I'm sorry, sir, I know you said you didn't want to be disturbed for a while, but I believe Heath Chapman has finally played his hand and proved what a vile man he is," and the general stared aghast as he realized Captain Putnam had no idea Heath was standing to his right, directly behind the open door. Mark had been on an errand for the general when Heath had arrived.

The general started to speak, but Heath motioned for him to listen. "Well," General Hull said as he looked again at Mark.

Mark straightened arrogantly. "I've suspected that he and my wife have been seeing each other all along, and I was right, sir," he confided boldly. "I've had a detail of men watching her, and less than half an hour ago he kidnapped her and took her with him into the woods. My men chased them as far as they could, but they don't know the area. I'd like to gather enough men to go after them and bring them back, sir, if it's all right with you," but now Heath stepped forward, his face pale.

"You fool, Putnam!" he blurted angrily from behind Mark, and Mark whirled around startled. "You stupid fool!" shouted Heath. "How could you be so damn dumb? You don't know what you've done, do you?"

Mark stared at Heath dumbfounded, his face white; then he glanced at the general in disbelief. "But my men . . ." He looked again at Heath. "They saw you drag her into the woods . . . your buckskins!"

"I'm not the only one who wears buckskins," Heath stated, his voice low and ominous. "I just hope you haven't signed her death warrant." Heath's teeth clenched viciously and his jaw set hard. "The British were trying to get your wife to act as a spy, Captain," he said. "She's been stalling them off with my help, and by God, if anything happens to her . . ." He looked at the general. "I'm going after her, sir," he said. "And I'm going myself, with my own men, and don't you dare let that ass follow me." He glanced quickly at Mark, then turned and walked hurriedly out the door, leaving them both staring after him, Mark shaking his head in disbelief.

"If he was here with you, General, then who has Janet?" he asked, bewildered, and the general shook his head.

"I don't know, Mark," he said softly, "but I can guess," and he sighed as he looked down at the reports before him that Heath had brought. The reports he'd been waiting for and dreading, and he shook his head, because the reports stated that General Brock was at Fort Malden and was preparing for an attack with enough Indians on his side to massacre the whole lot of them, and at the moment this news overshadowed the fate of one captain's wife.

It was dark already as Teak shoved Janet to the ground by the small stream and ordered her to drink. Sweat trickled down between her breasts and covered her legs, making her long silk skirt stick to her.

He looked about to make sure they were alone, then knelt beside her and dipped his hands in the water, quenching his own thirst. When he was through, he turned to her, his eyes hard and cold.

"All right. Now we talk," he said, and she gasped, her heart pounding.

He wouldn't believe her. He never would, and she

knew it. It was over. He'd take her back to Fort Malden and they'd put her on a ship and she'd never see Heath again. Never know the joy of being in his arms. Never feel the wonder of his lips on hers, his body possessing hers, and tears flooded her eyes, but she had to try. She had to try to make him understand. It couldn't end like this. Not like this! It couldn't!

"It was my husband," she sobbed anxiously. "It had to be. The other day he accused me of seeing Heath behind his back. He said he was going to have me watched. That Heath had been seen at our quarters." Tears streamed down her face. "I didn't betray you. Please, I didn't!" but he didn't believe her.

She was in love with Heath. She'd take any chance to be with him, even to trapping him, and what a feather in Heath's cap to have Warbonnet in his hands.

"I don't believe you," he said angrily. "You knew the men were there. I could see it in your face."

She shook her head. It was hopeless. He stood up and dragged her to her feet, and again they moved on until he found a place for them to spend the night; then, after making angry love to her, he slept with one arm about her, the other hand resting on his rifle.

Early the next afternoon Teak began to circle back toward the Detroit River, unaware that Heath, who was following not far behind with over a dozen braves, had anticipated his move.

Janet was exhausted and dirty. Her feet were sore, her dress ripped, but Teak was oblivious of it, his anger at being deceived pushing him on. He wanted to hate her, and he glanced at her coppery hair as he pushed her ahead of him. She was Heath's. Everything had always been Heath's. Everything that counted. Yes, he had the money and the title, but Heath had always had the love. From Rebel and from his mother. She'd always stuck up for Heath in everything. And now this woman too was Heath's. Oh, how he hated Heath!

He grabbed her arm and started to shove her again along the trail, when a voice behind him cut into his thoughts, and he whirled around.

"Let go of her," the voice cried, and Teak strained his eyes in the bright August sunlight that streamed down through the trees, and Heath stepped onto the trail behind him. "Let go of her, Teak!" he yelled again, his voice vibrating, and Teak straightened, then laughed.

"So you do know," he cried arrogantly as he still held her. "I thought as much." His fingers tightened on Janet's arms. "I wanted her to confirm it for me, but as always, your women are faithful, Heath."

Heath stepped closer and stared at the brother he hadn't seen for over twenty years. "Why, Teak?" he asked anxiously. "How can you fight for England? You were born here."

"Because England's given me everything I have. All this country ever gave me was a pair of buckskins."

Heath shook his head. "Let her go, Teak, please. Don't take your hatred for me out on Janet."

Teak looked at Janet, then back to Heath, and this time he saw them; there were Indians behind Heath, only they weren't Tecumseh's Indians, they were the few Indians loyal to Heath, and he'd brought them with him along with his friend Eli Crawford.

Teak stood still, motionless, like a tall blond giant, the sun glistening on his hair; then from behind him he heard the call of Tecumseh, and in that instant Janet, who'd been trying to follow the exchange of words between them, wrenched free of him and made a break toward Heath.

Heath watched her, her feet stumbling on the path, hair flying, and his heart stopped in his throat as a shot suddenly rang out from behind Teak, and he watched horrified as Janet crashed to the ground only a few feet from him, his name on her lips.

Teak watched dumbfounded as Janet fell; then he

turned, his eyes on the warrior behind him, but there was nothing he could say. He wanted to yell at the Indian. He hadn't really wanted Janet hurt. His threats had been only that. In truth he'd felt a softness toward her because she reminded him of Darcy. He would have taken her back for himself, not to send her away, but Tecumseh's eyes were blazing with hatred as he stood boldly, waiting for Teak to join him, and he had no other choice. Teak took one last look at his brother, his jaw tightening to hold back the words of condemnation he wanted to hurl at Heath for making Janet love him; then he turned and followed after Tecumseh without saying another word.

Heath watched Teak melt into the woods with Tecumseh, then motioned Eli and his men after them as he quickly knelt beside Janet and turned her over, holding her in his arms. She was still breathing, and her eyes looked up at him with love.

"I guess I should have stayed home this time too . . . shouldn't I?" she whispered softly, and Heath swallowed back the lump in his throat.

"Please, Janet, don't talk."

She coughed, a drop of blood at the corner of her mouth. "Who . . . who is he, Heath?" she asked, and he touched her hair, stroking it from her dirt-streaked face as she lay in his arms, and he felt the blood covering his hand where it touched her back.

"He's my brother, Janet," he answered softly. "And he'll pay for this."

Her hand tightened on his arm. "No, Heath, please," she said. "It's . . . it's best this way, really." There were tears in her eyes. "I knew that day at Fort Malden that . . . that I was going to die. I felt it, Heath." The tears flooded down her cheeks. "Mark . . . Mark would never let us be together."

"Janet!"

"Oh, Heath, I love you . . . I don't want to die!" She coughed. "I want to feel your love again," she said fervently; then suddenly her eyes widened. "Please, Heath, I don't want to leave you. I don't want to die ... I love you. Heath ... !"

He stared at her helplessly as she gasped for air; then her eyes rolled back in her head and the lids closed and she stopped breathing as easily as that, her head falling back limply. She was gone. In that one split second she was gone and he couldn't stop her going and something inside him died with her.

Heath laid her gently back on the bloodied grass and stood up, his eyes filled with tears, the blood on his hand from the wound in her back already drying in the hot, bright sun. Why, God? he asked softly to himself. What had he done that happiness should always elude him? What had Janet done that she deserved death? Love him? What was wrong with loving him? Two women he'd truly loved in his lifetime, and he'd lost them both. Was he destined to let love always slip through his fingers? To roam the earth until he was an old man alone and miserable? Was he always destined to love what he couldn't have? What didn't belong to him?

He straightened, the sun on his face glistening on the tears in his eyes, and he shouted to the forest around him. "You'll pay for this someday, Teak!" he yelled viciously. "I'll find you yet, and when I do, you'll pay for this!" Then he walked back and picked up Janet's lifeless body and started back the way he'd come.

He buried Janet that afternoon a short distance away, digging a hole for her in a plot of soft earth with his bare hands.

When Eli and the rest of his men finally came back empty-handed and they headed back once more for the fort, it was too late: on August 16, General Hull, surrounded by the British Army, with Tecumseh and his braves as their allies threatening a bloody massacre, surrendered Detroit to the enemy, and Heath, seeing the Union Jack flying above the fort, watched from a distant hill for only a short time. Then he and Eli disappeared into the woods again, the only two members of the march that had begun in Ohio who'd remained free.

❧ 8 ❧

For the next two years Heath and Teak played their own game of touch and go on the frontier, with Teak staying only a jump ahead of Heath, and more than once they barely missed meeting again face to face. Then slowly, as the months went by, after bitter American defeats along Lake Erie, the West once more gradually began to fly the American flag. Under the command of General William Henry Harrison, the American armies began to move forward instead of backward, and the tide began to turn.

Even the Indians saw the writing on the wall, and treaties were signed one after another until Tecumseh was exiled, taking refuge with the British, and the frontier was once more free of the bloodshed that had reigned in the Northwest for years.

Following Harrison's victories on land, the lakes began to reap their harvest, and the American fleet, with new ships to its credit, took over supremacy, enabling the armies to penetrate even farther, and by the spring of the year 1814, Detroit was once more in American hands, Tecumseh was dead, and the British were on the run. But though the Northwest was no longer in danger, the war had escalated elsewhere, and with it went Warbonnet, still free and still filled with bitterness and hate.

Teak had shed his buckskins for a business suit. His long white trousers enhanced the cut of his deep blue, elegantly tailored coat as he removed his hat on entering Mackgowan's Hotel. Washington at last. The ride had been a hectic one, but he was satisfied he'd covered his tracks well. He was posing as Mr. Giles Thompson, businessman and speculator, and from the moment he set foot in the Capital, the plans he'd made began to take shape. The people who made his acquaintance were sure he was planning to buy land nearby, the way he scoured the countryside on that horse of his, and the ladies who caught his eyes were praying he wouldn't change his mind.

Spring was in the air when he arrived, and by the eighteenth of August folks were so used to seeing him about that no one paid him a bit of mind when he rode down to a small town named Benedict some distance from the mouth of the Patuxent River, where he spent the night. But the next day they would have been horrified if they could have seen him standing on the shores of the river not far from town greeting an elite force of His Majesty's troops at the exact spot his reconnaissance had suggested they land. There were more than five thousand men with four line regiments and a detachment of marines, and their goal was Washington.

Satisfied that all had gone well, Teak turned his horse about and headed back toward the Capital, knowing that the maps he'd given generals Cockburn and Ross would be invaluable to them, his knowledge of the buildings in the Capital being extensive since during his few months in Washington he'd managed, through his dallying with the ladies, to work his way into the lives of many important people. And although he always kept one eye over his shoulder, he was adept at infiltration. His charm and good looks were a passport to many a lonely heart, and he stepped on them readily to achieve what he wanted, enabling him to wine and dine with the best. He'd even chatted and eaten with President Madison one evening, and now as he rode along, he smiled to himself at the success of his deception, quite pleased at this last feat, and a few nights later while the whole city erupted in a panic and

American forces tried to hold back the British at Bladensburg, he wondered what Heath would do if he knew where he was at the moment.

Teak Locksley, otherwise known as Warbonnet, had done his work well. He and his conspirators on the Washington scene had started rumors through a successful whispering campaign that made the American commanders believe the British were being led by Lord Hill, one of the greatest tacticians in Europe, and the false intelligence they'd sent out earlier had also caused General Stansbury to send his men on a wild-goose chase. By the time Stansbury's troops arrived on the scene, supposedly as reinforcements, they were too tired and exhausted to fight. In every way they could, Teak and the men who worked with him undermined the Americans.

But it wasn't the invasion Teak was waiting around for. Ordinarily he did his work and departed as quietly as he'd arrived, but his job wasn't finished. He had other orders today. Sealed orders given to him by General Ross, and only he and the London Foreign Office knew what those orders were.

Earlier in the evening, while the battle raged at Bladensburg, he had watched Dolley Madison pack up and leave, being hustled out to her carriage at the last minute by Colonel Carroll, with her little maid, Sukey, fretting, fussing, and in tears, while the president watched part of the battle from a vantage point near Bladensburg. Now, a few hours later, the battle all but lost, Teak stood again in the shadows behind the rioting crowds and watched as President Madison himself, with Attorney General Rush at his side, left the White House on horseback, relieved that his wife had already fled.

Teak moved his tall blond frame gracefully through the shadows, following once more as the president's horse made its way to the home of his wife's sister Anna Cutts, where he watched both men disappear inside; then he held his breath in anticipation. This was his chance. What he'd been waiting for.

The crowds in the streets were wild and in an ugly mood, and probably no one would pay any attention to what he was doing. Cautiously, he moved toward the house, hiding in the bushes so as not to be seen; then he straightened and looked through the window. Both men were in the kitchen, and although Anna Cutts had fled hours before, the servants were still in the house and the men were seated at the table drinking cider and eating.

He couldn't waste time. They could come out at any moment. Hurriedly he made his way toward the president's horse, patting its nose to keep it from getting skittish. Two pistols were in their holsters lying across the horse's saddle where the president had set them before going into the house, and he reached up, snatching them off quickly. But no sooner did he have them in his hands than a noise behind him made him whirl around, and his blood congealed as he found himself facing two stern-faced soldiers, their eyes hostile.

It took him only seconds to realize they knew what he was doing, and he was left with no other choice. He cocked the guns, one in each hand, as the men advanced on him, but when he pulled the triggers the hammers fell on empty chambers. He swore softly, disgusted, and threw the guns at the men, but they ducked and the guns sailed over their heads into the bushes, and were lost in the dark.

"It's a good thing the general told us to keep an eye on the president, ain't it, Ray?" one of the soldiers said, and the other one grinned.

"Eeeyah, but this here's a tall one, Heck. I think maybe I need a little help," and the soldier closest to Teak whipped out a knife, holding it high toward Teak's face.

Ordinarily two soldiers advancing on him wouldn't have bothered Teak, but both of these soldiers were tall and husky, as big as he was, and it was obvious as they squared off that they were veterans used to fighting. Teak reached behind him under his swallowtail coat and pulled his own knife from the sheath at the back of the waistband of his pants.

"One at a time, gentlemen," he murmured as the men advanced on him, but they didn't seem to hear as he backed away, moving toward the corner of the house, away from the president's horse. For a few minutes he was able to keep them at bay successfully; then suddenly both of them lunged at the same time as they moved around a corner, and the three men rolled over into the alley, straining against each other and pounding with their fists, the knives slashing viciously.

At first Teak held his own beautifully, his experience overcoming the odds; then he got careless. One false move was all it took, and a split second later he felt the other man's knife sink into his right shoulder burying itself to the bone. Enraged by the pain, he plunged his own knife home, catching the other man in the chest, and the soldier hit the ground in a pool of blood, evening the odds. But the wound had weakened Teak and he'd been unable to hang on to his knife in the struggle. A thrust to his groin from the remaining soldier missed and caught him in the upper thigh, plunging deep into the flesh, and he grimaced, groaning painfully as he tried to fight the man off.

Anger flared inside him at the irony of it. For two years Heath had chased him about the country, and never had anyone, including Heath, inflicted so much as a scratch on him, and now, here in what should have been a simple assignment, with the city in such an uproar, he was on the verge of being taken by two lowly privates. Well, he wasn't going without a damn good fight!

He doubled his fists, and they knuckled out viciously as he gathered a reserve of strength and caught the man on the chin. The soldier's head jerked abruptly as they rolled over in the dirt; then, another brutal fist to

the side of the head, and he flew back, dazed, collapsing on all fours, trying to keep from going under all the
way.

Half-crazed, Teak stared at the soldier, realizing
what would happen if he were caught, and the thought
of a noose around his neck spurred him on. He
struggled wearily to his feet while the soldier knelt in
the dirt road half-unconscious, and he glanced quickly
about. Then, without a moment's hesitation he slunk
into the shadows and began moving away as the soldier's head slowly cleared and he began looking anxiously about for his quarry.

Teak wasted no time. He kept moving, keeping to
the shadows, using trees and bushes for cover, ripping
off his telltale suit coat, tossing it aside, and mingling
with the crowd when he could, to throw the man off,
trying to conceal his wounds from the people scurrying
by. He could hear the private behind him, rallying
some fleeing soldiers to the cause, and his heart stiffened with fear.

He began to run now, staggering and half-limp-
ing as he left the worst of the mob and the close safety
of the houses, cutting across lawns and streets, heading
toward the river. He had to escape. Had to get away!

The river loomed up ahead of him in the night, dark
and deep as he reached its banks, and he breathed a
sigh. If he could find a boat and row to the other side
and reach the British troops, he could get help. Generals Ross and Cockburn would see he had medical attention. His hand moved to his leg, then examined his
shoulder. He was losing too much blood, and he knew
it.

His head began to feel light, unattached, and he
fought against the weakness that was trying to engulf
him. Straightening stubbornly, he stumbled on down
the riverbank, his eyes searching the darkness; then he
saw a small pier up ahead with a boat tied to it, bobbing gracefully in the water. A short flight of steps led
to the small pier, and he reached hurriedly for the rail,

but his hand, slippery from his own blood, slid on it and he plunged forward, landing on the pier with a crash, and he felt the bone in his leg crack and snap in two as neat as a twig as a muffled cry escaped his lips.

His face was white, and sweat poured from his forehead, sticking to his body, mingling with the blood, and he felt sick. Not here! He wasn't going to be caught here! He'd come too far.

He swallowed back bile, his breathing heavy, the pain from his broken leg and wounds unbearable, but he was only some two feet from the rope, and grabbed it with his fingers, hauling the boat in an inch at a time. When the boat was finally even with the pier, he gathered the last bit of strength he had and hauled himself to the edge, directly above the boat, using his elbows until he hung on the very brink. Staring down at the small boat, he made sure it was directly beneath him, then rolled, falling into it, and it tilted first this way, then that, as his body hit. He held his breath, motionless, praying it wouldn't capsize; then he felt it steady itself, floating out away from the pier again, bobbing on the water, the oars dangling freely in place.

He didn't have much time. His fingers reached out and he began working on the end of the rope that was still fastened to the boat, while some distance away he could hear the shouts of the private who'd managed to gather an excited group of patriots together. They were getting closer. Fear can bring on strength a man never knew he possessed, and now strength surged up in Teak, his blue eyes glazed in agony, and the rope slid from the boat, leaving it free. He felt the boat give a start, moving gently; then it caught in the current and he sighed as he tried to reach for the oars, but his arms wouldn't move. He was hot, flushed, and his head began to spin, the world around him becoming a whirl of noise and confusion. He tried to keep from succumbing, but it was no use. Slowly his fingers slipped from the oars, and in a moment of panic he fell flat on his face in the bottom of the small boat and a heavenly blackness engulfed him.

He had no idea how long he'd been drifting. It was daylight now, and he was soaked to the skin. A fine rain had fallen during the night, and although it had stopped some time ago, the sun had still not come out. He tried to lift his head, but was too weak. All he could do was lie in the bottom of the boat, in the water made pink from his own blood, and drift. The boat was moving fast, carried by the current that buffeted it along, and Teak lay motionless, feeling the strength slowly draining from his body.

Death was close now. He could feel it. Closer than it had ever been. He closed his eyes and tried to block his mind from it, but couldn't. He wasn't immortal. He'd been lucky so far, but a man's luck didn't always hold. Had his finally run out?

His eyes focused on his hand, close to his face, the fingers pale and blue-tinged, and he tried to send impulses to it to make it move, but it lay helpless, pink-stained water lapping at it lazily. To die here, with no one around, no one to care . . . never to see Locksley Hall again . . . never to ride through the fields and marvel at its beauty. Never see the Norman Towers rising on the horizon in their majesty, flooded by the evening sun. Tears flooded his eyes for the first time in his life. Where was he? What had he become? His head began to spin again, and he could hear voices calling his name. His mother and father, his sister, Heath.

Heath! The sight of his brother's face before him cleared his head somewhat, and he fought to live. Heath was alive, he had to be alive too, he couldn't die. He opened his eyes again, and the sky was dark already. Night? No, not that much time had gone by; then he felt the wind on his back, and the boat began to rock frantically and the sky darkened even more. He lay motionless for a long time, feeling the wind increasing its momentum as time passed, until now suddenly the storm hit with a violent thrust and he was being tossed about like a leaf on the water, the small boat almost capsizing as it dashed even faster downriver. His heart flew into his mouth and his stomach began to churn, and the last he remembered was a loud noise that sounded like a stampede; then everything went black again.

Some of the men were still clearing away debris, while the rest stood by watching the captain of the small sailing ship struggling to keep life in the man they'd pulled from the water after the small boat had smashed itself into their side. The worst of the tornado had hit farther north, probably near the Capital, but they'd felt the effects of it here as well.

"Maybe it'll scare those British troops clean out of Washington," said one sailor, his face snarling like a vicious monkey's. "Them bastards stole my kid brother and kept him for nigh on two years oncet while his wife and young 'un back here near starved to death. Grabbed him right off a merchantman, they did, said he was a deserter. Hell, he 'tweren't never outta the States. If I wasn't so old, with this game leg, I'd go upriver and show them redcoats what-for!"

"We know, Amos," said one of the other men. "You hates the British," and Amos snarled again.

"You bet I damn well do, and so do the rest of us, 'cludin' Cap there. You ne'er hadda put up with their arrogance. I tell you, I'll be glad when we've beat them at this bloody war."

Teak was trying to clear his head. He could hear the men talking, and listened quietly. They weren't British, that's for sure. He felt something hit his lips, then opened his eyes weakly as he tried to lift his hands.

"Steady, fella," said a rough, deep voice close to his ear, and he sipped at the whiskey being poured down his gullet.

Rosie—incongruously nicknamed Rosebud, or Rosie for short, because of the tattoo of a budding rose on his chest—leaned toward Captain Coke. "He looks like he must be a dandy with that fancy shirt and them pants, cap," he said surreptitiously, "and them boots ain't cheap 'uns like yours an' mine."

Captain Cokensparger, affectionately called Captain Coke by his crew, looked the man over slowly as Rosie talked. He was right. The man was undoubtedly a man of means, or had been before the fates had cast him adrift in that small boat.

Teak finished sipping the whiskey and lay back on the hard bunk, glad they'd thought to put a pillow behind his head. His eyes were open now, forced open by sheer will. "Where . . . am I?" he gasped, his voice barely audible.

"Well, we're running down the Potomac now, headin' for Chesapeake Bay," Captain Coke said. "The storm caught us short, but we outrun most of it. Folks north got hit worst, I reckon."

Teak looked over the faces staring at him, then glanced about the ship. It was a good size. A two-master, looked like a full crew. "Fishermen?" he asked, and the captain nodded.

"Headin' out to sea. That storm must have stirred up somethin' out there."

Teak's eyes narrowed as he watched the men. God! He felt as helpless as a sick puppy.

"What happened, mister?" asked Rosie, his sunburned face squashed into a frown, and Teak didn't answer for a minute. His story had to be good.

He tried to muster a half-grin. "I guess . . . I was robbed, gentlemen," he groaned softly. "All I remember is . . . stopping at a tavern for a drink," and they all nodded.

"Well, what do we do with you?" asked the captain, his face worried. "We're headin' out to sea soon as we get the mess from this storm cleared up, but we cain't take you with us."

Teak rested back, his eyes closed. They'd be heading out to sea through the Chesapeake. There'd be British ships somewhere near the Chesapeake, but he wouldn't dare try to get to them. How far down the coast were the Carolinas? He needed medical attention badly, but he also needed a place to hide out, and he needed it as badly as he needed a doctor. The Château was at Port Royal on the Broad River, but would his mother welcome him? He couldn't argue the point with himself. It was either that or die in some godforsaken shanty somewhere along the Potomac River.

He licked his lips, his voice husky. "Do you . . . know where Port Royal, South Carolina, is?" he asked weakly, and the captain nodded.

"Aye."

"I was . . . I was on the way to see my mother," he went on, "the Broad River . . . the Château." He paused to rally his strength. "If you take me there . . . there's money . . ."

The captain grinned. "Hey, look, my bucko, we've got fish to catch and bellies to feed," but Teak shook his head slowly.

"I'll . . . I'll pay you more!" he stated, his breathing labored, but the captain wasn't convinced as he rubbed the stubble on the end of his chin. "Loedicia Chapman at Port Royal . . . two thousand dollars . . ."

This time the captain's eyes grew wary. "You're sure of that?" he asked, and Teak nodded, barely able to talk.

"I'm sure."

His answer produced a grin from the captain and a question from Rosie.

"How we gonna keep him alive till we get the money, Cap?" he asked, and the captain's grin broadened.

"That, Rosie, is your job," he said, and he left the cabin to tell the men they'd be making a special run before starting to lay the nets.

During the next few days Teak drifted in and out of consciousness as his wounds began to fester. Rosie and one of the other men set his broken leg, but the knife wounds had been deep and the water in the bottom of

the small boat none too clean. The fishing boat made
its way down the Potomac, through the Chesapeake
and out to sea, completely ignored by the bigger ships
it passed, and as it plied its way down the coast, its
captain greedily thought of the money that lay at the
end of the run.

Teak prayed they'd reach the Château after dark,
and his prayers were answered, although he never
knew it. By the time the boat docked at the pier on the
Broad River, he was out of his head with fever, his big
frame barely breathing.

Loedicia sat in the library at the Château, reading;
occasionally she'd glance up at her husband where he
sat at his desk working on an assortment of papers.
How time did take its toll; but then, she wasn't young
anymore, either. Next year she'd be sixty. Lord, that
sounded so old. She didn't feel sixty. Yet, Roth was in
his sixties already. Still as handsome as ever, though,
she thought. So what if his black hair was now a beautiful silver white, it still waved and curled and it made
him look so distinguished. And his dark eyes still
sparkled with the glow of youth. He didn't look sixty-
six. Not at all, even with the white hair. He looked ten
years younger, and she knew he felt young too. How
often he told her that he'd been so afraid growing old
would be tiresome, yet here he was doing it, and it
wasn't so bad after all. In fact, things became sweeter
with time because you knew there wasn't that much
time left to enjoy them.

She set her book down, walked over and maneu-
vered behind him, then bent to kiss his neck, and he
scrunched his shoulders up as he dropped his quill pen
and whirled around laughing, catching her, pulling her
onto his lap.

"And just what do you think you're doing, madam?"
he asked, one eyebrow cocked at her sternly. "Trying
to seduce a poor doddering old man?"

Her hand flew to her breast in mock consternation.

"Oh, law, sir, but no," she squealed outrageously. "I was merely testing my lips to see if they still worked."

He eyed her lips seriously, examining the corners as they tilted up in amusement. "Hmmm. Maybe they are out of order. Shall we find out?" he said, and his mouth covered hers passionately, stirring a warmth inside her that brought a moan of delight from her depths.

She drew her mouth from his and looked into his eyes, running her finger along his hairline, feeling the silky softness of his once-dark hair, and she could see her own reflection in his eyes. Her hair too was no longer dark, yet it framed her face in a halo of frost with streaks of raven black here and there as if it were decorating a masterpiece by one of the famous painters of the day.

It was loose and curled haphazardly in billows, making her violet eyes even deeper, softening the lines that age was trying to mold into her face unsuccessfully, for she too still looked younger than her years, a condition she attributed to love. And how she did love this man. Who said passion and romance diminish with age? Her passionate love for Roth and the love he gave her in return was still as strong as it had been twenty years ago.

"You know you're a shameless man, Mr. Chapman," she quipped lovingly. "Taking a poor innocent maiden unaware."

His dark eyes sparkled back at her as his hands slowly caressed her, feeling the warmth of her pliable body that always seemed to amaze him, even after all these years. "An innocent maiden?" he asked, and she kissed him a long, lingering kiss.

"Remember when you found me at Fort Locke and shocked everyone when you picked me up in your arms and announced we were going to bed?" she asked, and his eyes softened.

"Have you ever regretted it, my love?"

"Oh, no!" Her hand caressed his cheek, and she

shook her head. "Never for one minute have I ever regretted my love for you, Roth," she whispered softly. "Without you, life would be dull and boring, without a purpose."

"And with you, my dear, life has been anything but dull," he said playfully. "Now, if you'll get off my lap long enough, I'll finish these papers, then take you upstairs and show you why I've come to that conclusion," and she laughed as they were interrupted at the door by Ann.

Ann had grown up into a fascinating young woman of twenty-five, but sometimes her quiet ways bothered Dicia. She had little interest in men, even though she seemed to enjoy their company when they did come calling. They courted her, but never too long, and Dicia was sure she knew why. Ann was very conscious of the Indian in her blood and probably made sure the gentlemen who came to court knew of it. Although her eyes were dark and sloe, it was the only thing about her that echoed the fact that she was half Indian.

Her hair, unfortunately, was straight, but thick and full, the color of burned honey, and she kept it long so it hung down her back to her tiny waist. She was taller than Dicia, yet delicate and willowy, her legs, spindly in her teens, filled out curvaceously, but they were well hidden beneath her long dresses. Dicia had been in her room one day when she was dressing and realized the girl's body was so well proportioned she looked like a living statue.

At the moment however, her sloe eyes were wide, her sensitive mouth quivering. "Mother?" she cried, addressing Dicia breathlessly, and they both knew by the anxious look in her eyes that something was amiss. "I'm sorry to interrupt." She was used to seeing them nuzzling one another, and if often warmed her inside to think two people could love each other so much; still, her face reddened. "There's a man at the back door," she gasped. "Says he's got Heath aboard his fishing boat."

"Heath?"

"Well, he says your son's aboard and he's hurt bad. I assume it must be Heath."

Dicia jumped up. "Oh, my God!" she cried as Roth stood up with her and they followed Ann from the room out to the back door, where Rosie stood, his weather-beaten face squinting in the light from the lantern one of the servants was holding up near the door.

"What is it?" asked Dicia, holding the skirts of her deep red velvet dress so she didn't trip, and Rosie stared at the lovely lady with the abundance of gray curls and warm, frightened eyes.

"We got a gent on board, ma'am. A big, blond bruiser," said Rosie. "He's hurt bad. Says he's your son and if we brought him here you'd give us two thousand dollars for our trouble."

Loedicia's eyes widened in alarm as she turned to Roth. "Blond? Heath's not blond!" Then she realized. "Oh, Lord!" Her hand flew to her mouth. "It must be Teak!" She turned back to Rosie. "Take me to him," she whispered quickly, and Rosie led the way into the star-filled night to the dock at the river's edge, where the small ship was tied.

The men watched curiously as they came aboard and Rosie introduced the captain. "This here's the lady, all right," he said simply, and Loedicia introduced herself.

"I'm Mrs. Chapman, this is my husband and our daughter. Now, may I see my son?"

"We got two thousand dollars coming to us, ma'am," he reminded her, and she nodded.

"You'll get it, sir. Now, please, take me to him."

He led them to the cabin where Teak lay muttering feverishly on the bunk, and as Loedicia stared down at him, a flood of memories washed over her. He looked so much like Quinn had looked when she'd first met him, and tears filled her eyes as she turned to the captain.

"I'll have some of the servants bring a litter and

carry him to the house," she said hurriedly, then looked at Roth, her eyes pleading.

"If you'll come to the house with us, Captain, I'll give you your money," stated Roth, and Loedicia smiled at him thankfully as she wiped the tears from her eyes.

They went on into the house, and Ann watched from the back hallway as Loedicia, with Jacob and three of the other men, went back down to the ship and Roth disappeared into the library. By the time the servants came back to the house with Teak, Loedicia following close at their heels, Roth was counting the last of the gold pieces into Captain Coke's hand and the captain was grinning from ear to ear.

"Glad to be of service, mate," he said as he glanced down at the money in his hands; then he bowed, saluting, and left the house, headed for his men, who were waiting aboard the two-masted sailing ship.

"Take him upstairs to Rebel's old room," said Loedicia, and she glanced at Ann, who was staring at Teak with a puzzled look on her face as they carried him away on the stretcher they'd made, using two brooms and an old blanket. "Ann, go tell Mattie to boil some hot water and bring bandages and towels," she went on, and Ann nodded as she slipped off toward the kitchen.

Loedicia and Roth followed the men upstairs, and she pulled the covers back on the bed for them so they could lay him down, wincing as she saw his wounds more clearly in the light from the lamps on the nightstand.

Rebel's old room was dainty, with roses, organdy, and pink fluff usually associated with a woman, and Teak looked lost in the softness of the delicately embroidered sheets with his filthy clothes and deeply tanned skin. The wounds were beginning to bleed again, and Loedicia frowned as she leaned over and pulled the filthy shirt away; then she examined his leg.

"My God, Roth," she gasped, tears trickling down

her face. "He's half dead. How could this happen? Where's he been?"

Roth shook his head. "I have no idea, but I suggest we get busy on him before he does die," and he started taking off his coat and rolling up his sleeves as Ann stepped in with a stack of towels and some bandages, followed by Mattie with a kettle of hot water.

Roth had nursed many a man back to health in his lifetime, but Teak was in bad shape. "I'm going to have to cauterize those wounds," he told Loedicia as he examined the putrid flesh, and Ann glanced quickly at her mother, seeing the terror in her eyes.

"I'll help him," she offered, trying to spare her mother, and Roth nodded, but Loedicia insisted on helping.

They worked on Teak for over an hour, washing and bandaging, cleaning out the wounds, and the smell of burned flesh hung heavy in the air after Roth put a hot poker to the pus and proud flesh.

"Throw these away," said Roth as he tossed Teak's torn clothes to Ann and asked her to leave the room for a few minutes while he washed him. When he was through, he pulled the covers up. The weather was still extremely hot, and Roth felt it was better not to try to put any clothes on his battered body, since the ones he'd had on had been cut off, so when he was washed and settled, he called Ann back in.

Teak was still moaning feverishly, and Ann had a cup in her hand when she stepped back in the room. "Mattie said to try to get some of this down him," she said as she held it out to Roth, but he didn't take it from her. Instead, he walked to the bed and sat on it, lifting Teak's muscular frame up, supporting him with his arm.

"You try to get it down him," he said, and Ann walked over to the bed and bent down, holding the cup to Teak's lips while Loedicia watched.

His lips were cracked and feverish, and he kept mumbling something about water, so it was easy to get him to drain the cup, although some spilled onto his bare chest.

Ann picked up a cloth as Roth laid Teak's head back, and she began to wipe the broth up from where it had spilled. His chest was broad, the muscles beneath the skin moving involuntarily as she sopped up the spill, being careful not to pull or catch the soft, curling blond hairs that covered him. Teak! Horrible, demoralizing Teak. Oh, how she remembered him. She remembered him well, too well.

She had been eleven then, and it had been her first trip to England, and she was anxious to meet the stepbrother she'd only heard about. He was a real earl, and she made sure she had on her prettiest dress, a frothy white with a pink satin sash and little tiny flowers in the front. And her shoes had to be special too. White patent leather with little faille bows, and her long braids were fastened with big pink ribbons.

She had stood in the salon at Locksley Hall between her mother and father, convinced that she was the ideal sister a big brother would want, remembering the fun she'd always had when Heath had been around, anxious for the chance to enjoy another big brother, and then he'd stepped into the room.

He was in his early twenties, extremely tall and good-looking, his clothes poured onto his body with a grace and elegance that would make him stand out in a crowd. Far from being effeminate, the frills at his throat only enhanced his blue eyes and emphasized his masculinity. Then he spoke, first to his mother in a cool, aloof manner, then to his stepfather, his voice bitter and resentful, but the blow was when he looked at her. His blues eyes studied her face as if she were something that had crawled out from under a rock; then: "And what on earth is this dreadful Indian brat doing in these ridiculous clothes?" he finally asked arrogantly. "Does she think by putting them on it automatically makes her white?"

Oh, yes, Ann remembered Teak. And she remembered the agonizing tears she'd shed because of his cruel words. That was fourteen years ago, but words were hard to forget even after fourteen years. She finished mopping up the spilled broth, then walked away.

With Mattie's broth in him, Teak slept peacefully that night, but for the next few days he was incoherent, mumbling about all sorts of things. Even violent at times, thrashing in the bed. His huge frame was hard to handle, and in the middle of this, Beau brought them news that the Capital had been invaded and the White House burned. However, the British had retreated after only a day, and were well on their way back to Britain, so everyone hoped, but not until after an unsuccessful try at Fort McHenry in Baltimore.

Roth sat at his desk in the library pondering over the news. He scowled. "Beau, do you think Teak had anything to do with what happened at the Capital?" he finally asked as he watched him standing across from him. "The captain of the ship that brought him here said they pulled him out of the Potomac about thirty miles or so south of Washington."

Beau looked startled. "You're sure?"

"That's what he told me while I was giving him the money. Dicia thinks he might have been one of the soldiers."

Beau walked over and looked out the window. He and Rebel had been in Charleston depositing Lizette in Mrs. Adams' Academy for Young Ladies for the fall term. She was all of fifteen now, and growing into quite a young lady. They'd stayed over a few days in their town house to go to the theater and visit with friends, and on the way back they'd stopped off to say hello, giving them the news that was shocking all of Charleston, and had discovered Teak in residence.

"Hmmm." Beau walked back from the window. "Has he been coherent at all?" he asked.

Roth shook his head. "No. Someone's been with him all the time, and when he isn't thrashing about, he's unconscious."

Roth turned his head as Rebel and Loedicia entered the room. Rebel was stunning in a pale pink traveling suit, her blond tresses piled beneath a small hat with pink chiffon veils that flew about her face, but for all her charm and poise, Beau liked her best with an old pair of riding pants and an old shirt on, her hair down blowing in the wind as she rode about Tonnerre, the name they'd decided on for their home. Tonnerre was French for "thunder," and Rebel thought the name quite appropriate.

"He's sleeping at the moment," said Loedicia as she joined her husband, standing beside him, then looked at Beau. "Where do you think he came from, Beau?" she asked anxiously.

He shrugged as he glanced at Roth. "It could have been anywhere, really."

"Was he in any kind of uniform?" asked Rebel.

Dicia shook her head. "No. A dirty old shirt that had once been quite elegant, and a pair of dress pants. There wasn't a bit of identification on him."

Roth stood up and put his hands on Dicia's shoulders. "Well, let's hope he wakes up soon so we can find out what's going on." He changed the subject abruptly. "Have you heard from Cole lately?" he asked.

Rebel frowned. "I don't like to think about it, Roth," she said. "The last we heard, he was still with Jackson's outfit. But I do worry so about him. Nineteen is so young to be out there fighting."

"He can take care of himself," commented Beau as he thought of his son. "I swear he inherited every Indian trait I didn't." He smiled. "If my father were still alive he'd probably try to talk him into taking over the tribe."

"It's so good to hear you talk about it so casually now, Beau," said Dicia. "I thought the day would never come when you'd realize it isn't what a man is that counts, but who he is and what he does."

Beau gazed at his wife; their eyes met, and he smiled. "Sometimes it takes the right woman to open a

man's eyes," he said softly, then turned to Roth.
"Would you like us to stay awhile, or do you think you
can handle Teak by yourselves?"

"I think we can manage," he answered. "But thanks
for the offer. If we need you, I'll send word."

They talked for a while longer before Rebel and
Beau left to go on upriver, while upstairs Ann took her
turn watching over Teak.

"The arrogant bastard," she whispered to herself as
she sat in the white satin boudoir chair, her dark sloe
eyes studying Teak. He was extremely attractive, she
had to admit. The fevered cracks were gone from his
lips now, and they looked soft and sensuous, and his
hair, cleaned of the dirt and mussed the way it was,
made him look young and vulnerable. She stood up
and walked to the bed, standing quietly looking down
at him, and suddenly she thought she saw his eyelids
move. Not frantically, as they usually did when he was
incoherent, but slowly, as if he was coming to.

Teak lay on the bed, his head pounding, the pain in
his body so intense he thought for a minute he was in
hell and the devil-demons were torturing him; then he
moaned and tried to open his eyes.

He shut them tight again, then opened them slowly
and stared through a hazy mist at a pair of dark sloe
eyes that were filled with hatred. Another demon to
torture me, he thought, then tried to lift his arms to
brush it away.

"Lie still!" the dark sloe eyes commanded, but the
voice that came from them was low and vibrant,
tingling his eardrums sensuously. "Please, I can't hold
you down. You're too big," the eyes went on. "If you'll
just lie still."

He relaxed and exhaled; then slowly the room began
to clear and the face that went with the eyes came into
focus, and he found himself staring up at a beautiful
young woman with a soft delicate mouth, small tapered
nose, and eyes so dark they looked like black coals, the
lashes on them thick, sweeping upward, softening their

intensity and unusual contrast to her amber hair that was pulled back and twisted into a chignon at the nape of her neck.

Ann looked directly into his eyes. She'd forgotten that they were so blue, and it startled her.

"Where . . . where am I?" he asked faintly, and she answered calmly.

"You're at the Château. Your mother is downstairs with Roth and your sister and her husband."

His forehead wrinkled as he stared at her. "Who . . . are you?"

"I, Lord Locksley, am Ann," she answered, her eyes filled with hatred, "Ann Chapman, but I guess you don't remember me."

Teak's scowl deepened. Ann? Ann Chapman? No, he shook his head weakly, he didn't remember her, and he stared after her as she left his side and gracefully walked from the room, closing the door behind her.

❦ 9 ❧

The constant sound of hammering could be heard as Heath made his way up Pennsylvania Avenue, then reined his horse to a stop and looked around. It was October, and already the Capital was on its way up again. The British had been beaten at Fort McHenry after their siege on the Capital, and the damn war was going well once more, but still he'd been unable to catch Teak. He persisted in slipping through his fingers like a slippery eel.

He nudged his horse in the ribs and rode on toward Blodgett's Hotel, where Congress was temporarily convening. Men were scurrying about and all was abustle. He sighed. They were still fighting over whether to move the Capital or not. How crazy, he thought. He gazed around. What's the difference, one city or another? They could easily rebuild, and it was all so handy here.

He smiled as he thought of the president's ingenuity. The State Department was operating out of Judge Duvall's old house, the Treasury Department was where the British minister used to live, the Navy was at Mr. Mechlin's near West Market, the Post Office was in one of Mr. Way's new houses and he headed now for the War Office, housed in a building adjoining the Bank of the Metropolis, and he reined up in front of it.

Dismounting, he tied his horse to the hitch rail and walked inside. The place was normal confusion, and he asserted himself, elbowing his way graciously toward a desk at the side of the room.

"Excuse me," he said to the man at the desk, interrupting a heated conversation he was having with a gentleman directly in front of the desk, "but I have an appointment. The name's Chapman. Heath Chapman."

The man behind the desk pushed his glasses back up on his nose and stared at the good-looking dark-haired man with the short, clipped beard, who was bending over in front of his face. The stranger wore a deep russet coat with brocade vest, buff trousers tucked into riding boots, and his brown hat sported a jaunty feather as he removed it, but it seemed rather strange to see a small gold earring in one of the gentleman's ears. Very strange, he thought, then dismissed it. People did strange things nowadays, it seemed, with the war and all. The man almost looked like a pirate or buccaneer.

"Chapman? Oh, yes, sir," he said anxiously, recognizing the name instantly, and dropped the pen he held in his hand. He looked at the man with whom he'd been arguing, and apologized. "I'll be back in a moment, sir," he said, and stood up, motioning for Heath to follow him.

They made their way across the room between the other desks and on through a door, then up a flight of stairs toward a room at the back. The bespectacled man knocked, then entered with permission from inside.

"Mr. Chapman, sir," he announced dramatically, then stepped back and faded down the hall again as Heath stepped into the room, shutting the door behind him.

One man and only one man stood in the room. He was small, almost delicate compared to Heath, but fire still flashed from his eyes as he greeted him. "Hello, lad," he said jovially. "I was afraid you couldn't make it."

Heath grinned. "And when did I ever ignore one of your requests for private audience, Mr. President?" he asked kindly.

James Madison grinned back; then his smile faded as he reached into his pocket and pulled out a folded piece of paper, handing it to Heath. "Here, read this," he said apprehensively. Heath frowned as he took the piece of paper from him and opened it up, his eyes narrowing as he read it.

"Good God, these are instructions to kidnap you," he exclaimed, and the president nodded.

"It was to have been done during the invasion, and it was evidently thwarted by one of our generals who sent two soldiers to keep an eye on me," he said. "One paid with his life, I knew nothing of the plot until I returned to Washington after the enemy had left and I sent for you right away."

"Warbonnet?"

"It sounds like it." The president clenched his fist. "Damn the man." His face reddened. "You know we even entertained him at the White House."

So this is where he disappeared to, thought Heath, but he wasn't surprised. "Nothing the man does shocks me anymore, sir," he said. "I only wish I hadn't lost his trail."

"Ah." The president's hand moved up in a gesture of attention. "But he failed in his attempt this time, Heath," he said, pleased. "And not only did he fail here, but word is that one of the reasons for the British failure at McHenry was that the maps they'd expected to receive telling about fortifications, strength, and other necessary details weren't forthcoming. Those maps and the information were to be supplied by the man carrying that letter, as you can see by the last line about proceeding to Baltimore. He never got there, Heath." His eyes narrowed anxiously. "But what I want to know, is where is he?"

"You've searched?"

"We've been from one end of the country to the other. He dropped out of sight and he was hurt. Both soldiers managed to wound him. The man's hiding somewhere. If you know anything about him that'll help, now's the time to use it. Find him so something like this can't happen again," and he gestured to the letter.

Heath studied it, then folded it over and handed it back to the president.

"You know," said the president, "the man was masquerading under the name of Giles Thompson. We found all his things at the Mackgowan Hotel after he'd disappeared, but by God, the night I met him his face was so damn familiar, and the other day I finally figured it." He scratched his chin as he stared drearily. "You know, he was a dead ringer for a man I met years and years ago in Philadelphia when I was visiting there with Tom Jefferson. The man had come east from the frontier. He was a friend of Tom's, but I can't recall his name. Hell of a good man, he was, fought in the war." He looked a Heath. "That scoundrel you've been chasing all over the country could pass for his brother."

"Or his son," said Heath softly, but the president didn't hear.

"What's that?"

"Nothing, sir, I was just thinking out loud," he answered, and James Madison sighed.

"Well, Heath, you have your orders and your work cut out for you. You know more about the man than anyone else. Find him."

Heath nodded. "Yes, sir," he said, and they shook hands as the president gave him a few last-minute instructions; then Heath left after examining everything that had been confiscated from Giles Thompson's room at the Mackgowan Hotel.

His first stop was to talk with the private who'd survived the fight with Teak.

"We lost him down by the river," he informed Heath when he was questioned, and that got Heath to thinking. As he left the private, he reached in his pocket and fingered a small piece of paper. It had taken a long time for that particular piece of paper to catch up with him. He and Eli had split a month ago, and Eli headed for Jackson's outfit. The message had arrived a few days later.

Strange the name should be so similar. Darcy McGill . . . Darcy McLaren? So Teak had gotten himself engaged before the start of the war, and to an American widow. Well, maybe, just maybe, that's where he'd headed when he'd left Washington. He could have made it across the river and worked his way south, or he could have joined the British. He might even be on his way back to England by now, for all anybody knew, but he had to know one way or the other. Not only for the president but also for his own peace of mind, because he hadn't told a soul, not Eli, not even the president, who Warbonnet really was, and he didn't know why except that he knew if people found out, his mother would be the one hurt, and he didn't want to hurt her.

He thought again about the address for Darcy McGill. Columbia, South Carolina. Coincidence? His stomach fluttered, then righted itself as a gust of wind whipped at his hat. Only one way to find out, and he spurred his horse, heading back down Pennsylvania Avenue away from town.

A week later he rode into Columbia, made his way to the nearest hotel, where he enjoyed a hot bath and had his beard trimmed while his clothes were being cleaned and pressed, then dressed again, feeling refreshed, went out to dinner, preparing himself to meet his brother's future wife.

The door to the house was painted blue, and against the white house with its blue shutters, it looked charming. Heath tied his horse to the hitch rail out front and walked up, using the big iron knocker that hung in the middle of the big blue door; then he waited for it to open. His stomach felt strange. Tight and constricted. What if it was really Darcy McLaren? What would he do? But the door was opened by a young girl of perhaps sixteen or seventeen.

Her hair was red, coppery red, and with the sun

streaming in a window behind her, it looked like it was on fire and a pair of deep violet eyes studied him quizzically. "Yes?" she asked as she stared at him, her pale gray muslin dress with embroidered rosebuds and gray satin sash barely edging her young ankles, and Heath smiled, startled.

"I'm looking for Mrs. Darcy McGill," he said, noting the saucy sparkle to the girl's eyes, but he was answered by an older woman who appeared suddenly and stepped in front of the girl.

The woman's hair was speckled gray, her face stern, the lips thin and severe. "May I help you?" she asked, and he repeated his request. "Mrs. McGill is away at the moment, sir," she informed him.

"Do you have any idea what time she'll return? I could come back later this afternoon."

The elderly woman clenched her hands together as if perturbed. "Mrs. McGill is gone for a few days, sir," she explained reluctantly. "Visiting friends in the south."

"Mother went to Beaufort," the young girl offered saucily. "We have a house there some friends are taking care of for us, and she's gone to visit them."

The older woman turned, frowning at the young girl's boldness.

"You're Darcy McGill's daughter?" he asked, and the more he looked at the girl, the more wary he became. There was something vaguely familiar about her. Her hair, her smile, especially the violet eyes.

"My name's Heather, sir, Heather McGill," she introduced blatantly, and Heath's stomach suddenly contracted and the lump in his throat stuck there, practically choking him as the older woman interfered.

"Heather, please," she retorted. "The man is looking for your mother, not you. You're not being a bit polite."

"Oh, Aunt Nell," the girl objected. "Maybe he won't need Mother. Maybe we can help him," and she looked again at Heath, her eyes flirting outrageously. "Is there something we can do, sir?" she asked.

He was staring at her, his face pale, and even Aunt Nell grew curious. "Sir?" she asked hesitantly. "Is there something? Perhaps we can help . . . ?"

He drew his eyes from Heather and turned them slowly on the little lady the girl had called Aunt Nell, and his face had a haunted look. "Was . . . was Mrs. McGill's maiden name McLaren?" he asked haltingly, and her eyes narrowed as she stared at him.

"Who are you?" she asked cautiously, and her eyes grew taut.

"I'm Heath Chapman, ma'am," he introduced himself and saw the frightened look in her eyes, and her hands fluttered nervously as she reached for the doorknob.

"I'm sorry, sir," she said, her voice trembling, "but we can't help you. Mrs. McGill isn't here. Good day," and she stepped back, closing the door abruptly in his face, leaving him standing on the porch, hat in hand.

He could hear the young girl through the closed door as he stood transfixed, trying to put together the pieces. "But, Aunt Nell," she was raging on, "he was so nice and so good-looking. You talk about me being rude. You practically slammed the door in his face."

"Heather," he could hear Aunt Nell, "please, I have my reasons. God knows, we may have said too much already."

"What do you mean, too much?"

"Never mind. Now, go back to what you were doing, girl," she begged, and their voices faded as he slowly lifted his hat to his head, then turned, walking down the steps.

Beaufort! A house in Beaufort! Heather? Heath and Heather! And the violet eyes, just like his mother's, and as he rode away he remembered a sunny meadow and a Sunday afternoon and Darcy aware for the first time in her life that her body could give her pleasure. How old was Heather? Sixteen? Seventeen? That had been the summer of 1796. It couldn't be . . . it was only coincidence, that's all, yet . . . He was tempted to turn around and go back, even stopped his horse once, then changed his mind. If it were true, he'd hear it from her own lips. If Darcy McGill was in reality Darcy McLaren, which he was sure now there was no doubt, he wanted to hear it from her, and he dug his horse in the ribs again and headed back toward his hotel, a sick feeling in the pit of his stomach.

Two days ahead of Heath, Darcy McGill, on her way south, sat in the coach feeling every shattering bump they hit. It had rained the day before, and the roads were a mire of mud and water, slowing them down considerably. She leaned her head back, trying to relax as best she could. The weather had turned cooler and the deep green velvet cape felt good about her shoulders, but she pushed the hood back from her face.

The message from Teak had been urgent. Since the start of the war they'd been unable to correspond, and now suddenly she had received a letter telling her to come immediately to Port Royal, to the Château, the home of former Senator Roth Chapman, but to tell no one of her destination or whom she was going to see.

If it had been anyone but Teak, she would have refused. To go back there, to the very home of the parents of the man who'd betrayed her . . . what was he doing there, and how could he ask her to join him in their home? But then, he didn't know . . . nobody knew . . . nobody knew she had any connections whatsoever with the Chapmans. How long ago that was.

She closed her eyes, remembering, and it hurt. A physical hurt that made her ache inside. She should have known. A young man as handsome as Heath was bound to have his pick of the ladies. She'd been such a fool to fall in love with him. She remembered the meadow and the violent passions he'd aroused in her. Passions that had brought Heather into being, and she also remembered the horror of learning that her lover was also her stepmother's lover. How cruel life could be.

She'd never really been the same since that night. Something inside her had dried up and died, and after her father's suicide she'd gone back to Columbia to forget, vowing never to love again, not knowing that already the seed of her love was determined never to let her forget what loving him was like. Aunt Nell had been angry at first, and humiliated, then understanding, and in the long run she had been the strength that had brought her through sanely. Aunt Nell had taken her to Boston, to an old friend, supposedly for a visit. It was at the friend's house where she'd met John McGill. Poor John. Sickly at fifty, almost on his deathbed, a widower for over twelve years, and childless, still he'd insisted she marry him to give her unborn child a name. He had died three months after the ceremony without ever having been able to consummate the marriage, yet she'd read to him and cared for him up to the last, and a month after his death, when Heather was born, she silently thanked him for his kindness.

She hadn't returned to Columbia for three years, living in the large house John had left her in Boston. She'd returned as the Widow McGill, but her only experience with passion had left her bruised in more ways than one, and it soon became apparent that she was unable to respond to the normal attractions of men. In fact she'd treated them coldly, their lust-filled eyes managing to drive her normal instincts even further from the surface until she forgot what it was like to feel or respond.

Then Teak had come into her life. She'd often wondered about Teak. He was more like a friend than a lover. Although she'd seen the desire in his eyes the same as in the eyes of other men, he'd treated her casually. A tender kiss, an arm about the shoulder, but never the passionate embrace other men always tried to bestow on her, and he'd never tried to get her into bed. Maybe that's why she'd accepted his proposal. The

thought of finishing life alone, when Heather married
and Aunt Nell was gone, frightened her. She didn't like
being alone. Not really. And after all, Teak was fun to
be with, and just think, she'd be a countess. The only
thing that frightened her was that he wanted children.
Could she do it? Could she give herself to another man
again? Could she have another man's child? As fond as
she was of Teak, was it enough for the kind of lovemaking she knew a man like Teak expected? And now!
What was he doing in Port Royal? Why was he at the
Château? How did he know the Chapmans? Well,
she'd soon find out, and her head banged hard against
the seat of the coach again as they hit another bump.

Teak had been at the Château for over six weeks
now, but his wounds were healing slowly.

"Ouch!" he yelled, grabbing Ann's wrist, holding the
razor that was in her hand away from his half-lathered
face as she shaved him. "Are you trying to kill me?"

Her mouth puckered angrily. "If your whiskers
weren't so tough. Besides, I'm not hurting you. You've
got the hide of an elephant."

"Oh, I have, have I?" He grabbed her free hand and
slapped it to the cheek she'd already shaved. "Elephant? Feel that. It's as soft as a baby's."

She flushed, and a warm glow went through her as
he held her hand to his cheek, his blue eyes bristling.

"Well, feel it!"

Slowly her fingers moved against his cheek, smooth
and faintly damp yet from where she'd just shaved
him. As her fingers moved, a slight tingle shocked their
tips and traveled up her arm, and a strange tightness
gripped her insides.

He grabbed her hand from his face and squeezed it,
still holding her other wrist. "Does that feel like the
hide of an elephant?" he asked. Her hair bristled.
"Well, does it?"

"No!"

"Then when you shave it, be careful. I bleed." She

shook his hand from hers, then looked down at her wrist.

"May I finish?" she asked.

He sighed as he let go. "When do I get to do it myself?"

"As soon as your right arm's completely healed," she said, glancing at the bandage that covered his right shoulder. "And if you don't quit trying to show off how strong you are, it'll never get better."

He stuck out his jaw for her to finish, and she took the last few strokes, then wiped his face clean.

"Who taught you to shave a man?" he asked suddenly as she started to clean up the mess, and she looked at him curiously.

"Why?"

He rubbed his chin. "You do a pretty good job, except when you get nervous."

"I wasn't nervous. You moved."

"I did not!"

"You did!"

"You get nervous a lot, don't you?"

She walked to the dresser and put the things in the drawer. "I told you, I wasn't nervous."

He moved, as if wanting to sit up. "Come here."

She eyed him skeptically.

"I want you to fluff up the pillows."

"You're not that helpless."

He pretended to try to reach behind his head without success, so she shrugged, walking back to the bed, the simple red cotton dress she wore accentuating her lithe figure, her full breasts amply exposed above the squared bodice, the deep velvet ribbons crossing below them making them seem even fuller. She reached behind him, pushing him forward, plumping up the pillows.

His face was close to hers and she could smell the clean fresh scent of him mingling with the masculine odor that she associated with him and had become accustomed to. How she'd ended up nursing him she'd never know, except that Loedicia had caught a cold, Roth had been busy, and Mattie said she didn't have time.

She still hated him. Every time she looked at him she remembered the stinging words and her stomach tied in knots while she trembled inside with a strange intense feeling. She didn't like hating, not so intensely. It did something to you inside and made you much more aware of the person you hated.

"There, is that satisfactory?" she asked as she straightened, and he laughed as he spoke.

"Don't you ever smile, Annie?"

She looked at him cynically. "Only when there's something to smile about, and taking care of you, Teak Locksley, gives me no pleasure."

"Oh, doesn't it?" he asked sarcastically. "Well, that's too bad, little sister, but it looks like they've stuck you with me, so you could make the task seem a bit more pleasant."

"For whom? You or me?"

"For both of us."

She ignored his words as she glanced toward the foot of the bed. "I forgot. Mattie said to check your toenails."

"My toenails?"

"She said they need cutting. Unless you intend to keep putting holes in the sheets."

"Oh, come on, now, Ann. There's nothing wrong with my toenails!"

She pulled back the edge of the covers and glanced at one of his feet, shaking her head, then walked to the other side and looked at the other foot.

"She's right," she agreed as she went to the dresser.

He straightened, watching her. "What are you going to do?"

"I'm going to trim your toenails."

He flushed bright red as she took a pair of nail parers from the drawer. "You're not!"

She walked back toward the bed. "I certainly am."

"Goddammit, they don't need trimming."

"They don't?" She pulled back the edge of the covers. "Look at them. I bet they haven't been trimmed for weeks."

"And you have to do it?"

"As you said before, I seem to be stuck with you."

"But you're not going to trim my toenails!"

She tilted her head back and her eyes steadied on him and for a moment neither said a word as a current seemed to flow between them and Ann's heart began to pound heavily.

"I can call Jacob and a couple of the other men to hold you down if you prefer," she said huskily, "or you can behave yourself. Which will it be?"

His jaw tightened angrily; then his eyes moved from her face to her bosom, where the skin vibrated to her heart's heavy beating, and he felt a twinge of desire as he watched the smooth flesh move. For the hundredth time since he'd discovered her hovering over him, he again realized that Ann was one of the shapeliest women he'd ever seen. He shoved his foot out toward the edge of the bed, and she glanced at him self-consciously as she moved to the foot of the bed and sat on its edge and began to trim his toenails.

She felt his eyes on her, studying her intently as she cut into the nails, and her hands began to perspire. Why was he staring at her like that? Trying to make her nervous again, that's what he was doing.

"Ow!" he blurted as she got too close, and she looked up innocently, then went back to her work. "Ow! Hey! What the hell are you trying to do, cripple me?" he yelled, and she pursed her lips stubbornly.

"I can still get Jacob."

His eyes flashed. "Get on with it!" he snorted, and lay back on the pillows, but this time he watched the ceiling and she finished without any more interruptions.

When she stood up and walked to the dresser, putting the nail parer back, he glanced at her furtively. Ann Chapman! Half-breed, that's what she was. A damn half-breed! But God, what a body beneath that dress. She had to be in her mid-twenties, and she was still unmarried. Most people probably considered her a spinster by now, but it wasn't possible a body like that had never ripened to a man. Her deep golden hair was flowing loose to her waist today, and he wondered what it would be like to wrap it around his hands and make those dark, sterile eyes of hers shine with desire. Some women were made for men to fondle, and he suspected, behind her cool surface, Ann was one of those women. Spinster? Not in the usual sense of the word, he'd say. His mother even said she had all kinds of beaux. Strange none had come up to scratch. Maybe because she was part Indian. After all, who, except his unconventional sister, wanted to marry an Indian?

He was jolted from his thoughts by her voice from across the room. "Is something wrong with me?" she asked abruptly, and he flushed, looking up into the mirror, where his eyes met hers.

"Not at all, little sister," he answered sheepishly, like a young boy caught with his hand in the cookie jar, and she turned to face him.

"Then don't look at me like that," she ordered breathlessly. "I don't like being undressed by your eyes or anyone else's." Her face was pale. "Now, if you have everything you need for the rest of the day, I have other things to do. If you need anything, just ring," and she motioned toward the velvet bell rope at the head of the bed, then left the room while he stared after her dumbfounded.

Ann was fuming as she hesitated at the top of the stairs. How dare he? Looking at her like that! Oh, how she hated him. It was impossible to imagine that he was related to Heath. She stood for a minute reminiscing. Heath! How long it had been since they'd last seen him. It had been eight years ago when he'd returned from his imprisonment in Tripoli. Handsome, adorable Heath with his warm smile and loving eyes. But he'd stayed such a short time, thanks to the narrow-minded people of Port Royal. If he'd only return. He'd said he'd come back when she grew up, and she'd waited for him just like she'd promised. He'd only been teasing her at the time, she knew, but she'd been serious, and she wasn't a seventeen-year-old girl anymore. She was a woman. She'd have something to offer him this time. Oh, why didn't he come home?

She stared down the stairs, then stopped. There were voices in the library, but it was someone else in addition to her mother and father, and it was a woman's voice. She started to continue down the steps, then stopped again as her parents and a strange woman stepped into the hall and looked up at her and she found herself looking into a pair of cool green eyes with little gold flecks that made them sparkle warmly beneath a mass of coppery red hair that hugged the woman's head.

"This is our daughter, Ann," Loedicia explained as they approached the stairs. "She's been nursing Teak beautifully. Ann, this is Teak's betrothed, the widow Darcy McGill. It seems Teak sent for her."

Without informing anyone, no doubt, Ann thought to herself, then greeted Darcy cordially. "Mrs. Mc-Gill."

Darcy flushed as she greeted Ann briefly, then turned back to Loedicia. "May I see Teak now, Mrs. Chapman?" she asked, her voice unsteady, and Ann frowned as she watched the woman.

Now, why on earth was she so nervous? "Is something wrong, Mrs. McGill?" she asked inquisitively as she looked down at Darcy, but Darcy shook her head.

"No, not at all. It's just that the trip has been a long one and I am a little tired."

"His Majesty's in the room at the top of the stairs on the left," Ann said sarcastically, gesturing upstairs, "but I'm afraid he's not in too good a mood. His crown's rather tarnished this morning, and I let him know about it." She glanced at all of them quickly. "Now, if you'll excuse me, I do have some things to do," and she finished descending the stairs, then disappeared down the hall.

"Your daughter's lovely," offered Darcy, trying to decipher Ann's puzzling remark as she watched her disappear, and Loedicia frowned. She too was surprised at Ann's sarcasm.

"Thank you. We're quite proud of her," she said, and glanced quickly at Roth. "Were you going up, dear?" she asked, but Roth declined.

"I have some things to do, so I'll let you present Teak with his surprise," he said, and she reached out, squeezing his hand.

Darcy saw the look on Roth Chapman's face while he exchanged his wife's affectionate gesture, and once more as she had when she first laid eyes on him, she felt a tremor deep inside. His hair was white, but the face . . . would Heath look like this when he aged? That the thought of him could still stir her was frightening, and she tried to still the memories as she turned toward Heath's mother and they started up the stairs and she continued wondering what on earth Teak was doing here.

Teak was propped up in bed resting his head back on the pillows with his eyes shut when Loedicia opened the door, and he thought it was Ann forgetting something.

"Came back to apologize, did you?" he asked as he started to sit up; then he straightened and his eyes widened and warmed as they fell on Darcy. "Darcy, I thought you were Ann coming back."

Darcy walked in, her eyes mocking him. "And what did you do to that poor girl that she said something you felt she had to apologize for?"

His eyes hardened. "I didn't do a thing. She's the one. Cutting my toenails!"

She smiled. "Did they need cutting?"

"Whose side are you on?"

"I happen to know you, Teak Locksley, and I can imagine the fuss you made."

Loedicia watched the two of them, and something bothered her. They were friendly and intimate enough, but it was a strange kind of intimacy, more companionable than passionate, and Teak hadn't made any attempt to kiss Darcy since they'd entered the room. Of course, maybe her presence could be what was hampering their reunion.

"Well, if you'll pardon me now," she said, making her excuses, "I've some things to do too." Teak sighed as she left the room.

Darcy pulled off her turquoise satin gloves and reached up, removing her matching hat with its nosegay of soft white feathers that matched the trimming on her turquoise silk traveling suit. "So," she asked anxiously, "now what's this all about, Teak?"

He scowled. "Not even a welcome kiss for your future husband?"

She walked to the bed and bent down, her lips on his, and he held her there for a long time until he was satisfied, then released her. "That's better."

She sat on the edge of the bed and looked at him. "All right, I'm listening."

His eyes suddenly grew distant, aloof. "Do I have to have an ulterior motive to come visit my mother?" he asked casually.

She stared at him, startled, not sure she was hearing right. "Your . . . mother?" she gasped.

"Loedicia Chapman's my mother," he informed her, not surprised at the shocked look on her face. "She and Roth married after my father's death. Of course that's not the whole story. It's a long one, if you'd care to listen."

She nodded. "Maybe I'd better," she said hesitantly, swallowing uncomfortably, composing herself as best she could. So he told her the whole story while she listened in chaotic silence, her heart pounding frantically as the words tumbled from him. He left out only his identity as Warbonnet and Heath's pursuit of him. That he'd tell her as soon as she absorbed this.

She stared at him transfixed as he finished, her mind in a whirl, trying to sort everything out. "Then you have a sister named Rebel and she's married to a man named Beau Dante," she said slowly, when he'd finished, making sure she had everything straight, "your half-brother's name is Heath Chapman, and the woman I just saw leave, the one named Ann . . . she's your adopted sister, right?"

"How did you get it straight so easily?" he asked. "Sometimes I get mixed up myself."

She looked down at her hands, the butterflies in her stomach fluttering violently. "Why didn't you tell me this before?"

He shrugged. "It didn't seem important in England."

She glanced up at him abruptly. "England . . . yes." She scowled. "That's something else, Teak. The last time I heard from you, you were in England. What are you doing here?"

He knew the question had to come, and he'd been waiting for it. He had to trust someone. Somebody had to be on his side. He took her hand in his and raised it to his lips, his eyes intent on her face. "Darcy, how long have we known each other?" he asked.

Her eyebrows lifted. "You like reminding me of my age?"

He smiled momentarily. "I'm not trying to be amusing." The smile faded. "I'm not a bad person, darling," he went on. "I'm just fighting for my country." He saw the hesitant look in her eyes. "I'm a spy, Darcy," he whispered softly, "and to make matters worse, my brother, Heath, is the man the men in Washington have hired to hunt me down."

His fingers caressed her hand, but she didn't really feel them. All she could think of were the three words that kept pounding in her ears. His brother, Heath! His brother, Heath! All these years, it was his brother, Heath. . . . What was she to do? My God, she couldn't tell him the truth. She'd seen the look of hatred on his face when he'd talked of Heath. She couldn't tell him. Not now. Maybe later, but not yet.

"You do understand, don't you?" he asked slowly as he watched her face, and she bit her lip.

"Why?"

"You mean why am I fighting for England?"

"Yes," she answered, trying to weather the shock.

He dropped her hand. "Because I live in England . . . because my loyalties are there. I don't want to lose the Locksley estate, my title, and everything that goes with it. Is that answer enough?"

She put her hand to his mouth to stop the bitter flow of words. "It's enough," she said softly. "But what will you do now?"

"I'll stay here until I'm able to travel, then disappear."

"Does your mother know?"

"No."

"You think it's fair to use her like this?"

"I'm sorry, Darcy, I have little respect left for my mother after what she did to my father."

"According to what you said, she was married to Roth Chapman."

Teak's eyes narrowed. "There's more to it, Darcy," he said vindictively, "but I don't like washing dirty linen. Please, believe me, my mother is not the virtuous woman she pretends to be."

Darcy stood up. "So you feel justified in what you're doing."

"Why not? I needed a place to hide. This is as good as any."

"If I didn't know you better, Teak, I'd swear you had no heart at all," she said, forcing herself to remain calm. "I just hope you're not the one to get hurt."

"How could I get hurt?"

She looked down at the bed where his tall frame rested uncomfortably. "They hang spies," she whispered softly, and he frowned.

"That's why you're to forget everything I just told you," he replied. "They also hang their accomplices."

She stared at him, her eyes frightened, and he reached out for her to comfort her, and suddenly she wished she hadn't come. What a mess to walk into.

Darcy stayed for supper that evening, and it was awkward for her, because every time she looked at Roth, he brought back so many memories. Memories that tore at her heart and made her weep inside. Then after supper they insisted she stay at the Château until Teak was ready to travel.

"We have plenty of room," said Roth, "so we won't take no for an answer," and there was nothing she could do except accept their hospitality and send to Beaufort for her trunks.

When Teak had regained consciousness, he'd told his family he'd been on a ship headed for the East Florida Territories, which were still in the hands of Spain, when a storm wrecked the ship he was on. He'd been picked up by the fishing vessel and asked them to bring him here, and the wounds he had were inflicted by debris whirling about during the storm. He had no way of knowing when he told the story that they knew he'd been fished out of the Potomac River, and if he had known, he might have played his hand differently. As it was, he sat back, relaxed, and let his wounds continue healing, confident he was safe.

It was early morning, the second day after Darcy's arrival. Teak's shoulder was comparatively better, although he still hadn't the strength to lift his arm high enough to shave himself, his thigh was healing, and his leg was still in a splint, where it would undoubtedly be for some time yet. Ann wanted Darcy to help take over part of Teak's nursing now, and she was willing, but he refused to let her, stating that she was a guest, not a nursemaid. Ann insisted that all there was to do was shave him, bathe him, and change his bandages and bedding, but Teak was indignant, so Ann continued her nursing, the servants took care of his bedding, and they let Darcy entertain him. He'd been at the Château for seven weeks this morning.

"And when do I get out of this bed?" he asked Ann when she'd finished shaving him and was changing his bandages.

She looked at him unsmilingly. "You can go downstairs today if you don't mind letting Jacob and the men carry you," she answered as she wound the bandage about his shoulder.

"Why would I care who carried me?"

"Because sometimes you're nasty," she retorted, and his teeth clenched as he looked at her.

She'd plaited her hair today in one long braid that hung down her back, and he caught the faint smell of cape jasmine that always lingered when she was near, and a strange sensation went through him.

"How do you get off telling me I'm nasty?" he asked as he watched her.

"Because you are."

"When have I been nasty to you? You come in here, cut me when you're shaving me, butcher my toes, and order me around. Who do you think you are?"

"I'm just giving you some of your own medicine."

He grabbed her wrist as she finished tying off his shoulder bandage. "What do you mean?"

She looked directly at him, her sloe eyes so dark they looked like shiny onyx, her thick lashes sweeping them gracefully. "You don't remember, do you?" she asked.

"Remember what?"

"I have feelings, Teak. I may be part Indian, but I do have feelings."

He pulled her wrist so her hand touched his cheek, and her fingers felt soft, like velvet. "Did I say you didn't?"

She gazed at her hand against his cheek, and a warm flush filled her. "I was eleven years old when I went to England with them," she said softly. "I stood in the salon at Locksley Hall, so proud because for the first time I was to meet the Earl of Locksley, who was my big brother. I wanted you to be proud of me and I had on my best dress that day. I'd already fallen in love with Heath and I thought this new brother would be someone else I could love. I was so happy. My heart was bursting inside me . . . and then you came in." Her eyes intensified as she stared at him coldly. "You were haughty and arrogant. You barely looked at me, Teak, and when you did, your only remark was to ask how an Indian brat thought dressing up like a white girl could make her white." She tried to pull her hand from him, but he held her wrist tighter. "I've never forgotten that . . . nor have I forgiven you."

He moved her hand to his mouth and brushed it with his lips, and she trembled. "Poor Ann, I must have been horribly stuffy," he murmured. "But then, how was I to know you'd grow into such a luscious woman?"

She let him hold her hand against his lips, the warm feel of it sending sweet sensations through her that she tried to ignore while she fought to keep her voice steady. "That's just the problem, Teak," she blurted breathlessly. "You weren't stuffy. There's a difference between being stuffy and being downright rude. You hated Indians then, and you still do, it shows in your eyes. You tolerate me because of your mother, but that's all. I saw it on your face the first day you were conscious. I'm not a sister to you, and I never will be. I'm merely some half-breed your mother happened to pick up along the way."

He took her hand from his mouth and toyed with it, studying the smooth, silky lines, noting the long tapered fingers and well-cared-for nails. "Am I that transparent?" he asked, and she pulled her hand away as he went on. "And here I thought I was being nice to you."

"Nice?" Her eyes narrowed. "I'm not your entrée for the evening, Teak, and I dislike being treated like one."

"I thought maybe Mother let you keep some of your ancestors' customs, like the gift of the virgin maid . . . ?"

"You're vulgar!"

A smile played at the corners of his mouth. "You dislike the idea of being offered for my entertainment?" he asked facetiously. "I see Mother's neglected her duties where you're concerned." Her eyes blazed and his hardened as he no longer looked amused. "After all, what else is an Indian woman for?" he slurred, and she exploded.

"I knew that's what you were thinking!" she snarled furiously through clenched teeth. "I knew it! I saw it the other day when you looked at me. You're despicable! I'm not good enough to be your sister, but I'd be good enough to vent your lust on, wouldn't I?"

"You expect me to accept you as a sister? A half-breed?"

"I'm good enough to nurse you, though, aren't I? And I'd be good enough to warm your bed. You're just like all the other men. I'm only an Indian, so it doesn't matter if I lose my virginity or not, do whatever you want because I'm only a stinking Indian! Well, let me tell you something, Teak Locksley," she retorted angrily, her eyes blazing. "You lay one hand on me, and so help me, you'll be sorry, do you hear? Your mother's been good to me, and I'd hate to hurt her, but I will if I have to. You want me to nurse you, fine, I'll do the dirty work, but you remember one thing, keep your hands to yourself from here on and keep your eyes and thoughts where they belong too. I'm not good enough to be your sister, I'm not good enough for anything else. You want to prove your manhood, do it with the woman you're going to marry. You understand?"

He laughed, sneering. "My, my, aren't you touchy? Who the hell do you think you are, anyway, telling me what I can and can't do?"

"I'm Ann Chapman, that's who I am," she yelled, "whether you like it or not."

"Well, I don't."

"Fine. Then we know where we stand, don't we? I don't like you and you don't like me, so let's keep it that way!"

He stared at her. What the hell was the matter with him? He was arguing with her as if she were an equal. He was an English lord. She was nothing but a lowly Indian. His sister! With those sloe eyes? His blue eyes met hers head-on, and suddenly as they clashed, a shock ran through him, exploding deep inside. A shock that shook him passionately and left him trembling, and he stared, bewildered, he couldn't look away. He couldn't tear himself from those dark, exotic eyes. They were tearing at him, smothering him, drowning him. He was spellbound, as if he were in a vacuum and it was hard to breathe. My God! She was fascinating like this, and he felt himself hardening, aroused by her sensuality.

Usually she walked around quietly. Very efficiently doing her job, being polite, unemotional, and unsmiling. He'd noticed her—how could he help it? She could be damned provocative in her sterile way, but now, with her eyes flashing, cheeks flushed, and breasts heaving angrily, the passion that lay buried deep inside her shone all too clearly and he felt a twinge of warmth surge through him that left him breathless. What the hell was she doing to him?

Ann's eyes fell before his smoldering gaze. She hadn't meant to tell him, but it was so obvious the circles his mind was running in. She'd caught him watching her over the past weeks as she moved around the room. Even the last few days, and while Darcy was present, she'd look up into his blue eyes and realize he'd been watching her, his eyes unconsciously outlining her curves. Yet there was hostility in his eyes whenever anyone mentioned that she was his stepsister.

Her chin tilted defiantly. "Do you still want to go

downstairs?" she asked unsteadily, and he scowled, his voice husky.

"I sure as hell better. I don't want to stay up here where you can accuse me of trying to ruin your virtue," he answered recklessly, trying to calm his emotions, and this time she didn't answer him, but took the shaving things back and put them in the drawer, then gathered the remains of the bandages up and left the room to get Jacob and some of the men to carry him downstairs.

He spent the whole rest of the day downstairs enjoying himself, trying to forget what had happened earlier. They couldn't put trousers over his broken leg, so he wore a nightshirt and robe, and he and Darcy amused themselves talking and playing piquet and cribbage. His mother and Roth visited with them off and on, and in the evening Rebel and Beau stopped by for dinner. Ann had made herself scarce most of the day, but now it was close to nine-thirty and she'd slipped into the drawing room, where they all sat talking, and she silently watched Teak.

He looked pale as he sat in one of the armchairs, his splintered leg propped up onto a footstool, his hands resting, clasped together, across his chest. He was tired, she could tell, but he was too stubborn to admit it. Earlier in the day he'd arrogantly declined her suggestion that he should get some rest, and now he was suffering for it. He hadn't seen her come into the room and walk to the big bay window, where she sat on the window seat, her pale blue lace dress blending in with the blue curtains, and he was surprised when she suddenly stood up and announced that she thought his first day up had been long enough.

He tried to protest, but Roth too had seen the effects his day out of bed had brought on, and with urging from his mother and Darcy, Jacob and one of the other servants were called in to help him upstairs. Jacob was a godsend, because although he was well up in years, he was as big as Teak, with still enough muscle for three men.

They all moved from the room as the servants carried Teak, everyone chattering as they stepped into the main hall, moving him toward the stairs, when the front-door knocker echoed through the marble-floored foyer and they all stopped hesitantly, Teak standing awkwardly on one leg at the bottom of the stairs ready for his ascent.

"Now, who the devil could that be this time of the evening?" exclaimed Roth as he glanced about to see if Mattie was going to come. The black woman was nowhere in sight, so he started for the door himself.

"Whoever it is, tell them it's too late," called Loedicia after him as he walked across the floor, and they all watched as Roth reached for the doorknob and slowly pulled the door open.

༨ 10 ༨

Heath stood motionless on the threshold, his tall frame outlined in the doorway as Roth opened it. His eyes were on the man wearing the robe, standing at the foot of the stairs directly in front of him. The light from the chandelier overhead in the foyer softened the man's features, but there was no mistaking the face. It was Teak!

Anger and hurt welled up inside Heath and he stiffened abruptly, but before he could make a move, his father was shaking his hand and hugging him and his mother was running across the foyer with arms open wide, her face wreathed in smiles.

"Heath!" Roth exclaimed as his arms loosened from about his son's shoulders, and Loedicia's violet eyes shone tearfully as she gazed up at him.

"Oh, Heath!" she echoed. He looked dark and forbidding to her, with his clipped beard and the earring still glistening in his ear, and she hesitated. This was Heath? This tall, swarthy man with the piercing eyes and unsmiling mouth? Then he looked into her eyes and his dark eyes softened.

"Mother!" he whispered softly, and she was engulfed in a hug that swept her off her feet, and his broad smile, the smile she knew so well, warmed her heart.

She felt so small in Heath's arms, and yet, except for the frosted hair, her face still held the strength it always had. She was still vitally alive, vivaciously animated, and he felt guilty for the times her reckless spontaneity had embarrassed him when he was younger.

Rebel and Ann were close behind Dicia with hugs and kisses, while Beau shook hands, slapping his friend on the back, but during the commotion, Heath never lost sight of Teak, who remained rooted to the spot, the hair at the back of his neck bristling.

Heath's eyes bored into his brother's now as Dicia pulled him farther into the plant-lined foyer toward the stairs as she talked.

"Just think," she was saying excitedly, her face beaming as everyone gathered around. "For the first time in over twenty years I have all of my children under one roof at the same time." She squeezed Heath's arm. "I can hardly believe it." She looked up at his rugged frame apparent beneath the trim cut of his elegant clothes; then she glanced at Teak, who was staring at Heath, his face pale. There was a strange look on Teak's face, and his mouth was set in a hard line. "Teak, I know it's been a long time," she said, frowning, "but . . . you do remember your brother, don't you?"

Teak's mouth twitched nervously as he stood on one leg, leaning against the newel post at the foot of the stairs, wondering what Heath was going to do.

They looked directly into each other's eyes, and sparks flew. Teak's first instinct was to run, and Heath's was to tear into him with his fists, but instead they stood glaring at each other, their eyes blazing defiantly.

Loedicia looked first at one, then at the other, puzzled, but it was Rebel who broke the tension. "Come on, Heath, I know Teak was only an ornery twelve-year-old brat the last time you laid eyes on him, but people do grow up, you know. The least you could do is shake hands."

Heath's breathing quickened as he stared at Teak, remembering Janet. Janet with her warmth and love. Janet, whose body lay somewhere in the Michigan woods where he'd had to bury her with his own hands. Janet, who'd be alive if it hadn't been for Teak. His brother! That he could be of the same flesh made his skin crawl. How could one woman bear two such different sons? How could he even be a small part of a man who'd do the things Teak did? His insides contracted, and a physical ache spread through him as he stared at Teak standing before him in his quilted robe, because although he wanted to cry out and condemn him for what he was, he knew if he did it would break his mother's heart, so instead, he held his feelings in check and nodded, acknowledging Teak, offering him his hand.

"Teak?" His voice was casual, as if nothing were amiss, and Teak looked at his mother's face, then to Heath, and reached out, taking Heath's hand apprehensively.

"Now, that's better," exclaimed Dicia happily, ignoring the looks that went with the handshake. "And this is Teak's fiancée," she went on, turning toward Darcy, who'd watched the exchange between the two men with her heart in her throat, "Mrs. Darcy McGill," and Heath's eyes left Teak's worried face as they dropped hands, and he looked at the woman standing at his brother's side.

Darcy hadn't changed, not really. She wore a pale gold dress of watered silk with gold velvet ribbons trimming the tight bodice and low décolleté. Her eyes were still the same cool green, her hair still like fiery copper, but there was a serene reserve that emanated from her, hiding the spontaneous warmth she'd possessed when she was a girl. Her eyes were steady on Heath, her lips trembling slightly as she spoke, pretending she was meeting him for the first time.

"Mr. Chapman?" she acknowledged softly, and he reached out, forcing her to reciprocate.

She lifted her hand to his, and a shock went through her as their hands touched, his dark eyes looking into hers. "Mrs. McGill. . . . A widow, I presume?" he said, and she flushed, her knees weakening as he bent over, his lips brushing the back of her hand lightly. "I'm charmed," and there was no doubt in her mind, from the intense warmth in his eyes, that he recognized her, but it was apparent only to Darcy. The others were too busy wondering what had inspired Heath to suddenly return.

"Teak's been quite ill, Heath, so I think it's best he goes on upstairs," Dicia said as she saw Teak's pale face and noticed him tremble slightly, and Heath relinquished Darcy's hand, turning toward his brother again while Dicia addressed Ann. "After you see him settled, Ann, come back downstairs," she said affectionately. "I know Heath will want to visit awhile before he retires, even if it is late."

"Why does Ann have to go upstairs?" asked Heath, glancing quickly at Ann, who'd moved to his side. His eyes appraised her appreciatively. She certainly had grown into a beautiful woman. When he'd left the last time, she was just seventeen.

"I've been nursing him," she explained, and her face lit up for Heath; then she looked at Teak. "He does look somewhat peaked tonight, doesn't he? It's his first day out of bed."

"Then please, don't let my coming interrupt things," he said. "Take your patient upstairs, but do come back down, it's been a long time."

She smiled. "I'll be down as soon as I can," and she motioned to Jacob and the other servant, who made a seat by crossing their hands, and Teak sat on them and they carried him upstairs.

Heath stood beside his mother, watching Teak disappear, with Ann behind him; then he turned to Darcy. "When are you and my brother planning to marry, Mrs. McGill?" he asked softly, and Darcy reddened.

"When the war's over," she replied, and Heath's eyes narrowed.

"Ah, yes, the war. Strange Teak should be here with a war going on."

"He was on his way to Spanish Florida when his ship was caught in a storm," said Dicia, "but come, tell us where you've been the past eight years, Heath. My heavens, it's been so long," and he followed them back into the drawing room, Darcy's presence making him uneasy, because she still had the power to arouse him with a look from those cool green eyes, and he was certain she too was far from complacent about his presence.

Upstairs, Ann was settling Teak into the large bed, fluffing the pillows for him to lie back on. "I suppose you're all happy to see Heath," he said irritably as he sat on the edge of the bed, and she smiled warmly.

"Why not?" The pillows were fluffed, and she helped him get settled back onto them. "Heath's always been wonderful to me."

"How nice."

Her smile faded. "You don't have to be sarcastic."

"I don't like Heath."

"How ridiculous. Your mother said it's been over twenty years since you've seen him, so how can you say either way until you get to know the man he's become?"

"I don't intend to get to know him."

"How can you avoid it?"

He tried to relax on the bed. "I'll keep my distance."

She stared down at him, annoyed. Sometimes he could be so exasperating and obstinate. "I wish I could understand you, Teak," she said, peeved. "How Darcy, as nice as she is, can love someone like you, is beyond me."

"Well, don't let it concern you," he said. "And when you go back down, tell her I'd like to see her if it wouldn't be too much trouble."

"Not at all," she replied. "She's welcome to you," and she left the room, unaware of the worried look on Teak's face.

Darcy was reluctant to leave everyone. Even though she and Heath had both acted as though they were strangers during the conversation in the drawing room, she caught him looking at her the way he had that night in her father's garden in Beaufort years ago, and the love she was sure she saw reflected in his dark eyes stirred her the same as it had then. She'd listened fascinated as he told of some of his exploits; then she trembled as Ann came down and told her Teak wanted to see her, and she was reminded that Heath was Teak's enemy.

It didn't seem right. None of it seemed right as she excused herself politely and went up to Teak's room. "What are you going to do?" she asked a few minutes later as she stood beside Teak's bed.

He glanced at her sharply. "What can I do?" He gazed at the hump his broken leg made beneath the flowered covers. "I sure as hell can't just walk out with this."

"Maybe he didn't come after you."

"Darcy, he wants me, make no mistake. The only reason he didn't say something downstairs is because of Mother. Heath's a sucker for sentiment. Always was." He reached out and took her hand. It was cold and lifeless, and he stroked it affectionately. "Don't worry, love," he said, "after seeing Heath with Mother tonight, I think maybe I'm in luck. But I want you to keep an eye on him for me. Let me know if he does anything you think maybe I ought to know about."

She shook her head. "I can't be a spy, Teak," she confessed lamely. "I . . . I'm an American."

His hand tightened on hers. "Did you intend to stay an American when you married me, Darcy?" he asked abruptly, and she scowled as she stared at the intricate patterns carved in the headboard of the bed.

"I . . . I hadn't thought. I guess I thought we'd live in both worlds. Yours and mine," she answered, but he shook his head.

"We'll live in England, not here," he said, "so you might as well get used to serving your new country."

He pulled her onto the edge of the bed beside him and released her hand, cupping her chin. "Darcy, you do still love me, don't you?" he asked.

She sighed. "You know I do," she answered breathlessly, and his hand moved from her chin to the nape of her neck, and he pulled her to him, his mouth covering hers. His lips were firm and possessive, and Darcy felt their strength, but as usual, that was all she felt. A slight warming, yes, but none of the passion that might have been there twenty years before. But then, a woman in her thirties wasn't supposed to thrill to the same giddy feelings she'd had when she was young. Passion was for youth. Teak's kisses proved that. They weren't the uncontrolled, passionate kisses of youth, either. They were tender, loving, and possessive, but never unbridled, passionate yearnings.

He drew back, looking into her cool green eyes. "I need you," he whispered softly. "Now more than ever. I have to know what Heath's planning to do."

"You expect me to find out?"

He licked his lips as if tasting her kiss. "You're a beautiful woman, my darling. You ought to be able to get him to tell you what he's planning."

"Don't be ridiculous. He knows we're to be married. He wouldn't confide in me."

Teak sneered. "Don't bet on it. He might think he's saving you from a terrible fate. Besides, Heath's always had an eye for the ladies." He thought of Janet, with regret; then his hand went up to Darcy's hair and he toyed with one of her coppery curls. Darcy looked a great deal like Janet, and Heath had been in love with Janet. "If anyone can get in his good graces, I think maybe it'd be you," he said softly.

"No!" She shook her head vehemently. "I can't do anything like that, Teak, and you know it," she said. "For one thing, I'm no good at flirtations. The original iceberg, and you expect me to get in the good graces of a man like Heath?"

He straightened, his eyes wary. "What do you mean, a man like Heath?"

That's right, she wasn't supposed to know what kind of a man Heath was. She swallowed hard, then answered. "You said yourself he's a ladies' man," she replied, and he smiled viciously.

"That should make it all the easier." His voice hardened. "I have to know if he's planning to take me right away. If he is, I'm getting out of here somehow. Leg or no leg."

She watched him anxiously. Why did he have to get mixed up in all this? Why couldn't he have told his superiors no? "He'll only track you down again," she said.

"Not if I'm in England."

"You think they'll let you quit?"

"I can try." He exhaled disgustedly. "I'm sick and tired of this whole mess anyway. All I want is to get back to Locksley Hall and my horses and all the comforts I've been missing."

Darcy studied Teak curiously. He meant it, and she knew he meant it. Teak loved the good life; that's why she'd been so surprised when he'd told her what he'd been doing the past few years, and it had been hard to imagine him living off the land, moving from one place to another with no real place to call his own. Teak wasn't a coward, far from it, but he liked life as well as the next man.

"Why don't you just wait and see what happens?" she asked, and his eyes darkened.

"Do you want me to hang, Darcy?"

She bit her lip as she looked into his blue eyes, stormy with vexation. "No," she whispered. "You know I don't want that."

His voice lowered, but his eyes were still dangerously alive. "Then do as I ask. Keep your eyes and ears open. I can't be downstairs, so I won't know what's going on. I have to have your help, darling, please."

He could be so gentle and loving when he wanted to be, and he reached out, pulling her into his arms, his voice vibrant. "You're all I have, Darcy. You're the only one in this whole crazy world who belongs to me. Don't turn away from me now, please."

Her eyes misted. They'd been friends for so long, and she did love him. Perhaps not the passionate love of her youth, but she did love him. He was reckless, spoiled, and arrogant at times, yet he had a charm that was captivating when he wanted to use it. She couldn't desert him. She had to help him. She couldn't let him hang, not Teak. "I'll try," she whispered. "Don't worry, Teak, I'll try," and he kissed her again long and hard, and for the first time in their relationship she felt a passion in Teak she'd never felt before as his kiss grew urgent and demanding.

His lips moved against her mouth, and he felt the familiar stirring inside him. God! How long had it been since he'd had a woman? Before, he'd always been able to curb his emotions when he was with her, because there were always other women willing to share his bed, but he'd lain here for weeks watching Ann, thrilling to the marvelous structure of her body. The exquisite way she had of tantalizing him with her low-cut dresses and seductive looks, yet he'd had no release from the desires she'd kindled in him, and Darcy's body suddenly became an answer to his longings.

His hand moved to her breast, and he began caressing her affectionately, his fingers dipping into her bodice, his lips still on her mouth. But at his touch he felt her body stiffen, and her mouth no longer moved beneath his, and she began to push him away.

"No, Teak," she gasped breathlessly, her mouth against his. "Please, don't. Not here on the bed. I can't, please!"

He stopped abruptly, his face close to hers, his breathing unsteady. "What is it? What's the matter,

Darcy? I only touched you," he whispered. "I've wanted to for so long. After all, you are going to be my wife."

She stared at him, her body unyielding. "Don't spoil it now, Teak, please," she whispered, trembling. "If you kiss me like that here alone in your room, anything could happen."

"I've got a broken leg, Darcy!" he whispered passionately, but she shook her head.

"I have a strange feeling that might not stop a man like you," she said, and he smiled.

"You flatter me, love."

"Not really." Her jaw set stubbornly. "But we're not married yet, Teak," she said, "and you have to admit there are things that could get out of hand . . . please." He sighed as his arms loosened from about her and she straightened. "Thank you," she said softly, and he held himself in check, his body aching as she moved from his arms.

"I'm sorry, Darcy. I . . . well, I'm sorry." She accepted his apology gracefully as she rearranged her clothes.

They talked awhile longer, trying unsuccessfully to decide what to do about Heath, and she finally left the room, tucking him in and blowing out the light.

He lay in the darkness for a long time after she left, wondering. He'd never tried anything like that before with Darcy, and for the first time since he'd met her, he began to wonder why. It wasn't that she was unable to arouse him, because there'd been many times he'd left her, aching so badly he was miserable. He'd kissed her often, yet never let the kiss get out of hand. Why? Because Darcy was Darcy, that's why. There was something about the way she carried herself that said a kiss is all I care to give, and even that with restraint. Yet behind her eyes, behind the cold reserve she clung to, he was sure there lay a woman of strong passions. He'd caught rare glimpses of it many times since he'd known her. Perhaps her first husband had smothered her emotions to the extent that she was afraid to feel anymore. One thing for sure, it would be interesting to watch her come out of the protective shell she'd built around herself. He only hoped he'd live to see it, and once more his thoughts centered on Heath's unexpected arrival.

He stirred, getting into a more comfortable position, listening to the occasional sounds of laughter that floated up from downstairs; then slowly he heard the voices diminish as Rebel and Beau left, the rest of the family went to bed, and the house grew quiet.

In a room down the hall, Heath sat on the edge of the bed, pulling off his boots one at a time, his mind racing over the past few hours. He'd known. Somehow, when he'd lifted the knocker on the door to the Château, he knew he'd find Teak inside. He'd gone to Beaufort first, to the house where he'd met Darcy McLaren, learning from her friends that she was at Port Royal. Darcy McLaren . . . Darcy McGill. He wondered when she'd married. What had happened to her husband, and when had she met Teak? Darcy and Teak! It didn't make sense, and he set his boots aside, standing up, beginning to shed his clothes. There were so many answers he wished he didn't have to hear.

The room they'd given him was luxurious, with thick green carpeting, fancy furniture, and delicate white accessories. It was the room that would have been his had he decided to make the Château his home, and it was used as a guest room. He stripped to his underwear, then walked to the window, pulling back the sheer white curtain, and stared out into the cool November night. Winters in the South were warm compared to the North, but still there were often cool nights, and occasionally in the dead of winter, light snow covered the countryside. When this happened, the camellias' pink and red blooms would thrust their heads above it to wink colorfully at the world in defiance, and he wondered what his life would have been if

he'd defied life in the same way and had stayed in Port
Royal instead of running away.

There was no use wondering. He had run away. He
closed his eyes, his hand involuntarily seeking the gold
earring, and he remembered the violet eyes of the
young girl named Heather back in Columbia. She was
his daughter. She had to be. There was no other explanation, and he cursed softly to himself as his hand
dropped from his ear and his eyes opened again, his
thoughts filled with Darcy.

She was still as beautiful as she had been the night
he'd first laid eyes on her, and he felt an ache in his
chest because he realized how much she and Janet
were entwined in his feelings, and thinking of Janet
hurt. He'd loved her as much as he'd once loved
Darcy. Janet had been what Darcy should have been to
him, and remembering her was painful. Sweet, lovely
Janet. They'd had so little time together, and she was
gone because of Teak, and now Darcy belonged to
Teak.

He turned abruptly from the window and walked to
the dresser to blow out the lamp, his mind passing over
the plush surroundings, his bare feet noiseless on the
carpet. He blew out the lamp, then stood poised, his
thoughts on the man who'd caused Janet's death. Right
now Teak lay in a soft bed in the other room, and
Heath's mind skipped back to that moment when the
door had opened and he'd seen him at the foot of the
stairs.

His first instinct had been to attack. To smash in
once and for all the face that had haunted him since
that day in the woods two years before. Heath had
hardly felt his father's handshake and hug and his
mother's kisses. He'd been almost oblivious of everything tonight except Teak's startled countenance there
in full view, and it was all he could do to control the
urge to accuse him in front of them all, yet he'd sub-
merged his anger and hatred beneath a veneer of
measured calm.

It wasn't the time. He couldn't see his mother hurt. Happiness shone in her eyes as she spoke of having all her children together again. He couldn't disillusion her. To arrest Teak and accuse him there in front of her, for her to learn that her younger son was to be hung as a spy, would tear her heart to pieces, so he'd played along, pretending nothing was wrong until he could think of an answer.

Even meeting Darcy was like playing a game. Pretending they'd never met, kissing her hand and talking to her as if she were a stranger, but would it work? Would Beau remember him talking about seeing Darcy McLaren and put all the loose ends together? And what was he to do now? His mission was to take Teak back to Washington, but he knew that was impossible at the moment. He didn't want to hurt his mother, and besides, at the moment Teak couldn't go very far with a broken leg, so he climbed in bed and lay thinking for hours, trying to figure out a solution.

The next morning he left his room early, his mind finally made up. There'd been no easy solution for the dilemma. Even now the thought of what he knew he'd eventually have to do, hurt. After all, Teak was his brother. As much as he'd come to hate him, they were of the same flesh. He hadn't always hated him. There'd been times when they were both young that life had been good for them. When they'd roamed the wilderness with Tcak's father, Quinn Locke, and learned the skills that had brought them both to what they were today. How time could change things.

Heath shrugged as he headed for the stairs, meeting Ann on her way up to Teak's room to dress his wounds. Ann had certainly turned into an attractive young woman, and he'd enjoyed the soft way her eyes had looked at him last night, and the kiss she'd bestowed on him on his arrival had been anything but sisterly. "How's your patient this morning, Ann?" he asked casually, his eyes admiring the deep burgundy dress she was wearing.

She sighed. "His leg's mending fine," she said, hefting the clean bandages onto her other arm, "but his wounds are taking a terribly long time to heal. They were badly infected. Even after Father cauterized them, they were seeping. I guess they were deeper than we thought."

He studied her face, noting the worried look in her eyes, and he frowned.

"Something wrong, Heath?" she asked, but he shook his head.

"No. I'll see you later," and she watched as he went downstairs; then she continued on to Teak's room.

During breakfast Heath acted normal, playing the part of the wayward son coming home for a visit, talking jovially with his mother and father, who were the only ones at the table; then after breakfast he joined Roth for a ride about the Château.

"Is the duchess still around?" he asked Roth as they left the stables and headed their spirited mounts toward the cotton fields.

"She never gives up," Roth replied. "She's still running River Oaks with an iron hand."

"Has she married Alan Minyard yet, or has he left?"

"Alan took off a few years back, but Rachel took her schooling from him well. She runs the whole place by herself. Although she still manages to hire the wrong men. I hear tell her new overseer is the meanest she's had yet."

Heath glanced at his father affectionately. He was still a virile man, handsome and distinguished, and he imagined Rachel was extremely vexed over her inability to seduce him away from his wife. Her attempts over the years were so obvious it had become a private joke among many of Roth's friends and contemporaries, but he'd never given her any reason for encouragement, and although she'd tried her best to shake Loedicia's faith in him, she'd failed miserably. Roth loved his wife with a passionate love that shone from his dark eyes whenever he looked at her or mentioned her name, and the years had only deepened that love. A twinge of pain struck at Heath's insides as he glanced at his father enviously.

When they had covered all the grounds at the Château, they rode upriver to the Tonnerre to visit Rebel and Beau, arriving in time for lunch, and Heath was pleased to see the success Beau had made of his life. The plantation was beautiful, the small house where he and Beau had once spent lonely nights had expanded into a white columned Georgian mansion with magnolia trees gracing the lawn beside fields of peach trees, their russet leaves glistening in the sun, and maple trees, shed of their leaves in the cool November air, lined the drive that circled up to the front door.

They had built a big house, planning on a large family, but had had only the two children, Cole, now nineteen and a soldier somewhere with General Jackson's army, and Lizette, named after Loedicia's dear friend. Lizette was a young lady of fifteen attending finishing school in Charleston. Beau no longer fought his Indian heritage. He'd learned to accept it and proved it made no difference in his abilities. He made as much money as his neighbors, even more, and had become one of the leading men of the community. At forty, with a touch of frost at his temples, his face handsome and swarthy, emerald-green eyes passionately alive, he was a far cry from the restless young man who'd left Fort Locke with Heath in search of Heath's father and had once captained a ruthless privateer. He was a happy, contented man, and once more as Heath watched his friend, the pangs of jealousy couldn't be stilled.

Later, as Heath and his father rode back toward the Château, he realized how empty his life was. Even Teak wasn't alone; he had Darcy.

"What's wrong, Heath?" asked Roth, interrupting his thoughts as they jogged along the dusty road.

Heath glanced at his father in surprise. "I didn't know it showed."

"Something's troubling you."

"Nothing I can't handle."

"You're not planning to leave us again?"

"No." Heath shook his head. "Not for a while anyway."

Roth's eyes studied his son. "I was hoping you'd make your stay permanent this time."

"Permanent?"

"Don't you think it's time you stopped roaming and settled down?" he suggested. "I'm not going to last forever, you know, and this place is yours when we're gone. It's time you started learning how to run things."

Heath felt his stomach tighten as they rode along. "I didn't earn the Château, Father," he said, causing Roth to shake his head.

"One doesn't earn an inheritance, Heath," he answered, protesting. "It's simply there. Teak didn't earn the Locksley estates, he inherited them when Quinn died. The same as you'll inherit the Château, the shipyards, and everything that goes with it when I die."

Heath looked at his father gravely, his dark eyes like burning embers in his tanned face, his lips severely taut. "I can't stay," he answered bitterly.

"Can't or won't?"

"There's more to my coming here than just a visit, Father," he said. "Besides, you and Mother have a lot of years left."

"A lot?" Roth laughed. "What are you doing, making us immortal or something?" He leaned over and patted his horse's neck as the mare tossed her head. "Most of my friends and contemporaries are gone already," he continued as he straightened. "I'm sixty-six, Heath, a young sixty-six perhaps, thanks to your mother and the happiness she's given me, but let's face it, life could end at any time for me. I'd like to think you'd be around to help your mother if she needed it, and take care of things. Besides, it's time you settled down to a place of your own. You should have a wife and family. You're not getting any younger either. This wandering about is fine for a while, but a man needs roots. A place to call his own. I know. A man needs someone to love him, and someone he can love in return."

Heath glanced from his father off toward the road ahead, where white fences began to herald the start of his father's property, and Roth saw the haunted look in his son's eyes. Roth was sure he'd hit on part of Heath's trouble, but still something else was wrong. Heath was always unsettled and restless whenever he came to visit, but this time it wasn't the same. The easy charm and carefree banter seemed forced from him, and his eyes refused to relax, as if they were used to observing everything about him and instantly spotting danger, that they feared even to blink, afraid they'd miss something. Beneath the casual air he tried to emanate, he was like a coiled spring, ready to fly at a moment's notice, and there was a hardness about him that had never been there before.

"Heath, please, what's the matter?" he asked as they rode side by side, and Heath looked at him abruptly. "You said you had other reasons for coming here besides a visit."

Heath rubbed the soft hairs of his beard with one hand as they reined up alongside the white fence and moved up the lane toward the house, and he wondered if he should confide in his father, then decided against it for the moment and smiled cynically instead.

"Forget it," he answered as they rode back toward the stables. "It isn't really important," and Roth shook his head as he saw the forced smile fade from Heath's face and an intense gleam spring to his eyes as Darcy McGill emerged from the house and stood watching them.

She was wearing a deep green satin-lined cape, her coppery hair flowing freely about her shoulders, and Heath couldn't take his eyes from her.

"She's a lovely woman, isn't she?" Roth said as he watched Heath's eyes pour over her like a hungry bear at the sight of honey.

"Very lovely," Heath answered softly. "I wonder if Teak appreciates her."

Roth scowled, then let the words that had been at the tip of his tongue all day come forth. "What is it between you and Teak, Heath?" he finally asked. "Even your mother noticed the enmity between the two of you last night, and it's upset her."

Heath drew his eyes from Darcy, who was heading toward the stables, and he studied his father critically. "Has Mother said anything to you?"

They neared the stable doors, and Jacob met them, holding the horses while they dismounted. "She's in a quandary, Heath," he answered. "She loves you both, yet she knows something's wrong. She tried not to let it bother her, but she could see it in your eyes when you shook hands, and sensed it as you watched him go upstairs to his room." Roth patted his mare's flanks as Jacob led the horse away. "She knows there have been a lot of years between, and it's hard to go on loving someone who's like a stranger to you instead of a brother. . . . I hope that's all it is, Heath," he said, and Heath straightened, his face expressionless, his eyes on Darcy as she walked toward them, pulling her cape closer about her to ward off the cool late-afternoon air, and there was no chance to answer his father except with a quick assurance that nothing was the matter; then Darcy stood before them, her pale green eyes hesitant as she spoke.

"Mrs. Chapman said one of the stableboys could post this letter for me," she said, holding a small white envelope in her hand, and Heath's eyes steadied on hers, warm and full.

"Why not post it yourself?" he suggested. "We can hitch a buggy, and I'll drive you to Port Royal."

"Oh, I can't put you out," she said, her face flushed, but he disagreed.

"I have some errands in Port Royal myself," he said, his eyes boring into hers, "so you're not putting me out." He turned to Roth. "You don't mind, do you, Father?" he asked, and Roth shook his head.

How could he refuse without sounding ridiculous? But he wasn't sure he liked the idea. It was bad enough Heath seemed to dislike Teak; now he was taking an unusual interest in his brother's fiancée, and the look in Heath's eyes as he talked to Darcy was far too revealing. Minutes later, as the small buggy headed down the drive and Roth sauntered toward the house, he shook his head apprehensively, and if he could have heard the conversation that was going on between the two people in the buggy, he'd have been even more upset.

Heath flicked the reins as they pulled out onto the road. He was more than mildly aware of the woman at his side. She was no longer the happy-go-lucky girl he'd once known, but neither was she a cold unfeeling woman. He could sense it in every move she made. She was as aware of him as he was of her. Neither of them spoke for a few minutes.

Then: "I don't believe it," Heath said angrily as he headed the buggy toward the small town spread out on the banks of Port Royal Sound. "I just don't believe you're in love with Teak, Darcy. Why?" he asked.

Her lips quivered slightly as her hands clutched the letter in her lap. "Why not?" she retorted, her face flushing nervously. "I have a right to live my life as I want. I can fall in love with whomever I wish."

He glanced at her, his dark eyes coveting her shapely figure, warming to the youthful lines still gracing her face. "We have to talk, you know that, don't you?"

Her lips parted, and she sighed. "If you insist," she said softly, and as soon as they were out of sight of the Château, he pulled the buggy to the side of the road, then turned to her.

They just stared quietly, letting the years pass between them, remembering what had once been, and Darcy's heart was beating violently in her breast. Heath touched her cheek, the skin soft beneath his fingers, and the cold reserve began to fade from her eyes.

"Please, Heath," she whispered softly, her voice breaking, "we can't go back."

"I don't want to go back," he said gently, "not to what I was then. I'm not a spoiled, conceited youngster anymore, Darcy. I'm a man, I'm lonely, and I want what should have been mine all these years."

She looked at him, puzzled, her eyes wary. "What do you mean?"

"I want you and my daughter, because Heather *is* my daughter, isn't she, Darcy?" he asked, and he saw her flinch at the mention of Heather's name. "Isn't she, Darcy?" he asked again.

She pursed her lips as she gazed into his pained eyes, and she was suddenly transported back to that day in the meadow when love had been so sweet, and tears filled her eyes. What was she to do? She could lie to him, but he'd know she was lying.

"Yes," she whispered softly, her lips trembling, "yes, Heath. She's your daughter," she replied, "but she doesn't know, nor does Teak. I didn't even know he was your brother until I came here." Her eyes saddened. "How did you find out about Heather, anyway?"

"By accident. I was looking for Teak and discovered he'd become engaged to a Mrs. Darcy McGill."

Her eyes dropped from his, and she gazed down at the letter in her lap addressed to Heather McGill.

"Tell me about it, Darcy," he demanded, and she looked away. He took her chin in his hand and turned her face to him. "Darcy?"

She told him everything that had happened since the night he'd said good-bye and left her standing in the garden of her father's house in Beaufort. "Heather has no idea you're her father, Heath," she finished. "She thinks her father was a man named John McGill who died in Boston years ago."

Heath studied Darcy's eyes, their cool green replaced by flecks of gold that warmed them and made them come alive. To look at her coppery hair brought an ache to his loins, and he was reminded of Janet and the love she'd given him. A love that mingled with the love he'd once given this woman when they were both young and vulnerable. A love that seemed to be springing back to life within him whenever he looked at her.

"Do you love Teak, Darcy?" Heath asked, and she sighed.

"Yes."

"You don't sound very convincing."

"Why shouldn't I love him?"

Why? He knew why. "You don't know what he is."

"Don't I?"

His face darkened. "You can't know what he is!" he retorted, but her next words proved him wrong.

"What are you going to do with him, Heath?" she asked cautiously, and his face paled. "You see, I do know, don't I?" she went on. "He told me what he's been doing." Her hand moved to the lapel of his black velvet coat, and her fingers stroked it intimately. "Heath, he's only been fighting for his country, the same as you," she said. "Don't do this to him."

Heath's eyes narrowed as he stared at her. She knew! She knew what Teak was, and still she could defend him. "Fighting for his country?" he blurted angrily. "He's a traitor, Darcy. How can you defend a man who's done what he's done? How can you love a man like that? My God, have you changed that much?"

"If I have, I had a good teacher, Heath," she said. "I discovered a long time ago to love with my head and not with my heart. Teak's been good to me, and he cares, and he's not what you think." Her chin went up defiantly. "Yes, I love him."

"Enough to hang along with him?"

Her eyes widened as he went on. "Darcy, he's a spy. He's caused the deaths of hundreds of men, and anyone aiding him is equally as guilty. If you help him in any way, you're guilty too."

She stared into his eyes, her body trembling. "What am I to do, Heath, forget he exists?" she cried. "Forget the love he's given me? In spite of everything we've been to each other, I'm to turn on him now just because he's English, is that it? Maybe you can hate like that, I can't, Heath. Maybe you can turn against your brother simply because he chooses to live in a different country, but then, you never did know what loyalty was, did you?"

Her words struck deep, and he reached up, his hand covering hers, and she clutched his lapel. "You've never forgiven me, have you?" he asked bitterly, and her mouth twitched.

"Forgiven you? Why should I? You told me you loved me, and all the while you were making love to Cora." Her eyes grew hostile, the warmth in them replaced by cold calculation. "I'm not a naive young girl anymore, Heath. Maybe Teak isn't perfect, but he's been honest with me. He's never tried to be anything but himself. He didn't have to tell me what he's been, but he did. Were you ever that honest with me, Heath? If you had told me about Cora from the start, I might have been able to forgive you."

His hand tightened on hers. "Would you, Darcy? Would you have forgiven me?" He sneered. "I doubt it!"

"Did you give me a chance to try?"

"I asked your forgiveness."

"Afterward, yes. But did you ever once stop to think that I deserved to know the truth from the beginning? You knew I loved you, but you didn't love me enough to share with me. That's where you and Teak are different. At least he's honest with me, Heath. I know I'm not the first woman in his life, and perhaps I won't be the last." She smiled cynically. "I see that shocks you. Don't let it. Teak's told me he loves me as much as he's able to love anyone. Neither of us is young anymore either, we both know it, and I'm not sure I can even give him the love he needs. You see, I made up my mind a long time ago that I'd never let a man do to me what you did, Heath, and now I'm not sure I can even give myself to a man anymore. So if I fail Teak, I imagine he'll find a mistress somewhere to satisfy his needs, but knowing Teak, he'll never go behind my back."

"And you'd be satisfied with that?"

"Satisfied? Oh, no, Heath, I wouldn't be satisfied, but I could accept it. I'm no longer looking for what can never be anymore. The passions you kindled that day in the meadow died the night my father shot Cora, and I'm not sure I ever want to feel them again. Besides, love like that is only for the young."

He stared at her dumbfounded, and suddenly he knew what he'd sensed from the start. She wasn't in love with Teak, not the way a woman should love a man. She'd grown cold and unfeeling over the years, letting her head rule her heart, and the love she had for Teak was the logical love a woman talks herself into acecpting when real love has eluded her. Heath's hand began to caress the fingers still touching his lapel, and his eyes softened as they looked into hers.

"Is that what I've done to you, Darcy?" he whispered softly. "Have I ruined you for love? Was I the only one to ever make you feel?"

She shuddered, and her eyes faltered before his smoldering gaze. "Please, Heath, take me to Port Royal," she pleaded anxiously as she felt the warm vibrations emanating from his fingers as they caressed her hand, but he paid no attention to her faltering request.

His hand moved into her hair, and she looked at him sharply as he leaned toward her, his swarthy face beneath the clipped beard warming her inside with its nearness. He was so close, his breath touching her face, and his eyes devoured her.

"Darcy," he whispered softly, "has no one made you

come alive since I touched you last?" His hand curled about her neck, caressing it, turning her blood to liquid fire.

She didn't want him to do this to her, not again. Why did his nearness affect her like this? She fought violently against the sweet sensations he was stirring inside her. "Take your hands off me, Heath," she gasped frantically, her face pale, and his fingers stopped on the nape of her neck, their touch burning into her flesh.

"You don't like it?"

"I'm not seventeen anymore," she murmured bitterly, pushing both hands against him now to keep him away. "You can't just walk back into my life and take up again where you left off, Heath, I won't let you."

He could feel the vibrations passing between them and saw her lips quiver as she tried to make her protest sound convincing. She was fighting. Fighting to keep her rigid self-control. Fighting the natural instinct he knew she was feeling. She was still angry and hurt, but behind that anger and hurt somewhere was still the passionate woman he'd once known. He'd seen it in her eyes only moments ago.

He leaned toward her, bending to kiss her, but she turned her head quickly and his lips touched her cheek, searing their brand on her soft skin as she cried out. "No, Heath!" She couldn't let him. She wouldn't, not again! He wasn't going to break down her barriers. He was no different now than he had been then. He was a wanderer, a charmer. Hadn't she seen the way Ann looked at him, her eyes warm with desire? "Not again, Heath," she whispered stubbornly, trying to push him away, her body stiff and unyielding. "Maybe once I was taken in by your charm and looks, but not again." Her eyes flashed, and his lips eased against her cheek, then moved to beneath her ear, sending sweet shocks flooding through her, but she wouldn't give in, in spite of the yearning that was kindling in her loins. She pushed harder against him, struggling until she finally freed herself and he settled back, staring at her.

"Take me to Port Royal, Heath," she gasped breathlessly, on the verge of tears, and his jaw tightened obstinately.

"And what of us? Nothing's been settled, Darcy, nothing at all."

"Hasn't it?" she asked grimly. "Things were settled for us years ago, Heath."

"And Heather? What of her? I suppose I'm just supposed to ignore the fact that she's my daughter?"

Darcy shook her head. "I'm sorry, Heath." She glanced at the letter in her hand. It was bent and crushed from when she'd struggled against him; then her green eyes searched his anxiously. "Please, can't we talk about it later when we're both not so upset?"

His eyes softened cynically. "I'm not upset."

"Well, I am!" She straightened and sniffed in wiping a stray tear from her cheek. "I feel like my head's about to explode." She smoothed the letter, rubbing her fingers across Heather's name on the front of the envelope, then looked back up into Heath's eyes. "Let me have time to breathe, Heath, please," she whispered softly. "The past few days have been one shock right after another. Let me catch my breath, and then maybe we can talk rationally about Heather."

Heath stared at her, at the desire he saw masked in her eyes, and he sighed. Maybe she was more right than she realized. Maybe he had come on too strong, but, oh, God, she was so lovely and he'd felt so alone for so long, like a drowning man reaching for a lifeline to stay afloat. She had been his once, and he wanted her again; he knew that now. The more he looked at her and talked to her, the more he realized he'd never stopped loving her. He smiled warmly and watched her scowl as he took the reins, driving the buggy back onto the road, and for the rest of the ride to Port Royal the conversation was stilted and cool as Heath told Darcy of his plans for Teak and she argued heatedly against them, unsuccessfully.

ॐ 11 ॐ

The head of Teak's bed was directly next to the window, and it was near dark when he leaned over and pulled back the rose velvet drapes and sheer white curtain, looking beyond the huge white columns that crossed the veranda at the front of the house, watching the buggy come up the drive and disappear around back toward the stables.

All morning he'd fretted. First over Ann's nasty remarks, then Darcy's preoccupation with private thoughts she wouldn't share with him, and now he wondered what she might have learned in her drive with Heath. He shifted in bed nervously half an hour later when Darcy finally came into the room, and she could see he was irritated.

"Did you have to go all the way into town with him?" he asked as she entered. "When I told you to try to find out what his plans were, I didn't mean for you to throw yourself at him."

She glanced at him quickly as she closed the door behind her. "Don't be an ass, Teak," she snapped, still shaken by her encounter with Heath and in no mood for Teak's arrogance. "I've found out what you wanted to know. Aren't you interested?"

He glanced at her suspiciously.

"For heaven's sake, do you trust me or don't you?" she said, recognizing the look on his face.

His eyes narrowed as he studied her flushed face and the strange, almost glazed look to her eyes. "I don't trust my brother," he answered emphatically, and she pursed her lips, then shrugged as she sat on the edge of the bed.

"Well, do you want to hear it or not?"

He nodded.

"Your brother was quite frank with me, Teak," she replied. "He told me you were a spy known as War-bonnet and that as soon as your leg's healed, which Ann says should be in a few days, he's taking you back to Washington to hang as a traitor, and if I try to help you escape in any way, I'll hang right beside you."

Teak stared at her angrily as he listened to her blunt words; then he clenched his teeth together viciously, remembering the threat Heath had shouted that day in the Michigan woods. "Damn him!" he said, wincing as he moved too quickly and the wound in his shoulder pulled. "He's never going to forget that woman!" He laid his head back on the pillow. "Oh, I wish to God I could bring her back to life. That I could have stayed Tecumseh's hand."

Darcy stared at him, puzzled. "What on earth are you talking about?" she asked, bewildered, for neither Teak nor Heath in all they'd told her had mentioned a word about a woman.

So for the first time since that fateful day two years before, Teak talked of Janet and told Darcy the whole episode. "I didn't want her dead," he explained as he finished the story. "I never wanted Janet dead, but he'd never believe me." He sighed. "My threats were only that, threats." He reached out and touched Darcy's cheek, running his finger along her jawline affectionately. "She reminded me so much of you, my love," he confessed wearily. His hand moved beneath her chin as he straightened against the pillows, and he turned her to face him and saw the tears in her eyes. "Are the tears for me or him, Darcy?" he asked huskily, and she shook her head.

"Neither, Teak," she whispered softly, her heart in a turmoil, "they're for me," and she pulled her chin from his hand and stood up, walking to the dressing table to stare at herself in the mirror.

Downstairs, Loedicia, pretending to read, watched from the other side of the drawing room as Heath and Ann sat before a gaming table battling over a game of cribbage.

Ann was wearing a deep blue dress with tucked bodice, leg-o'-mutton sleeves, and a full skirt caught up with blue velvet ribbons to reveal a pleated petticoat, but Heath was dressed more casually in white silk shirt, buff breeches, and soft doeskin boots. Ann's eyes followed Heath's face adoringly as she hung on every word he said, and Loedicia glanced at Roth standing near the window, who nodded and also watched the exchange between the two, but neither player seemed aware of being watched.

"You always win," complained Ann as they finally put the cards away, and Heath smiled.

"Because you don't concentrate, my dear sister," he replied, settling back in his chair. His dark eyes gazed into hers. "You're always too busy asking me questions."

"That's because you never tell us anything without our asking first," she countered. "You're getting as bad as Teak. I swear he's as closemouthed as you are." She shrugged as she looked across the gaming table at him. "Are you hungry?" she asked abruptly, conscious of his eyes on her, and he admitted to being starved, since it had been hours since he and Darcy had dined unharmoniously in Port Royal, so they excused themselves and headed for the kitchen arm in arm to talk Mattie out of an evening's repast before retiring.

Ann and Heath spent the rest of the evening in the kitchen talking intimately over wine, biscuits, and cold chicken and were still there when Darcy came back downstairs to bid everyone good night, and they were still there when Loedicia and Roth followed Darcy upstairs.

"Aren't you tired too?" Heath asked Ann as he

watched his parents disappear from the kitchen door, where they'd stood to wish them good night only a few minutes before. Ann sighed as she stood up, walking past the huge fireplace that graced the kitchen wall, her dress swishing softly as she walked, the deep blue of it enhancing her golden amber hair.

"Tired? Yes, I'm tired," she said, looking about the familiar room, now empty except for herself and Heath. "I'm tired of Port Royal and I'm tired of the Château and everything else around here."

The glass of wine he was raising to his lips stopped in midair as Heath watched her move over to look out the window above the sink where Mattie always cleaned the vegetables.

"I wish I could do like you do, Heath," she went on, her back still to him. "I wish I could come and go as I please. I wish I didn't have to account to anyone for what I did or didn't do. I wish I weren't me."

He stood up, setting down the half-empty glass of wine, and walked across the room to stand behind her. The lamp on the table cast a soft glow, and it caught the golden highlights in her loose flowing hair that hung to her waist. "What's the matter, little sister?" he asked playfully, and suddenly she turned on him, her dark eyes wide, lips trembling.

"Will you stop that!" she cried unhappily, and her heart went out to him. "For God's sake, Heath, I'm not your sister! Not really," she blurted angrily. "Do you always have to think of me as your sister?" Her voice lowered as her long-lashed eyes gazed into his. "Can't you think of me as a woman just once? Please, Heath," she pleaded. "I'm not your little sister anymore!"

Heath stared at her, dumbfounded, and slowly felt a stirring inside. His eyes traced the delicate lines of her face and stopped on her mouth, warm and inviting. She was right. She was a woman, soft and desirable.

Her hand touched his beard, then moved to his lips, brushing them lightly. She had waited so long for him to return. Heath, with his warm eyes and loving heart. He was special. Not one man in Port Royal had ever measured up to him. Even when she was little and he'd teased her, it had made her feel important. He'd never treated her like a nuisance or mocked her heritage. He was so different from Teak. Her fingers pressed his lips and she felt weak and giddy inside, wondering what it would be like to feel those lips on hers.

"Heath," she whispered softly, "I've been waiting so long for you to come home."

He reached up, his hand enclosing about her fingers; then he kissed their tips lightly before releasing her hand again and letting his arm creep about her waist, pulling her hard against him, and suddenly Ann wasn't Ann anymore. She was Janet and Darcy and all the women he'd ever made love to, and her body was yielding against his, molding to him passionately, dredging all his hidden desires to the surface.

Her sloe eyes focused on him ardently as her heart pounded against his chest. "Love me, Heath," she murmured breathlessly, and Heath felt himself hardening against her.

"You don't know what you're asking," he whispered.

"Don't I?" She trembled against him. "Why do you think I've discouraged all the men in Port Royal who tried to court me? I didn't want them, Heath. I wanted you. I knew that one day you'd come back, and I've been waiting. Heath, I love you," she confessed, "I've always loved you, and not as a sister. I need you, Heath!"

His hands were on fire as he felt her well-formed body beneath his fingertips. She was a sensuous woman, and his body was responding to her. My God! What was he to do? This whole thing didn't make sense. He knew she'd been infatuated with him when she was younger, but he thought by now she'd outgrown it. He should have known by the greeting she'd given him last night and the way her eyes melted when she looked at him.

"Ann, we have to be practical," he began, his desires warring with his common sense. "It wouldn't work."

Her face flushed crimson, and he knew she was close to tears. "Don't you want me, Heath?" she asked helplessly as she stared into his face, then she gasped and shook her head in disbelief as she thought she read his eyes. "You don't! Oh, Lord, Heath, you don't, do you?" she cried. "I can see it in your eyes," and she pulled away, turning her back to him. She'd been so sure. She'd wanted him so badly for so long, the thought that he might not want her hadn't crossed her mind until now. She was so embarrassed. Why didn't he want her? Teak did! Why not Heath? Every day she felt Teak's eyes on her, stirring her, wreaking havoc with her emotions and making her aware of the fact that her body was overripe for love.

She'd felt the first stirrings of desire in her loins years ago when Heath had been home, and after kissing him good-bye when he'd left again, she'd vowed to herself that only Heath would ever fulfill her dreams, and now he didn't even want her. Wasn't she desirable enough? Her body ached with longing. She wanted to feel what love was like. To know the intimate happiness it could bring and to quiet the urgent passions within her that were becoming almost impossible anymore to restrain. If she didn't soon, she'd go mad.

Her head flew back violently and her eyes closed as Heath leaned forward, his lips brushing her ear.

"It isn't that I don't want you, Annie," he murmured, his voice strained. "It's . . ." He reached for her shoulders, but she pulled away from him frantically, not wanting to hear lame excuses. Not wanting to listen to hollow words that had no meaning, and she half-ran across the room, stopping at the kitchen door only long enough to take a deep breath that held back a sob; then she walked sedately into the foyer, head held high, her heels tapping lightly on the marble floor, and started up the stairs.

Heath clenched his teeth stubbornly, his body desperately trying to forget the sensuous feelings her intimate pleadings had aroused, but it wasn't that easy. It had been a long time since he'd made love to a woman, and Darcy's rejection of him earlier in the day had left him vulnerable. He was already tingling inside. Quickly he moved to the table and picked up the lamp, shielding the flickering candle within as he followed her, trying to overtake her, and his hand shot out, covering hers, holding it tightly beneath his as he caught up to her and they reached her bedroom door, opening it.

"Annie!" he whispered huskily. "Don't run from me, please," and she stiffened.

Her room was directly at the top of the stairs, opposite Teak's room, and she turned to Heath, her voice hushed. "Don't pity me, Heath," she said, forcing her hand out from beneath his. "Please. I couldn't stand pity."

His eyes thrilled at the sight of her. She was lovely with a natural beauty that made him wince. "Oh, God, Annie, I don't pity you, I pity me," he gasped. "Do you know what you've done to me?"

"Don't Heath. Don't pretend."

"Pretend?" He reached out with his free hand and pulled her close against him and she felt his hardness through the soft folds of her full skirt, her body molding subtly against him. "Does this feel like I'm pretending?" he asked, and he kissed her deeply, moving her through the doorway into her room, shutting the door quietly behind them with his foot, as his lips held her captive.

She moaned beneath his mouth, her body yielding, then gasped breathlessly as he finally drew his lips from hers. "Why?" she asked heatedly, her eyes glazed with desire, and he sighed as he set the lamp on the bureau beside the door, his eyes never leaving hers.

"Mother!" he explained in one word, and she brushed the explanation aside as easily as he had given it.

"She'll never know," she whispered, and he groaned helplessly as his lips covered hers again and his hands moved behind her, beginning to unfasten the hooks on her dress.

He let her clothes flutter to the floor slowly as he kissed and fondled her; then he picked up her warm, naked body and crossed the floor, laying her gently in the middle of the bed, where the light from the lone flickering candle in the lamp on the dresser shone on her, turning her skin to creamy velvet, her firm full breasts rising and falling seductively.

Heath's hands caressed her, his fingers hardening her nipples, his lips on her breasts and mouth, arousing her to a fever pitch until she wanted to crawl inside him; then slowly her hands moved beneath the silk shirt he wore, and she thrilled to the feel of his body beneath her fingertips. Her hands kneaded his flesh erotically, and she murmured her longings against his mouth until he knew she was ready, her body opening for him, and his hand between her thighs captured the throbbing of her desire.

His hands released her momentarily, and he straightened, pulling his shirt hurriedly from his pants, unfastening the cuffs; then suddenly he froze, his eyes glued to her body as a series of bumps and bangs, followed by a half-muffled cry and a loud shattering crash, echoed from the hall outside her bedroom door. His fingers stopped on his shirt as he stared at her, her mouth open, eyes widened in fright.

"What was that?" she gasped, her voice breaking. Heath whirled toward the door, his shirt forgotten, and he grabbed the lamp as he pulled the door open. Ann quickly moved from the bed toward her dressing gown, her body shaking violently, as if someone had thrown cold water on it.

Heath stepped into the hall gingerly, his desire for Ann forgotten, the lamp held away from his body, his eyes searching into the shadows; then he inhaled sharply, the hair at the nape of his neck prickling anxiously as he saw the banister broken in several places as it still tried to cling tenaciously to the stairs. He moved to the top of the staircase, then stepped hurriedly but cautiously down them, the lamp he carried bringing the shadows to life, and there, at the foot of the stairs, his battered body sprawled on the marble floor of the foyer, lay Teak.

Heath saw Teak wince and knew he was still conscious; then he glanced quickly at his brother's leg. The splints that had held it were shattered into a dozen pieces, scattered about the floor, and the leg lay limply in an awkward position, and there was no doubt it had been broken again. Heath leaned forward, the lamp lighting Teak's face, and Teak's bright blue eyes were filled with hate.

"Well, were you going someplace, brother?" Heath asked sarcastically as he stared down at Teak, and Teak's lips curled viciously, the pain from his leg goading him on.

"None of your damn business!" he snarled back; then his eyes shifted up the stairs, catching sight of Ann descending them hurriedly behind Heath.

Her hair was disheveled, the ribbon that usually held it away from her face was missing, and the warm flush, barely discernible on her cheeks, was beginning to pale. Her hands trembled nervously, tightening the sash on her scarlet dressing gown, and Teak knew instinctively she was naked beneath it.

"My God, what happened?" she asked as she slipped deftly by Heath and knelt beside Teak, unaware that Teak's eyes had settled back angrily on Heath.

He knows, thought Heath as Ann examined Teak's leg and Heath watched Teak's eyes narrow, looking first at him, then back to Ann. Teak knew that he and Ann had been in her room together, he was sure, but he brushed it aside quickly as his parents and Darcy, awakened by the noise, joined them at the foot of the stairs and the place was suddenly turned into bedlam.

Even Mattie came scurrying from the servants' quarters and Jacob lumbered in to see if he could help.

Not only was Teak's leg badly broken, but he was bruised and sore all over from the fall, and although he was thankful to be alive, he cursed himself for his clumsiness as they carried him back upstairs and sent for the doctor. He explained to them lamely that he must have been sleepwalking, a habit he'd had for some years now, because he had no knowledge of why he'd tried to navigate the stairs in the dead of night without even a lamp to light his way.

Heath, however, knew better. He could bet that Teak knew exactly what he was doing and had never sleepwalked in his life. He'd been trying to get away. If he could have managed to sneak from the house and hide out for just a few days, he'd have been in the clear, his leg completely healed, and the hunt would have started all over again. Yes, Teak knew exactly what he'd been trying to do.

"Maybe you should have helped him," Heath sneered under his breath at Darcy sometime later as they all moved away from the bed to let Ann give Teak some laudanum to help ease his pain until the doctor arrived.

Darcy pursed her lips angrily. "I would have if he'd asked me," she whispered low enough so only Heath could hear, and their eyes locked dangerously as they followed Loedicia and Roth out into the upstairs hall. "But he didn't, so I didn't," she went on. "So now what are you going to do, Heath, drag him off anyway, even though he's half-dead?" and Heath stopped, his eyes intent on her face.

What was he going to do? He'd had everything planned so well and he'd steeled his body and his mind to accept the inevitable. He'd planned to break the news to his mother, knowing it would break her heart, yet knowing she'd have Roth to comfort her; then he was going to take Teak back to face whatever awaited him, even though he knew once it was over he would never return, because his mother would never forgive him.

He loved his mother so very much, yet he had a duty to his country and a score to settle that went far beyond his own feelings. What he'd planned to do wasn't only for Janet, but for all the men at Detroit, Fort Dearborn, and all the other outposts in the Northwest Territory who had suffered because of Teak, and for Bladensburg and the president too. His decision had been a hard one to make, and in making it he'd condemned himself to more years of wandering the face of the earth alone, but he'd had to make it, and had finally consigned himself to the inevitable.

He'd watched his mother when they'd carried Teak upstairs and laid him on the bed, and he glanced toward her now, standing in the hall as she talked with his father, and the misery in her eyes hurt him deep inside.

"Well, what are you going to do now?" asked Darcy again as she stared at Heath's pale face, and he glanced away from his mother, back toward the open door to Teak's room, his eyes gazing beyond, into it, where Ann still hovered over the bed, trying to make Teak more comfortable, and he had no answer. Instead, he turned and walked toward the top of the stairs.

"I'll go wait for the doctor," he said forcefully, leaving her no chance for further comment, and there were tears in Darcy's eyes as she watched him slowly descend the stairs.

There was little sleep at the Château that night, and the days that followed were hectic. At first Ann spent all her spare time nursing Teak again, and Heath was grateful, because the day after the accident, remembering the fateful results of his earlier indiscretions with Darcy and Cora, he'd thanked God for not letting him make the same mistake again with Ann, and he tried to avoid her as much as possible. Her constant preoccupation with Teak was a blessing. Still, there were times she'd catch him alone, her eyes inviting him, her words holding double meanings as she toyed with him seductively, and he had a terrible time fighting to keep his desires in check. He couldn't be rude to her, and he never wanted to hurt her, but he was determined not to let his emotions run away with him again.

The ridiculous part of the whole affair was that it wasn't really Ann he wanted, it was Darcy. Yet each day that he and Darcy were thrown together, the animosity between them deepened until they began to snap at each other for no apparent reason at all, the air between them often sending up visual sparks that neither made any attempt to quell. So it was inevitable that they began to try to purposely ignore one another.

The days dragged on slowly through November and on toward Christmas, and in spite of the war, a festive air began to fill the Château. Heath had decided, under the circumstances, to forgo dragging Teak bodily from Port Royal for a while, and was glad he could postpone the ugly scene with his mother that he knew lay in the future, without really feeling guilty about reneging on his duty. After all, you couldn't move a man with a badly broken leg all those miles back to Washington. Besides, with Teak immobile, Warbonnet was no longer a threat, so he'd bide his time until the splints were ready to come off Teak's leg again, and in the meantime, even though Darcy and he always were at odds, it gave him a chance to see her and be near her, although he was the last to admit it, even to himself. Instead, he spent his time visiting Rebel and Beau and getting to know his niece, Lizette, who came home for the Christmas holidays, capturing her young, romantic heart with his magnetic charm. And he spent a good deal of time with his mother, trying to make up for the sorrow he knew he was going to bring her. He was actually overly attentive, and he even reluctantly accepted his father's eagerly given knowledge about the running of the plantation, although he knew there was no future in his knowing, and all the while Teak lay in his room fuming, practically chained to his bed, because the doctor warned him if the leg didn't heal right he could lose it, and he felt as helpless as an old woman.

Darcy visited with Teak every day, and as Christmas neared, they began trying to think of a plan for his escape, and as Teak lay abed watching the world moving around him, his thoughts too began to roam, and more often than he wanted to admit, they were centering on Ann.

Even in his dreams she was always there. Always Ann. The little minx was getting under his skin. He found himself watching the bedroom door anxiously every morning for her to gracefully slip in, regretting the little time she gave him, thinking of all kinds of excuses to keep her near him longer so he could look into her dark eyes and feel the warmth that crept through him clear to his toes. Strange, he used to hate sloe eyes. But then, that was before he discovered the strange depths that dwelt in them.

And her hair. God! It was beautiful. Like an amber cloud, long and full, and he loved to smell the cape-jasmine scent that lingered on it when she leaned close to him. It was intoxicating. Sometimes it almost drove him mad when she fluffed his pillows, her full breasts brushing his arm, her lips so close to his he had all he could do to keep from crushing her sensuous mouth to his, and he wondered if she knew the effect she was having on him. Even Darcy had never aroused the wild passions this so-called sister of his was kindling in him, and yet her actions, her verbal abuses, always left him in an emotional turmoil so that he snapped everyone's head off, including hers. Just once! If she'd only treat him decent just once. . . .

Christmas Eve brought Teak downstairs for the first time since the accident. The huge house was decorated for the holidays with pine boughs, holly, and an enormous Christmas tree that adorned the front window in the drawing room, where packages galore were spread

bencath its boughs, and with the aroma of savory
smells filling the halls, the atmosphere reminded Teak
of Locksley Hall and the last time he'd been home. Oh,
what he wouldn't give to have it all back again. To
walk about the majestic halls and gaze out from its
Norman towers across the countryside.

He sat in the overstuffed chair near the tree, wearing
a dark green robe, his bandaged and splinted leg
propped on a footstool in front of him, and watched
the goings-on with a critical eye and a glass of brandy
to soothe his usually irritable disposition.

Roth was resplendent this evening in long buff
trousers, ruffled shirt, and a deep red velvet coat that
made his hair look all the whiter, while it matched the
color of the dress Loedicia wore. The red clashed with
her violet eyes, thought Teak as he sipped his brandy,
but it enhanced her frosted hair and made her look
even younger, and he realized again what a beautiful
woman his mother was. Then his lips curled in a sneer.
Beautiful and deceitful, he thought, and his eyes caught
Darcy as she walked into the room and stopped to talk
to his mother.

Darcy wore a dress of emerald green, her copper
hair piled atop her head, the combination of colors
striking with her fair complexion, but it was Ann who
startled him as she followed Darcy into the room, carrying a bundle of packages she deposited under the
tree. Her amber hair was caught up and twisted into a
full chignon at the nape of her neck, the hair pulled
back softly from her forehead, emphasizing her al-
mond-shaped eyes, and the stark white silk dress she
wore with its draped bodice and yards of billowing
skirt revealed her shoulders and darkened her creamy
skin, giving it a tawny hue. She looked like a goddess,
all golden and white, and as his heart thumped inside
of him, he downed a large gulp of brandy. Then suddenly his throat constricted and he almost choked on
the brandy as Heath, immaculately dressed, his gold
brocade coat offsetting dark trousers and vest, walked

in and joined Ann at the tree. He handed her a present to put under it, and she looked up at his dark bearded face, the gold ring in his ear shining unusually bright, and she smiled warmly, her face soft and desirable.

"Damn him!" cried Teak to himself as he watched them together, and suddenly he didn't feel like Lord Locksley anymore. He wasn't an earl, he was only Heath's younger brother, living again in his shadow, envying Heath's charm with the ladies. Hadn't it always been that way? He had never truly been himself until the day Heath left Fort Locke. Even then he'd never really been Teak Locke, he'd still been Heath's younger brother, until England. Then there'd been the money and the title, and he'd had his own identity with people who had never known Heath. Now, staring at Heath's handsome face again, Teak once more felt what it was to be second-rate, and he looked away quickly, trying to forget as Rebel and Beau arrived and his eyes stopped briefly on their daughter, Lizette.

Lizette was all of fifteen, mature for her age, wearing a dress of a deeper green than that worn by Darcy, her ebony hair piled atop her head, and except for her gorgeously green eyes, she was undoubtedly a replica of what Loedicia must have looked like when his father had first met her. The thought was painful, so he looked away quickly to Rebel, who managed to capture and hold his attention as she hurried toward him. She was carrying a huge white-tissue-papered and red-ribboned package, and when she reached him she held it out for him to see.

Her coloring was his coloring, golden and fair, and even though they'd fought as children and he'd resented her closeness to Heath, at the moment she was the only one who really made him feel as if he belonged. They were both so much like their father, and her periwinkle-blue dress was a brilliant contrast to the reds, golds, greens, and white of the others.

"This package is especially for you, Teak," she said

as she teased him with it, smiling, and he forced a return smile he didn't really feel.

"What did you do, buy me a new leg?" he quipped, and her eyes frowned.

"I wish to God I could," she said, then whisked the package to the tree, joining Heath and Ann, but it was Beau, suavely dressed in black velvet, who saved the evening, taking an edge off the tension he saw building rapidly between the two brothers. In his inimitable, stony-faced way, he began reminiscing about Fort Locke and the crazy things they all did when they were young, and after a while even Heath and Teak forgot that they were enemies. They relived adventures long forgotten, when Quinn was still alive and their lives had been less complicated, and Beau's emerald-green eyes shone brightly as he watched the brothers actually laughing together over some of their escapades. By the time the eggnog was passed around and Lizette seated herself at the piano to accompany their caroling, Heath and Teak were frowning at each other, puzzled over their actions, and wondering where the years had gone and how they'd ended up like this.

Teak leaned his head back in the chair as everyone gathered about the piano, and he listened with eyes closed to the voices that rose in song; then suddenly he made the mistake of opening his eyes and straightening in the chair. It was just in time to catch a glance that passed between Darcy and Heath. It was a glance he couldn't understand, that held her heart in her eyes, giving Heath an open invitation, and Teak stared at them in disbelief. In all the years he'd known her, she'd never looked at him like that, and he felt betrayed. The anger inside him rose once more. First Ann, now Darcy. Was no woman safe from his wandering eye? He remembered Janet's words, thrown at him when his body had finished taking her. Even Janet had told him he could never compare to Heath, and Teak looked quickly from the piano, staring at the

Christmas tree, the warmth that had filled his heart only moments ago replaced by a cold dread.

Rebel, Beau, and Lizette were staying the night, so they'd be there in the morning to open presents, and later that evening, after everyone else was in bed, Loedicia and Roth sat quietly on the floor in front of the fireplace reminiscing, the only light in the room coming from the crackling flames before them.

Loedicia leaned her head back on Roth's shoulder, feeling the sweet strength from him filling her, and she sighed. "How do you think it's going to turn out?" she asked softly, her voice hushed, and his answer was vague.

"Who knows, love? They're both unpredictable."

"But they're brothers. They shouldn't hate so." She stared into the flames. "For a while tonight I thought Beau had bridged the anger between them, but I guess it's never that easy to make people forget. I'm sure Teak's still blaming Heath for Quinn's death, and Heath's still blaming Teak for his treatment of me over the years. Sometimes I could throttle them both."

"Maybe it's deeper than that. Who knows?" he asked, and she looked at him, startled.

"You think maybe I was right, then?" she asked. "That Teak was one of the soldiers who raided Washington? After all, he did lie to us," she reminded him; then she frowned. "But that doesn't make sense either. If he had been one of the soldiers, why wasn't he wearing a uniform? Those fishermen said he was still in the same clothes he had on when they'd fished him out of the water." She shook her head. "Besides, what would that have to do with Heath? I know he works for the government, but he'd have no reason to suspect or even know Teak had lied to us. I just don't understand it." She leaned closer against him, nestling her face against his neck lovingly. "I just don't understand. All I know is that for the first time in years I have all of my children together again, and nothing's turning out as it should!"

Roth's lips brushed her forehead and his arms went about her, holding her close as he looked over her head toward the Christmas tree, its ornaments glittering in the light from the dancing flames, and he knew she was right. Something was bothering Heath, and something was bothering Teak. What it was, he had no idea, and whether it had anything to do with Teak's mysterious appearance or not, he had no way of knowing, but he was determined that if there was any way to find out, he would.

The next day Teak again joined everyone downstairs, the gifts were opened, dinner enjoyed, and Christmas festivities begun. For the rest of the week they entertained company at the Château and were entertained at the homes of friends, but always Teak was conveniently absent. His reason for not accompanying them to visit friends could be understood: he was unable to travel. But his stubborn reluctance to come downstairs when guests arrived bothered Loedicia. Finally, by New Year's Eve she had taken all the excuses she could handle. A number of guests were expected the next day for dinner, close friends, and she was determined that he was going to make an appearance, and Roth caught her heading for Teak's room with fire in her eyes.

"Just once my son is going to do something I want him to do, or he's going to give me a good explanation why he can't," she said angrily as he stared at her. "I have two sons and two daughters," she went on firmly, "and it's time our friends met them all."

"He won't come down," insisted Roth.

"Then I'll know the reason why."

"Do you want me to come with you?"

She shook her head. "No. You'd better get dressed," she said impatiently. "We're to leave in less than an hour for the ball, and you're not even ready."

Roth smiled. "But I see you are," he said, and took her by the shoulders, examining her thoroughly. "And a more stunning wench I've yet to see," he whispered softly, watching the amused tilt to her mouth, for she was lovely in spite of her anger. Her dress matched her violet eyes, and the diamonds at her ears and throat gave a regal command to her coiffured hair with its topknot of ringlets. She looked far younger than her years, and her eyes betrayed the joy she found in his teasing words.

"You're impossible, sir," she quipped softly, and he laughed, folding her into his arms, kissing her long and hard.

"Now, go play mother," he said amiably, releasing her, and she licked her lips sensuously as she gazed into his warm dark eyes; then she turned without saying another word and continued on her way to Teak's room, while Roth went to the master bedroom to dress for the New Year's ball that was being held at one of the neighboring plantations.

Teak was lying in bed with a book, trying to keep his mind on the words before him, when Loedicia knocked and entered. He stared at her curiously, aware from the moment she came in that she was upset. She walked to the bed first and glanced down at the book he was reading, then clenched both hands together and wandered to the window, her conversation trite and casual; then suddenly she turned on him, tilted her head defiantly, and confessed what was on her mind.

"Tomorrow afternoon, Teak," she said abruptly, "Roth and I are having dinner guests. They're old and close friends, and I know you haven't come down to dinner before when we've had guests, and I haven't made a fuss either, but I'm afraid this time it's different. I'm afraid if you don't appear tomorrow, Teak, this time I will make a fuss." Her eyes flashed as she stared at her younger son, now a grown man in his thirties.

"What's so special about tomorrow?"

"I told you, they're old friends."

"Mother, I'm from England," he tried to explain. He didn't want to meet their friends. With Roth once a senator, he was afraid he'd run into someone from Washington who'd recognize him. "This country is at war with England. Won't your friends think it's strange?"

"They don't have to know where you're from."

"You mean you've never mentioned that your son's an English lord?"

"Well, yes, I have, but I've already told them about the shipwreck and . . . they know you're here, Teak, people talk . . . they're anxious to meet you."

"Why?"

"Because you're my son. I've told them about you over the years, and they know I'm proud of you. I'm proud of both my sons, not just Heath."

"Are you?" he asked, his eyes studying her sardonically. "How strange. Are you really proud of me, Mother?" he asked again. "That's certainly a surprise, because, you see, I'm not proud of you."

"You're . . . ?" Her eyes faltered, unable to believe the words that fell from his lips, and she stared at him dumbfounded. "You're . . . What do you mean? What on earth are you talking about, you're not proud of me?" and he laughed, his voice close to a sob.

"All these years you've fooled everyone, haven't you, Mother?" he said, his eyes blazing. "Even Heath and Rebel." His voice was filled with sarcasm. "Loedicia Locke, faithful wife and mother. How quaint! 'Whore' is more like it, isn't it, Mother? Or maybe 'adulteress' is a better word. Which is it, Mother, 'whore' or 'adulteress'? Which one suits you best?" He seemed to gloat over the shocked look on her face. "Oh, I imagine you were pleased when my father was killed, weren't you, or did it really happen the way you say? Maybe it wasn't really an accident. After all, I wasn't there to dispute it, I was back in England. And you couldn't even wait to mourn him, could you?" He snarled angrily. "You and Roth!" His voice was hard, cold. "Oh, I wish to God you weren't my mother, then hating you wouldn't be so hard."

Dicia's mouth fell, and she shook her head slowly, the venom of his words taking her breath away. "My God, Teak!" she finally gasped, finding her voice again, and she stared at him incredulously, her mind confused at his attack. "Will you please tell me what you're talking about?"

Teak swallowed hard, straightening against the pillows, his fingers toying nervously with the book in front of him on the bed.

"I was there that day," he began softly, and she stopped him.

"You were there what day?"

"The day my father was released from London's Newgate Prison," he answered slowly. "And that evening when both of you were getting ready to go back to the palace at St. James's for the dinner party the king had invited you to, I came to your room to ask if I could go too, but before I had a chance to knock, I heard you and Father quarreling."

She stared at him in confusion so he went on.

"I heard you admit to my father that you'd slept with Roth Chapman the night before," he said angrily. "I heard him accuse you, and I heard you admit it." His look was contemptuous. "My mother!" His face contorted with bitter pain. "The mother I'd cherished all those years. My mother no better than a whore! How could you do it to him?" he cried bitterly. "How could you do something to a man who'd never hurt you? He loved you with all his heart, Mother. He worshiped the ground you walked on. How could you do something like that? How? Why?"

She bit her lip, the full impact of his words sinking in. All these years he'd treated her shabbily. Now she knew the answers. Now she knew why. He'd felt betrayed. She stared into his blue eyes so like his father's, and a tear reached the corner of her eye. Yes, he was like his father. Exactly like his father had been at his age, stubborn and violent, but could he be tender and forgiving too, as his father had been? She found her voice again, her words barely a whisper.

"You ask me why . . ." she said slowly. "If you heard the quarrel, Teak, I shouldn't have to give you an answer, you should know why."

He shook his head, his eyes puzzled. "All I know is you slept with another man."

"And your father slept with another woman!"

His eyes narrowed and his jaw tightened savagely. "No! You lie!"

"Lie? Oh, now I lie. You say you heard your father accuse me. Well, then, didn't you hear me accuse him?"

Teak shook his head hesitantly.

"Didn't you hear the whole quarrel?" she asked, and he continued to shake his head.

"No," he answered reluctantly. "I was fifteen years old, Mother. When I heard you admit your guilt to him, I couldn't stay and listen to any more, and I ran to my room."

Dicia wiped the tear from the corner of her eye as she stared at her son. She'd never wanted him to know. She'd never wanted any of her children to know of Quinn's betrayal, but Teak already knew enough to warrant knowing the rest. There were times when the truth had to come out, because the living were far more important than the dead.

"Teak," she tried to explain, "the night before your father was arrested and put in prison accused of his cousin's murder"—her voice lowered—"he slept with Rachel Grantham." She saw his eyes widen in shock. "If you don't believe me, ask Rachel," she continued. "She lives next door to us here, as you know, at the River Oaks plantation, and I'm sure she'd be ever so glad to gloat over the deed, since she's tried her best to accomplish the same thing with Roth over the years, only it hasn't worked. Your father and I had quarreled, yes, and he was drunk at the time, but it was still no excuse." Dicia watched her son's face as he looked away and stared at the dainty flowered wallpaper on the wall across the room, and she went on. "Two wrongs don't make a right, I know," she continued slowly. "We were both wrong, Teak, but at least Roth had been my husband once. The duchess meant nothing to your father."

Teak didn't answer, he just kept staring straight ahead. Was she telling the truth? Was she really telling the truth, or was it a play to reap his forgiveness? She had married Roth, hadn't she? For twenty years he'd warred with his emotions, and now . . .

"Don't believe me, ask her," she said softly. "I loved your father, Teak, very much, and you're so like him that every time I look at you it hurts a little inside, and I love you too, even though maybe I haven't been the mother to you that I should have been. Forgive me, please," she pleaded, and he frowned, his eyes turning slowly toward his mother, his blond hair almost reaching to his collar, reminding her so much of Quinn, especially the way his eyes were darkening like a blue summer sky before a storm.

"I may come down for dinner tomorrow, Mother, if I can see your guest list first." She started to protest. "I have my reasons," he went on firmly, his anger barely held in check. "But if I do, it'll be on one condition, and one only."

"And that is?"

"That you invite Rachel Grantham to dinner so I can learn the truth." Loedicia stared at him unhappily. "I don't believe you, Mother," he went on. "I have no reason to, because I know what kind of a man Father was and I know how much he loved you, but I loved you once too, and because of that I'm willing to give you a chance."

Loedicia didn't say another word. She just turned and walked out of the room.

❧ 12 ❧

The New Year's Eve ball was going beautifully, even though Dicia's heart wasn't really in it. Nor would her heart be in the dinner tomorrow. She'd run in to Rachel earlier in the evening and invited her to dinner and had seen the woman's hazel eyes covet Roth at the unexpected invitation.

Rachel, who was a good ten years younger than she was and whose chestnut hair was just starting to turn gray, was the last person in the world Loedicia had wanted to spend New Year's Day with, but it couldn't be helped. In spite of everything, Teak was her son, and she did love him. She gazed about at her other children, surprised to find them all on the ballroom floor.

Rebel and Beau weren't dancing, however. They had just stopped and were standing to one side talking with friends who also had a boy Cole's age stationed with General Jackson's army, and they were comparing notes, worried because neither parents had heard from their sons for some time and it was rumored that Jackson's army was going to try to take New Orleans. A rumor that was sweeping through the ballroom.

She frowned as she saw Ann dancing with Martin Engler who still vainly pursued her when he thought his wife wasn't around, and . . . Well, of all things, Heath was dancing with Darcy. That was a rare sight indeed. Her frown deepened. Darcy hadn't even wanted to come, but Teak had insisted it wouldn't be right for her to miss out on the festivities, so she'd come, to please him, and had looked unhappy right from the start. Well, at least at the moment she didn't look too unhappy, but then, one never knew. Loedicia shrugged. Maybe she and Heath had decided to start the new year off by trying to be nicer to each other for a change. It was certain the past few weeks they'd treated each other like enemies because of Teak. Well, maybe if they started getting along, it was a good sign, and she smiled as she turned back toward Roth, joining the conversation he was having with friends.

Across the floor, Heath looked into Darcy's eyes, and her face turned crimson. "You're blushing again," he said softly, and she scowled.

"I didn't have to dance with you, you know, Heath," she retorted as they whirled about the floor. "I only did it because I didn't want to embarrass you. I had no idea Arnold would suggest you change partners."

"Arnold's engaged to Steffie."

"And you were dancing with Steffie." She nodded. "That explains it, then, but I still want to apologize for forcing myself on you."

Heath's mouth twitched. "I assure you, ma'am," he said, amused, "it's a situation I've suddenly found most pleasing," and again Darcy blushed.

"Will you stop it, Heath," she said self-consciously. "You know we've done nothing but snarl at each other these past few weeks. Don't let's start pretending now."

He grew serious. "Darcy, please, can we talk?" he asked, and she looked around her at the people, not really seeing them, and once more she felt a stirring deep inside as she had that day in the carriage, and it frightened her.

"Haven't we talked enough already?" she answered, her voice strained, but he refused to listen. Instead, he danced toward the French doors that led outside, and whirled her through them into the star-filled night.

The ballroom overlooked the river, and flower gardens bloomed all the way to its banks. The cool, rainy weather that had preceded Christmas had left a warm spell in its wake, and it was exceptionally balmy for New Year's Eve, with the strong scent of roses on the wind, and the magnolia trees were in bud waiting impatiently to burst into bloom. Heath ushered Darcy past them.

"Where are you taking me?" she asked, protesting.

"Where we can talk."

"But we have nothing to talk about."

"Don't we?"

"No!"

He grabbed her hand, pulling her reluctantly after him; then suddenly, when he was so far from the house and the ballroom that they could barely hear the music and laughter, he stopped and pulled her to stand in front of him, staring at her.

Her eyes were wide in the moonlight, and fearful. Her soft hair, cascading down the back of her head, contrasted delightfully with the pale green dress that frothed about her, and the sharp rise and fall of her breasts beneath the sheer material that held them was enough to excite any man, especially one who'd done nothing but dream of her for days.

Heath faced her now, his dark eyes on her lovely face, and he sighed. "Darcy, I can't go on like this," he said softly. "I thought I could, but I can't. I've fought it all the way . . . I can't fight it anymore."

She stared at him helplessly, her heart in her throat. "Heath, I'm engaged to Teak," she reminded him, but he didn't care.

"To hell with Teak," he said angrily. "When I left Port Royal years ago, I said I'd never stop loving you, and I haven't."

"Don't lie."

"I'm not lying."

"You aren't? Then what of this woman you're so anxious to avenge by arresting Teak? This Janet?" she asked. "You say you never stopped loving me . . . you loved her, didn't you?"

Heath's eyes faltered. He hadn't known that Darcy knew about Janet, and for a moment Darcy's red hair reminded him of Janet—or had Janet reminded him of Darcy? The two were mixed up together terribly in his emotions. But Janet was dead. He'd buried her in the Michigan woods, and with her death had gone a part of him. He'd been dead too until he'd met Darcy again. He had to be honest with Darcy and with himself.

"Yes, I loved Janet," he said softly, in answer to her accusation, and she smiled sardonically as he went on; then slowly the smile faded from her face as he spoke. "Janet was everything to me you should have been," he said. "She gave my life meaning and warmed my heart when I thought there was no room left in it for loving." His voice lowered. "I wandered about alone for years without you to love . . . and without you to love me in return. . . . Janet gave me what you weren't there to give me. Would you begrudge me those few months I had with her?"

Darcy's lips trembled, and he went on.

"Why do you think it was so easy for me to love her, Darcy?" he asked as he reached out and pulled her into his arms. "She was you all grown up as you are now, and when I held her in my arms, I was young again." His dark eyes devoured her as he held her close.

"Oh, Heath, I wish it were all that easy," she murmured unhappily, "but it isn't. I'm not the young girl you left in the garden in Beaufort anymore. That Darcy died when you walked out of her life, and the Darcy who took her place is a cold, unfeeling creature with no heart left to love with. Not the way you need loving."

"Let me be the judge of that."

"You don't know."

"I know I love you."

"Heath"—she had to make him understand—"when I realized that Heather was on the way, I vowed never to let my emotions get the best of me again, and I didn't. I told you before—I'm not a woman anymore. I'm dead to the kind of love you'd expect."

"Are you?"

"Yes. I freeze up inside every time Teak's kisses start to get out of hand."

"I'm not Teak!"

"It's no good, Heath," she whispered. "It's too late for us."

He bent his head and kissed her just below the ear and felt her body stiffen in his arms. "Relax, Darcy," he whispered passionately. "I won't hurt you."

"I can't!"

"You can." His lips were against her ear, and she felt a shock run through her and she inhaled sharply. "See," he whispered, "you felt that, didn't you?"

"Yes . . ."

His lips burned their way across her cheek to her mouth, his breath warm against her lips. "You'll feel this too," he murmured huskily, and his mouth touched hers, lightly at first, then becoming hungry and more demanding, and Darcy felt a sweet sensation of pleasure begin to fill her, tingling through her body, exploding in her loins. Her first instinct was to fight it, but he wouldn't let her. "Relax, darling, let yourself feel," he whispered against her mouth. "Remember what you felt once before in my arms, and remember that I love you," and Darcy felt a wild thrill of passion seize her.

Tears welled up in her eyes as he kissed her. This was Heath, the man whose daughter she shared. The man she'd loved for years with all her heart. She wasn't young anymore—did she dare let herself feel again? Was the ecstasy there as it once had been? His hands gave her the answer as he began to caress her, and slowly she began to respond to him. Heath was right. They could fight it from now to eternity, but they couldn't deny the love that still existed between them, and she found herself answering his kisses with a passion she'd thought died with age, and she felt young and full again.

Inside the ballroom, Ann danced the next dance

with Martin again, then insistently excused herself and began looking for Heath. She'd made him promise to be with her when the clock struck midnight, and there was only ten minutes left. She was a beautiful sight in black lace with diamonds at her ears as she searched the huge ballroom, asking discreet questions, then sighed when someone said they thought they'd caught a glimpse of Heath out in the garden.

She frowned as she started outside, then shrugged her shoulders and stepped through the French doors. It wasn't polite or considered decent for unescorted ladies to step outside alone at social affairs, but she wasn't going to be cheated. She'd waited all night to dance the first dance of the new year with him, and he'd promised.

The air felt fresh and alive after the stuffy ballroom, and Ann took a deep breath as she began to move slowly among the flowerbeds, following one of the paths. She searched in the dark, listening for some sound that would warn her that Heath was about, but everything was so quiet; only the sounds of music floating out from the ballroom windows and the occasional soft laughter of the people inside could be heard.

She'd walk some, then stop to listen. Walk some more, then stop again, the warm breeze lifting the layers of black lace on her skirt and whipping a few stray strands of hair from her plump chignon. She pushed the stray hairs back into place and moved on; then suddenly she turned toward a high wall of bushes from where a faint sound carried to her on the night breeze.

"Heath!" she whispered to herself, relieved. He was always wandering off alone, complaining about disliking crowds. He'd told her that's why he spent so much time in the wilderness, and she smiled, quickly moving forward, starting around to the other side of the shrubbery. Then suddenly she stopped in the shadows, the smile fading abruptly from her face. Her eyes strained in the darkness, and her heart started pounding frantically as she stared dumbfounded, recognizing the two people standing on the other side of the bushes not more than ten feet from her, and her hand flew to her mouth, muffling a gasp.

Heath and Darcy didn't even see her, they were so absorbed in each other, and the agony of what she was witnessing made her stumble back quickly into the deeper shadows, where she stood rooted to the spot, staring at them in disbelief, her eyes filled with tears. Darcy was in Heath's arms, and while she watched, he kissed her over and over again, talking to her of love, telling her she was the only woman he loved, that he couldn't go on anymore without her, and Ann's hand tightened on her mouth to stifle the sobs that were beginning to choke her.

Darcy and Heath! She'd never dreamed! The sight of them together like this seared itself into her heart, and she wanted to die. Why? Wasn't Teak enough for Darcy? Did she have to go after Heath too? Ann stood in the darkness for a long time, unnoticed by the two lovers, her eyes glued on them, the reality of what she was seeing numbing her as Darcy returned Heath's loving words; then slowly, when she could stand it no more, she melted even deeper into the shadows again, and turned, reluctantly retracing her steps back toward the ballroom.

She was like someone in a trance, not hearing the music or voices of the people coming from the ballroom, or even seeing the gardens surrounding her anymore. All she could think of was the sight she'd just witnessed. Even the bell that rang, tolling loudly across the plantation, heralding in the stroke of midnight and the new year of 1815, went by without her even hearing.

It wasn't fair. It just wasn't fair! She sobbed deeply as she stopped a few feet from the French doors, tears streaming down her face. She couldn't go in. She couldn't face all of those happy people. Ever since she'd been a little girl with her front teeth missing, she'd loved Heath so very much. All her dreams, ev-

erything she'd ever wanted, had been wrapped up in
Heath, and she'd lived for the few letters he wrote,
waiting patiently for him to finally return and discover
that she was grown up, and what good had it done
her? Damn Darcy! Damn her anyway! Why did she
have to come and spoil everything?

Her fists clenched, and she sniffed in, then gently
wiped the tears from her cheeks, and suddenly her face
reddened as she remembered how she'd thrown herself
shamelessly at Heath, and that night in her room.
What must he think of her? The misty clouds of shock
gradually fell from her and were replaced rapidly by
humiliation, anger, and hurt. Teak was right! He'd
cursed Heath often for being a bounder and a cad—for
having a way with the ladies, he'd called it—and she'd
defended him. Oh, what a fool she'd been. And Teak,
poor Teak thinking Darcy belonged to him, that she
loved him.

The first shock was over, and Ann became aware
again of the merriment inside the ballroom, barely a
few feet away. Everyone sounded so happy, and a
physical pain pierced her breast, making her wince.
She couldn't stay at the party. Not now. Not like this,
with her heart breaking. She had planned to be with
Heath; now that was all over. She had to get away to
think, to sort out her emotions. There was nothing
more for her here, nothing at all.

Her mind made up, furtively she eased back into the
ballroom, accepting the New Year's greetings, of her
friends as she filtered back through the crowds, trying
to smile and act normal, wishing them a Happy New
Year in return, yet moving hurriedly toward the entrance, where she managed to slip out quietly and re-
trieve her black velvet cape from one of the servants.
Her father's carriage was outside with the others, and
she hurried, instructing the servant who helped with
her cape to tell her parents she wasn't feeling well and
had returned home, but would send the carriage back;
then she went outside and climbed in the carriage,

leaning her head back dejectedly, and had the driver return her to the Château.

The drive back chilled her in spite of the warm night, and she pulled the cloak tighter about her on the way to the door, explaining to Mattie as she entered that she wasn't feeling well.

The housekeeper followed her to the foot of the stairs. "Well, you just get a good night's sleep, Miss Ann, honey," Mattie said affectionately as she squeezed her arm. "You was probably dancin' too much, that's all," and Ann nodded as she bid the old black woman good night and ascended the stairs, dragging her feet wearily.

She reached the top of the stairs and stopped, glancing down casually at the light filtering through the crack at the bottom of Teak's bedroom door; then suddenly she froze and stared at it, frowning. She watched it again for a while, then rubbed her eyes and squinted, looking again. She had noticed a light from the window in his room as the carriage came up the front drive, and now, as she watched the crack of light from under his door, it was blocked out momentarily and dimmed, as if someone had walked across in front of it. But Mattie had said Teak was upstairs alone, and everyone else was at the ball.

She strained her eyes and stood motionless, continuing to watch, and again someone walked between the lamp and the door, casting a shadow across the crack. If Teak was supposed to be upstairs alone and someone was in his room . . . something was wrong! Her heart fell to her stomach. Forgetting momentarily about the shocking surprise she'd already received once this evening by intruding where she hadn't been invited, Ann smoothed back a stray strand of hair, then tiptoed gingerly to Teak's bedroom door, her heart pounding, holding her breath. She grabbed the knob, turned it quickly, and flung the door hurriedly open, then stood gaping in disbelief.

Teak whirled unexpectedly from in front of the

dresser, his eyes round as he stared at Ann's stricken face. Then, before she could catch her breath and say anything, he limped briskly across the room, grabbed her arm, and pulled her inside, shutting the door behind her.

"You're walking!" Ann exclaimed incredulously as she glanced first at his leg protruding from beneath his nightshirt, then at his face, and Teak towered over her, his eyes darkening.

"But you weren't supposed to find out."

She shook her head. "I don't understand . . . all those times you tried to stand and couldn't . . ."

"I faked it."

"Why?"

He straightened, looking even taller. "I have my reasons."

Ann's hand clamped onto her forehead, and she closed her eyes. For a minute he thought she was going to faint. "Here," he said as he took her arm and ushered her to the bed, "sit down," and she sat on the edge, bewildered.

Everything had been too much. First Heath, now this.

"Are you all right?" he asked, loosening the ties of her cloak, letting the cloak fall back off her shoulders.

She looked directly at him. "Yes, I'm all right." His eyes sifted over her appreciatively. "But," she went on, shaking her head hesitantly, "I don't understand, Teak." She'd managed to compose herself somewhat. "How long have you been able to walk . . . and what's going on?"

He walked to the chair, limping only slightly, and snatched up the green robe, slipping into it, his face unsmiling; then he turned back to face her as he tightened the sash. "I can't tell you," he answered calmly, and walked to the window, staring out through the sheer curtain that hung beneath the heavy drapes.

"You can't tell me?" She stood up and walked over to stand behind him. "I nurse you for months, taking care of you the best I know how, giving you all of my time, losing Heath in the process, and you say you can't even tell me!"

He turned. "What do you mean, losing Heath?" He glanced at the small porcelain clock on the dresser, realizing it was only twelve-forty-five, too early for her to be home. "What happened? Why aren't you still at the ball with the others?" he asked.

She bit her lip. She couldn't tell him about Darcy. She couldn't hurt him like that. Not even Teak. As much as he always angered her and she hated him, she couldn't do that to him. "I'd rather not talk about it," she replied, but he didn't like her answer.

"What's happened?"

"Nothing."

"It had to be something."

"It doesn't matter, really." She tried to shrug it off nonchalantly. "I just discovered that I mean nothing to Heath, that's all."

"Ann . . . I'm sorry."

Tears once more began to filter into her eyes, and it was hard to stop them. She felt a sob beginning to tighten in her breast. "Don't be sorry. It's my own fault," she said suddenly, not caring what he thought. "I should have known better than to try to compete with all the other women he's known. After all, what do I have that I could possibly hold a man with? Nothing!"

Teak laughed. "Nothing? My dear sister"—his eyes caressed her sumptuous figure—"if you consider what you possess nothing, I'd certainly like to see what you consider something."

Her face reddened angrily. "You're worse than he is," she stated vehemently. "To you I'm nothing but a goddamn half-breed!"

Teak's face sobered. "Hey, wait a minute. Did I ever call you that?"

She scowled, her lower lip pouting. "No!"

"That's right!"

"Not to my face, anyway," she snapped. "But you've thought it. I know you have. I've seen your eyes watching me. I know what you've been thinking."

"What have I been thinking?"

She stared at him insolently; then her eyes lowered from his gaze. "Never mind," she half-whispered, but he grabbed her arm, pulling her close against him.

"What do you mean, never mind?" His voice was low, husky. "You're so smart, I want to know. What have I been thinking?" he asked again.

Her face paled, her dark eyes staring into his stormy blue ones, and she felt a strange shiver run through her. "I asked you a question," he said softly, and she tried to shrink away from him, only to feel his other arm encircle her waist, and her voice died inside her.

"I'll tell you what I've been thinking," he said when he realized her heart was pounding so hard against his chest she couldn't find her voice to answer. "I've been wondering what it would be like to run my hands through your hair," he said, and released her arm, reaching up, taking the pins from her hair, releasing her chignon, the flesh at the nape of her neck tingling excitingly in every spot where his fingers touched, and in seconds his hand was buried in her long amber tresses and they felt like silk. "And I've been wanting to touch you anyplace and every place and feel your velvet skin beneath my fingers."

His hand left her hair, dropping onto her bare shoulder, his long fingers moving sensuously up to curl about her neck, then cup her face, and all the while his eyes never left hers. "And I've been wondering what it would be like to feel your gorgeous mouth against mine," and before she could protest, his mouth touched hers, lightly at first, barely touching hers; then suddenly at the touch of his lips Ann went all hot and weak inside, and her mouth moved against his in response, and Teak wasn't just kissing her, he was devouring her, the kiss deepening passionately, and Ann's

arms crept slowly about his neck as he pressed her to
him.

Ann trembled as Teak finally eased his lips slightly
from hers, but they were still barely touching, and a
groan surged up from deep inside him. "Ann," he murmured against her mouth, "how long I've wanted to do
that. I've been going crazy wanting to touch you, to
hold you."

She swallowed hard, her whole body on fire. What
had he done to her? Even Heath hadn't made her feel
like this. He had no right to do this to her! She hated
Teak, had always hated Teak!

"No!" she cried, her voice breaking. "Please, Teak,
no!" but he couldn't stop now.

He swung her into his arms and carried her to the
bed, laying her down, his hands caressing her, her body
responding in spite of her protests as he undressed her
hurriedly, brushing aside her weak, halfhearted attempts to stop him, his desire for her driving him on.
He kissed her softly, hungrily, passionately, each kiss
silencing her, each caress an agony as it thrilled her in
spite of herself.

He slipped hurriedly from his robe and nightshirt
and climbed into the bed beside her, looking down into
her face, and Ann closed her eyes. She didn't want to
be here, not with Teak, but she couldn't move. Her
body was primed, crying for what she'd denied it for so
long. Yet to surrender without a fight . . . She had to
fight him.

"Teak, leave me alone," she begged, trying to push
him away, but her hands on him only fired him all the
more. "Please, Teak, I can't, I don't want to, please!"
she cried, but instead his mouth touched her breasts,
and she moaned, twisting and turning beneath his
hands until he couldn't stand it anymore.

Teak was hard, like a ramrod, his desire for her
sweeping him on. He couldn't wait any longer, and he
moved above her, spreading her legs, his hands
beneath her hips, her weak protests blocked out by his

need for her. Urgently he lifted her hips to meet him and with one hard lunge drove into her, and with the force of his entry he felt that momentary obstruction before it gave, and he froze, his manhood deep inside her, and stared down into her face.

She had bitten her lip with the pain to keep from yelling, and she was crying, her tears falling, wetting his pillow beneath her head, and Teak felt sick.

"Oh, Ann, my little Ann," he cried, mortified at what he'd done, "and all the time I thought you and Heath . . ." He shook his head, then bent down, his lips warm on hers, his hand stroking the hair back from about her sweaty, tear-streaked face. "I had no idea you were still a virgin," he whispered softly. "That night I fell down the stairs, I wouldn't have fallen, I'd have made my escape if I hadn't heard the sounds coming from your room. I thought Heath was making love to you, and I was blinded with rage, trying to get the sounds of your lovemaking behind me as quickly as I could. All these weeks I thought you and Heath . . . Oh, my darling, can you forgive me? I wouldn't have taken you like this, I'd have been soft and gentle, but I was angry. I thought if you could give yourself to him willingly, why couldn't you give yourself to me. I didn't know."

Ann stared up at Teak, trying to sort through his words, and all the while she could feel him inside her, and it was a strange sensation. Now that the hurt was gone, and for some reason she couldn't understand, it felt good. Suddenly it occurred to her that she liked what Teak was saying, that she liked what he was doing to her, and she didn't want him to stop, but she couldn't find any words.

She reached up slowly and touched his face, her fingers near the corner of his mouth, and he saw the tears stop seeping from her eyes.

"Ann, I love you," he whispered softly, and Ann couldn't believe her ears. "I didn't want to admit it even to myself," he said, "but I do. Please, I've been such a fool." She felt him begin to move against her, moving inside her, thrusting in and out gently, causing sweet rippling sensations to flow through her, and she sighed.

"Teak!" The throbbing surrender in her voice caressed him, and he knew she'd no longer fight him. Instead, she responded to his movements as they grew more abandoned, arching to meet him passionately, using her hands and body to please him, enjoying every moment even when the pain in his leg made his love-making rather awkward. Instead, she tried to help him, assuring him everything was all right, and he wouldn't relent in spite of the pain in his leg, not until a wave of ecstasy tore through her, making her cry out. Then he exploded inside her, collapsing on top of her, spent and breathless.

They lay for long minutes, neither saying a word; then slowly Teak nuzzled her neck, feeling the warmth of her flesh beneath his lips. "Ann!" he murmured softly, and it was as if he couldn't get close enough to her as he held her body beneath his.

Ann lay with her eyes shut, her mind racing, and for the first time in her life she didn't know what to do. Her body had cried out to this man, and he'd fulfilled its need, and now, although she'd been so sure she hated him, the thought that he might move from her and leave her lying here naked and alone made her ache inside.

Was this love? Was this mad sweet pain that coursed through her love? Could she have been in love with him all this while, yet been so blinded by Heath's charm, she hadn't realized it? Whatever was happening to her was strange and new, and then suddenly she remembered Teak's leg and the deception, and a sickening dread began to grip her insides.

Teak felt her body stiffen beneath him as she reached up, touching the scar on his shoulder. He raised his head and stared down into her lovely face, still flushed with desire, her sloe eyes frowning. "What is it?" he asked softly as she stroked the deep scar, and she didn't know how to answer him. What could she say?

"I don't know," she said softly. "I . . ." She turned her head sideways to avoid his eyes. "I shouldn't be here with you. Not like this."

"Why not?"

"Because of everything . . . your leg . . ."

Teak stared at her for a long time, his heart in his throat; then slowly he slipped from her and stretched out beside her on the bed.

"I have to know, Teak," she said, looking at him as she pulled the covers up to hide her nakedness, knowing the tender moments between them were gone and feeling the loss already, but she had no choice. "I can't forget what I saw when I walked in here, simply because you've made love to me, Teak," she said softly. "I can't," and his eyes met hers and he felt sick.

She was right. There was no way he could pretend it hadn't happened. There was no way he could change things. He was what he was. But he didn't want to tell her. For the first time in his life he knew what real love was all about, and now if he told her, there was every chance he'd lose it. Yet, he had to tell her. There was no other way. He turned from her questioning eyes and stared at the ceiling for a long time; then in faltering words he told her the story of his life, from the day he'd received the letter from his mother telling about his father's death, to the message from Castlereagh and what had happened.

Ann listened, with pity at first, sympathetic toward the young boy who'd felt betrayed, then surprisingly jealous as he told of the many women who'd moved in and out of his life, and finally with shock as the weight of his words of confession revealing himself as a spy hung around her neck like a millstone, trying to choke the life from her.

She shook her head slowly in disbelief as he finished, her eyes filled with tears. Then, "No," she cried softly as the words tumbled from his mouth, and she winced. "No, Teak, no! Tell me it can't be true, please, not you," she begged. "Tell me you're making it up, please, not this . . . not you," but he turned to her, his eyes grave.

"Why not me? What's so different about me?"

"You're an American."

"Am I? I've been an Englishman since I was fifteen, Ann."

"But a spy! Oh no, please . . ."

He reached out and touched her face, wiping a tear from the corner of her eye. "Does it really matter what I am, Ann?" he asked lovingly. "Does it matter where I was born or whose side I'm on? Does it, really? Can love be measured that critically? Can you tell your heart to hate me simply because I'm not an American? Can you?"

She muffled a sob and jerked her head from his hand, trying to turn from him, but he wouldn't let her.

"Ann!" he cried, moving over her, grabbing her face with his hand, forcing her to face him. "I asked you a question. Does it make a difference?"

"Yes!"

"Why?"

"Why? You ask why?" Her face paled. "I'm an American, Teak. That alone should answer your question. How can I love you?"

"But you do!"

"No!"

He stared down into her eyes, stubbornly cold. What was it about this woman that haunted him? Why couldn't he get her out of his system? Why couldn't he just say to hell with her? What did it matter what she thought? Damn her! The little minx was in his blood, and now that he'd bedded her, he knew he'd never be happy with anyone else. Never had his abandon been so complete, his heart so full. She had to love him. She had to.

"Dammit, Ann, you can't shove me aside because of this," he said. "I won't let you."

She sneered sardonically, her mouth twitching. "You won't let me? I thought you hated Indians," she said bitterly, but he shook his head.

"It won't work, Ann," he answered. "I don't give a damn whether you're Chinese or Indian or what you are, and I know you feel the same about me. It's you that counts, and I won't let this stand between us."

"How can you stop it?"

"Like this!" His mouth covered hers, and his kiss was wild at first, with all the pent-up passion that surged within him. Ann tried to fight her feelings, but it was useless, and her insides were torn apart as the realization of her love for him surfaced and she answered his kiss with a sob in her throat. Oh, God, what was to become of them?

By the time the others arrived home from the ball, Ann was in her own room, her body satiated with the love Teak had surrendered to her, yet her mind was warring savagely with her conscience. While across the hall Teak, safely in bed with the splints back on his leg, was feigning sleep, trying to think of a way to tell Darcy that he didn't love her and also trying to think of a way to end this whole mess once and for all. All he really wanted was to go back to Locksley Hall and take Ann with him, and yet, at the moment, both goals seemed so far beyond his reach. If he could only have seen through the door to his room and out into the hall, however, and watched the conversation between Heath and Darcy as they said good night, his heart would have eased some, for Heath and Darcy were also trying to figure out a solution to the mess they found themselves in, but they couldn't and he couldn't, and instead he fell into a restless sleep, waking in the morning with a heavy heart.

The dinner party for New Year's Day was scheduled for late afternoon, and Teak squirmed restlessly in bed all day, upset over the fact that his mother instead of Ann had come to check on him that morning.

"I let Ann sleep," explained Loedicia as she examined the bandage on his leg. "She left the ball last night because she wasn't feeling well, and when I stopped by her room this morning, she looked like she'd had a bad night."

Teak stared at his mother uncomfortably, wondering if perhaps she'd guessed what was going on, but she acted normal toward him.

"By the way, Teak," she went on as she finished and tossed the covers back over him, "the duchess will be here for dinner, and I'll bring her up when she arrives. Will that suit you?"

His eyes narrowed. Had he done this to her? Had he put the cold, bitter look into his mother's eyes? Those beautiful violet eyes that were usually soft and full of love? Oh, that he could have understood love years ago, he might have understood her. He thought for a moment of Ann, then sighed.

"I'm sure it'll be all right," he said meekly, and Dicia glanced at him for a moment, surprised at the lack of animosity that was usually present in his voice when he spoke to her; then she shrugged and went out.

The day dragged by for everyone, including Heath and Darcy. They'd thought of no solution for the situation they were in, and were at each other's throats again because Heath was still determined to take Teak back to Washington, insisting that it was his duty.

It was afternoon, Teak was out of bed, sitting in the overstuffed chair in his bedroom wearing his nightshirt and robe when Loedicia and Roth walked in with the duchess. It had been years since Teak had last seen Rachel Grantham, and she had changed a great deal. Although her chestnut hair was only tinged with gray, the lines in her face had deepened. Perhaps there were some men who would still consider her attractive in her pink frills and froth, but to him, with all the artifice she used to try to make herself look younger, she looked old and used. Her eyes fell on Teak, and she scowled curiously as she stepped into the room, studying him from head to toe.

Seeing him was a shock for Rachel, really, because Teak was a double for his late father, and Quinn Locke had been a handsome devil. Tall and strong, Quinn had been a blond giant of a man with a magnetic personality, and there was no denying that this was his son. Even the grim line of his mouth made her remember far too well the father. Rachel smiled as Loedicia introduced them, reminding them that they'd met before when Teak was a boy.

"Ah, yes, I remember," said Rachel. "You were the young man who had all the girls in London agog," she said. "How could I forget Quinn's son." She turned to Loedicia as Roth put his hands on his wife's shoulders possessively. "Strange you didn't tell me he was here," she said, "and it seems equally strange to find a British peer in the home of an American when we're at war with England."

"That's why we haven't really announced his visit," Dicia explained nervously, glancing back up at Roth, who nodded his approval of what he knew she was going to say; then she looked back at Rachel. "He was on his way to the Spanish-held Florida territory when his ship was caught in a storm," she explained. "When I told him you were coming to dinner, he expressed his desire to see you." She looked at her son. "If you want, Teak, we'll leave you alone," she said solemnly, but Teak shook his head.

"No need," he replied sharply, "since the answer to the question I intend to ask the duchess concerns you, Mother, it's best you stay," he said, and glanced at Roth. "You might as well stay too, since your indiscretions with my mother are the real reason for all this." Rachel looked at mother and son bewildered; then her eyes settled on Roth.

Now, what could have prompted this? She knew there was an ulterior motive to Loedicia's dinner invitation. Had Teak requested it? "My, how mysterious," she said curiously, and once more looked at Teak. "Just what answer is this I'm supposed to have?"

Teak straightened in the chair and clasped his hands in front of him, gazing at his fingers intently; then looked up abruptly into Rachel's hazel eyes. "I want a simple answer to a simple question," he said coldly, his voice steady but strained. "Did you or did you not sleep with my father years ago when he was staying at Bourland Hall in London?"

Rachel's hand flew to her breast as her face turned color. "My heavens, sir," she blurted self-consciously, glancing at Roth, then back to Teak, "what a thing to ask a lady."

"Nevertheless, I'm asking it," he snapped.

She clenched the front of her sheer dress helplessly as she felt Loedicia's accusing eyes on her, and for a moment she remembered that night very clearly and the look that had been in Loedicia's eyes at the sight of Quinn in bed beside her. How she'd love to see Loedicia squirm then, and she gazed at her hostess harder. Loedicia was squirming now too. Had she known ahead of time that Teak was going to ask such a question? Probably not. What woman wants to admit to her children that her husband preferred another woman's bed?

Loedicia's eyes were grave, her breasts beneath the deep green satin of her dress rising and falling heavily with the beat of her heart, and Rachel dropped her hand, throwing back her head arrogantly as she stared at Loedicia for a long time, then turned to Teak, very aware that Roth was watching her closely.

"A simple answer for a simple question, Teak," she said, her voice like velvet. "Yes, I slept with your father." She glanced at Dicia. "I suppose your mother denied it."

Teak's eyes sought Loedicia's, and she saw a strange new light in them, a light filled with warmth and forgiveness. "On the contrary, your Grace," he told her

slowly as he stared at Loedicia. "I was the one who denied it," and he continued to look at Dicia. "I'm sorry,
Mother," he said. Tears welled up in Dicia's eyes as
she felt Roth's hands tighten on her shoulders; then
Roth excused himself and Rachel, ushering the duchess
reluctantly out of the room to join the guests arriving
downstairs, leaving the door open behind him for
Loedicia to follow.

Mother and son stared at each other for some time;
then Loedicia spoke. "Are you sure you understand,
Teak?" she asked.

Teak shook his head. "Not really," he said pen-
sively. "All those years Father said he loved you. Yet,
the duchess. Why?"

"As I told you before, he was drunk, and also he
was trying to prove he didn't need me, but it didn't
work. We both needed each other, Teak, and when he
died, a part of me went with him."

Teak reached out his hand toward her, and she
stared at it hesitantly. "Truce?" he asked, raising his
eyebrows.

Dicia reached out, tears in her eyes. "More than
that," she said affectionately, and instead of grabbing
his hand, she bent down and kissed her son on the
cheek, giving him a big hug, and Teak flushed at her
show of affection. But as she straightened, a voice from
the open doorway startled her, and she turned abruptly
to face Heath.

"My, my, what a cozy scene," Heath said casually as
he stepped in, and she frowned. Something was wrong.
She had seen it in Heath's eyes earlier in the morning,
and now they were dark and brooding as he looked
directly at Teak. "Another conquest, Teak?" he asked
sarcastically, and Teak's jaw tightened.

"What's that supposed to mean?"

"Darcy's already on your side, now Mother. That
leaves only Ann to go. But then, the women are always
the easiest for you, aren't they, Teak? My father won't

be so easy, though, will he? How are you going to get him on your side too?" he asked.

Dicia was confused. "Heath, what on earth are you talking about?"

He sneered. "I'm talking about Teak, Mother," he informed her angrily. "I'm talking about my brother, a man who's turned against his country—"

"My country?" interrupted Teak from his chair. "Since when is this my country?"

"Since the day you were born in it."

"This country's given me nothing," stated Teak. "My title, everything I have that means anything to me, has come from England."

"So that gives you the right to come over here and get even?" countered Heath. "You can turn your back on your family, on the men who fought with your father for the freedom you're trying to take from them? Using friendships for your own vicious ends?" He looked at his mother. "Don't you know what Teak's become, Mother?" he asked, disappointed. "Don't you care what your son has done? He's not an American anymore. He's an Englishman clear to his bones." Heath looked fierce, the charm and warmth gone from his face, and Dicia stared at him, almost afraid of the ferocity that drove him.

"Heath, I know what you're thinking," she said unsteadily. "We know Teak lied when he arrived, but . . . he was a soldier doing his job, Heath. He had no choice."

"A soldier? Is that what he told you?"

"He didn't tell us anything," she said. "We suspected it from the start, when the fishermen told us he'd been picked up in the Potomac right after the raid on Washington." She reached out and touched Heath's arm. "Heath, a soldier does what he's been ordered to do . . . he can't help where they send him. He has to obey orders."

Heath pulled his arm from her grasp. "So does a spy," he said viciously, and Dicia shook her head.

"Spy? Teak wasn't a spy. How can you accuse your brother of being a spy?"

Heath saw his mother's face whiten, but there was no turning back, the words were out. "Because I've chased him across this country trying to catch him, that's how," and Dicia turned from Heath slowly and looked down at Teak, still sitting in the chair.

"Tell him, Teak," she begged, grabbing his hand, holding it tightly. "Tell Heath he's wrong, Teak. Tell him," she blurted frantically, but Teak swallowed hard.

"I can't, Mother," he answered, relieved that she finally knew. "Heath's right. I am a spy."

Loedicia's startled eyes filled with tears as she shook her head. "Why?" she asked, still holding his hand, and his fingers tightened. "God in heaven, Teak, why?"

"Because I had no choice. I love Locksley Hall, Mother," he explained. "I always have. It's been more of a home to me than here. If I'd refused to do what they wanted, they'd have called me a coward. I'd have lost everything that meant anything to me. Everything that Father left me, including my friends, and I couldn't stand that. Was that so wrong?"

"Well, was it, Heath?" asked Roth from the doorway, and all three pairs of eyes centered on him as he walked across the floor. He'd come back upstairs to find out what was keeping Dicia, and had heard the whole conversation. "Was it wrong for Teak to fight for his country as you did yours, Heath?" he asked.

Heath frowned. "You're on his side?"

"No, I'm not on his side," Roth answered. "But I remember once years ago when they called me a traitor and a turncoat because I fought with the colonies. A man does what he has to do, Heath, but that doesn't make him any less a man."

"You were a soldier, Father," he said, eyes blazing. "And everyone knew you were a soldier. You didn't turn on people who loved you, pretending to be friends while shoving a knife in their backs. I've followed Teak for two years, seeing the havoc he's rained across this country, vowing someday to even the score, and now my orders are to take him back to Washington to pay for all he's done. I have my duty."

Roth saw the hurt in Loedicia's eyes, and it tore him apart. "Heath, can't we talk about this calmly?" he asked. "Do we have to hate?"

Suddenly the memory of Janet wavered before Heath's eyes, and a hoarse sob escaped his lips as he looked at his father. "You ask me do I have to hate," he said, eyes flashing. "And I say yes, I have to hate. I hate the man who killed the woman I loved. I buried her with my bare hands." He held up his hands. "My bare hands, Father, do you understand? Could you do that and then forgive her murderer? I vowed I'd kill him the next time I saw him," and his fists clenched.

"I didn't kill Janet, Tecumseh did," cried Teak, but Heath turned on him.

"If you hadn't used her, none of it would have happened. And now you're doing it again, taking Darcy away from me too, and she's going to suffer too for what you've done, just like Janet did. How much am I supposed to take just because you're my brother?"

Teak's eyes widened as he stared at Heath. Darcy? Heath and Darcy? "What do you mean, I'm taking Darcy too?" he asked.

"Darcy's mine," said Heath nastily. "She's always been mine. I should have married her years ago, but I ran away instead, and now you're spoiling everything again for me. She said she'd never forgive me if I take you back."

"But . . . Darcy . . . ?"

"Darcy's the mother of my daughter!" cried Heath, and this time they all stared at him incredulously as his face went white beneath his beard, and he turned from them, staring out the window.

"I think perhaps there's going to have to be a lot of explaining done before this whole thing is settled," said Roth wisely as he slowly glanced one at a time at all of them, "but I think Darcy'd better be here too."

"And Ann," said Teak, and Dicia glanced at him sharply, then frowned.

So while their guests waited impatiently downstairs, being entertained by the duchess, Teak's room was the scene of a family discussion that should have taken place months before, and after the air had cleared and the facts were brought into the open, Loedicia stood quietly looking about, surveying her family.

Heath stood with his arms about Darcy, trying to comfort her, and Ann sat at Teak's feet with her head in his lap, afraid to let go, while he stroked her hair and tried to assure her that no matter what happened, he'd always love her.

"I guess we've really done it up right this time, haven't we?" Loedicia said as she brushed a stray gray hair from her forehead and looked at her husband. "And I thought my life was complicated years ago." She glanced at Heath, and her eyes filled with tears. "Heath, what happens if you don't take Teak back?" she asked.

Heath scowled as he felt Darcy stiffen against him. "I don't know," he answered truthfully. "President Madison gave me special orders. . . . I don't know."

"Can't you pretend you didn't find him?"

"Mother . . ." Heath's arms tightened on Darcy. "I'm a special agent. I've sworn allegiance to my country."

"And what of your family? What of your allegiance to us?"

His hand caressed Darcy's back hesitantly as his mother's question penetrated. What of his family? What did he owe them? Anything? Was there a special code, one for your country, one for your family? He gazed at Teak and Ann and remembered how shocked he'd been when Teak had confessed that he'd fallen in love with her. And now Ann was so afraid of losing Teak. It was written in her eyes as she looked up at him.

"If I knew the answer to that, Mother, I wouldn't be

standing here torn between love and duty, would I?" he answered.

She turned to Roth. "Darling, help us, please," she begged, but Roth shook his head.

"I wish I could," he replied. "But I'm at a loss too." He looked at Heath. "I know how Heath must feel, yet—"

"Damn the war!" cried Ann as she looked up at all of them, her heart breaking at the thought of what might happen to Teak. "If there hadn't been a war, none of this would have happened. Why can't we forget there ever was a war!"

Teak put his hand on Ann's head, and she turned to look into his blue eyes. "Ann, don't," he said softly. "Nothing can change what's happened."

"But I can't lose you now," she murmured softly. "I want to be with you . . ."

Roth watched Ann's eyes fill with tears. If there was no war . . . He turned to Heath. "Heath," he said, "if the war ended, would taking Teak back be so important? If there was no war anymore, would your conscience care then?"

"What are you getting at?"

"We all know that Senator Bayard and Albert Gallatin, along with Henry Clay, John Russell, and John Adams, are at Ghent working on a treaty, and Beau said when he picked Lizette up in Charleston just before Christmas that the British are expected to sign for peace any day now. If this is so, then why don't we wait? Since Teak can't travel yet anyway because of his leg—"

"But I can," interrupted Teak.

Ann protested. "No, Teak, please," she begged, putting her hands on his so he wouldn't try to remove the splints. "You know you're not well enough to stand on your leg yet, and traveling would be too much for you," and his forehead wrinkled at the lie she was telling, yet he couldn't brush her plea aside, and for Ann's sake he bit back the truth.

"As I was saying," continued Roth, "wait, Heath. You've waited this long, what matters if it's a little longer, and by the time Teak's well enough to travel, perhaps we'll have an answer. I've already sent inquiries to find out how the peace talks are going, and it shouldn't be too long now."

"Two weeks," pleaded Dicia. "Only two weeks more, Heath?" she asked, and Darcy looked up at him.

"Please, Heath," she asked, and Heath shrugged.

They were right. What was two weeks more? Maybe by then he'd have an answer.

When he nodded agreement, Dicia sighed with relief.

When Loedicia and Roth finally joined their guests downstairs, greeting Rebel and Beau's late arrival, and they all paraded to the dining hall for dinner, it was with reluctance that Loedicia excused her other children from the table.

"They have commitments of their own I knew nothing about when I said they'd be present," she apologized as they were all seated, and it was only Beau and Rebel who noticed the betrayal in her voice and knew all was not well.

For the rest of the week after the dinner party, tensions at the Château were stretched almost beyond the limit as Dicia watched her family trying vainly to work things out. Finally it was Ann who broke. She couldn't stand it any longer. The thought that she might lose Teak almost drove her crazy, and one afternoon she saddled her horse and took her usual ride, she headed upriver, and without consciously realizing it, ended up at Rebel's front door. She and Rebel always got along beautifully, and Rebel wasn't surprised at all to see her younger sister, since she'd learned from her mother about their troubles, and she felt sorry for Ann, remembering how horrible it was to love someone and worry about losing them.

"Come, sit down," she said as Ann paced the flagstone walk of the beautiful terrace at Tonnerre, looking out over the river with a keen eye as she walked, studying the boats sailing up and down its breadth. "Worry isn't going to help, Ann," Rebel went on, but Ann bit her lip.

"I have to talk to someone, Reb," she said, tugging at the waist coat of her black riding suit, snapping the riding crop against her gloved hand nervously. "Please, Rebel," she asked, "do you really love Teak?"

Rebel half-laughed. "Well, naturally I do, Ann, don't be so upset. No matter what he's done or been, he's still my brother."

"Then I know a way out," she finally said as she stopped and knelt anxiously by Rebel's chair. "I know a way Teak can be safe and Heath won't have to live with his conscience condemning him for the rest of his life. It's the only answer."

Rebel's eyes widened. "How?"

"Promise you won't say anything to anyone about what I'm going to tell you," she said, and Rebel promised. Ann took a deep breath and leaned closer to her sister. "Teak can walk, Reb," she confided furtively, her eyes shining. "There's nothing wrong with his leg anymore. He has a slight limp, but he can walk." She hung her head. "He wanted to tell them, but I wouldn't let him. I was afraid Heath would take him back right away." She looked back up at Rebel. "Now it can be a way out, Reb, I know it can," she said. Reb stared into Ann's sloe eyes gleaming suddenly with anticipation.

"How will that help?" she asked calmly, and Ann sighed.

"Don't you see? Reb, we can run away, Teak and I. With your and Beau's help, Teak and I can escape and go to England, and Heath won't be at fault. He can't very well blame himself over something he'll know nothing about, and once we're in England, there'll be nothing he or anyone else can do," and she went over her plan.

Rebel stared at Ann in awe, letting the idea sink in, and the more she ran it over in her fair head, the crazier it sounded, yet it could work. And if it did? Beau still had his private ship, the *Duchess*. But how could they keep Heath from finding out? And he'd be mad, terribly mad, when he did find out, yet, what could he do? Nothing. He surely wouldn't arrest his whole family as traitors.

The more she listened to Ann on the terrace that afternoon, the better she liked the idea, and that evening after supper while she and Beau settled down for a quiet evening together, the strangest plot of the whole war was instigated, and on January 10 it came to fruition.

Heath had been restless all day, sensing rather than knowing that something was in the wind. Ann was exceptionally nice, and so was Teak, yet he couldn't put his finger on anything, and on top of it all, the captain of Beau's private ship, the *Duchess*, had docked the ship at Roth's pier with the excuse that something was wrong with the rigging and it was ridiculous to go all the way back upriver when they could fix it here, then head straight out to sea in the morning as planned.

During the past week or so Heath had fought valiantly with himself and yet had come up with no solution, and to make matters worse, he'd begun to understand a little more the brother he'd been separated from for so many years. They spent hours together talking, and he discovered that Teak wasn't such a bad sort after all. They were different, yes, as different as two brothers could be, and he'd learned that Teak had always hated him because of his father. For Teak the reasons seemed logical at the time, but now that hate was gone on both sides . . . Damn! Why couldn't he go on hating the man? It would make things so much easier, because every time he closed his eyes, he could see the men who'd suffered because of Teak, and it made things worse.

Bedtime came and went that evening, and still nothing happened, and Heath began to think his intuition was failing him. He and Darcy took a late walk outside before retiring, and all seemed well. Yet he had the strangest feeling, as if he were walking a tightrope, and when he finally fell asleep, it was a restless sleep filled with nightmares.

It was still dark out, only a few hours before dawn, when Ann slipped from her room and moved across the hall to Teak's room. He was already awake and dressed in the pants and shirt she'd secretly given him earlier in the day, the splints from his leg resting on the chair, and when he took her in his arms and held her close, she felt as if her heart would explode. This had to work, they had to get away.

Most of Ann's clothes had already been smuggled aboard ship in barrels the crew had been told contained barley, and the crew were all sleeping, with the rigging fixed, waiting for dawn to set sail. Now all they had to do was get on board.

Even Mattie was still asleep as Teak and Ann blew the lamp out in the room and crept into the hall, descending the stairs in the dark, afraid a light might rouse someone and the noise wake the rest of the household. Ann led Teak through the hall and out the back door, and they melted into the shadows, heading for the dock.

The night was warm, the air clean, and Teak breathed in deeply as they moved toward the edge of the water, his heart in his throat. He hated to think what might happen if they didn't get away, and the thought of losing Ann, of Ann having to watch him hang as a spy, had haunted him for days. He jumped suddenly as they stumbled onto the gangplank and tripped over the captain, who was waiting to smuggle them on board.

"Shhh," cautioned the captain. He breathed a sigh of relief as he helped them up the gangplank, across the sleeping crew, and both held their breaths until they reached the cabin beneath the quarterdeck and the captain ushered them inside.

"This is it," whispered Ann as the captain closed the door behind them.

They stood in the dark, hardly believing that they'd made it. They hadn't even dared tell the crew what they were doing, afraid one of them would talk.

Teak looked down at Ann, then pulled her toward him and tried to see her face in the dark. "You're not angry because we have to leave like this, are you, Ann?" he asked anxiously.

She shook her head. "Mother and Father will understand, Teak," she replied. "And Heath will be upset, but in a way I think he'll be relieved. Now he won't have to make any decision either way."

"You're going to like England, you know," he said softly. "Lady Ann, the Countess of Locksley. How does that sound for a title?"

"Oh, Teak," she cried, her arms entwining about his neck. "I don't care about titles. All I care about is you."

He kissed her sensuously, then carried her to the bed, where they spent the rest of the time making love until dawn.

Everything had been thoroughly thought out. Only Rebel, Beau, the captain, and the two fugitives were in on the plan. Beau felt that the fewer people who knew what they were doing, the less chance of detection. If Loedicia knew they were leaving, she'd probably have cried her eyes out all the day before and given it away. This way they'd be safer.

The ship was to sail at dawn, before anyone would have a chance to discover they were missing, and once out of Port Royal, the captain was to marry them. Then they were to be taken to the Spanish city of St. Augustine, where they would find passage aboard a ship sailing to England and safety. The plan was a good one, yet Rebel had been apprehensive. She had to be sure things would go on as scheduled, so the first golden rays of dawn found Rebel and Beau on horseback, out for a morning canter, riding across the fields of the Château as the field hands began to emerge, and all eyes were on the ship in the river as its sails began unfurling to catch the wind.

Heath stirred in his bed, his eyes flew open, and he sat up straight. Something had wakened him, but what? It was barely light in the room, shadows slowly beginning to fade. Then suddenly he knew what it was. He could hear in the distance the familiar flap of the sails and creaky rigging, along with the shouts of the men trying to get the ship under way. It had been years since he'd sailed, but the old familiar things always came back, no matter how long they'd been absent.

He threw back the covers and got up, walking to the bedroom window, leaning on the sill, watching the big ship as the lines were cast off, the anchor raised, and she eased from the dock. Then abruptly his eyes caught a movement near the bank, and he stared, stunned. Rebel and Beau were astride horses, watching the ship leave. Now, why on earth would they be here before dawn watching the *Duchess* pull out, unless . . . ?

He swore softly to himself as he grabbed his pants and pulled them on, then sat on the bed and jerked on his boots. If his suspicions were right . . . His shirt was half on, half off as he bolted toward the door and threw it open, then raced down the hall to Teak's room.

He yanked open the door, then stood for a minute and swore as the faint outlines of the splints on the chair and the empty bed were all that remained in the shadowed room. He yelled for the rest of the household while he crossed the hall and opened Ann's door, and yelled again, louder, when he found her closets empty.

By the time he stepped back into the hall, his parents had emerged from their room, still half-asleep, and Darcy was just opening her bedroom door.

"Good heavens, Heath, what is it?" asked Dicia, staring at him sleepy-eyed.

Heath let out a roar. "He's gone, by God!" he shouted angrily. "Teak's gone!" He glanced toward the back of the house, then ran down the stairs, taking them two at a time, while the others followed in consternation, but it was too late as he reached the back veranda.

The first rays of the sun hit him full in the face as he stepped from the veranda onto the walk, and he moved slowly, hesitantly toward the pier, watching the ship maneuver into the current, and for a minute his heart sank; then suddenly it was as if a weight was lifting from him, and he stopped, staring after the ship, his eyes weary.

He stood motionless, watching the *Duchess* drifting downstream, knowing that somewhere in one of the cabins Ann and Teak were on their way to England, and for a few minutes he could only stare. Why did he feel this way, angry yet relieved? Maybe it was better this way after all. He turned his head as Rebel and Beau rode to the stables, dismounted, then joined him.

"Whose idea was it?" he asked, staring at his sister, and Rebel's violet eyes looked totally innocent beneath the wide-brimmed hat that covered her flowing mass of blond hair, and for a minute he remembered her in buckskins, riding the trails at Fort Locke with carefree abandon.

"Why, I don't know what you're talking about, Heath," she answered guilelessly, and suddenly Heath smiled.

"I might have known," he said as he turned and watched Darcy come out of the house and start down the walk, tightening her dressing gown about her, her red hair like a homing beacon as the sun hit it. "All I want to know is, are you sure Ann will be happy?"

"What do you think?" asked Beau as he put an arm about his wife's waist, and Heath sighed.

"Teak's gone, Darcy," he said as she approached, "and Ann's gone with him, and I suppose it's all for the best, really, because God knows I didn't know what to do." He looked toward the house, where his parents stood on the back veranda, then frowned abruptly as a man on horseback tore down the road, pulling in at the front gate, and rode round back to the stables, leaving his horse's back on the run. It was Roth's man Jacob. He'd been in Beaufort overnight on special business for Roth, and now he studied all their faces as he slowed his pace.

"It's over," he cried breathlessly, loud enough so Roth and Loedicia could hear, and he saw the startled look in their eyes. "I thought you'd all want to know right away, so I hurried back," he went on. "The war's over. A messenger's on his way to Washington, but the word's got this far. Jackson's army beat the British at New Orleans, and they've surrendered. There's no more British Army to fight!"

Loedicia grabbed Roth by the shoulders, her face aglow. "Oh, God, darling, it's over," she cried jubilantly. "It's over. Now Teak will be forgotten, and there's no more reason for fighting." Her eyes lit up. "And Cole will be coming home! With the war over, our grandson will be coming home."

Roth smiled as he gazed into her dancing eyes. "And I wonder what mischief he can get us into?" he said facetiously as she laughed, tears of happiness filling her eyes.

"Probably between Cole, his sister Lizette, and now Heath's daughter, Heather, we'll be kept busy enough for the rest of our lives," she said. "That is, if our children are any example of what our grandchildren will be like." She shook her head ecstatically. "But I don't care, as long as I have you to share it with." She wrapped her arms about his neck, pulling his head down to meet hers, and she kissed him on the mouth passionately, seductively, right there on the back veranda for all to see, and without the slightest bit of shame.

Heath watched his mother, and his face reddened. "Would you look at that," he said as his arm went around Darcy's waist and he pulled her close. "You'd think they were on their honeymoon or something, wouldn't you, and right out here in the open." He turned to Rebel. "You know, Mother's lack of conventionality used to embarrass me when I was younger," he said, "but I guess she's never really going to change, and I guess Father wouldn't want her to, and neither would we." He shook his head. "I only hope when we're their age that we can still enjoy life and love as much," and all of them laughed, heading back toward the house, their troubles over as Roth picked Dicia up in his arms and carried her inside and on up to their bedroom while the *Duchess* slowly sailed down the river and out of sight.

About the Author

The granddaughter of an old-time vaudevillian, Mrs. Shiplett was born and raised in Ohio. She has been married to her husband, Charles, for thirty years, and has lived in the City of Mentor-on-the-Lake for twenty-five years. She has four daughters and two grandchildren.